LOCKS

LOCKS

ASHLEIGH NUGENT

PICADOR

First published 2023 by Picador
an imprint of Pan Macmillan
The Smithson, 6 Briset Street, London EC1M 5NR
EU representative: Macmillan Publishers Ireland Ltd, 1st Floor,
The Liffey Trust Centre, 117–126 Sheriff Street Upper,
Dublin 1, D01 YC43
Associated companies throughout the world
www.panmacmillan.com

ISBN 978-1-5290-9789-4 HB
ISBN 978-1-5290-9790-0 TPB

Originally published in a different form by RiseUp, 2020.

1 3 5 7 9 8 6 4 2

A CIP catalogue record for this book is available from the British Library.

Typeset in 11.5/15.5pt Dante MT Std by Jouve (UK), Milton Keynes
Printed and bound by CPI Group (UK) Ltd, Croydon, CR0 4YY

Visit **www.picador.com** to read more about all our books
and to buy them. You will also find features, author interviews and
news of any author events, and you can sign up for e-newsletters
so that you're always first to hear about our new releases.

Dedicated to my dad
who has truly lived by his favourite saying:
Triumph over adversity

And to my mentor, Ted Devlin,
who taught me that in times of success,
humility is our best friend

True teachings last forever

PROLOGUE

It is a sign of how far we have travelled that just to repeat the terms that were common parlance to anyone growing up in Britain in the 1970s, 80s, and 90s requires this precursory note. Why repeat those terms, so offensive now: racist, homophobic, sexist and downright insensitive? Why? Well, because we have to be honest about where we have been if we are to adequately chart the next stage of our journey.

It is beyond the remit of this little prologue to explain how these terms were normalised, why, and by whom. But, hopefully, by pointing out that they were, and by showing how such a world shaped dangerous tenets in our collective and individual consciousnesses, I will contribute something meaningful to the conversation on where we are going.

I had to do something.

Something had to happen.

Ashleigh Nugent
August 2022

. . . *contradiction is a ruling principle of the Universe. And*
everything in phenomena, whether it's the physical world
or the biological world or the social world, has its internal
contradiction that gives motive to things – that internal strain.

Dr Huey P. Newton, Co-founder of the Black Panther Party,
in an interview with William Buckley

Something had to happen.

Loads of things had happened to my cousin Increase. Nothing ever happened to me.

'Well, we will be in Jamaica in just over ten uncomfortable hours,' said Increase looking at his watch as we walked through Departures, Terminal 2, Manchester Airport. 'This should be great,' he said, exaggerating a toothy grin at me, 'apart from all the niggers, of course.'

He said it loudly enough that the two big Black girls walking in front of us could definitely hear.

I wondered what they must have thought.

It was Friday the 16th of July, 1993; fifteen days before my seventeenth birthday.

1993 was the year that Spike Lee asked me where I came from on 'Malcolm X' and Snoop Doggy Dogg bow-wow-wowed the world in 'Dre Day'. Black people were popping up all over the place. There was a time when the only person on telly that everyone in school could say that I looked just like was Trevor McDonald. By the time 1993 came around, I'd been told I that looked like Frank Bruno, I'd been accused of looking like Andi Peters, and once someone even said I looked exactly like Mr Motivator.

I thought Joe Shirley was genuinely trying to be nice when he'd said, 'Don't worry about it, Aeon. You don't look nothing like Mr Motivator.' But he went on, 'You're not even a proper Black. You're like more like that other fella . . . ah, what's his name?' His eyes lit up: 'Gary Wilmot,' he chuckled.

Gary fucking Wilmot!

1993 was the year that Stephen Lawrence got murdered by racists, and I became an angry Black lad with a 'chip on his shoulder'.

Mum and Dad were at a 'function' the night I heard about Stephen Lawrence. So I took Dad's Ford Granada and drove around Huyton playing my N.W.A. tape, *Niggaz4Life*, at top volume – 'Real Niggaz Don't Die' – snarling at gangs of White lads like I'd fuck them all up. On my own.

'I can't believe you've talked me into going to Jamaica,' said Increase. I stared out the window of the Boeing 737 at the clouds billowing up into white empires over the Atlantic Ocean. I hadn't talked him into anything. He'd invited himself.

My favourite primary school teacher, Miss Elwyn, used to tell me that a hero's journey always starts with the hero having to leave home and go off on a mission, a quest, an adventure. At first, though, the hero doesn't wanna go. Like Sarah Connor or John Rambo. They never wanted any shit, did they? But the 'other' brought it to them: 'They' sent *The Terminator*. 'They' drew *First Blood*. Forced the issue. And now it was Increase saying that he didn't wanna go to Jamaica.

Increase was trying to write himself in as the hero of the story.

And this was supposed to be my story.

'Jamaicans perform worse than Whites in just about every

endeavour,' said Increase, 'apart from running and rapping and . . . pimping.'

I stared at a tower of clouds; tried to make it crumble with my mind.

'No Black person has ever created anything of epoch-making significance.'

What's an epoch?

'Who invented steam engines and aeroplanes, telephones and the atomic bomb, Aeon?'

How would I know?

'White men! Why do Jamaicans perform worse in academia than any other demographic in Britain?'

What's a demog . . . ?

'Why do we have the lowest-paid jobs; I mean, how many Jamaican doctors or lawyers do you know?'

The way Increase looked at me when he was ranting this shit; as if he thought it was all, somehow, my fault. What could I do? I just shook my head and went a bit red in the face.

'Why do Blacks have the highest levels of recidivism, higher levels of domestic violence, the most single-parent families – where the fuck are our fathers, Aeon?'

Mine was probably at work. His was dead. Maybe he was right? I needed a retort.

Maybe I should have read some books; books about slavery and stuff. I reckoned that stuff was probably to blame for all this stuff. Problem was, most of what I knew about slavery came from Bob Marley songs, and, even then, I didn't really understand what they were on about. And there was that song we used to sing in Miss Elwyn's class:

'Oh Lordy, pick a bail o' cotton
Oh Lordy, pick a bail a day

3

Up, down, turn around, pick a bail o' cotton

Up, down, turn around . . .'

And that was it. That was pretty much the extent of my knowledge on the Transatlantic Slave Trade after eleven years in Searbank schools, and Increase knew it.

Suffice to say, there was no way I was gonna attempt to argue with Increase. Especially not here, now, with those two big Black girls sat in the seats directly in front of us, and him just dying to make me look like a tit.

A new tower of clouds took shape underneath us.

Something had to happen.

And as we stepped off that plane in Montego Bay, and my black Adidas shell suit puffed up like a mushroom cloud in the hot breeze, I knew what it was.

Sort of.

'What is you carrying?' said the customs guy, his voice a monotone drone.

'Pardon?' I said, a trickle of sweat escaping from underneath my woolly black Gio-Goi bobble hat.

'What-is-you ca-rry-in?' he said, enunciating each syllable as if *I* spoke a foreign tongue.

'Er . . . just, er, clothes, like.'

He rolled his eyes and sucked his teeth – 'Pttts!' – as he unzipped my black and red Head bag.

'Will you be visiting people in Jamaica?' he asked as he rifled through my stuff. I wondered what he was looking for.

What would I be trying to smuggle *into* Jamaica?

He picked up a T-shirt with his fingertips and thumbs and sneered at it. It was my favourite new one. It had N.W.A. slashed red across the top, like fresh wounds hanging over a photograph of a shrouded body at some murder scene in South Central LA.

'Family?'

'Eh?'

'Fam-il-ee? Will you be visiting family in Jamaica?'

'Er, yeah, yeah. Family, like.'

That answer had him suddenly more upbeat for some reason.

'So, what gifts do you have? For your faaamily.'

'Erm.'

Increase was leaning over the next desk, touching the elbow of his inspector and grinning. He handed him something with a shady handshake, and the inspector gripped Increase's elbow and laughed. Increase glanced over and winked at me.

'Gifts,' said my inspector. 'What gifts do you have? For your family.'

'Er, n- n- nothing, like.'

The inspector sucked his teeth an extra-long, loud time: 'Pttttssss, cho! You have no gifts.'

Mum used to say that my hair was a gift; impossible to get a brush through but a gift all the same. Mum said that I had a double crown. She said that I had hair that had a mind of its own.

Some of the kids at school started calling me Wog Head.

At the time, I didn't know what any of that meant.

Increase waited in the shade as I lugged my black and red Head bag through the double doors, already drained.

Increase grinned: 'You should've just given him something. "Gifts",' he said, copying the customs man. 'These people all want something from you, Aeon. And remember what I told you: if you're dealing with anyone in a position of authority on this backward island, you need to either have great charm and humour or, as in your case, you need to learn how to be obsequious. They all have designs on making you a supporter of torpidity, a patron of indolence – please give generously, hahaha,' he laughed.

He'd lost me on that word: ob-seek-we-us?

I just stood there wobbling in the heat like the sea of tarmac rising and falling in front of my eyes.

A huge and enthusiastic bloke came bounding towards us. No one could rush under the weight of this sun, but this fella was giving it a good go. He handed off a competitor like Martin Offiah in slow-mo. 'Welcome to Jamaica,' he said as he landed before us. The high-pitched voice sounded wrong coming from this giant. Just imagine Mike Tyson but taller and camper, as a bell boy, with flamboyant wrists, in a threadbare waistcoat, and he's called Jeremy.

'Jeremy. Jeremy's the name! Where are you from? Wait, wait, I can guess, I can guess. Erm, Canada? No, no, wait, wait . . . Holland? Not Holland, no, no.' Jeremy would have made a very good medium – 'England. London. London, England.' – with a bit more practice.

'May I?' he asked, passing a hand over our bags.

Increase waved his hand to show that Jeremy could carry the bags to the taxi rank if he wanted to.

'Irie. Come, come. Irie man. Welcome to Jamaica.'

We followed Jeremy to a blistering queue of decrepit cars, all the colour of a bygone paint job. Jeremy lifted the bags into the boot of a car.

The driver tied the boot shut with a shoelace. 'Good British Hillman Hunter,' said the driver.

I had no idea what that meant.

'Two dollar, sir, two,' said Jeremy holding out his hand.

I could feel Increase's grin goading me, even through the back of his head as he turned away and got in the front seat.

I rummaged around in my JD Sports shoulder bag. I was too scared to take out the envelope with all my money in just in case Jeremy tried to rob me; which sounds stupid but you didn't see many Black people back then. Not where I was from.

And I was too embarrassed to admit that I didn't know what two dollars looked like. Which is stupid. I wasn't from Jamaica and I'd never been to Jamaica. But I wished I was, or at least that I had. I was suffering from an attack of not-Jamaican-enough shame syndrome. I pulled out what felt like the biggest coin in my pocket and pressed it into Jeremy's palm. He glared at the coin.

Thinking about it now, it looked like a 50 pence piece, which would have made it a Jamaican 50 cent coin. In 1993, the exchange rate was forty-three Jamaican dollars to one English pound. So that large coin, therefore, must have been worth, well, fuck all.

Jeremy huffed something under his breath as he walked away: 'Bumberclaat!' A word I'd never heard before, but was soon to become very familiar with.

'Welcome to Jamaica,' smiled the driver. 'Irie man. Where to?'

'Peach's Paradise Hotel, please,' said Increase.

'Peach's Paradise.' He lilted it up and down like a lyric. 'No problem.'

We were barely out of the airport when the driver reached into his shirt pocket and pulled out a fat little cone-shaped spliff.

'Enjoy Jamaica,' he said as he offered the spliff to Increase. 'Local produce.'

Increase backed away from the spliff like it was something Princess Diana wouldn't have shook hands with. He never used to refuse spliffs. It was Increase who'd introduced me to weed three years earlier. 'No, thank you.' And now this. 'I don't touch the stuff.' This new Increase. 'The Devil's weed.'

What the fuck!

'No true,' said the driver. 'De herb is a gift from God.' His voice went up in pitch on the word 'God'. 'Behold,' he said, paraphrasing God as quoted in the King James Version, 'me has given you every herb bearing seed which is upon de face of all de earth. And God saw de tings him hath made and, behold, twas good. Mm-hmm, true.'

'You can interpret a book any way you like,' said Increase.

'Now dat true,' said the driver.

'The weed is the great ambition-killer.'

'Dat true too.' The driver nodded grimly.

He turned to me and smiled: 'You are too striving for a smoke too?'

Now, it seemed rude to say nothing. But to answer the question honestly would have been to concede a defeat in Increase's favour. So I just said, 'Thanks, mate,' and took the spliff.

The driver passed me a packet of Peach's Paradise matches, clearly enjoying the coincidence: 'Peach's Paradise. No problem. Make clear heat upon de herbs, dem. Irie man.'

I sucked and inhaled a mouth full of earth, tree, and ether. I eased the smoke out through my nose.

Increase grinned at the driver: 'I have a foolproof plan to implement exponential growth in the Jamaican economy, reduce crime, and lower the mortality rate,' he said.

'Haha. How dat?' said the driver, already amused.

'You take half of the population of Jamaica and move them to Japan; then you replace them with a million Japanese people.'

'Mm-hmm,' mused the driver. 'I think you is right, yunno? Dat plan would probably work.' He exploded into laughter, rocking back and forth, slapping the top of his steering wheel.

'The only downside would be the problematic rise in Japan's crime rate.'

'Haha.'

'And in Japan's mortality rate.'

'Yeah man, dat also true, bredrin. De Japan man be in for a shock,' he laughed.

'And the Japanese woman too, brother.'

'Too true, brother.' The driver grabbed Increase's thigh. 'De Japan woman get a good old shock from de Yard man, eh-eh.'

How does he do that; charm people while insulting them?

I passed the spliff back to the driver. 'Irie man,' said the driver. 'No problem. Enjoy Jamaica.'

Am I supposed to smoke the whole thing?

I sucked, inhaled, and eased the smoke out through my nose.

A spring in the back seat rubbed right in the middle of my sweat-drenched back as we wobbled along the potholed road.

And it was so hot.

The radio pumped out a deep and earthy sound that shook the seats and reverberated right to my heart.

BOOM – dum-dum, dum-dum, dum-dum, dum – BOOM, BOOM . . .

I sucked, inhaled, and eased the smoke out through my nose.

Sounds jabbed rhythmic whip cracks in the wrong place.

Suck, inhale, ease . . .

Dum-dum, dum-dum, dum-dum, dum – BOOM, BOOM . . .

And the high-pitched voice swelled over me:

'The weak don't follow the water
The weak don't follow the water
The weak don't follow the water
The weak don't follow the signs . . .'
Dum-dum, dum-dum, dum-dum, dum – BOOM, BOOM . . .
The rumbling, rattling, and rolling motion of the motor melded with the music as I sucked and inhaled.

Then another voice, like no voice I'd ever heard before, roared over the music like a heartbroken lion-boy chanting:
'De weak don't follow de water or de signs
Johnny never know what him got, until it dies
Johnny didn't do it love, but for de lies
De weak don't follow de water or de signs . . .'
The engine rattled like no car I'd ever been in.

Why is it so hot?

Sweat ran down the inside of my leg.

My head hung to the left, and blood rushed in my ear like the sea in a shell.

I was getting a bit paranoid, so I decided I should finish the spliff before we arrived at—

'Peach's Paradise Hotel.'

What the fuck?

Suck, inhale, ease – stop. Slow down. Don't get paranoid. This isn't Searbank. No one cares about a spliff around here. Weed's legal here. Isn't it? Just act normal and get out the car.

But I couldn't just act normal and get out the car because the door had no handle. It didn't even have a window winder or any interior panelling.

And it was so fucking hot.

OK, just try to look normal – just smoking this spliff.

The driver's door had a little latch, like the ones you get on a rabbit hutch. He lifted the latch, shook the door, cursed it, leaned back into Increase, and booted it till it dropped open. He got our bags out of the boot before shaking our doors open.

The heat rushed in.

Shit, it's even hotter outside the car than in?

Increase headed off towards reception, leaving both bags by the car for me to carry.

'Five dollar,' said the driver. He held out his hand as I rustled a bunch of notes from the envelope in my JD Sports bag, found one that said five, and gave it to him.

'Another five dollar,' said the driver.

He wants paying again?

'For de smoke.'

He wants me to pay him for the spliff? Five quid? For one spliff?

Increase was already in front of the reception area, grinning back at me like – *You wanna deal with niggers, boy? Deal with that, nigger.*

A billion unseen creatures rattled and croaked in the bushes behind me.

I slipped a large coin out of the envelope and held it out in front of me. The driver snatched it from my hand and sneered at it: 'Bumberclaat.'

That word again.

'Rassclaat teef.'

And some new ones.

I picked up the bags and headed off towards Increase.

'Hotfoot!' shouted the driver.

An old baldy bloke built like a bison got up from a green plastic garden chair facing the reception area and snarled at the driver. I had no idea who he was, but it seemed he served the role of protecting foreigners from angry locals.

The driver sounded almost tearful as I trotted off: 'Rassclaat.'

My woolly black Gio-Goi bobble hat was heavy with sweat. Of all the new things I'd bought especially for this mission, the woolly black Gio-Goi bobble hat was the only one I'd dared to wear for the outward journey. But apparently, black gets hotter than white. It felt like I was wearing the sun on my head. I thought my face was gonna disintegrate into a cloud of vapour.

My heart thumped, pulling oxygen from my lungs, pumping adrenalin to my thighs.

My sweaty hands were losing their grip on the bags.

'Bumber-rass fucking hotfoot teef.' The cursing continued.

Increase stepped down to give me a hand up the steps leading up to reception. I shrugged him off, but he put his hand on my back. '"Hotfoot".' Increase mimicked the driver, giggling like a kid – he must have been stoned from the fumes. 'Hotfoot? Fucking hotfoot?'

I tried to push him off again, but my body shuddered with a burst of uncontrollable laughter. I laughed so hard that my eyes pulsed and bulged out of my head, like Arnold Schwarzenegger in *Total Recall*. I laughed till I cried, and we collapsed into a quivering two-bodied heap on the hot stone steps before reception. Those same stone steps which, that very same night, would become the cold and comforting perfect place to die.

The Jamaican cover version of Rod Stewart's 'Da Ya Think I'm Sexy' was unlike anything I'd ever heard before. And worse. And it was that obvious omen of doom which was blurring up from the poolside bar into our room.

I unzipped my Head bag and considered unpacking my new image: tapered black corduroys; red, yellow, and green string vest; excessively long shorts; stupidly baggy jeans; a range of different coloured bandanas all patterned with the same paisley teardrops; a T-shirt with a picture of Malcolm X holding a big gun, the words 'BY ANY MEANS NECESSARY' written across the bottom.

It's weird to think that I only got to wear most of the stuff in that Head bag once – or not at all.

'We should take some pictures, for posterity,' said Increase. He assumed a pose on the balcony: back straight, chin up, head slightly to one side. 'Ah, wait.' He reached under his plaid tank-top, pulled out a pair of round Armani glasses from the top pocket of his short-sleeved Ralph Lauren polo shirt, and smoothed them over his face. Increase had 20/20 vision. But Increase also had a new image, of which these stupid fucking specs were just another aspect, along with the chino pant-style shorts and tas-selled brogues worn with Yves Saint Laurent socks – pulled all the way up (for fuck's sake).

'Hurry up,' said Increase.

'All right, la, I'm just getting the camera, like.'

He tried another pose, a mid-distance intellectual-type face, as he said, 'You really need to stop talking in that ridiculous Scouse accent, Aeon. Especially if you expect to be taken seriously as a Black man. You're in the woods now, nigger. You can't talk to Jamaicans in that la-la voice, no one will understand a word you're saying.'

How could I change my voice now? I'd spent years perfecting my Scouse accent. Searbank's a small place. Perfecting the art of being someone you're not is something to do.

'Camera, nigger, come on,' said Increase. 'It's in your hand luggage, Aeon. See, now that's what the evil weed does to your brain: decimates brain cells, diminishing your short-term memory.' He clicked his fingers to hurry me. 'Camera, nigger, come on.' He puffed up his chest and his biceps bulged through his short sleeves.

I wound on the disposable camera and quickly clicked in his direction.

'Go on, I'll take your picture now.' He motioned for me to move onto the balcony. 'You may as well get a memory of your first day at Nigger University.'

'All right, in a sec, la. I just need to, er, thingy . . .' I didn't want my picture taken. But as it was unavoidable, I sloped off to the bathroom to do a few press-ups first, get a bit pumped. I was never gonna look like Increase, but I had to at least make an effort.

The receptionist at Peach's Paradise was the most beautiful Black woman I'd ever seen. You didn't see Black women like that in those days. Increase's mum was the only Black woman I had ever seen in Searbank. And the only Black women you saw on the telly when I was a kid were Floella Benjamin, Rustie Lee, and Moira Stuart. And no disrespect to any of them; but I'm just saying, this receptionist was well fit. Her long coffee-bean fingers pointed us in the direction of the tourist trail.

'Turn left out of the hotel, and walk down the declivity.'

Declivity?

Her voice was dark and rich, like the lips in *The Warriors* movie, and her accent was a clipped Americany-posh-English that would swing for brief moments into Jamaican twang.

'There you shall come to a roundabout. You must make sure that you always turn right at the roundabout. Do not go left.'

'What will happen if we go there?' said Increase.

Her hair was as all straight and shiny like the Timotei girl's.
How does she do that?

She stroked some shiny loose strands behind her ear.

'If you go left at the roundabout, that road will take you downtown. You do not want to go downtown – it is not a place for
tourists.'

Why did she look at me when she said 'tourists'?

'You must turn right at the roundabout, and this road will take
you to all of the local tourist attractions.'

Increase leaned over the counter slightly. 'The road is like the
sunrise, then:' he said, 'it gets brighter and brighter until the daylight comes.'

'The road of the wicked, however, is as dark as night,' she said.
'They fall but cannot see over what they have stumbled.'

What the fuck are they on about?

She looked at me, all professional, and proceeded. 'Turn right.
Here you can visit Gloucester Avenue, locally known as the Hip
Strip. You will find all of the tourist beaches along the Hip Strip.
Be vigilant to avoid the first beach you pass because it is for local
people only. Also along that road, you will find respectable tourist
shops and many fine eateries. Just remember,' she said, 'do not go
left.' And then, in her strongest Jamaican accent yet: 'Only go
right.'

Part way down the hill, we passed a market perched on an
embankment that was a shortcut to the Hip Strip. A man popped
up from the steps that led through the market and shouted to us:
'Canada? America? You want to buy vest, hat, cane?' I really did
want to buy vest, hat, cane. They looked amazing; proper Black
stuff, especially that cane. But I needed to get my confidence up

before I could don any vest, hat, cane. For now, I was just trying to get comfortable in my new oversized baseball shorts.

As we approached the roundabout, a guy pointed at us and shouted, 'Holland. Hey, Holland.' And another guy waved at us and shouted, 'New York.'

In the middle of the roundabout at the bottom of the hill stood a slick looking dude surrounded by some rough looking skinny women in boob tubes and super-short shorts. The dude was wearing a silver suit jacket and a pink shirt with the buttons open like Tubbs out of *Miami Vice*.

'Hey, guys, I'm Randy,' he said holding out his hand, 'Randy Priest. Where you guys from?'

'Liverpool,' I said, shaking his hand. Searbank, of course, isn't really Liverpool, but no one's ever heard of Searbank. And besides, there's something about saying Liverpool that gives you a sort of confidence, a kind of 'so don't fuck with me' ticket.

'Liverpool?' he said. 'John Barnes, The Beatles.'

I nodded.

Increase rolled his eyes and walked away.

'Hey, you guys looking for girls today?' said Randy.

'Deep pits,' said Increase heading leftward, 'and wide wells.'

'Ooh!' said Randy. 'That's tough, tough Christian talk, man. But remember, brothers,' he shouted after us as I followed Increase, 'I am the priest at the roundabout, and my whole congregation is Christian. Maybe later,' he shouted as we both headed leftward. 'After a drink, maybe then you come see the priest for some guilty indulgences.'

So we've just turned left, haven't we?

I didn't know what Increase was thinking.

Has he noticed?

As for me, I was happy with it. I was in Jamaica to see my real home, my people, the place where I belonged, fuck 'tourist attractions' and 'fine eateries'.

'The hero must dare to cross the threshold,' Miss Elwyn used to tell me.

The sun felt heavier once we'd crossed that threshold. It weighed down on my shoulders like a ship, but heavier. It was like the weight of a ship full of people, their shit and piss and blood and pain all weighing down on my shoulders.

The feeling reminded me of a dream I used to have. I'd be carrying matchsticks in my arms – all the matchsticks in the Universe. But I could manage the weight OK, until I wondered whether I could. Until I wondered whether I should be scared about the danger of being crushed under the weight of a whole Universe worth of matchsticks. What if lack of fear was more dangerous than fear itself? Then I'd force myself awake.

'Hey, Germany,' said some bloke as he walked past.

'USA?' asked another.

The painted plaster on the downtown shop fronts flaked. It had once been some bold and confident colours. Now the colours were all faded and defeated, like the skinny fawn patchwork of a mongrel dog that took a death stroll into the road. Fatalistic like the long, affected drone of the cop as he drove the car in slow motion and cursed the dog but didn't swerve to miss it. Detached, like the way the dog ricocheted off the bumper and just hobbled on. Dangerous, like the eyes of the cop in the passenger seat, which, although concealed behind mirrored shades, seemed to be glaring at us, his antique British army issue rifle resting on the frame of his open window.

A car with no doors revved loudly but didn't change speed.

A topless, skinny yet well defined shoeless old man fried a fish on a grill over a metal bin in the middle of the street while smoking weed. The smell of burning plastic, burning weed, and cooking fish was trapped in the street's atmosphere by the weight of the hateful sun.

I thought about the weight of those matchsticks.

I wondered if I should turn back, abandon the mission.

I heard Miss Elwyn tell me: 'Once our hero has crossed the threshold, there is no turning back. For now our hero has entered the world of the adventure.'

We walked on.

Music swelled through windows and doors and bounced off every wall.

People stared at us from the windows of slow cars, and from shops full of people standing around talking, laughing, not buying shit.

'Canada?' said one fella.

And someone said, 'Africa.'

I became super-conscious of how I was walking – forgot how to walk naturally. I wanted to walk like the lads with one trouser leg rolled up. But right now, it felt like I was walking like Pinocchio – a marionette trying to be a real boy.

Someone shouted, 'Hey, Chinaman.'

Chinaman?

A mad man wearing nothing but an off-white towel around his waist drew a symbol with his finger in the dust on a barber-shop window. The barber came out and slapped him across the back with the flat side of a machete. The sound cracked right across the street. We flinched. The mad man didn't. He strolled on to the next shop and drew his symbol on the window with his finger.

Young men made of marble wore bandanas shaped as tilted crowns and eye patches.

Old ladies with stone faces wore bandanas with the knot tied at the front.

An old man with grey dreadlocks waved his right hand in the direction of his selection of string vests on display on a torn-up cardboard box partly propped against a wall. He opened his left hand to show the bud of weed that was also on sale.

A man's dirty sandals slapped the conked-out concrete. He was wearing a pair of sagging old blue jeans with one leg rolled up. His T-shirt looked as old as him and it read:

IT'S A BLACK THING

MARCUS

MARTIN

MARLEY

MANDELA

AND ME

YOU WOULDN'T UNDERSTAND!

The sun didn't lose any of its weight in the shadows of the shops.

A rustle of humans gathered in a doorway. Some of them were laughing, some pointing, some looking around nervously. Some of them just stared without expression at some limp thing in a doorway.

A man?

We've gone too far.

A woman with a half-melted face bumped into me without reacting, as if she didn't feel the collision.

We came to a place where one-storey houses had bars on the windows and doors, like tiny prisons.

A lad with scars all over his body stood at his front door wearing nothing but baggy jeans and a gun. I tried not to look at him, but his primitive face, like a Neanderthal, and his tiny body, like some sort of pygmy, bothered me. Even in a passing glance I could see that there was no expression behind his eyes. It was the most unsettling face I'd ever seen.

There was a long wall along the road facing us. The wall had little shacks leaning against it made of corrugated zinc propped up on scraps of timber. People were hanging around outside the shacks, sitting on bricks, chatting, washing themselves out of buckets, cooking stuff, as if they actually lived there.

Neither of us had said anything in what could have been an hour, two hours, ten minutes, thirty-five minutes? At some point Increase must've taken his watch off. And besides, watch time doesn't apply in dreamlike states on the edge of reality.

I felt Increase's gape skate over the side of my face. 'What the fuck is this?' he whispered.

I whispered back: 'I don't fucking know, la.'

An old Rasta appeared from a niche in the side of an abandoned theatre. 'Go straight, then right,' he said. 'Straight, then right.'

'Don't Break My Heart' by UB40 was, surprisingly, crooning, clicking, and clapping through the radio at Peach's Paradise poolside bar.

Increase shook his head at the two huge Black American kids who bobbed up and down in the shallow end of the pool, throwing a ball in each other's direction.

The bartender had his head in the fridge.

Increase cleared his throat: 'What soft drinks do you serve?'

The bartender hoisted himself upright and loomed over us: 'Lilt.'

'Lilt?'

'Lilt. You only drink Lilt when you're in Jamaica.'

'OK,' huffed Increase. 'One Lilt, then, please.'

'I'm joking, man,' laughed the bartender. 'We don't serve no Lilt. We have Tango, Sprite, Pepsi, 7-Up, and Coke.'

The dad of the two kids in the pool waddled up to the bar and said, 'Gimme a Budweiser, please, bartender.' He slopped down on the seat next to Increase.

'We were next,' said Increase. 'One 7-Up, please.'

'I beg your pardon?' said the American. He looked like Bill Cosby but vast – huge chest, face too big for his eyes. He kept his hands slightly folded like he was trying to make his arms even shorter. It all added up to what looked like a kind of bull-man – a Bull Cosby.

Increase ignored him as the bartender poured 7-Up.

'I was brought up to believe that English people have impeccable manners,' said Bull Cosby.

'Then keep watching, you might learn something,' said Increase taking his logoed paper cup.

'And you, sir?' said the bartender looking at me.

'Beer, please. What beers have you got?'

'Red Stripe.'

'No other types, like?'

'Just Red Stripe. You only drink Red Stripe beer when you in Jamaica.' He wasn't joking. 'I, myself, prefer a warm Guinness in the evening. But this is not the evening, this is the afternoon. And we don't serve no warm Guinness, because this bar is here to serve you, and you don't drink warm Guinness.'

I am happy to try a warm Guinness.

He pushed a can of cold Red Stripe over the bar. 'You drink Red Stripe. Thirty dollar, please.'

I must have looked confused because Increase said, 'Don't

panic, Aeon. Thirty dollars is only about, what,' he looked at the bartender, 'seventy-five pence?'

The bartender shrugged.

'In England it would cost three times that much for a beer,' I said.

The bartender leaned over the bar. 'That is the tourist price of course. If I paid that much for a beer and I drank eight beers one night, that would be a whole week's wages gone.'

'Hey, guys, can I get my Bud now? Before you continue your fascinating conversation?' said Bull Cosby.

The bartender handed him a Red Stripe.

'Put it on my tab,' said Bull as he waddled off to his lounger.

'You earn two hundred and forty dollars a week?' said Increase.

'Something like that. And that's not a bad wage, considering.'

'Considering what?' I asked.

'Considering Jamaica.' The bartender looked into Increase's eyes, then mine. 'You wondering how anyone survives on so little money?' he said. 'We work two jobs. Some people work more than me. Others just get by, yunno. Don't buy many clothes. Just wear the same ting day in, day out. Keep wash the same jeans, T-shirt. Make it last, yunno, year in, year out. People just get by. Or don't. Survive or don't survive. You do whatever you have to do, yunno?'

Increase had to seize the opportunity. 'That's what I love about Jamaica,' he said.

'What's that?' smiled the bartender.

He waited a few seconds for added impact, – 'No, sorry, it's gone.' – then grinned off to sit by the pool.

I cringed and sipped at my Red Stripe.

'So,' I said eventually, 'do you know where I can get some weed from, man?'

'Ganja?' The bartender frowned. 'You don't ask me for ganja, man. You don't ask just anyone for ganja just because you're in Jamaica, yunno.'

Really?

'But if you're really that desperate, you may want to try the Rastas in that room.' He nodded to a ground-floor balcony on the far side of the pool. 'Something tells me they may be able to assist you.'

I looked over as Bull Cosby jumped into the pool. Increase raised his hands and shook his head as water splashed up onto his khaki shorts.

'Sky,' said the bartender.

'Eh.'

'Sky. That's my name. It's not my real name. Around here most people have a name that describes the way you look or act or something. So people have always called me Sky.' He straightened up so his head nearly touched the canopy over the bar. 'For obvious reasons, yunno?'

'Oh, right. I'm Aeon.'

'Ian?'

'Aeon. Like EE-ON. Aeon McMenahem. And that is my real name.'

'Aeon McMenahem,' said Sky, raising his eyebrows.

He looked thoughtful, as if the name meant something to him. It meant nothing to me. It was just another thing that made me stand out – who's ever heard of someone called Aeon McMenahem?

Sky leaned forward and lowered his voice, like we were sharing some secret. 'That is a very powerful name, Aeon McMenahem. A Maroon name. Nobody ever tell you that?'

I shook my head.

'Well you must have chosen it,' he said, shrugging his shoulders. 'You will have to learn what it means. It is your chosen fate.'

Out of the smoke that billowed from the patio doors, a small guy with red eyes, dreadlocks, and a few patches of whiskers on his jaw and upper lip appeared.

'Yes, brother?' he said in an American-ish accent.

He had a massive bogey clinging to a hair that hung from his left nostril. The bogey put me off my stride.

'Er, sorry, mate, I was just, er . . . You got any weed,' I pushed the boat out and added a 'dread?' at the end.

'Indeed,' said Bogey. 'Enter.'

Music rattled out of a portable Sanyo tape recorder on the dressing table. Its speaker sounded like it was being beaten to death by a bassline that distorted the voice that sang 'Natty Dread Taking Over'.

There were two other lads in there, slouched in white wicker chairs at the far end of the room. One had spiky little locks and skin like tar, the other had a messy afro, light brown skin, and a dazed grin. They were sticking skins and grinding weed on the white wicker table in front of them, preparing a spliff so big it took two of them to make it.

Bogey sat on a third wicker chair by the dressing table, a posh one with armrests. He opened the top drawer, which was full of green stalks puffed up with buds of brown weed. 'We ain't got enough to sell,' said Bogey. 'But you can take this.' He snapped a chunky bud off one of the stalks. 'And please,' he said, passing me a Kingsize Rizla, 'do join us in a ceremonial smoke of the sacred herb.'

As the only one standing up, I felt a bit out of place. But I didn't feel at ease enough to sit on the bed. I licked along the length of a Regal Kingsize, tore away the seam, and sprinkled two-thirds of the tobacco into the Rizla.

'Stop, brother. No, no,' cried Bogey.

What?

'You're not seriously gonna mix that poisoned Babylon tobacco with our weed, man?'

'Er . . .'

'Look, young brother.' Bogey stood up, grinning over at Baby Locks and Bad Fro. He walked behind me and put his hand on my shoulder. 'I've got a drawer full of your finest sinsemilla, grown in the verdant Jamaican hills, harvested yesterday, cured in the sun, and purchased for the equivalent of twenty-five Canadian dollars.'

'How much is that worth, then?' said Increase, appearing at the patio doors just in time to catch me being made a cunt of. Bogey stiffened a bit, and the two stoned minions very nearly flinched over their gargantuan construction.

'I've never been up on the Canadian exchange rate,' said Increase as he closed the patio door behind him. 'But to be fair, most people don't even know that Canada's got its own currency, do they? That it's even a country?' He pushed Bogey's hand off my shoulder, saying, 'He knows how to make a spliff, don't you, cuz?' Then sat down in Bogey's wicker throne.

'You can insult Canada all you like, brother,' said Bogey. 'I'm not Canadian as much as you are not English.'

'No, "brother", I'm English. I am definitely from England. I don't know what you are.'

'I am,' said Bogey, 'we are African!'

Increase rolled his eyes. Even I could tell that this guy wasn't from Africa.

'I'm Alone in the Wilderness', sang the Rasta in the Sanyo.

Bogey sucked his teeth and said, 'Just as you call dis likkle light-skinned brother your cuz, I call all of you my African brothers. You overstand? Cho!' He must have been putting on his best Jamaican accent now. 'Tis a motley razza Babylon cook up inna England; masters o' de waves and home o' de slavers.' He paced up and down between us. 'England a bloodclaat.'

As he spoke, he grabbed a handful of weed and ground it into a fine dust with his fingers.

'Twas de angel of de Lord dat spoke to Samson mother,' he went on, 'and say: "No shall he know a strange woman, but only a woman of him father's house, dem."'

He produced a Rizla from somewhere, laid it on top of the pile of weed in his palm, turned it over, rolled it, licked it.

'Samson disobey de Lord and gave in to temptation due to de beauty of Delilah. Delilah, thereby, weaved de seven locks, dem, from him head with her web.'

He fired up a lighter and puffed on the spliff till his face obscured giving him a mystical air, like Obi Wan Kenobi's ghost, but Black, and with a bogey hanging from his nose.

'Dem dat sow iniquity, reap de very same; so shall you sow, so shall you reap.'

What is he on about?

'Samson gave up his power. And, rude bwoy, you want to mek sure it clear what side of de dividing line you stand upon when judgement drop upon de iniquitous head of de White man. Then shall de original man, de Black man from Ethiopia, we de Annu-naki rise up again and rule all Earth in righteousness and divinity. Jah Rastafari.'

It seemed possible that we were being insulted. It was weird, because if some White lad in a party in Widnes or St Helens had gone on at me like that, I would have punched him in the face by now, even if I didn't know what he was on about. But I wasn't insulted by this guy; I was just embarrassed that I didn't understand. I wanted to understand. I wanted him to explain it all to me. But I couldn't say that – not with Increase there.

Increase wasn't impressed.

I thought it best just to make my spliff for now. I emptied the tobacco into the ashtray, took a bud of weed and tried to grind it up the way Bogey had.

'And we,' Bogey said as Increase sat back, shaking his head and getting more vexed by the second, 'as prophesied by Marcus Mosiah Garvey, shall be repatriated back to Mother Africa by our Moses, our Christ, our God incarnate, de Most High, conquering lion of de tribe of Judah, Haile Selassie I, Jah Ras Tafari.'

I finished rolling my spliff and tried to light it. It hadn't turned out like Bogey's. His was a big Bob Marley thing. My effort looked like the things they smoke in Vietnam War movies.

'Fucking bullshit,' said Increase. He had his hand over the base of a lamp on the dressing table as if he was about to pick it up and hit someone with it. He let the lamp go, and I noticed he was shaking slightly.

'You think Rasta philosophy is not genuine?' said Bogey.

This Bogey fella didn't seem to realise that he was in genuine danger.

'I know it's not genuine, Rasta.' Increase took a deep breath to calm himself before he went on. 'I know you're desperate to create a version of history that propagates the myth of Black superiority. You need it to tackle your own sense of emasculation and inadequacy. I understand that, trust me, Rasta. I know we ain't got a history, religion, or culture to call our own. We can't rely on our ancestors because no one knows who the fuck they are.'

I puffed hard on my bumpy little spliff.

The Sanyo blurred out something about someone who was here first – it sounded like he was saying the Awawaks, but it was all gobbledegook to me.

Increase sighed real heavy. 'It's sad, Rasta, but slave-bred Blacks like us aren't superior to anyone. We'll never rule the Earth, and we're certainly not the original man. We're outcasts, denigrated even by the Africans, who are only the descendants of the first murderer. And why would anyone want to live in Africa anyway – it's a conglomerate of shitholes? They've allowed the White man to destroy it. And what makes you think they'd want the likes of you and me there making them look even worse, Rasta?'

A tiny trail of smoke rose up from the end of my little spliff as I puffed with tight lips.

Baby Locks struck his lighter, and Bad Fro puffed on a spliff the size of a rounders bat till the end fired up.

'It makes no sense to you why we would believe things which, to the brainwashed Babylonian, seem implausible,' said Bogey. 'So tell me, what do you believe?'

Increase glanced at the clock on the wall.

'Ha!' said Bogey. 'You believe in that! The Babylonian clock. You believe that the Babylon clock says tick and tock?'

'Yes! Come on, Aeon,' said Increase. 'This is bullshit, let's go.'

'Does it?' said Bogey looking at me. I shrugged my shoulders and wobbled my head. 'You see?' said Bogey. 'This is how Babylonian ideology gets inside you, so insidious it a mere duppy that makes you believe what it say without question. Every day it whispers its silent whisper into the dream you call reality, until you can only but agree. Listen to that clock.'

Increase pulled his hands down his face as if he was trying to get rid of something.

Bad Fro passed the massive spliff to Baby Locks.

'Hear it saying tick-tock, tick-tock . . .'

My spliff was only burning down one side, so I licked my finger and wet the burning portion to balance it out.

'. . . tick-tock.'

To be honest, I was starting to feel a bit embarrassed for Bogey.

What is he on about?

Still, we all listened to a few more rounds of tick-tocks, until Bogey raised his hand and made a new suggestion.

'Now imagine,' he said, 'that the clock is not saying tick-tock, it is now saying tock-tick, tock-tick, tock-tick.' And it did. Like magic, the pattern of tick-tocks changed to tock-ticks.

How did he do that?

Bogey relit his spliff, looking all happy with himself. 'May I suggest that the clock says tock-tock, tock-tock, tock-tock.' And it was; the clock was only saying tock.

Baby Locks and Bad Fro nodded behind a wall of weed smoke: 'Tock-tock, man!'

'Yeah, tock-tock.'

'Noooo,' shouted Bogey raising his hands and bellowing out thick plumes of smoke. 'It says tick-tick, tick-tick.'

You have to bear in mind that Jamaican weed is nothing like the rocky-black we used to buy from Shelly Tracky in Searbank flats. And even though I couldn't get a good drag on this spliff, I was still, already, absolutely fucking wrecked.

'Nooo. It says cack-cack-cack.'

Totally twatted.

'Or does it say kick-kick-kick?'

Unbelievably bollocksed.

Bogey's voice wobbled like the Holy Ghost was in his throat, and opaque weed smoke almost obliterated his face. 'So what does this mean?'

Shit, is he asking me?

'Erm . . . the clock doesn't go tick-tock?'

'For Christ's sake, Aeon,' said Increase. 'He's talking nonsense. Utter weeded claptrap. Come on, let's go.'

Bogey looked at me, ignoring Increase. 'I don't know. I ain't never worked with no clocks.' He suddenly had a Canadian accent again. 'Point is, it never occurred to you, or to your "cuz" here, that a clock may only make one sound, until it was suggested to you. You believe that every clock says tick-tock just because you were taught to believe it. Without question. Common sense, is it not? It is not! Because, you see, that word, that sound could be any one of a number of suggestions, if you just opened your mind to the possibilities.

'Imagine, for example, a world without the European empires, a world without Transatlantic Slavery, the Industrial Revolution. Now imagine that in that world, nobody had ever decided to cat-egorise human beings by the colour of their skin. The associations of Black people with badness would not exist. When you saw a Black man, you would not immediately associate that man with the inferences implanted by Babylon: uneducated, uncivilised, savage; you would not be unconsciously reminiscent of blacklists, blackballs, and black sheep, black markets, black magic, and black death – or blackened reputations.'

I wanted to say something, but all I could think was:

Stop looking at that bogey.

Increase stomped over to the patio doors, waving his hands and growling, 'I'm going.'

I followed him. And as I stood at the patio doors, the net curtain closing around me, I turned back to Bogey who eyed me and said, 'When judgement come, make sure you on the right side, rude boy. You overstand!'

'I'm Not Ashamed', sang the Sanyo Rasta.

'The right side.'

'The hero will meet a mentor,' Miss Elwyn used to tell me.

But how was I gonna meet a mentor with Increase always hanging around, sticking his nose in? Just like that Bogey situation. I thought about it as I lay back on the bed. Bogey could well have been a mentor, but I could never be myself when Increase was around. And yeah, maybe Bogey was a bit of a tit, but maybe that was just the weight of Increase's shadow hanging over the situation.

I bet he's made up he ruined that for me. I could still be down there now, getting stoned with Canadian Rastas and learning how to build proper Bob Marley spliffs, if it wasn't for Increase.

I had to make something happen.

Kissy Sunshine believed that the world you see is just a reflection of your own beliefs: 'An outer projection of inner perception,' she used to say. Kissy didn't have normal beliefs.

I could've just told Increase from the start that I didn't want him with me. That I was going to Jamaica on my own. I was nearly seventeen and I had to make my own decisions. Find my own way. I had to shake off the expectations of Searbank, of Mum and Dad, of Increase, of my mates: Joe Shirley, Jay Reynolds, Matty Lamb, Lollipop, Tommo, and the rest. Other people's expectations had me frozen in ice. I'd to come to Jamaica to melt the ice of Searbank.

But I'd failed in the mission before it even got started because I couldn't bring myself to tell Increase that I didn't want him to come to Jamaica with me. But you can't tell people that you're going to Jamaica on your own. That's just too weird. Who goes on holiday on their own?

I had to make something happen.

I needed, at least, to dare to be honest with myself about what I wanted. I had to remind myself that there was no big man sat on a cloud judging my thoughts; I could think whatever I wanted to think.

I can do whatever I need to do.

I could have happen whatever I wanted to have happen.

I wanna get rid of Increase.

I wanted to start this story again. I wanted the night so that I could wake up and start again, without Increase.

It felt like it had been daytime for ever. Where was the night? Where was the adventure? It was time to run through a burning building and rescue a beautiful maiden, or drive a fast car through a pile of cardboard boxes in a crowded marketplace, or run into battle with a pug in my hand like Jean-Luc Picard in *Dune*. Well, maybe not that last one, but you know what I mean; I just needed something.

Something that was mine.

Not theirs.

Not his.

I'll write my own story. I'll write killer lines like 'Fuck tha Police' and 'Real Niggaz Don't Die'. I'll write lines long enough to wrap around a neck; lines strong enough to hang a human body from the ash at the front of Searbank High School; lines with so many layers that you can make of them whatever the fuck you choose, mate.

And I'll be the hero; me, Aeon.

I run through a burning building. The maiden is waiting for me. It's the receptionist from Peach's Paradise. She swings her beautiful silky hair from her face.

But the building shrinks and turns into one of those tiny houses downtown with bars on the windows and doors.

I can't run any more.

There are icicles hanging from the ceiling, and there's frost on the bars over the windows.

But it's hot.

The heat of the place is zapping all my strength.

I'm stuck.

My feet are frozen to the floor.

I'm stuck and the maiden is weaving my hair with her web.

My hair is heavy and it's pulling me into the ground, right through the cracks.

Then I'm gone, into the darkness.

I can hear the sound of chanting, a lion-man roaring, and I sink into the bliss of the chant; into the black and peaceful earth; as black as her hair; as black as the night; as black as the beginning.

I opened my eyes and it was night-time.

There was a voice crooning somewhere.

What the fuck? Is that the theme tune to *Prisoner: Cell Block H*? But a reggae version? Where the fuck am I?

I sat up on my bed. It was really dark. Increase had gone.

Peach's Paradise was a small hotel – four storeys, three stars – and there weren't many places he could have been.

Our door opened onto an outdoor corridor with rocks running alongside it with plants and bushes alive with the rattles, clicks, and clacks of creatures you couldn't see. To the left, and at the end of the corridor, there was a large plastic chest that was supposed to be full of ice. The ice was melted. I filled my jug with plastic-tasting water and went back to the room.

I looked over the balcony to the poolside bar. No Increase.

I got a shower. I didn't wash my hair though. I hadn't washed my hair for three months. I thought that if I never washed my hair it would matt up into dreadlocks easier.

Kissy was the only person I actually knew who had dreadlocks. I never understood how Kissy grew perfectly neat dreadlocks even though she was White. She always washed her hair. And here I was, on my third attempt at growing dreadlocks. I'd tried plaits, I'd tried sleeping in a hat, I'd tried VO5 wax; nothing had worked. It was like my hair was being awkward. Kissy said it was probably trying to tell me something. Kissy didn't see anything the way a normal person would. How could your hair be trying to tell you something?

I slipped on my favourite new pants, the baggy black corduroys that tapered in at the ankle. I left the gold rope chain that Mum had bought for my fifteenth birthday hanging over the N.W.A. T-shirt. I used to keep Dad's serpent key on that chain. One time I left my chain and key on Kissy's dressing table and she tried them on. From then on she wore them every day.

The day Kissy gave the rope chain and serpent key back to me – that fucked me up.

Over the T-shirt went an oversized denim shirt from Burtons, unbuttoned.

My hair just needed to be kept out of sight for now. That's why I wore the woolly black Gio-Goi bobble hat. But the time had come to exchange the woolly hat for one of the bandanas I'd

34

bought from the place un-affectionately known as the 'Paki Market' in St John's, Liverpool. I chose a black bandana folded up and wrapped around my head with the knot at the front, like Ice Cube in the video to 'It Was a Good Day', like the old women downtown. I shifted the knot of the bandana to the left side of my head and positioned my new white baseball cap with the brim to the right-hand side.

I checked myself in the bathroom mirror.

Now that's a double crown.

I looked well Black.

I slipped on the big red Ellesse boots.

Still no sign of Increase.

'You, in Jamaica?' Increase had chuckled as we cruised along Turnpike Road into Searbank Village. 'For one,' he sneered, 'how would you survive Jamaica?'

I scowled and shook my head.

The guy in the white van had probably seen us approaching and estimated that we would be well past him by the time he pulled out from behind the sandstone wall. He probably wasn't expecting us to suddenly slow down. Or maybe he wasn't paying any attention to us. Maybe he'd also seen the two girls in psyche-delic leggings, crop tops, and hairspray perms walking towards the traffic lights. Maybe he was also leaning over his passenger seat to wind down the far window of his white van, getting ready to shout something at these two girls.

I was just sat there like: No, no nooooooo!

Increase was now leaning over my chair, so close to me his body touched mine.

Nooooooo!

'Look at the state of these two – put some clothes on.' He was already raising his voice – as if it was me who was wearing a crop top.

Him touching me, along with the prospect of him shouting something at these two girls, who probably knew me because everyone knew everyone in Searbank, and me being stuck in between him and them – it had my sinews ready to snap like tattered mooring. Then, just before shouting something at the girls, which would probably have been some number about the whore of Babylon or some shit, Increase decided to finish getting his digs in on me:

'And for two,' he said, 'how on Earth are you going to afford to . . .'

CRASH!

We were shunted across into the next lane. An oncoming 10A bus swerved to just about miss us as the passenger-side door crushed into my left shoulder. Ten thousand tiny portions of shatterproof glass exploded into my face, my hair, and all over my red Nike tracksuit. Increase's jaw bounced off my right shoulder before he wheeled across into the driver's side door.

The shock aroused some sleeping beast in the caverns of my mind. The beast ordered me to fly through the window, grab the guy out of his white van, and beat him over the head. I took a breath and tried opening the door instead. Then I shook it violently. It was stuck dead. I looked at my shaking hands and took another breath.

It was interesting, how Increase framed it. I remembered the Ten Commandments well, and one of them was definitely: 'Thou shalt not steal.' And pretending to have whiplash when your neck was perfectly fine was definitely a way of stealing £2,000 from the insurance company (a very common way in Merseyside). But

Increase said he was just taking what he was owed because he'd paid money to the insurance company since he was seventeen. I, on the other hand, had not paid anything to anyone and was, as Increase kept reminding me, breaking the eighth commandment.

He didn't seem too concerned about fraternising with a sinner the day the cheques came through the post, though.

'Now we can afford to go to Jamaica,' he grinned.

We?

—⚬

I straightened up my back, sucked in my cheeks, and pouted trying to look taller, older, and blacker, but the beautiful receptionist wasn't even there. Instead, there was this large orange woman. She smiled a smile that never reached her eyes. Next to her stood a thin yellow ghost of a bloke with a bald head. He vanished under the counter as the woman started talking.

'Hello, dear, I'm Peach,' she said, 'and this is my paradise. Is this your first time in Jamaica, honey?'

'Yeah.'

I tried to not look as freaked out as I was. It had just never occurred to me before that Jamaicans speak with Jamaican accents, even if they're not Black.

'Have you given us all of your money and sensitive documents yet, honey?'

'Eh?'

'Your cousin has already done so,' she said.

'Er. No, I'll be OK thanks.'

The bald yellow head of the man popped up from underneath the counter. 'You do not trust my wife?' he said.

He spoke quickly, which was weird for a man who looked dead. And his voice went up and down in pitch every few syllables. The voice really reminded me of someone, someone off the telly; I just couldn't quite grasp who it was.

'Why do you not trust my wife? Is it because of her colour?'

What, orange?

Peach looked hurt.

Confusion piled upon confusion. I knew it was because she sounded Black that I didn't trust her with my money. And that made me as racist as the police who were always searching me, as racist as the security guard who always followed me round HMV in Liverpool – he was Black too.

Mr Merryfield, head of history at Searbank High School, reckoned that White people had evolved to be more civilised than Black people because they ate more fish. I never could figure out why they'd have eaten more fish. I was sure Africa had rivers. Then 'Do They Know It's Christmas?' would come to mind. I loved that song, and that said that there weren't any rivers in Africa. So maybe Mr Merryfield was right. And maybe I couldn't trust this woman who looked orange but definitely sounded Black.

She reached under the counter and produced an A4 envelope, handed to her, I supposed, by the yellow fella, who'd disappeared down below again.

'See?' She showed me the join across the top of the envelope where it was signed multiple times with Increase's signature. 'It is best to keep all travellers' cheque, passport, money, and so on, secure in our safe, just in case,' she said. 'Penelope should have already told you such this afternoon. I will have words with her when she returns.'

Penelope. So that's her name.

I remembered Penelope's coffee-bean fingers, her shiny hair flowing over her long neck. If Penelope had asked me to put my stuff in an envelope I would have done so without question. Maybe I wasn't that racist after all.

Cars were rattling down the hill to the sound of an omnipresent reggae bassline.

Men still worked under the straw roofs of the wooden stalls of the marketplace, some packing up, some still trying to sell stuff. One man was sat at the side of his stall carving a sculpture from a log with a piece of broken glass: a beautiful dreadlocked woman smoking a pipe.

I decided that before I went home I'd buy things from these stalls: dark brown carvings of lions that would hang from my walls; fat black leather hats with red, yellow, and green bands that would crown a head of neatly dreadlocked hair. And I'd definitely buy one of those canes, a beautiful walking cane with Rastas, lions, and ganja leaves carved down its length. I imagined myself strolling through Searbank with my hat and my cane. I wondered how I could justify walking with a cane.

Fuck it!

I saw myself walking with a limp and a beautiful cane.

This time, I turned right at the roundabout, like Penelope had told us.

I passed a couple of bars on the right side of the Hip Strip, one of which had been burned down.

Over the road there was a beach with an outdoor bar where Blacks and Whites, tourists and Jamaicans talked and danced, drank and smoked. A sweet reggae tune was blasting, then it stopped, suddenly, with the sound of a foghorn and a man shouting aggressively. Gunshots rang over the sound of his voice, and some of the people dancing threw up their hands and made gunshot sounds – 'Bop, bop, bop' – and even some automatic weapons – 'Brrrrrrrap' – as the foghorn brought in a new song. It was that voice again; the lion-man chanting:

'Fiyah!

Bun up de whole of a Babylon

Fiyah!

Bun de iniquitous and wicked one

Fiyah!

Feh end all de old and wicked ways

Fiyah!

Feh turn these dark nights into day.'

I so much wanted to get over there and dance.

Soon, Aeon. Just walk and soak it up. This is it. This is Jamaica.

The song was interrupted, after just one chorus, by another foghorn. More shouts. More gunshots.

A tall dreadlocked man came bouncing down the road singing 'Running Away' by Bob Marley, dead loud. I noticed that no one was staring at him – apart from me.

I wanted to be like that. So many times I'd had the urge to sing out loud, or to rap the words of some De La Soul or Ruthless Rap Assassins song, or even some of my own little raps, while walking through Searbank village.

But Searbank wasn't the Hip Strip. If a bloke as big and Black as this dude bounced through Searbank singing Bob Marley dead loud, the whole village would know about it. The old fellas would mutter at each other. The old ladies would step aside. And the lads would have no option but to resort to extreme violence as a veil for their own insecurities.

In fact, if such a big Black dude lived in Searbank and did something as shocking as singing out loud in public, he would be doing so in full knowledge of the reaction he'd likely provoke. He, therefore, could be said to be exciting a public disturbance. And if that situation ended with that man hurting someone, it would, let's face it, be the big Black dude who would get arrested, locked up, served with a Section 3, secured in a B Unit for 'his own safety', and administered medication to aid with the 'mental health issue' with which he would be swiftly diagnosed.

A short Black man with tiny dreadlocks strolled past chatting to a tall man with the smallest sunglasses I'd ever seen in my life perched on the very tip of his nose. The way these fellas walked – strong and bold; the way they laughed – loud and fearless; all those things Searbank would never let me be.

As a kid, I'd lost count of the number of times an adult had commented on how 'cool' I looked or how I was so 'laid back'. By the time I was old enough to see some benefit to being 'cool', I'd already perfected the art of being frozen in ice just so I could fit in.

That was why I was in Jamaica: to find the things I'd lost. And maybe this was them; those hidden aspects of me expressed as a serpentine swing of the hip, a feline roll of the shoulder, a wild roar of rampant laughter. The Jamaicans had something I craved: the defiance in the eye, the pain in the voice of the lion-man, the danger in the dance. And now I could feel it: the determination of bass-driven music with its whip-crack-at-the-wrong-time rhythm, always somewhere in the air.

This was me.

I would have put money on it that no one here ever listened to any of the shit my mates listened to: The Smiths, Orchestral Manoeuvres in the Dark, INXS, fucking Joy Division.

Fuck Searbank music.

Fuck Searbank High School, and fuck Mum and Dad for bringing me up in that fucking racist backwater.

I decided then that I was gonna be like a proper Jamaican: cool and proud of it. I would feed the fire in my chest that would finally melt the icicles dripping from the walls of this cave. I felt to roar like the lion-man.

Yeah, mate, fuck 'em.

And suddenly, I was at the end of the Hip Strip. The distance looked dark, with just a few houses dotted along the length of the road. There was just one more building, at my right, a white-washed thing that looked like an old ranch with a veranda upstairs. I could see diners up there in suits and dresses, eating and drinking wine. No gunshots and foghorns here.

As I turned to walk back, I peeped up for a sneaky look at a woman sat at one of the tables. I had this fleeting fantasy moment: seeing myself sat there facing her from the other side of the table; her smiling at me the way she was smiling now; laughing at my joke, like the way she was laughing now; flirting with me, like the way she pushed her long silky hair behind her ear.

Miss Elwyn used to tell me: 'Sometimes the hero is fate bound to fall for a forbidden love. Percival and Angharad, Romeo and Juliet, Maria and Tony. Such heroes will risk everything to pursue their true love because – and this is what so many have missed,' she used to say, '– the forbidden love represents the part of oneself that "they" don't want you to know about.'

Aeon and Penelope.

It didn't have quite the same ring, but I tried it out anyway.

I imagined her as Penelope. Imagined she was sat there with me. She turned and I saw that she really did look like . . . I turned away for fear of being caught watching her, but I glanced back up just to check.

Oh no. Of course it is. It's her. And, oh fuck off. She is. Obviously she is. With Increase.

HAVING CROSSED OVER INTO the world of the adventure, the hero will be challenged by 'various wee beasties', as Miss Elwyn used to call them.

I uncrossed my legs. I never understood how other kids seemed happy to sit on the dining-room floor for assembly in Searbank Primary School. It hurt my bum bones, the parquet floor was cold on my thighs, and the spiky little hairs on Anthony Davis' leg used to prickle my knee as I wriggled about.

'Stand up,' Miss Elwyn used to say, slipping her hanky from under her sleeve. 'Stand up, you wriggly wee beasties.' She was the only teacher in that school who could get 'wee beasties' like me to pay attention. Because she understood what the beastie was, what we were.

'None of you would have made it as far as your mother's womb if you didn't have the little beastie in you;' she used to say, 'making you push harder to beat all the others. And that is why you are all the hero of your own story. Because you are the ones who made it.'

Obviously, I never knew what she was getting at – they didn't cover reproduction in fourth-year juniors, and Mum and Dad weren't much up for discussing it. But everything Miss Elwyn said did, somehow, make sense.

'Inside each and every one of us lives an angel and a beastie,' she used to say. 'And it is the friction between the two that generates the very drama of life.'

'In the olden days,' she would say, 'before big cities, before cathedrals, before Kwik Save and Toy & Hobby, our ancestors had to be able to care for their babies. They had to access what we now call love – that's the angel. But they also had to protect and feed the babies; kill the odd sabre-toothed tiger, hunt the wise mammoth, swing an axe at the occasional invader – that's the beastie. One had to learn how to cradle a baby in one hand and brandish a spear in the other – the angel and the beastie,' Miss Elwyn chuckled.

'Some so called grown-ups,' she would say, 'may not want you to roll in the mud or get a bloody nose, to stomp your feet and scream, and sometimes, my poor wee beasties, you just have to go along with their rules. But you must remember that just because they call themselves grown-ups, that does not necessarily mean that they know best. And if you ever find that their rules don't suit you, you may just have to scream and stomp your feet and roll in the mud whilst they are not watching. For the beastie will always find a way out of the cave. Beasties need to breathe as any other creature does. And if the beastie is not allowed to come out of the cave the easy way, it will always find another way.'

'Weed! Coke! Girls!'
 Sounds promising.
 'Yes, mate, you got some coke?'
 'Come.'
 'Rewiiiind, selectaaaaa!' came a shout from the beach just

yards behind us. The record spun backwards, and the crowd shouted, 'Bop, bop, bop' and 'Brrrrap' as a foghorn blasted.

'Run it baaaaaack!' screamed the angry voice, and the tune started all over again.

The poster was red, yellow, green, purple, and orange, and it said that this thing on Walter Fletcher beach was a SOUND-CLASH. The soundclash, something I'd never heard of before, could be likened to *Name That Tune* on ITV, but outdoors, and louder, and with a greater threat of violence, and no Tom O'Connor.

'Coke?' He was wearing a fistful of massive rings and a huge chain, all of which looked like they were made of gold tinfoil. He rummaged underneath a rock behind some long dry grass at the side of the road.

'Hold this.' The coke was tied up in a corner torn off a carrier bag. 'Get down, man!' he said, ducking lower behind the grass as a couple of White tourists ambled past.

'Two hundred dollar,' he said holding out his hand. It looked to be about two grams. That would have cost eighty quid back home.

Forty dollars is about one quid. So two hundred dollars is about – I calculated – not very much. I passed him the money.

'Now, what's that in your hand?'

'Eh?'

'In your hand, man, what is it?'

'Charlie. Coke.'

'Exactly. Now you under arrest.'

What!

'But that's OK. You just give me two hundred dollar, and me let you go. But I must confiscate the cocaine.' He shrugged. 'It's illegal.'

Scenarios passed through my mind faster than thought.

Pay him. Run away. Punch him in the face.

'And don't try anything funny, Liverpool,' he said, patting something underneath his oversized baseball vest.

How does he know where I'm from?

'News travel fast in Jamaica,' he said, reading my eyes.

I was gonna have to act quickly because when my heart pounded like that my legs would shake, and that carried the risk of making me look scared.

Do it.

'OK, OK,' he said holding up his hands. 'Don't get excited, Liverpool. I'm only testin', man.' He leaned in closer and said, 'But that the type of shit that go on in the Yard, man. So be careful! Watch yourself, Liverpool.

'Now.' He glanced over each shoulder. 'You want some weed?'

'Er . . . yeah.'

The soundclash was getting livelier. Two rums and a Red Stripe down, I sloped off to the toilets. I untied the bag of coke and scooped a bit onto one of those large coins.

If you bought some coke in Liverpool, it would have been chopped and mixed with something: maybe just teething powder or some other benign product, maybe Vim or something equally unsuitable for nasal consumption. The result is a finely chopped and toxic powder, easy to balance on a coin and sniff up your nose. This stuff was different. This was tacky clumps of yellowy-white stuff. I had to hold my nostril and rub it into the sensitive skin inside my face to stop it from dropping out. I sniffed back and the coke slid down my throat with an instant numbing effect.

As I walked back through the soundclash, a sharp as ice clarity got hold of me. The sounds and shapes were all the same, but I was more aware of them; too aware to really be part of it; but too separate too; too much of a boy preserved in ice walking through a world dissolving in flames.

And what's more, the coke had completely cancelled out the rum.

I necked a few more rums and two cans of Red Stripe, then tried my best to dance to the stoppy-starty music. It was hard though. When the music's that good you wanna hear the whole song. You want a chance to get into it, to dance. But how can you dance when the songs keep stopping and changing, and some angry-sounding geezer keeps shouting pointless shit over the top of them?

I decided I didn't much like the soundclash after all. I bounced out of there and headed off along the coast road in the direction away from Increase and Penelope.

A long, lone figure with his head down nearly passed without noticing me.

'Sky. All right, lad. Where are you going, mate?'

'Aeon McMenahem, the Liverpool Maroonian.' He looked me up and down and frowned. 'What have you been taking?'

'Why, do you want some, lad?' I sniffed and swallowed.

'No. No thank you, Aeon.'

'Do you fancy coming for a bevvy, then?'

'A what?'

'A bevvy. A drink. Come on, mate, you must know where all the clubs are round here. I can't be arsed with that mad shit on the beach. It's too fucking shouty,' I shouted.

'Haha, yes. The soundclash. Where is your cousin, Aeon?'

'Him? Ah, fuck him; I don't know, mate. I'm not arsed. Come on, let's go and get a drink, I'm spitting fucking feathers, here.'

'No thank you, Aeon. I have just finished work. And the clubs are very expensive. I told you today, I cannot afford to go to clubs.'

'Fuck that, mate, I'll pay innit. Come on, I can't go out on my own.'

'OK,' Sky smiled. 'Maybe just one drink.'

We walked on, side by side; me leading Sky because I don't think he really wanted to go for a drink, Sky leading me because I didn't have a clue where I was. I wasn't even sure which way we'd turned at the roundabout; I supposed it must have been the way in between the other two.

Sky was clearly tired, not saying much, which left space for my thoughts to fester.

An aggressive horn honked.

The headlights bounced from some bloke's gold teeth and the whites of his eyes as he sideways stared me out, grinning.

Somewhere in the mid-distance a woman screamed.

The warm, dark, and heavy night breeze, and the putrid fumes of ancient cars thawed the ice clarity of the coke; cracks ran down the walls of the cave; and the beastie stirred.

A police car rolled past us. I didn't dare to look at them, but paranoia told me they must have been staring at me because I looked fucked.

Shit, shit, shit . . .

I had to get rid of the coke.

I pretended to cough a bit and put the bag of coke in my mouth. There was a small hole in the bag, and some of the coke was spilling out and mixing with my spit. But I couldn't take the bag out my mouth now so I just had to go with it.

Tingling swept from the back of my throat, across the base of my skull, and danced on my scalp.

The weed! said the paranoia. Throw it! No, eat it!

Calm down, it's OK. It's all going according to plan.

But maybe that was the problem: that my plan to make

something happen was actually gonna work. That Kissy's 'outer projection of inner perception' belief was right.

I swallowed another stream of salty medicinal oblivion as we walked through the car park of the Pier 1 nightclub.

Of all the girls hanging around cars, getting chatted up or waiting to be chatted up, two stood out from the rest. They were standing by the open door of a car chatting to a couple of Jamaican lads. Usually, as I approached two girls, I would get a moment of trying to work out which one to look at first. Because if you clock the wrong one, and she likes you, that could ruin your chances with the other one, who might turn out to be fitter, or easier.

This was different. Sometimes you just know. Like when you're about to turn thirteen and Vanessa Paradis comes on *Top of the Pops* singing about Joe the Taxi. Sometimes you just know. And I fell in love with the brunette instantly. She was one of the most beautiful women I have ever seen, anywhere. She had something about her; Kissy probably would have called it a special energy; Joe Shirley would have said she was a dick-tease. She turned and smiled at me. I instinctively looked away, immediately hating myself for doing it. In the second it took me to recover, she'd already turned back to the Jamaican lads she was talking to.

I felt Sky smirk down on me.

Two big fellas stood in the entrance of the club making sure everyone's footwear was in order. Sky's work shoes and my big red boots passed muster.

The bar was at the far right of the entrance, and everywhere else was dance floor. After the bar, there was a wide exit leading onto a pier.

My face was numb: gums, tongue, cheeks, teeth, chin – all of it as thin as a ghost. I wondered if I could still talk. Only one way to find out.

'What are you drinking, lad?' It seemed I could talk even better than usual, if not a bit loud.

Sky yawned. 'Appleton with ice, please.'

'Apple what?'

'Rum, Aeon. Rum and ice.'

The music was all scandalous bass and rhythms in the wrong place. The singers' voices were set to split the heart, others roared dangerously to stake it, and one – a voice which did both – had to be the voice of the lion-man.

The dance that went with the music snaked the limbs like strips of ribbon. People pointed to the sky, waving finger guns at the gods. Hands suggested shapes of the bodies they weren't touching. Hips wound around each other, not quite making love.

A muscle man, no taller than me but stupidly wide, writhed around with a tiny woman attached to him, her legs making a circle around his waist, her feet crossed on his lower back.

The whole scene was so far removed from memories of doing 'The Hokey Cokey' at the Grafton in Liverpool, or 'The Time Warp' at Top of the Town in Widnes, or doing the right-heel-to-left-toe, left-heel-to-right-toe dance to the 'Wham Rap' at Cindy's in St Helens.

At the Pier 1, a mass of bodies writhed as one; a scene of sex, rebellion, and elevation all in one and all at once.

A lanky man with buck teeth and limp wrists jerked about like the last man on Earth. His half-hinged limbs swung from their joints, held on by the rust of a storm-worn history.

I tried to get into the winding dance. But the more the bass poured into my nerves, and the sweat poured out of my face, and the lump in my stomach fluttered about like free-floating atoms, the more I knew I had to get away.

I went back to the bar. She was there, the girl from the car park, turning from the bar with two glasses. She smiled at me again. I held her gaze this time, and I think I even managed a smile.

'What are you doing later on?' she said.

'I, erm . . .' I swallowed. 'I don't know, I mean, I'm just, erm . . .'

She laughed and disappeared into the crowd.

Aeon, you dickhead!

This was hardly a new experience for me: to be in a nightclub, obsessed with just one girl, too shy and/or too fucked to talk to her.

Tonight, though, I was a special kind of fucked. The kind of fucked a person gets when they need to forget the choices they've made.

I thought some more rum and a spliff on the pier might at least help induce some sensation other than empty dread.

When that didn't work, I went back to the bar.

But drinking double rum and Coke . . . double rum and ice . . . quadruple rum with no ice . . . just a load of fucking rum in a glass, knocked back swiftly with another spliff on the pier, on my own, then that again with a ciggy made no fucking difference whatsoever.

Sky came strolling down the pier with two Jamaican girls, one on each arm. 'Here he is. Aeon McMenahem, the Liverpool Maroon man.'

He's livened up.

He palmed one of the girls off on me and danced off with the other one.

We sat on the rocks for what felt like hours. The girl talked and talked, rolled a spliff, and talked some more. Voices murmured along the pier, and basslines boomed in the background. I'd never met anyone who could talk more than my mum, until now. She wanted to know all about England, about White people, about rich people. What could I tell her? I was fucked.

She was a nice girl, a pretty girl, a clever girl. She was exactly the kind of girl I wanted to meet in Jamaica – a Black girl. But I just could not do it. And it didn't help that she really reminded me of the girl from the porno.

Joe Shirley's dad had a limitless collection of porn.

We argued over whether they were really doing it in softcore *Playboy* movies. We tilted our heads and squinted at a woman shaving between her legs over a kitchen sink. We squirmed in disgust at the 'Readers' Wives' compilations and said things like, 'Ee, that's your ma, that.' And we ogled in awe and argued and tussled over who would be the first or next in line to borrow the latest hardcore movie featuring group sex, anal penetration, masturbation with fruits and vegetables, and some weird stuff too.

Pornography was a fundamental feature of our passage into manhood. It was educational. No one else was teaching us how to be men, how to treat women, how to get a woman to enjoy swallowing sperm so much she masturbates at the same time. Porn was all we had. Not that we actually thought of it like that at the time. Thought isn't possible when all the blood that once circulated your brain has been relocated to your dick.

We used to spend ages perusing the top-shelf material in the local Asian-owned shop – 'the Pakis' as everyone called it. And there was no shame in it because, as Joe Shirley used to say, 'Who gives a fuck what a Paki thinks anyway?'

I used to stash the magazines under my bed. I knew the cleaner would find them while she was heaving the Kirby up and down my red, grey, black, and white IKEA rug or Mr Sheen-ing the wooden legs on my double bed. I just didn't care because, as Joe Shirley once said, 'Who gives a fuck what a cleaner thinks anyway?' And I knew she wouldn't mention it to Mum, because I was the cleaner's blue-eyed boy.

Once, some of us had a group wanking session while sleeping rough on Searbank Primary School field. That was the night that spawned the myth that I had a huge cock. It seemed strange to me because we had compared cock sizes, and it was clear that Tommo's was the biggest, followed by Lollipop's, then mine; Joe Shirley's and Jay Reynolds' were about the same – the others never joined in. Yet, from that night on, it became an in-joke for the lads to mention my 'big black mamba' at every opportunity. There was no truth in it, but I was happy to go along with the illusion.

Porn was a ritual, a bonding force, and a shared interest without taboo – until that day in Joe Shirley's bedroom.

It was about a week or so after the first time I got off with Kissy. Joe Shirley reached round to retrieve a video from behind his two-in-one TV/video recorder in the shape of an American football helmet.

'Wait till you see this bitch, Macca,' he said. 'You're gonna love this bitch, lad.'

I wondered why he was only talking to me when there were four other lads there.

And why he was calling me Macca? No one ever called me Macca. I didn't like it. Aeon was my name, and I didn't want anyone calling me anything else. Especially not Shirley. When Joe Shirley chose a name for someone, it stuck. There was a lad in the year below us who everyone called Rodney, simply because Joe Shirley noticed one day that he bore a fleeting resemblance to Rodney off *Only Fools and Horses*. And What-a-Mess was only known as What-a-Mess because Joe Shirley reckoned she looked like the cartoon dog, What-a-Mess. And Splat was only called Splat because Joe Shirley decided that his birthmark looked like a splat of shit on his face.

Joe Shirley pushed the VHS in – CHK-K-CHVVVVV-CHK – the machine swallowed it. Tommo, Lollipop, Jay Reynolds, and Matty Lamb were all sat on the bed leaning towards the screen as Joe Shirley bounced into his space in the middle and pressed number 8 on the remote control.

The picture was wobbly and hard to make out, so Shirley leaned forward and turned the tracking knob.

The picture stopped wobbling.

I stopped breathing.

The man on the right of the screen had his face all screwed up and aggressive. He rammed himself deep into the woman's throat so she choked and gagged. The man on the left of the screen grunted like a pig as he clawed at the woman's hips and pulled her back onto him, slapping her hard.

It wasn't much different to a lot of other videos we'd seen, maybe a bit more aggressive. The only difference was that the woman was Black. I'd never seen a Black woman in any of Joe Shirley's dad's videos, or in any of the *Club*, *Men Only*, or *Razzle* magazines under my bed. I had once seen some pictures of Mel and Kim from a *Penthouse* magazine. But this girl was different; this girl was proper Black, almost jet black, shiny black, real exquisite black. And the men were white-legged, pink-bellied, and red-faced.

Joe Shirley nudged me and giggled: 'What do you think of that bitch, Macca? You fucking like her, don't ya, lad?'

Jay pushed himself back on the bed, looked into his lap, and folded his arms. Tommo and Lollipop looked sideways at me. Matty Lamb said, 'Yeah, fuckin' sound that, lad.' As if nothing had changed.

That was the very night I stopped having the dream about Hattie from *EastEnders*. White porn stars had not put me off White women; on the contrary, they'd made me lust after them even more so. So what was the difference?

I didn't know.

And I couldn't talk.

She talked. She went on as if she hadn't noticed that I was only partly there with her on the rocks. She talked about how much she wanted to go to England, marry a rich White man, and have loads of money.

The red rum water before us shimmied off in every direction, and then dropped off the end of the world.

I finished my drink and rolled back to the bar, past the dance floor where the crowd wound around each other as some dude sang, 'Murder She Wrote'.

She was there again, the girl from the car park. There were some lads next to her. She giggled at me, and I said something to her – God knows what. She flicked her hair away from her face and leaned into me. I actually put my hand on her waist and said something in her ear. Maybe I stumbled a bit, maybe she tottered on her heels. I secured myself on her hips. Someone accused me of spilling my drink on them or their drink on me or something. Someone pushed me.

I got hold of someone's shirt or someone got hold of my shirt. I saw a face in front of me, an almost inhuman face with no feeling behind the eyes. My arm lashed out without me telling it to, and I hit him in the side of the head with my rum glass.

Someone had me in a headlock. I struggled, but he had arms like a fucking vice. He dragged me outside and shoved me to the ground. I jumped up to run at the doorman, but someone grabbed my arm. I turned to swing at them.

'Stop.' Sky bent down to get level with my face. 'Stop, Aeon. That's enough. It's over.'

I felt another hand on my arm. It was her.

'You are crazy,' she giggled. She brushed the hair away from my face. My white cap had gone and my black bandana was hanging off the back of my head.

'Great hair,' she said.

'Hey, fuck them,' said her friend. 'Let's go to the Cave.'

We passed through the reception of a hotel that must have been two stars up from the class of Peach's Paradise, into the Cave nightclub.

At the bar, Sky insisted he didn't want any more alcohol. I guessed he was probably embarrassed about letting me pay for everything, especially now that we had two White girls with us. So I considered slipping him some money so he could get some rounds in. Increase popped into my head, the thing he'd said at the airport: 'These people all want something from you . . .' I took my rum and sat down with the girls.

If countless rums and cigarettes and spliffs and a lovely girl on the rocks by the pier can do nothing to shift the horrible paranoia inflicted by cocaine, a fight works wonders.

And now I was about to chill and have a drink with this stunning bird. She had caramel tanned skin and long wavy hair. Her tight little shapely body was landscaped in a just above the knee silver dress, her long legs spiked at the ends into silver high heels. She had the face and body of five hundred years of good breeding, and she was definitely, by far, the most beautiful woman in the Cave.

'I'm Angel,' she smiled. 'What's your name?'

'Aeon.'

The four of us were sat upstairs, secluded in a fibreglass cove painted to look like rocks. Sky already had his arm around Angel's friend – a blonde, plump, and very sexy girl.

Angel was nineteen, she told me. She was from Miami. She was a model who had recently appeared in *Playboy* magazine. The two girls were in Jamaica to export cocaine back to America on behalf of a gangster friend of theirs. They were staying in one of his villas, just along the coast. And later that night, they were going to take us there and introduce us to the beautiful private beach, where we would, it was suggested, go skinny-dipping by moonlight.

Well fuck me!

She was, without a doubt, the most flawless-looking girl I had ever talked to, and she was gonna go skinny-dipping – with me!

Heaven.

It should have been heaven.

All I had to do was stop thinking about Kissy Sunshine.

Kissy wasn't one of the popular girls in our school. She didn't wear normal clothes and she didn't have normal hair. And she was in the year below us which made it even worse.

Kissy didn't hang about on Searbank Primary School field. I didn't know what she was doing there that day.

I was sat on the hill rolling a spliff, not watching my mates play heads and volleys on the playground. I'd recently given up on pretending to be in the least bit interested in football. And now I didn't have to worry about being shit at it – I just didn't play. Kissy was sat about twenty yards up the hill, listening to two floppy-haired sixth-formers try to impress her, while ignoring her ugly mate, by spouting every fact that they knew about some band called The Cure. It all sounded very gay to me.

Then the Kentons came through the little wooden gate, and the sixth-formers got up and literally ran from the field.

Ben and Richie Kenton were brothers from Huyton. Huyton lads considered themselves to be proper Scousers, while they considered us lot from Searbank to be plassy Scousers, woollybacks from the sticks – about four miles from where they lived. And the likes of the Kentons liked to come to Searbank to prove how Scouse they were by hitting people and robbing their shit.

Angela, Kissy's ugly friend, clearly wanted to leave with the sixth-formers, but she wouldn't leave without Kissy. And Kissy would not leave.

We couldn't go anywhere, obviously. Lads like us, who didn't listen to gay-sounding bands, didn't have such options. For us lot, running away from the likes of the Kentons was even more humiliating than being spat on (as Matty Lamb was), having your football popped with a butterfly knife (this was Lollipop), being punched in the head (Tommo), or even being forced to climb onto the school roof and sing 'Material Girl' by Madonna with your pants around your ankles and the word BITCH written on your forehead in pink lipstick (Joe Shirley).

Kissy Sunshine didn't wear make-up – it was Angela's pink lipstick that ended up on Shirley's forehead.

And now, as my mates floated around the playground like litter in a light breeze, the Kentons came stomping up the hill to see who else's day they could ruin.

I smoked my spliff and watched Angela shudder and cry as the Kentons commented on the size of her arse, rooted through her bag, pocketed the gold chain and locket that she said was a gift from her dead grandmother.

But they didn't say anything to Kissy. It was like she was invisible to them, like she was too weird for them to even comprehend. So they just ignored her as she stared at them through curtains of mad hair.

Then they turned to me. 'And what the fuck are you looking at, you nigger?' said one Kenton.

Kissy got slowly to her feet.

'Yeah you, you fucking coon,' said the other one. 'What are you fucking looking at?'

Kissy walked straight at the Kentons, chanting something that sounded like a spell. None of us had ever heard or seen anything like it.

The Kentons giggled and tried to look unfazed, but you couldn't blame them for being scared. Everyone had seen *Carrie*, and Kissy looked just the part: long woollen skirt, something that looked like a yellow nightie, a scarf that reached her ankles, and dreadlocks flowing down and sticking out in all directions.

The Kentons stood their ground for a minute.

I was scared for the girl, but what could I do? The Kentons were cunts. There was a rumour that one of them had bitten a lad's eyelids off while in a Borstal – which sounds implausible now, but you didn't question these things back then.

My heart thumped.

Kissy stepped even closer to the Kentons. My legs were shaking, but I took a couple of steps forward and stood at her side. Kissy threw her hands up in the air and, as a finale for her mad chant, shouted directly into the Kentons' faces: 'Leave, swine! Vacate this place!'

Wow! We'd never heard anyone from our school use words like 'swine' and 'vacate'. And – this is the God's honest truth – the Kentons just stood there, looked at each other like they were sharing a bad trip, and then actually vacated the field.

Then Kissy, this mad girl, drew an imaginary circle with her finger around where we were stood. She stopped right in front of me and stared into my eyes. She was shaking hard.

'You really don't remember me, do you?' she said.

What do you say to something like that? I lit the spliff and took a toke.

'If you don't know what to say,' she said, 'you could just give me a go of that spliff. You don't recognise a damsel in distress when you see one?' She smiled.

I passed her the spliff. She pushed her mad hair away from her face and took a drag, looking at me with her big, too-far-apart brown eyes.

'Damsels in distress also like hugs,' she said, smiling her big gap-toothed smile at me.

I could feel the lads staring up the hill at us.

And no, Kissy wasn't a popular girl.

But I already had a rock-hard erection.

How many men in the Cave wanted to be where I was that night? You don't have to see who's looking to know you're being watched. When you're dancing with a girl like Angel, the stares are so intense you can feel them boring into you.

Before we left for the girls' villa, a song came thudding through the speakers. The whole club reacted. Everyone threw their hands up and wound them over their heads. People made finger guns to shoot the gods – 'Bop, bop, bop.' Everyone who wasn't already dancing made their way to the dance floor, including Sky and the girls. So I followed.

Sky knew the song. The girls knew the song. Everyone there seemed to know the song, apart from me. I recognised the voice though; that lion-man was everywhere.

The bass goes: BooM, *BOOM*, Ba – BooM, *BOOM*, *BooM*. The beat baps and snaps at empty space. The vibe gets close, it gets inside you, slides through the holes in your bones, owns the walls and polystyrene rocks of the Cave. The Cave quivers as the bass pulses waves through the floor, vibrates around your ribcage, soaks into the ligaments, nerves, and lymph nodes of every dance-floor dweller, moving us all inside and out.

Either I could suddenly dance really well or the Cave was doing the moving for me. Angel had her legs either side of my right leg so her crotch nearly touched me every time she wound in at me, spiralling up and down like a snake, shivering in my skin, making simulated love.

And that voice, the voice of the lion-man – young and wounded but proud, an alpha male awaiting a destiny that may never be – a rounded sound that growled into words I couldn't grasp, apart from the odd one: '. . . lead . . . head . . . dead . . . battyman . . .'

And the bass goes: BooM, *BOOM*, *BooM*, Ba . . .

Everything I knew about making love I'd learnt from Kissy Fortescue-Sunshine. So I thought that sex would always be the way it was with Kissy. But that first French kiss with Jemma Simpson at the Searbank Youth Club disco should have signalled a warning. There are quite a few lads from Searbank who can say they had their first proper kiss with Jemma Simpson. She just opened her mouth and engulfed my lips – which is a proper achievement considering the size of my lips. I didn't have a clue what to do, and people were watching.

The girls were all lined up along the benches on one side of the Youth Club, the boys on the other. I always sat in front of the DJ box.

We, the supposed lucky ones – the ones who'd copped-off – were in the middle of the dance floor doing a slowy, in front of everyone. We all swayed in the same way: side to side, padding our feet around small circles, maintaining that old right-heel-to-left-toe, left-heel-to-right-toe pattern. The DJ had just stopped the 12 inch single 'Especially for You' by Kylie and Jason and was fading in 'Nothing's Gonna Change My Love for You' by Glenn Medeiros, when Jemma Simpson started slobbering all over my chin and probing her tongue around inside my mouth. It was horrible. I didn't enjoy the kiss much either.

Kissy Sunshine didn't kiss with an open mouth, not straight away anyway. And she never writhed about with her tongue out or screamed and moaned like the women in Joe Shirley's dad's videos. Not unless lots of other stuff had happened first.

She used to make me give her tiny puckered kisses all over her neck and ears, and then kiss gently down the front of her body, legs, toes, up her inner thighs, guiding me, eventually, in between her legs, kissing and touching, stroking and making little circles, building up slowly.

62

Or she'd do it for me: massage my back, stroke my head, lick my nipples till I could feel her inside me, till the roof of my mouth tingled when my tongue hit the spot that completes the circuit.

Quite a few boys from Searbank can say that they had their first sexual experience in the alley at the side of Jemma Simpson's house. It was drunkenly clunky and awkward. I was almost relieved when her mum came rolling down the alley with a rounders bat. I removed my fingers from her daughter and legged it, holding my jeans over my half-hard cock.

Then I went to Kissy's house.

Kissy never did anything clunky and awkward.

The first time we made love, we were up in Kissy's bedroom in the loft, while her parents, two floors below us, smoked weed and played 'After the Goldrush' by Neil Young over and over again, and louder each time. Kissy didn't have normal parents. They didn't listen to normal music. It seeped through the walls and vibrated the floorboards, making Kissy's bedroom feel like another world, a different dimension. When Kissy took me inside her, their music faded.

We'd done everything else we knew of in the three-month build up to that first time: touched and played, tickled and laughed, stroked and yawned together with the sun in our eyes, making shapes in the cornfields.

But then the summer holidays ended, and it was never gonna be easy, going out with someone in the year below. But no matter what anyone said about me and Kissy, every time we made love it went deeper, and we got to know something new about each other, about ourselves. There were no barriers, no fear or embarrassment. We could say anything, try anything, do anything together – and we did. We rocked harder and slowed down together, swelled and released together, at the same time every time. That was just the way it was with Kissy Sunshine.

Angel's friend was called Sara. She and Sky made a nice couple, him long and dark, her plump and light, both laughing and sharing stories. What Sky lacked in money he more than made up for in charisma and conversation, which saved me a lot of effort.

The four of us glided from the Cave. I felt like a boy king, happily drunk and untouched by the dangerous stares that come with walking out of a place like that with a girl like Angel.

Angel and Sara had a private car waiting for them outside the Cave; a proper car, a posh one with a well-dressed driver whose neck tapered into his shoulders.

He drove us to a beautiful one-storey villa in a street of villas, a place unlike any I'd seen on the island so far; the kind of place you only saw on *Wish You Were Here* with Judith Chalmers.

Angel kicked off her high heels to cool her perfect feet on the stone tiles, walked through to the open plan kitchen, and opened a fridge full of champagne.

Sara reached under the settee and pulled out a mirror smeared with leftovers of lines of coke and a still open, still sizeable bag of the stuff. She put the mirror on her lap, arranged four healthy lines with a credit card, rolled up a note, and offered Sky the first line.

'No. Not for me, baby. But you enjoy yourself.'

Sara snorted a line, passed the mirror to Angel, and then jumped back onto the couch to snuggle into Sky. Angel went next, then me. I sniffed, swallowed, and winced. 'Nice one.'

'Nice one,' Angel copied, mimicking the Scouse accent and

giggling. 'You are so cute. Isn't he cute?' she laughed over to Sara. Sara cut another line.

I'd been called that word, cute, so many times by girls that it started to piss me off. Why always cute? Heroes aren't cute, are they? Heroes are handsome.

Increase was handsome. His dad, according to that one photograph, was handsome. My dad was definitely handsome. None of them were cute.

I needed another line.

I glanced over at Sky as he drank champagne from a glass that looked like a toy in his giant hand. That's what a hero's hand should look like: big and strong. My hands were no bigger than a girl's. They were, actually, exactly the same size as Kissy's.

I rolled up a note with my cute little-girl hands, sniffed, swallowed, and winced.

'How do you like the coke?' said Angel.

'It's better than the stuff we get in Liverpool,' I said. 'I feel hypo already.'

'Hypo?' laughed Angel copying the accent again.

Hypo? Hypo?

'Hypo? Hypo?' Increase had said as he walked into our kitchen. 'Hypo means underneath or deficient, Aeon. You mean hyper. You are always hyper. You should read a dictionary. Or just a book, any book,' he laughed.

And Dad laughed with him saying, 'You're right, Increase. I keep telling him to read the books in the study, the way you do. You know, I've gathered that whole collection for his benefit. He's got the entire set of the *Encyclopaedia Britannica* at his disposal, *The Complete Works of Shakespeare*, *The Thomas Hardy Collection*. And I don't think he's ever read a single word of any of them. He won't listen to me; he thinks I just talk shit for the fun of it. Maybe he'll listen to you, Increase.' They walked through to the dining room together, both of them looking like heroes: tall, dark, handsome, and intelligent and both of them laughing at me.

Angel stroked my hand.

She's laughing at you. Cute!

Even Kissy never called me handsome. Kissy called me beautiful, but I don't think she meant the way I looked. Kissy thought everyone was beautiful. Kissy even thought the fucking Kentons were beautiful, so that meant nothing.

'You'll have to be gentle with Aeon. He's confused about his sexuality,' Increase had said the first time he met Kissy.

'Who isn't?' said Kissy. A typical Kissy answer.

But with that one comment, Increase uncovered some dusty corner in a cavern in my mind. A place no lad from Searbank wants to go; least of all a lad with my history. And I tried to ignore it, but he kept saying it every time Kissy came round, until I didn't want him anywhere near my Kissy.

I could feel the mocking gaze of Sky and the two girls burning into the back of my head as I got up and walked across to the patio doors. I turned back to the couch and no one was looking at me. But when I turned away I could feel them again.

I was gonna need another line, which would only feed the paranoia, obviously, but so it goes.

What else can you do?

And that girl, Angel, who would make even women stop and turn their heads because she was just so fucking beautiful, she wanted me. She walked over to me and touched my arm as I stared out to where the black sea ended with one white shimmering line. She stroked my chest and smiled saying, 'I can tell that you work out a lot. You've got a really good body.' I tensed up my chest muscles. I didn't know how long I could keep that up for, but it was gonna have to be a while because then she said, 'Let's go for a swim.'

The girls ran off together down the private beach towards the sea, holding hands and giggling, then not holding hands but shimmying and wriggling out of their clothes. There she was, about two hundred yards in front of me, slipping her knickers down over her ankles.

It was like being in a movie. I was the boy. She was the girl. This was the story.

It wasn't supposed to be a psychological horror.

Sara and Angel ran off into the water giggling, splashing each other and screaming.

Sky folded out of his clothes. His long, toned body caught the light of the moon. He was a giant running down the beach, shrinking into water, splashing the girls and laughing.

I stripped down to my boxer shorts, walked to the shore, and dipped my toes into the sea as if to test the temperature.

Then I remembered the condom in the pocket of my baggy black cords. I wondered if I should go back and get it, put it somewhere concealed but easy to access, which was quite a challenge under the circumstances. But AIDS was all over the news back then. I didn't know anyone who had it, or anyone who even knew anyone who had it, but a foreigner seemed to carry more threat, for some reason. I went back and got the condom, holding it to my palm by my thumb. I stepped out of my boxer shorts and headed to the sea.

Sky was splashing and laughing with the girls as I waded in. As Angel swam over to me, I adopted the crouch position to hide my shrivelled cock and balls in the water.

Angel lay on her back, where the water met the shore. I hovered over her and twisted the condom into the sand. My un-tanned arse poked out of the water as the tide receded, and as it returned it washed over me and made my balls go even tighter. I really hoped she wouldn't touch them until they'd warmed up a bit.

It would have been good to just lie there for a bit, to talk, and to touch. Then go for a shower, lie in bed, talk more and get to know each other. It would have been good to start with some gentle stroking and kissing, to take my time, to feel her nipples go hard under my tongue, to kiss up and down her body.

But the beastie stalked the back of the cave, bewildered. I had to move quickly to prove him wrong. But maybe he was right. For the past three years, it had only ever required the sight of a naked woman in a magazine, or a woman in a bra in one of my mum's catalogues, or a fully clothed woman innocently trying to teach French to thirty teenagers to turn my cock into a throbbing blood bandit. And now I couldn't get it up.

Angel smiled: 'That's OK, we'll try later. It's probably the coke.'

I don't know how long I spent in that bathroom trying to get a reaction out of my cock. I shook it up and down, I wobbled it side to side, I even banged it against the sink just to get some feeling into it.

Sky was in Sara's bedroom now.

Angel was in the front room waiting for me to reappear.

I was sneaking out of the front door.

In the few weeks from meeting Kissy on Searbank Primary School field, Joe Shirley had changed my name a number of times. It was too fleeting for anything to stick so no one else ever did call me Macca. And only a few people caught on to the Migger thing. It was supposed to be like Digger, which was John Barnes' nickname – someone else who I looked nothing like – but it started with an M, like my surname, hence, Migger. And I'm sure that Joe Shirley sometimes changed the M to an N, but it was impossible to say.

Kissy had always managed to slip beneath the radar of the likes of Joe Shirley, but being with me had made her visible. Shirley came up with a thing for her: 'Gypsy Woman' by Crystal Waters was a big hit at the time. So now they sung it at her every time they saw her: 'La da dee, la dee da. La da dee, la dee da.' To be called a Gyppo was a big insult in those days. Kissy quite liked it.

I couldn't figure out why Shirley had started treating me like I was one of the plebs. But he was always turning on people, getting everyone to back him in a campaign to make someone's life a misery. So I didn't take it personally.

But that day, when all kinds of people I'd never spoken to before started approaching me saying how sorry they were for me – all pissed off on my behalf – I started to consider whether I really should be more offended. Even if Joe Shirley had laughed it off saying, 'I was just calling her a Migger lover. Because she loves our Migger, innit, hahaha.'

Now, this was 1991, during Increase's second Nation of Islam phase. His first began shortly after his dad died and he moved in with us. It must have been a huge adjustment for Increase: from living in a Black community, to living in Searbank.

Apparently, during the two years that Increase was at Searbank High School, he would get called nigger every day; and Black bastard and coon, wog, midnight, and Chalky, and, apparently, even jungle bunny. This would happen while he was walking to school, in school, and walking home from school. And these slurs would be spat at him by pupils and parents, by teachers and dinner ladies, by shop owners, and even, so he reckoned, the lollipop lady.

It didn't take long before Increase started getting the 10A into Liverpool and hanging around in Toxteth to be around other Black people. That was where he met Graham X. And Graham taught Increase the 120 Lessons, the Twelve Jewels, the Supreme Alphabet, the Supreme Mathematics, and the Five Percent Theory of the Nation of Islam. For a short while he even wore a black suit with a bow tie and a funny black hat.

There was only eight years' difference between me and Increase, but things had changed quite a lot in those eight years. There were still little incidents. Like the way Paul Richardson's dad used to shout, 'You're not going anywhere with that fucking nigger,' every time I knocked at their house. But his dad was always drunk, wasn't he? Or the time we had some Germans over on an exchange trip and one of them was a dark, dark Black girl with tight, tight afro hair. And while they were all building this nature reserve, a load of lads from a couple of years above us stood at the other side of the school pond chanting, 'Trigger, trigger, trigger. Shoot that nigger. Trigger, trigger, trigger. Shoot that nigger . . .' And not one teacher tried to make them stop. But they weren't talking about me, were they? Or the time that other girl had to get off the 10A bus before her stop because some smack heads kept calling her an ugly Black bitch, a Black slag, and a gorilla. But they never said anything to me, did they? But the way she looked at me as the bus drove off, leaving her alone in Page Moss. And the way that German girl scanned the crowd and caught my eye. And the way Paul Richardson's mum came to the door and looked at me as if it was my fault. And that was the last bus, wasn't it?

Increase told me that he overcame all the shit they gave him by making sure he became someone that people were scared of. It was when he started wearing the bow tie and the weird hat that people got too scared. Increase ended up in hospital with the Reebok logo still imprinted in his face.

'But Joe Shirley's the second cock of our year,' I said.

Increase had cut himself off from Graham X after that. And not soon after he joined the Royal Regiment of Fusiliers.

'You need to catch him off guard, then,' said Increase. 'Get him when he's not expecting it. Act normal, smile, be nice. Catch him when he's sitting down outside the Spar eating his cheese barm. Walk over all casual, like it's just another day, then kick him as hard as you can.'

I wasn't fully convinced. It was the first time I'd ever really considered attacking someone – I'd never seen the point of violence.

All sorts of people suddenly wanted to support me in my new-found fight against racism. Tristan Murphy saw fit to remark on the racist comments written on my school bag. But it was me who'd written them. One of them was the name of my favourite rap group, Niggaz With Attitude, and another was the name of their new album, *Efil4zaggin*. I could see why he thought they were offensive. But I could not grasp why he thought the NF logo was racist. That was just something everyone wrote on their books and bags, and on walls, and on the back of seats on the bus. I never thought it actually meant anything.

Increase had gone AWOL from the army after his tour in Northern Ireland. That was when his second Nation of Islam phase started. But this time it came with big shirts, a zig-zag pattern in his hair, and a constant scowl.

He gave me a lecture on the history of Black people and racism. It was a very strange history that started with a mad scientist from Africa who'd invented White people as a social experiment. It wasn't anything like the history Mr Merrifield taught us.

I bunked off school and stayed in my room until Mum had finished talking to the cleaner and gone to the shops. When I heard the cleaner coming up to do my room, I grabbed my ciggies and jumped out the window. I waited on the old quarry field, knowing the cleaner would leave at 10:30 on the dot, and then I went back to the house. I knew no one would see me – the neighbours on both sides were doctors, so no one was ever in their houses.

I couldn't stomach any food or even another ciggy, so I just waited – waited and listened.

I played the song, rewound it, and played it again and again and again for the next two hours. 'Real Niggaz Don't Die' by N.W.A. is more than a song. The beat kicks you in the head. The bass drops down and down, down like a rock falling for ever, down like a man who's been knocked over and over and over again, rolling over. Sounds ring high and dirty and repeat over and over and on and on, and you can almost hear the sounds chanting: I WILL NOT STOP, JUST WATCH ME – I WILL NOT STOP, JUST WATCH ME – I WILL NOT STOP, JUST WATCH ME . . . And the pain behind the words seems to scream POWER TO ME, by any means necessary, POWER TO ME, the powerful, immortal, POWER TO ME . . . The power that's built of years, lifetimes, and generations of being pushed down and down and down, and kicked and kicked, and spat on and whipped.

It's not a fucking song, is it?

I followed Joe Shirley down from the shop at dinner time till he noticed me. He turned around and said, 'What?' with a mouthful of cheese barm.

I said something lame like, 'What you, ya fucking fucker?' and started swinging punches. We exchanged some blows, and soon everyone had run down from the shop and they were all stood around us shouting and pushing.

I had Joe Shirley trapped against a high fence where he couldn't get a good swing at me. I cracked him with a right hook, and another. I even tried a kick to the stomach, which failed, but I was winning, or at least we were about even, which was better than I could have expected.

Suddenly, he stopped fighting and just stood there with his back against the fence. So I stopped too. He actually looked a bit scared. I was just glad it was over.

Then he said, 'Down on the field after school, you nigger,' and walked off. Jay Reynolds and Matty Lamb walked after him. Tommo and Lollipop stayed with me.

What-a-Mess touched my shoulder and asked me if I was all right.

Splat said, 'Fuckin kill him, Aeon. Please.'

Even Ratty Rawlinson smiled at me. Ratty never smiled at anyone.

But Joe Shirley was second cock of the school, not me, and it was his to have. I just didn't have enough violence in me to even want to fight him again.

It was just another disappointment, I suppose, for the likes of What-a-Mess, Splat, and Ratty Rawlinson, when I fell down on the school field and let Joe Shirley bounce around me stamping on my back – 'Get up and fight, you little coon.' – kicking me in the head – 'Get up and fight, you Black bastard.'

The beastie was biting at my mind as I staggered back along the coast road towards the roundabout. He hammered at my chest and lingered in my breath. I could feel him seeping through my pores. He was in the palm of my left hand, making it wanna squeeze the breath out of something. He was in the knuckles of my right fist, making it wanna pummel the fucking thing till it dies. He was trying to scream his way through my skull and claw his way through my eyes.

'Hundred and fifty dollar, man,' said a shoeless Rasta holding a carved wooden cane out towards me, extending it like a ceremonial sword.

I tipped some vodka straight from the bottle onto my furry tongue so I could speak: 'Nah, al aalight mate.' It didn't help much.

'Hey, man, come on, Liverpool?'

They all want something from you.

'Hundred and twenty dollar, man. Three English pound so a poor man can eat. Look, friend, see.'

'Nah, mate.'

'To give a likkle something in return, may well save your life tonight, likkle rude bwoy. Tek the cane and pay me.' The Rasta looked at me like he knew something I didn't know, then said, 'Just tek it.' But I pushed his hands away from me, and the cane fell to the floor.

'A magical amulet will be offered to protect you,' Miss Elwyn used to tell me.

Bullshit. It's all fucking bullshit.

Another stranger sauntered by and chuckled at the scene. 'Hey, Liverpool,' he said, extending a fist in my direction. I instinctively extended an open palm, when it was supposed to be a fist, so paper covered stone instead of stone colliding with stone, it was all wrong – I even shook his fist. He laughed at me and walked on saying, 'Bumberclaat.'

'How would you like to play tonight?' said one of the girls on Randy's roundabout. 'Come on,' she said, walking in my direction but never leaving the roundabout. 'You want some of dis?' She pulled down her vest to reveal a long, dark nipple. A horn beeped as I staggered into the road, then back onto the pavement, shaking my head.

'Hey what's up, Liverpool, you a battyman or sometink?' she shouted.

'Yeah, he only likes boys,' shouted another.

'Hey, fuck you, battyman,' shouted the first one.

'Fuck you, you fucking slags,' I shouted as I made my way to the hill.

The beastie burst through my skin, wrapped around my shoulders, and whispered at me, slobbering in my ear.

I put the bottle down on a wall halfway up the hill. I fumbled a half-smoked spliff and a packet of Peach's Paradise matches from my pocket.

'Yo!' said a lad as he appeared from behind the wall. 'Where you from?'

'Eh?'

He was wearing no shoes.

'Er, Liver—'

He reached out and snatched the gold chain from my neck.

I grabbed his wrist with one hand and yanked at the chain with the other. The chain snapped in half. Dad's serpent key bounced on the gravel with a clink that clanged around my skull.

Suddenly, I didn't feel so drunk. I swung my right fist at him and it connected with his jaw; the spliff crushed against his face in a shower of hot sparks. He dropped to one knee, then stumbled straight back up, ready for me.

He reached into his pocket and pulled out a butterfly knife. He unfolded the blade and locked it in place.

I just stood there watching him, like it was all happening in slow motion.

Then I punched him again.

The impact of the blade felt like two hard punches to my left inner thigh. I screamed, not with anger or pain or fear; this scream was sheer energy, an edge of reality ecstasy.

My body was on Superman form, pumping me with adrenalin, doing all it could to keep me alive.

I swung my fists about, hoping for a strike.

Warm blood welled up in the holes in my thigh, and then cascaded down my leg like I'd pissed myself.

We stumble and fall together.

I landed on my back with him on top of me. I deflected a blow to the body, but the knife slid down across my ribs.

He raised the knife and jucked down again. This time, I somehow managed to grab the knife by the blade. It sliced into my palm as I whacked him in the nose. I tried to force him over to be on top, but it didn't work.

Then, for some reason, I turned and looked down the hill.

Time had slowed right down now. A car had stopped at the bottom of the hill, and Increase was stood by the open passenger-side door. Maybe time had frozen because Increase wasn't moving. Or maybe Increase was standing still because he was stunned, or scared, or maybe Increase wanted to see me die.

I screamed down the hill at Increase, 'Come on, then!' I screamed it at the shoeless boy on top of me. I screamed it at the beastie. I screamed it at Randy and the girls on the roundabout. I screamed it all the way back to Searbank, to Mum and Dad. I screamed it to right here, right now, Jamaica. I screamed it to America and its Black movie gangsters and pimps. I screamed it at wide-eyed Black men screaming in abject terror as they're thrown over ravines by Tarzan – the White 'King of the Jungle'. I screamed it to all White people – a people I can never be a part of because it's already too fucking late. So I screamed it to all the Black people – 'Come on, then!'

Increase was moving now. He sprinted up the hill and snap-kicked the lad in the ribs.

I still had hold of the knife by the blade. I wrenched it from the lad's hand, rolled away from him, and got up. He tried to run, but I crunched his knee with a kick and, as he dropped, I kicked him hard in the head so his face bounced and scraped along the gravel. He was shitting himself now, trying to scramble to his feet. I decked him with a side-kick to the body, and he fell into the wall.

I turned the knife around and lunged at him with the blade, and then . . .

Nothing.

A warm breeze blows through me into the sheer, dark, tender nothingness.

Music – a sonorous rhapsody of bass envelopes me. A voice, exactly like the voice of the lion-man, chants a wordless and repetitive rhythm.

'Come on, Aeon. Oh shit.' I opened my eyes to Increase pulling up my T-shirt to see if any vital organs had been punctured. 'Right, you're not dying, cuz. Can you hear me, Aeon? Look at me. That's it, look at me, Aeon. Aeon! Aeon!'

'What?'

'Can you walk?'

'Yeah man . . . I'm sound, la, let's just . . .'

I slipped back into the blackness, following the blood that soaked into the earth under the small stones, and I was gone.

And everything is perfect.

The music is perfect.

The darkness is perfect.

'Come on, Aeon. You're gonna be OK, cuz. Look at me, cuz. Aeon! Come on, look at me, Aeon.'

'What? I'm OK, la. I'm OK.' I just wanted to be left to sink away from the night into the real blackness waiting for me. 'Just leave me here. I'm OK, mate.'

My eyes opened again as Increase hauled me over his shoulder. The jerky journey up the hill stopped me from sinking down again for anything more than a few eternal seconds at a time.

Increase sat me down on those cold steps before reception at Peach's Paradise. Perfect. I drifted away.

'Come on, sit up, cuz. You're gonna have to sit up, Aeon. Aeon! Stay awake. Look at me, Aeon. Aeon! Look at me.'

'It's OK, ya know. It's sound, mate. I'll just chill here for a bit.'

And it is OK.

Dying is easy.

If you accept it.

The chant takes me deeper: the Universe's pulsating rhythm, the first hymn; the supreme wordless psalm, the first word; the pre-eminent protest of primeval particles pulling apart, remaining as one; the great mother's endless lullaby; like the perfect repetition of a reggae bassline, backed by the simplest, most honest proclamation of the lion-man; two songs in one; one moment a birth, each moment a death.

Who wouldn't choose this?

Noise.

Shouting.

Increase pulling me up by my arm.

'I'm OK, y'know. Just, just let me sleep for a bit.'

And I'm gone again.

One more long second in the song.

Increase shook me awake again. There were men there now – two, I think – policemen, and a car.

'He needs an ambulance,' shouted Increase. 'What's wrong with this fucking place?'

The two men were shouting at him. One of them was a big man with a booming voice and exaggerated syllables. Someone had me propped up against a car, but the big man wouldn't let them put me inside.

'Him not bleeding Hall over the back of my work veHicle,' said the big man. 'You Hinglish boys cannot come to Jamaica and Hact like rude boys. See wha' Happen?'

Increase pushed him and shouted, 'Just get him in the fucking car.'

I slide down the side of the car, and I'm gone again.

Someone picked me up. Increase was taking off his shirt and shouting, 'Give me something to cover the seat with, then.'

Someone manoeuvred me onto the back seat. It was covered with newspaper and shirts.

'You will pay for Hany damage to my patrol veHicle,' said the big man.

I close my eyes and drift back, back, back – ah, blackness.

THE FLICKERING STRIP LIGHT made little rainbows around my eyelashes.

A beautiful round face with big round eyes and round cheekbones smiled down on me. Her white nurse's uniform blended in with the white walls and white ceiling tiles so that her face hung in space.

She checked the tube sticking out the back of my hand and said, 'Everything is OK.'

She smiled again.

She left.

I slept.

Increase blasted through the door shouting up a storm in a once silent room. 'I've been sat up in this hellhole all night because of you.'

I thought I'd got rid of him.

'This is the last time I do anything like this for you, Aeon.'

Then I remembered – he came back.

'If you get yourself in any more shit from now on you're on your own.'

I saw him stood there by the open door of a car, staring up the hill, dead still like time had stopped.

'I'm gonna get someone to stitch you up so we can get out of this shithole.'

He'd carried me up the hill.

'Jesus! I can't believe you talked me into coming to this fucked-up country!'

I didn't.

'They've got tramps sleeping on the benches out there. All kinds of degenerate fucking niggers,' he was talking in a kind of shouty whisper, 'screaming and arguing and moaning in that horrible defeatist Jamaican fucking drone.'

He'd saved me.

'I don't know how you've got a room to yourself. It must be because you look like a foreigner. They've left me sat out there all night, because I'm obviously not foreign-looking enough for special treatment.'

But he'd wanted me dead, I was sure of it.

I often wondered why Mum didn't like Increase. He was tall, handsome, clever, he read books; Dad loved him.

Mum did once mention the time I'd stopped breathing as I lay in my Silver Cross pram in the front room (she always mentioned that it was a Silver Cross). Apparently, it was Increase who had found me. That was the only time Increase had been to our house when I was a baby. And that was the only time I'd stopped breathing.

But when I asked Mum to tell me about that day, she just looked uncomfortable. Then she did what she'd always do when asked about something she didn't want to talk about: she gave a lengthy monologue on something only loosely related; like the day I was born:

Ooh it was hot that summer wasn't it hot tell him how hot it was Love wasn't it the hottest summer on record 1976 there was a plague of ladybirds that summer and they were rife in Yorkshire where we lived ooh we had a lovely little place there didn't we Love Beverley was a such a quaint little village ooh it was lovely parochial and bucolic and you you were four weeks overdue you just didn't want to come out did he Love and you were so fat wasn't he fat ooh you were fat I used to just sit there in the garden all obese and sweating ooh I sweated profusely didn't I sweat Love . . .

Dad nodded.

. . . and I used to just sit there in our lovely garden watching the ladybirds and sweating and I knew you were fine but they got worried at the hospital they were worried weren't they Love lovely little hospital that wasn't it Beverley Westwood much nicer than Hull Infirmary that's where I did my nurse training Hull Infirmary that's where all the commoners were born but you wanted something a bit special didn't you so you got Beverley Westwood Hospital well they were worried weren't they Love they wanted to induce the birth and you know what it was like you knew I could feel that you just knew and you didn't want them messing about with you so when they went to get the Pitocin you just popped out and when they came back into the room because I had a room all of my own didn't I Love imagine that nowadays a room of one's own and when they came back in you were there already feeding like crazy big fat thing you were no crying no fuss smiling you were from the moment you popped out just like that well they must've thought I'd been having an affair or something mustn't they Love because you were White ooh you were so White you were so White you were the Whitest baby on the whole ward wasn't he White Love . . .

82

Dad nodded.

I had to get rid of him again.

'It stinks of death in that corridor.' He looked genuinely disturbed as he said it. 'I fell asleep sat upright on a bench and woke up to a body being dumped off the back of a truck, completely chopped up.' He was almost in tears.

I've gotta get rid of him?

'God help me, I hate these Black bastards.'

The storm whorled out of the white room.

I slept.

A metal trolley clattered through the door guided by a hunched old lady with a brown cardigan over her nurse's whites. She stopped by my bed and looked me up and down real close, nose scrunched up as if she was sniffing for shit. 'Where you get stab?' she croaked.

'My leg.'

'Well tek off your pant and show me, then.'

I slid the baggy black cords down. She looked at the wounds with her face about an inch away from my thigh. She sucked her teeth as if I'd done something to annoy her, while prodding the holes in my leg.

Ow!

Ow!

'Ow!'

She rummaged around in some plastic trays on her trolley with her face almost touching them, then pulled out an enormous sewing needle and a roll of plastic thread.

You are fucking joking.

Without any warning, or anaesthetic, she poked the needle

into the skin of one wound. She pushed and pushed so the skin stretched and stretched. I stretched my fingers and shut my eyes tight waiting for the pain to shoot through the numbness. When I opened them again, I saw another white nurse's dress in my peripheral vision. It was the round-faced angel. She put one hand on my shoulder and squeezed my hand with the other as the needle broke through to the other side. Cardigan tied one stitch through the middle of the wound so it made a figure of eight. The lower wound was bigger. So she did two stitches on that one.

The taxi driver who took us back to Peach's Paradise knew all about us. 'News travel fast on the island, rude bwoy.'

Increase said he'd given all of his money to the policeman who drove us to the hospital – which seemed unlikely.

I dug into my pocket and pulled out a bloodstained two-dollar note. 'Me seh news travel fast, rude bwoy,' said the driver. 'Pay me now.' And there was something else in there – half a gold rope chain.

When did I pocket that?

Then I remembered – Dad's serpent key. I remembered, even in the midst of being attacked and defending myself, I'd been aware of the sound of it clanging on the gravel.

'If you let him go to the room,' said Increase, 'he'll get your money. I'll wait here till he gets back.'

'No mind dat, just pay me now.'

Whatever little energy I had was being sucked out by the driver. He turned in his seat and shouted, 'You pay me now, bomboclaat Englishman.'

'Here, here,' said Sky appearing at the driver's side window. He handed the driver some money. The driver shook his head and sucked his teeth, bemused, but took the money anyway.

Sky put his hand on my arm to help me out the car.

'I've gotta look for the key,' I said.

Sky frowned like I'd gone mad. 'Key?'

Increase stomped off shaking his head.

'My dad's key. It fell last night. In the fight. I've got to find it.'

'I will go look for the key, Aeon. You need to get clean up.'

'I'm OK, mate. I just need to look for the key.' I was already walking off down the hill.

'OK, Aeon McMenahem,' said Sky striding behind me. 'Wait, I will help.'

The hill seemed steeper now, and the sun was heavier than ever. We reached the little wall where the lad had appeared. There was still blood all over the gravel; motionless rivers between the cracks, coagulated clumps over the small stones.

No key.

My heart started to beat so fast, and it was so hot, and I was so tired, so thirsty, and so hungry I thought I might faint. But I had to find Dad's key.

'Come, now,' said Sky.

'I . . .'

I was down on all fours on the broiling gravel.

'Come, now.' Sky put his hand on my shoulder.

I knew it was gone, of course. And what was worse, I knew what that meant.

Something.

Dad never spoke about the key. I'd found it while rooting through his top drawer looking for bus fare. I just decided I liked it and wore it on my chain from then on. Dad had never mentioned it, so neither had I.

But I knew it meant something. And I knew that now it was lost, the something I was making happen was not gonna be as straightforward as diving through a glass window, jumping from a car just before it explodes, or surviving a stabbing incident.

I was so tired I could hardly keep my eyes open. I could hardly stand up.

'Come, now, Aeon. Come.'

Sky led me back up the hill and along the open balcony that led to our room.

Increase had already gone in and shut the door. A maid was stood at the door waiting for us. The three of us stood there looking at the door all sheepish, as if we were about to invade someone's private space. I opened the door before the awkwardness got too tense. Increase was sat on the balcony facing out towards the swimming pool, in silence.

'Tek off your pant,' said the maid.

She got a jug of warm water and a flannel from the bathroom as I sat down on the end of the bed. She wiped around the two wounds. She looked into my eyes and smiled with mild and tired eyes. She looked back down and wiped. 'Jesus wept,' she said, reviewing the shoddy stitch job on the wounds. 'I think you should get into the shower and clean yourself up.'

The mirror in the bathroom reflected the white door, the whitewashed walls, and me with a dark mask of cracked blood.

The amount of times I'd stared in the mirror at home and practised looking hard, looking angry, looking like a psycho. And now, with the blood of two boys encrusted over my face like a dried-up river bed, I looked like a true warrior. It didn't suit me.

My favourite pants lay on the floor, ruined.

Blood and bubbles flowed from me – as I rubbed the tiny soap bar all over my body again and again – and spiralled down the plughole.

I discovered a slash across my ribs and into my left lat.

My right hand stung where the knife had sliced deep across the palm from the forefinger to the mount of Venus.

I stepped out the shower and wiped the steam from the mirror. The blood was gone from my face and all that was left behind was the tired and scared-looking kite of a kid who didn't even shave yet.

Well, I had kind of shaved. Once. When I was five years old.

I'd been told so many times that I was coloured. It was always some comment from a kid whose mum or dad had told them I was coloured because my dad was foreign.

Coloured?

I just could not get it. For one thing, I could not see how my dad looked any different to anyone else's dad in Searbank. This was in the early 80s when Dad was seven foot, two inches tall – one of those feet being pure afro. And his afro flowed seamlessly into his huge afro beard so his whole head looked like one of them big fluffy 70s microphones. But my eyes told me he looked no different to anyone else's dad. I could not see that there was a difference.

And to the five-year-old stood on the upturned bin, the mirror in our bathroom said that I was definitely not coloured. There were definitely no stripes of colour – red, yellow, purple, and all that – across my face.

Dad's shaving stuff was kept in the cupboard underneath the

mirror: shaving brush, soap dish, and beautifully enticing shiny silver cut-throat razor. Every five-year-old boy wants to be like their dad. But this clumping together of me and my dad into some imperceptible club that made me coloured had made me extra-determined.

Obviously, then, I did as Dad did. I wet the brush. I lathered up the soap and dabbed it all over my face (that felt so good). I took Dad's cut-throat razor and unfolded it. I ran it down the side of my face.

The popping sounds of ten thousand tiny bubbles. The shock of cold of steel on my cheek. The warmth of red blood, staining white suds and dripping off my chin.

Increase had left the room by the time I sloped out of the bathroom wrapped in a towel skirt.

The maid sat me down on the bed. She took a small pot from the pocket on the front of her apron. It had a dark paste inside. She scooped some onto her finger and wiped it over the stab wounds on my leg. 'Maroon seed,' she said.

That word again: Maroon.

There was something in the way the maid touched me, the way she looked at me, caring, just like the round-faced nurse.

I wondered why she was helping me. I knew what Increase would say: 'They all want something from you, Aeon.'

And I knew what Miss Elwyn would say: 'At this stage in the journey, the hero must determine: who are his friends, and who are his foes? Angels and beasties,' she'd chuckle, 'inside and out.'

Sky served me a can of Red Stripe at the poolside bar that evening. It was Saturday night and I could hear Montego Bay bubbling with life and reggae in the background. But I was so tired.

'I'm sorry I left you,' said Sky.

'You didn't leave me. I left you, mate. I'm sorry, I was being a—'

'A bumberclaat?' he smiled.

'Yeah, one of them.'

'No, it's my fault,' Sky grimaced. 'I should have kept a watch on you. Especially after what happen at Pier 1.'

'Do you think it was to do with the fight?'

'You were fighting?' said Increase appearing behind me. 'Before the stabbing?'

'It was nothing, la,' I said. 'Some dickhead started on me. He said I spilt his drink or something.'

'What kind of place did you take him to?' Increase snarled at Sky. 'Some ghetto hole where you and your desperate friends could set him up?'

'No, no it wasn't . . . It's a place where tourist go, a safe place,' said Sky.

'A safe place? On this island? Are you joking?'

Sky raised his head and looked down on Increase. 'So why weren't you there to look after your likkle cousin?'

'Because I'm not here to be his fucking guardian.'

Sky sighed: 'So why are you here, Increase McMenahem?'

'Where are you going?' Mum had frowned. She was not impressed.

'Jamaica,' I said. Mum's eyes moved side to side like she was looking for something inside her head. 'And just when do you think you're going to Jamaica?'

'Erm,' I said, as if I needed to think about it, 'July, I think.'

'Next month?' She was not happy. 'And just who exactly do you intend to travel all the way to Jamaica with?' Increase walked in just as she said it. Mum's face was all tight as she looked at Increase. She wasn't comfortable.

And that was the last time she mentioned it.

I spent as much of Sunday as possible sunbathing on the beach, absorbing as much heat as I could take. This was in the days when I used to rush home from school on summer afternoons to lie down on my Ocean Pacific towel, inching down the garden to follow the last of the sun – sometimes even missing *Neighbours* and *Home and Away*, I was that determined to get darker. And now I was in Jamaica. I tried to convince myself that I'd fulfilled the first part of my mission: to make something happen. Now all I had to do was chill out and get Blacker.

Walter Fletcher beach was a tourist beach that you had to pay to get onto. It was all right for a bit; watching the Italian bloke parading up and down in his leopard-skin thong, skinny legs dangling down like loose threads; watching some other European fella's wife un-strap her bikini to sunbathe topless, side-eyeing her bullet-like nipples. It was OK.

The only local people allowed on Walter Fletcher beach were the ones who worked there. And, by far, the most entertaining of them was a creased-up old geezer who hobbled up and down the beach all day singing, 'Bag Juice' (which is literally some juice that comes in a bag) and 'Joe' (his name) and his little jingle, 'Joe me sell the bag juice.' You just don't see people like Joe in Searbank.

'Is a beautiful place,' said Joe, as I took a bag of warm juice from him.

'Yeah,' I said.

And it was beautiful, the sand was almost white and the sea was crystal clear.

'What's that for, though?' I asked pointing at the line of netting than ran across the sea about five hundred yards out.

'That,' said Joe. 'That is to stop White people from getting eaten by shark.'

Oh!

'Dem only like to feed dem Black bodies.'

What?

'Two dollar. Irie man. Enjoy Jamaica.'

That day, on that beach, I noticed for the first time just how light my feet were. Looking at those feet, you'd have no way of knowing that they walked a Black man around. They could have been the feet of any tosser from Searbank.

There was also the beach Penelope had told us to avoid, where no tourists went because it was free and, therefore, frequented by Jamaicans. I decided I'd try that one at some other point, when I was feeling a bit Blacker. That was the plan anyway.

In between those two beaches was Doctor's Cave beach, where I'd bought the coke at the soundclash. There you saw cool tourists mixing with cool locals. The dreadlocks giant I'd seen singing in the street on Friday was there, crab-bouncing through the sea singing 'Time Will Tell' by Bob Marley.

Someone had once told me that salt water helps to matt your hair together. It didn't seem to be making any difference so far.

I lay there a bit longer, tanning my feet, listening to the dread-locks giant sing 'Exodus'.

At the market, I bought a fat leather Rasta hat with red, yellow, and green around the rim. You see those colours everywhere in Jamaica, so I thought they must be the colours of the Jamaican flag. I did wonder what this green, black, and yellow flag I also noticed was all about – I thought it must've been African or something.

I also got myself one of those canes. It was a beautiful thing: a carved walking stick with detailed faces of Rastas and lions representing the fighting spirit that wards off the temptation to evil. It had a woman on it – the Goddess and guardian of the garden. And it had a serpent with wings bringing the energy and knowledge of the gods. There was a leaf carved around the apple of knowledge that leads to hubris and chaos, and to humility and wisdom. And there were children playing in the first garden where humans once walked. The whole story right there, carved on a walking stick.

It was painful walking on my bad leg. Not quite painful enough to warrant the walking stick, but I was sure it made me look cool, in a Black kind of way.

At one of the tourist shops on the Hip Strip, I browsed over the knives and played about with a big Rambo knife in a leather sheath. No fucker would be mugging me if I had that on my belt. I thought about buying it but backed out.

On the way back up the hill to Peach's Paradise, I bumped into Increase and Penelope walking slightly separately, pretending to not be in love.

'Where are you going?' Penelope smiled at me.

'Him walking the crooked path,' said Increase sounding a bit Jamaican.

What the fuck!

They both laughed.

Fuck them.

I went back down to the Hip Strip and bought the Rambo knife. No one's fucking laughing at me any more.

Back at Peach's Paradise, it was time to get bad-boyed up. Everyone in Montego Bay was bound to know about the stabbing, so I had to show them that I wasn't scared. Most of all I had to convince myself. So I had to go downtown. I had to go downtown and I had to look the part. To look the part and feel the part.

I squashed my messy 'wog head' into the fat Rasta hat and donned some canvas slip-ons from Top Man on my slightly browning feet. The Rambo knife sheathed nicely on my leather belt from Dickie Lewis's which held up the scruffiest jeans I had, which had patches of brown leather around the pockets that were now peeling off. Scruffy was good; the look I was going for. I stuffed my black bandana into my back pocket so it hung out, the way I'd seen people donning them downtown. I tried rolling one trouser leg up, but I wasn't quite ready for that. The top I wore was a red, yellow, and green string vest I'd bought from Trash 'N' Ready on Granby Street in Toxteth.

Increase knew people that lived in the Granby area in Toxteth, proper Black people. I'd never known anyone from round there apart from Mani and his family, who I only knew because they went to our church.

Every Saturday, after church, Dad used to stop off at Granby Street to buy food stuff from the Jamaican shops: yam, plantain, ackee, saltfish, black-eyed peas, breadfruit, hard-dough bun. It was another world. I used to lean over to the front of the Ford Granada and lock the doors while Dad was in the shop. Then I'd try to soak up the sights – while avoiding all eye contact.

As I got older, I wanted to know more. And it was obvious that

Increase was never gonna take me down there to meet any of his Black mates. So I jumped the 10A bus to town, asked someone the way to Toxteth, and walked there in my black and white Troop tracksuit and SPX boots.

Trash 'N' Ready, the shop where I bought my string vest, was like a mini-Jamaica. They played music like I'd never heard, had amazing colourful clothes like I'd never seen, sold proper nice weed, and sucked their teeth at you for no apparent reason.

The mirror in the bathroom said I was looking proper bad boy. Defo looking darker. I imagined that my hair was already starting to matt under the magic hat.

Yeah man. Something had to happen. Who else has got a story like this? Who else can say that they've glassed someone in a Jamaican nightclub, shagged a *Playboy* model – well, she wanted me to shag her – got stabbed in a street brawl, took the knife off the attacker and stabbed the fucker back?

Something had to happen.

I tried hard to convince myself that it already had.

Kissy once said, 'The world around you is sculpted by energy that resonates from your emotional body, which is seated in your heart. And what the heart pumps out into the world is directed by your thoughts. So you know what that means, don't you?'

'I haven't got a clue what you just said.'

'It means be careful what you wish for, Aeon.'

'Right. Well, I just wish you'd pass me that spliff.'

The walk downtown went well. Hardly anyone harassed me or shouted the name of a random country at me.

It started to feel like I could almost fit in, like I could actually learn to be, no, I already was one of them: a Jamaican; a Black man; especially with my new story; with my stab wounds; with my cane, my fat hat, and my crooked new walk.

Sunday was nearly done and I'd avoided Increase's for most of it. But I got trapped with him down at the poolside bar that night. He caught me by surprise as I supped a rum and Coke and pre-pared to enjoy my own company. Then that hefty American, Bull Cosby, came and sat on the other side of me. I was ambushed.

'Terrible thing that happened the other night,' said Bull.

'What thing was that?' said Increase.

'The thing with your cousin, here. Hey, how are you doing?' said Bull.

'Oh, I'm OK, thanks,' I said.

'Terrible thing,' he repeated. 'Well, I suppose you English boys just aren't prepared for the harsh reality of a place like Jamaica. It's not like where you boys come from, here.'

'What do you know about where we come from?' said Increase.

'Well, I'm just saying, England is different.'

'Different to what?' said Increase.

'Well, in the US, for example, we carry guns to protect our-selves from such incidences.'

'Can I see your gun?' said Increase.

'Hey?'

'Your gun, can you show it to me?'

'Well, I don't take a gun on vacation.'

'You don't have your gun?' said Increase, raising his eyebrows in pretend surprise.

'Well, no I—'

'You'd better shut your fucking mouth, then, hadn't you?'

'Well, I, I mean, I, I—'

'I mean, I mea, mea . . .' said Increase as he got up and swaggered off.

And Increase wasn't the only disappointment. My back was peeling. It had gone pure dark after just one day on the beach, and now, the same night, my tan was peeling off in big strips like old wallpaper. I tried to stick it back on with after-sun lotion – who's ever heard of a Black man who peels?

Monday night was carnival night on the Hip Strip: beach barbecues, live music, bogle dance competitions (whatever one of them was); all manner of cool sounding shit that I was destined never to see.

The knife got sheathed in the belt of some stupidly baggy red jeans from Stolen From Ivor. I put on the Malcolm X 'BY ANY MEANS NECESSARY' T-shirt with a green and yellow hooded mesh top from Trash 'N' Ready over the top. I tucked in the laces of my big red Ellesse boots so the boots hung loose around my feet. I tied a black bandana around my head with a corner pointing down over my right eye like a pirate's eyepatch. The fat Rasta hat went over the bandana. I put three readymade spliffs in a ciggy box and – 'Yeah man.' – I was ready.

It was still early, and just a few locals and tourists were starting to trickle down to the Hip Strip. Reggae music was reverberating from all angles of the near distance, and the air was electric with expectation. At the bottom of the market, the man still worked on his Rasta head with a piece of glass, while his portable radio sang of 'Slavery Days'.

Just ahead of me, two police cars pulled up followed by an old truck with an open back. They took a couple of bollards from the back of the truck and made a roadblock with some rope. They left a gap between the truck and one of the bollards for pedestrians to pass through.

Now they were searching a young Jamaican lad, while a few White tourists and a couple of Black girls passed through, unchecked. The police took something out of the lad's pocket, threw it onto the back of the truck, and let him through.

Then they stopped me. 'What dis for?' said one officer grabbing my new cane.

'It's to help me walk,' I said keeping tight hold. 'I got stabbed. I need it to walk.'

'Pttts.' He sucked his teeth and eyed me like he was Dirty Harry – "Go ahead, make my day." – and all that.

The first time I ever got arrested I was fourteen. I got nicked for having a go on Lollipop's bike. (Lollipop was named, by Joe Shirley obviously, for his skinny body and big round head.) The policemen followed me onto Penny's Pit, skidding on the grass like they were Starsky and Hutch – like one of them was gonna slide over the bonnet in a knitted cardy. Matty Lamb slipped a bumnut of rocky under his tongue, Tommo chewed and balked on a half-smoked spliff, Joe Shirley slid a roach-ripped Rizla packet into his turnups.

The police said that a bike had been stolen from outside Ali K Babi's takeaway.

'So?'

'We think you took the bike, lad.'

'Me? This is his bike,' I said, pointing at Lollipop.

'We'll have to take you in under suspicion anyway, lad.'

'Suspicion of what? It's his bike.'

'It is, it's my bike, mate,' said Lollipop. 'It's got a serial number on it. Radio it in and my mum's address comes up.'

'If it's your bike, son, then take it. But your friend's coming with us.'

'Why? He's just told ya,' snarled Joe Shirley. 'It's his bike,' he nodded at Lollipop.

'I'll tell you what,' one of the policemen said to me. 'We'll take you to Ali's. One of the girls who works there saw the lad who took the bike. If she says it wasn't you, we'll bring you straight back here to your mates. All over. How's that?'

'All right,' I shrugged.

But when we got to Ali's, they kept on driving. 'I thought you were gonna ask the girl in the chippy.'

The policemen didn't answer.

They drove me straight to Prescot Police Station. They made me empty my pockets and put everything I had into a plastic bag: twenty-seven pence and a Michael Jackson keyring. Then they made me take off my belt so my jeans sagged down over my arse, and take my shoelaces out so the tongue on my Reebok Pumps stuck up over the bottom of my jeans. They banged me up in a cell for the rest of the afternoon, until Mum could get out of work.

They did, eventually, catch the kid who'd stolen the bike. He was a local lad, and a well-known thief from a family of total head-the-balls, all of whom had blond hair and blue eyes. I'd never robbed anything in my life.

I started nicking money from Mum's purse shortly after that.

He was no Clint Eastwood. He was more like a fat Mexican primed to get shot in the opening scene of some spaghetti western, but Black. He yanked the cane from me and threw it onto the back of the truck. He ordered me to put my hands up in the air and patted me down.

'Why you carrying this?' He unsheathed the blade.

'Er, well I got stabbed and . . .'

He threw the knife onto the back of the truck, sucking his teeth: 'Ptts, you get stab.' He nodded for me to walk on.

I was about to walk on, gutted about my new cane and my new knife, when a huge hand grabbed my shoulder. I turned to face the white shirt of a man so big his chest was level with my face, and millimetres away from it.

He glared down at me with spiteful delight – huge smile, wide eyes. It took a few seconds to sink in; it was the guy who'd taken us to the hospital three nights earlier, the guy who Increase had shouted at, the guy whose 'work veHicle' had been drenched in my blood. He lowered his head so his horse-sized face was level with mine, so I could smell his shadowy breath.

'Let me see what you Have in your pockets. What's this?' he said as he pulled out the cigarette box and opened it. He sounded excited.

'Dem's me roll-ups, man,' I said, trying to sound casual and . . . well I don't know what, it was just a shit answer.

He broke open the end of one of the 'roll-ups', held it to his nose, sniffed long and hard, then boomed with pure joy in his voice: 'Hit's ganja!'

Maybe an hour or so later, I was still stood on the same spot watching these two pigs search every young Black Jamaican man that passed through the roadblock.

Why are they keeping me here?

I was starting to wonder if weed was illegal in Jamaica after all.

It's not likely.

But here I was.

The second time I got arrested in Searbank it was a weekend. Everyone was out on Penny's Pit getting pissed, getting stoned, fingering Jemma Simpson, that kind of stuff. The pigs pulled up next to us as we walked out of Cosmo's Offy. Tommo pegged it across Penny's Pit, groping in his jeans for a sheet of double-dip MBS trips. Matty Lamb put a fiver's rocky in his mouth. A plastic bag dangled behind Joe Shirley's legs as if the pigs couldn't see it or even hear two bottles of MD 20/20 jangling against a bottle of Thunderbird.

The female pig squealed at me: 'Where did he go?'

'Who?'

The male pig put his trotters all up the front of my Campari ski jacket shouting, 'You know who, lad. Why did he run off?'

'I don't know. Why would I know?' Obviously I knew, but why were they asking me?

'Get in the car,' the pig-woman screamed. She grabbed my arm, and the man pushed my head down and forced me into the car.

'Leave him alone,' shouted Joe Shirley. 'He hasn't done anything.'

People started running over, shouting at the police. Shirley threw a half-brick that hit the back of the car as it skidded off the park.

That was when I was fifteen.

When Mum and Dad came to get me from Prescot Police Station, the pigs told them that they had 'observed' me walking down the street drinking a bottle of cider, carrying a bag of booze, shouting at them, and gesticulating in their direction all at the same time. As if! I didn't even know what gesticulating meant. And only pussies drank cider.

The Montego Bay pigs didn't search any women or tourists, even Black ones, just young Black Jamaican men. And me.

Kissy popped into my head again: '. . . be careful what you wish for, Aeon.'

The back of the truck was filling up with confiscated knives and machetes. And I was still the only person who'd been arrested – if that was what was happening.

The third time I got arrested I was sixteen.

The pigs told Mum and Dad that they thought I'd escaped from a local care-in-the-community home, because they had 'observed' me 'sat looking at a pond, with a sweaty face, while wearing a vest'. It was July. I'd been for a jog. I was looking at a pond.

Anything that didn't fit in Searbank did not belong.

I wasn't too bothered at this point, more bored than anything. A few hours in the cells and a £60 fine plus court costs were the worst you could expect if you were arrested with a bit of weed back in England. And this was Jamaica so, surely, even if weed was illegal, they'd just let me go. The big pig probably just wanted to scare me or something.

They wouldn't lock you up for a few spliffs, would they?

The police station was one room – a dark and dusty polygon with a desk in the middle and two cells in a left-hand corner.

One cell was empty. Two lads were in the other. One was a young kid with his face up against the railings. He had the wide, desperate, and eager eyes of a puppy. The other lad was sat on a concrete slab at the back of the cell shining up a huge white Nike boot with a flannel.

The other pigs had left, all apart from Big Pig who was now behind the desk showing me his massive teeth. He told me to take off my hat. He looked at my hair, sighed, and shook his head. 'Why you people don't wash your filthy Hair? Put it back on.'

My stuff sat on the desk: one belt, cigarette packet, a lighter, five hundred dollars, half a gold rope chain, and a bloodstained two-dollar note. Big Pig put it all in a big zip bag – all except my five hundred dollars, which remained on the desk.

'What Hother money do you Have?' said Big Pig.

'None, mate, that's it.'

He smiled his broad, mean smile at me.

'Come, now, Hinglish boy. You must tek more money than this to carnival.'

'Nah.'

He rolled his eyes around the room before landing them on mine. 'But you must Have more money.'

'I haven't got any more money,' I said, holding up my baggy red jeans so they didn't fall down.

He leaned forward as if to share some secret. 'Are you sure you Have no more money?'

'Yeah,' I said.

'Surely you, a Hinglish ragamuffin, must have some more than just this?' He frowned.

The conversation went on like this for a good while; him never saying what he was getting at, and me never guessing.

Why would he be bothered how much money I've got?

Sky had advised me to always keep some money in my sock so if I got mugged they wouldn't get everything. But there was no way the police could have known about that.

He gave up on his line of questioning when another pig came in. He put the bag with my stuff in it under the desk. He put the five hundred dollars in his pocket.

They don't do that at Prescot Police Station.

He turned to the new pig and said, 'I Have given Him a chance.'

What chance?

'Him just Haffe go a court.' He sucked his big teeth and left the room.

The new pig looked like a Black Rab C. Nesbitt: flabby and bored, with BO stains under his arms, and a white string vest under his see-through white shirt. He led me to the cell with two lads in it. He opened the gate and gave me a little shove and a suck of his teeth as if I'd done something to annoy him.

The cell was tiny.

The wall at the back of the cell had small, randomly spaced brick-sized gaps. I could still hear faint ripples of the fun shit I was fated never to see, seeping through from somewhere out there.

Boots stood up, suddenly animated by the new arrival. 'Irie, friend,' he said, still polishing his boot. 'What di babylon arres' you for?'

'Weed.'

'How much?' Polishing.

'Just a few spliffs.'

'Where you from, rude bwoy?' Rubbing.

'Liverpool.'

'Englan?' Wiping.

'Liverpool!'

'It lucky dem arres' you tonight,' said Boots. 'Tomorrow you go a morning court, early, early. You get a fine, and dem let you go.'

'Sound,' I nodded.

'If them would of arres' you on Friday, dem would have kept you all weekend in this tiny cell, man.'

'Really?'

'Feh real, mon. Dat wha'ppen to me.'

'Fuck that, man.'

'Indeed, rude bwoy.'

'So what are you in for?'

'Dem say that me harass di tourist. Dem say dem want to keep me off di street.'

'Right.'

'Me tell them me no harass no tourist. Me have no need feh harass no tourist, dem. Me was just chatting to a nice English gal and dem no like it. Dem get jealous and arres' me.'

He looked me up and down. 'How old are you, rude bwoy?'

'Sixteen.'

'Oh!'

'What?'

'You already tell dem you is sixteen?' he asked, wiping.

'Yeah. Why?'

He shook his head and sighed. 'That mean you will go a court with the yute here.' He nodded towards Puppy, rubbing. 'You will go a family court.'

'Oh right. What time's that, then?'

He stopped polishing his boot. 'Thursday.'

Thursday?

It was some time in the night, and no one had said anything for ages. The only way to monitor the passing of time was by the swelling of my bladder. 'Can I use the toilet, mate?' I said to Rab C., who was now sat on an upturned bucket near the cell, staring at his hands.

'No. Me cannot open the cell. It past time,' he said, staring at his hands.

'Past what time?' I said. There was no clock in the room, and he wasn't wearing a watch. 'Whatever time just pass,' he said, staring at his hands. I did a little need-a-piss dance, but little dances held no sway with him. He spat on the floor and sucked his teeth.

It got unbearable, so, in desperation, I went into the corner furthest from Puppy and Boots, nearest Rab C., and pissed on the cell floor. They all went on as normal – Boots polishing a boot, Puppy twisting a clump of hair, Rab C. staring at his hands.

Time passed.

Big Pig returned at some point in the night. He had a Black English girl with him. 'Another Hinglish who don't know when they are given a chance,' said Big Pig. She'd been nicked with weed too. Rab C got up from his bucket, unlocked the empty cell, and led her in, his hand lingering on her arm. She eyed him with a frown.

Boots got all excited at the sight of a woman. 'Hey, Fatty,' he said, 'you should come an' see me before you go back a England.'

'You what?' she snapped in a cockney accent.

Then Puppy joined in: 'Hey, Fatty. Your batty really nice and fat, yunno?'

'Pardon? What did you just—?'

'Listen, Fatty, when we get out a 'ere we can go a do a likkle something, me and you,' said Boots.

'Sorry?'

The two of them kept at it.

We didn't get it, me and her. But after a while it started to sink in, for both of us I think. The Jamaican lads weren't trying to insult her. She was fat, they liked the fact she was fat, and they thought it was appropriate to say so. The same way a scally in the 051 nightclub in Liverpool might think it perfectly normal to chat up a girl by saying, 'Fit arse on you, girl,' a Jamaican rude boy will say, 'Me like your big fat batty.' It must work sometimes. I've seen it work in the 051.

Fatty was having none of it.

Time passed.

I opened my eyes and turned my stiff neck to the left. Puppy and Boots were top and tail on the concrete slab; Boots polishing a boot in front of his face, Puppy snoring lightly.

The concrete step that I'd spent the night on was just about long enough to support a spine, so my legs were propped up at forty-five degrees against the wall. I'd taken the fat Rasta hat off and doubled it up so it acted as a cushion against the edge of the step.

The smell of piss drifted up from the floor.

Boots took a break from polishing his boots. He stood up on the sleep slab, positioned himself in front of one of the brick-shaped holes in the wall, unzipped his jeans, and pissed out into the open air.

He could've suggested that last night.

He lay back down and snarled at me, muttering something about 'stinking fucking pissy floor' as he picked up a boot to polish.

I sat up on the cold step and rolled my neck, wincing as my vertebrae clicked into position.

Rab C. was relieved of duty by his doppelganger, Rab 2, who sat on the bucket and stared at his hands.

Puppy woke up and twisted a clump of hair. His scruffy little afro was already turning into a cool little head of baby locks – just like that.

Boots was still muttering to himself – 'Pissy fuckin' English bombo . . .' – polishing a boot.

Time passed.

At some time, Big Pig returned with Fatty's parents and released her without charge. Big Pig spoke loudly as he unlocked the cell: 'Hif only all Hinglish tourists knew how to do business in Jamaica. Life,' he said, turning to me, 'would be a lot Heasier all around, would it not?'

And I still did not have a clue what he was getting at.

Boots shouted at Fatty from his slab, something about how nice and fat her 'batty' was, and Puppy joined in: 'Me like how it wobble when you walk.' Her mum looked horrified.

Time passed.

Puppy rocked back and forth on the slab with his hands around his knees. Boots mumbled to himself as he polished a boot: 'Dem jus' a keep I man lock up in a cell . . . me nah harass no tourist, dem . . . dem jus' a lock up I and I with a pissy fuckin' English bombo . . .'

Time passed.

'. . . bloodclaat, dem jus' a keep I man for no reason, mon . . . dem jus' a bombo pissy fuckin' English mon . . .'

Time passed.

Boots' mumbling was getting unbearable. I shouted at him, but he never responded.

Rab 2 stared at his hands.

Puppy twisted a clump of hair.

Did I actually shout then, or just imagine it?

I shouted again, really loud: 'Shut the fuck up, dickhead.' I must have been a foot and a half from Boots' face. Nothing.

Are these people all mad?

Is it me?

I tried another tack and shouted, 'Bunch of fucking cunts.' Nothing. 'Ah! Jamaica's a shit-hole.' My breath came heavy and my body was trembling.

Time passed till I stopped trembling.

Just as the heat and light were fading outside, two pigs came for me and Puppy.

Rab 2 handed back my belongings, which were now reduced to half a gold rope chain and a bloodstained two-dollar note.

Boots mumbled to himself from the slab, sniffing down at the floor: 'Pissy English bomboclaat.'

I thought I'd been in the police station all day, but it was still hot as they drove me and Puppy through the dust and dirt of downtown Montego Bay.

The smell of exhaust fumes.

Earthy basslines, whip-crack beats, whining guitars.

I decided I didn't feel like part of this place after all. I'd never felt so English in my life.

'Where are you taking me?' I said.

No reply.

I'm still on mute, then, am I?

I looked over at Puppy. He just sat there twisting a clump of hair and staring out the window. Shouting 'bunch of cunts' didn't seem like the best idea this time, just in case I wasn't going mad and they could actually hear me – these pigs looked quite hard.

They turned into a place with a yellowed sign: Barnett Street Correctional Facility. They stopped the car at the top of the track and got us out. One of the pigs took Puppy off somewhere to the right, and the other one led me down the rest of the dusty dirt track.

At the end of the track was a long concrete animal pen over-flowing with topless blokes.

'Red Man,' an angry-looking bloke shouted at me. He gripped the bars like he was gonna bend them and run straight at me. 'You with me, Red Man,' he shouted, 'hahaha,' shaking the bars. 'Red Man is mine.' He had a head like a bowling ball. 'Red Man.' He was frothing at the mouth. 'Your pants are mine.' Spittle sprayed from his mouth. 'Hahaha. You mine, Red Man. Your shirt is mine.' He had muscles in his face. 'Red Man!' His eyes widened as he caught sight of my boots. 'Mine, Red Man. Dem boots is mine.'

Come on, feet.

I'd folded over the waist of my baggy red jeans to make them a bit more secure, but I still had to pull them up now and again to prevent them from falling down at badly timed moments – this one, for example.

I hadn't eaten or drank anything since the Spanish omelette I'd had at Peach's Paradise on Monday afternoon. It occurred to me that I might just faint and wake up next to Bowling Ball.

Just keep going, legs.

We stopped just short of the animal pen and turned right into a small building between two blocks of cells. I allowed myself to breathe out. The pig led me to a small office and left me there with two screws standing either side of me. There was one man sat behind a desk, long fingers splayed over the vinyl surface. His face looked young but his eyes were severe. 'Where are you from?' he snarled.

'England.'

'England,' he chuckled.

The voice of Bowling Ball boomed through the walls: 'Red Man!' Bars rattled.

Just stay standing.

'Take off your hat,' demanded Fingers.

I took off the Rasta hat.

He looked at my hair, shook his head, and sighed. 'Where are your parents from?'

'My dad's from Jamaica,' I said, as if that might help the situation.

'Oh good,' he said, grinning at the two screws and tapping his long fingers on the desk as if he was excited about something. 'You know,' he said, screwing up his face, 'your type of people disgust me. You disgust all right-thinking Jamaican people, do you know that?'

'Er . . .' I shrugged my shoulders. I didn't even know what type of people he was talking about.

'You people should wash your dirty hair.'

My hair? He's on about my hair?

'How old are you?' he asked.

'Sixteen.'

'Hmm.' He seemed a bit disappointed. 'Take him to juveniles.'

They led me past the animal pen. Bowling Ball screamed and shook the bars even harder in protest at me not being put in with him. 'Give me dem shoes, Red Man.' I tried to not look at him. 'Dem my shoes, Red Man. You don't deserve dem fucking shoes, Red Man. Red Maaaaaaan.'

Breathe.

I had no idea where the screws were taking me, but juveniles sounded better than Bowling Ball's cell, any day.

Juveniles, as it turned out, was a row of cells on the upper storey of a two-tier concrete box with railings.

Every cell was the same: two concrete slabs jutting from the left-hand wall, one slab jutting out of the right-hand wall. On the back wall of the cell there was a concrete toilet with a small barred window above it on the right and a thin metal shower nozzle popping out of the wall on the left.

And juveniles, as it turned out, had girls in every cell.

Girls in every cell!

Fuck you, Bowling Ball.

A tall and big-boned girl smiled kindly as we passed the first cell. Behind her there was a girl with her head in her hands. It was a White girl in a tight silver dress, like Angel's. She had light brown hair, like Angel's, but her hair was tangled and unwashed, and it covered most of her face. I could see gauze and surgical tape poking out from under her small hands with long nails, like Angel's.

A screw pushed me on.

A pretty young girl hung her arms through the railings and watched as we passed the next cell. Her cellmate followed me with her eyes as we passed, her body dead still on the sleep slab.

In the next cell there was a girl in pink hot-pants, a white boob tube, and a blonde bob-style wig. 'Hello, rude bwoy,' she simpered as we passed. 'Where are you from? Canada? England?' She twisted herself sideways to reveal the contours of her thin waist and round arse.

Another girl was sat on the toilet at the back of the next cell. She widened her eyes like – *You getting a good look?* – as one of her cellmates plaited another's hair.

I started to wonder whether Bowling Ball was a safer bet.

We came to the end cell and there was Puppy. Opposite him there was another shoeless lad, about my age. He had the face of a tortured breeze block.

This was clearly my cell.

Best of a bad world, I supposed.

The gate clanged behind me. The lock clunked in the strike. The shoes of the screws clip-clopped away.

Puppy nodded from the other lad to me as if to say – *Look, I told you so*. Breeze Block looked me up and down, maybe amused, maybe angry, maybe waiting for me to do something. 'Where you from?' he said, pointing his chin at me.

'Liverpool.'

He grinned at Puppy, like they had some secret agreement, then he smiled at me.

'Why dem put you in here,' he said, 'if you from England?'

'Dunno, mate.'

'Tek off your hat,' he said.

For some reason, I obeyed him.

'You think you a Nyabingi dread?'

'Eh?'

'Me bet dat why dem a lock you up with us.' Breeze Block explained to me that the cells downstairs were reserved for foreign men who were, mainly, caught with drugs. 'Some big English man down there,' he said, pointing with his chin and eyeing me up for muscles.

He paced up and down the cell asking questions. He wanted to know what it was like where I came from. He wanted to know if I was in there for drug-smuggling like so many other foreigners. He wanted to know what was wrong with my leg. The limp wasn't really necessary, but I knew that a spot of exaggeration would make people ask, which would give me a reason to tell them about the stabbing, which would make me sound dead hard and make them less likely to fuck with me.

'. . . so I took the knife off him and stabbed him in the face,' I lied.

Breeze Block was quiet for a bit after that. He soon started up again though. He asked me if I lived in a mansion, if we had maids and servants.

'What? No!' I didn't mention the cleaner, obviously. Or the gardener.

He asked if it was true that everyone in England was rich.

'No.'

Maybe he didn't believe me because then he came out with it: 'What you have in your pocket?'

'You what?'

'In your pocket. Empty your fucking pocket, man.' He didn't look that threatening now that he was trying. There was something about his miserable angular face that made it seem more intimidating when he was pretending to be nice.

Then Puppy joined in: 'Empty your fucking pockets, English man.'

Fucking hell, now he's a tough guy? The little shit.

'There's nothing in my fucking pockets.'

'Now he fucking swear at us?' Breeze Block turned to Puppy, then back to me. 'You fucking threaten us, you pussyclaat?' He got up on top of the toilet, reached through the barred window for something stashed on the other side, and pulled out a long flat piece of metal. It was thin but sharp at one end. He jumped down and jabbed the makeshift weapon at me. 'Empty your pussyclaat pocket, red motherfucker.'

'Look,' I said, turning out my pockets.

I showed him the half a gold rope chain and the bloodstained two-dollar note. Big Pig had stolen my five hundred dollars, but I still had the rest of my money stashed in my right sock. I raised my hands in a gesture of surrender, allowing myself to look pathetic with white pockets hanging out of my baggy red jeans. 'See.'

'Pull down your pant, man,' said Breeze Block.

'You what?'

'Do it now, pussyclaat.'

'You have money in your shorts,' said Puppy.

'And take off your shoe.' Breeze Block side-snarled Puppy a split second to make sure it was clear who was having the big red boots. 'Don't test me now, man,' he said, turning back to me. 'Take off your pant and your fucking shoe,' he snarled, jabbing at me again.

'Look,' I flinched to defend myself, 'I'm not gonna drop my pants, and I'm not gonna give you my boots.' I'd already sacrificed my favourite pants to this story, and there was no way this brick-faced bastard was getting my red Ellesse boots. I loved those fucking boots.

Breeze Block lunged at me with the metal thing and caught me with a glancing jab that stung just under my left ribs. 'Fucking hell!' I jumped back. He jucked at me again. 'Ee-ar, fuck off.' I stepped back against the gate. 'Just fuck off, la.'

'Juck him,' shouted Puppy all excited. 'Juck him, man.' Breeze Block caught me again, in the belly this time. I thought blood might be trickling down my stomach. I moved along the cell, a concrete bunk at my back. He jucked again, and again, and then waved the thing by my face.

I caught his wrist and twisted his hand so the weapon pointed at his face. He screamed in pain as I shouted, 'It's not even a fucking knife, you knob-head.'

His body swept around as he tried to escape the pain. The weapon dropped to the ground. I grabbed him by the afro and slammed his rectangular face against the railings. He tried to turn around to fight, but I grabbed his face, sunk my thumb into his eye socket, and held him tight against the cold metal: 'I'll fucking kill ya, ya cunt.'

'It's OK, English, calm down, man,' said Puppy. 'We won't hurt you.' I let go of Breeze Block. He looked scared.

My legs were shaking, and I had to let them know it wasn't out of fear. I picked up the metal thing and handed it to Breeze Block, raising my eyebrows like – *Go on, lad, have another go.*

He climbed back up to his stash and put his weapon away, then climbed onto the top bunk and sat there, staring at his feet.

Feeding time involved buckets of mushy stuff that the screws left along the corridor. They opened the boys' cell first. Puppy got a plastic cup and an empty cardboard milk carton from under his bunk and gave the milk carton to me.

'What's that for?'

'What else you have to eat from?'

Breeze Block had a little Tupperware box.

I watched Puppy scoop some mush out of the nearest bucket

and take it back into the cell. Then Breeze Block filled his box. So I filled my milk carton. One of the screws left a two-litre bottle of tepid water just inside the cell. He closed the gate and locked us back in before letting the girls out.

I thought my stomach must have shrunk because I had no appetite, which was a relief because I didn't really fancy eating mush from a milk carton. It looked like over-soaked rice mixed with tiny bits of brown and orange stuff. The two lads scooped the stuff into their mouths with their fingers. I decided I should join in. I scooped some up in my fingers. It tasted of nothing. I scooped some more, then a bit more, and, the next thing, the carton was empty.

We passed the tepid tap water between us as the girls mingled in the corridor, chatting and scooping up tasteless mush.

The big-boned girl from the first cell came bouncing over to our cell with a huge smile. I wondered how someone like that could be in prison, someone so positive. 'Where are you from?' Three thick braids bobbed as she cocked her head to the side.

'I'm from England, Liverpool,' I said. 'You?'

'Florida.'

'Florida?'

Hot Pants had followed Big Bones over. She kept looking at me, tilting her head, adjusting her wig, doing her best Mariah Carey – *And this is my arse* – pose.

'Mm-hmm,' said Big Bones. 'A lot of the girls in here are from America. Mostly they have been caught trying to smuggle drugs to America.'

'What kind of drugs?'

'Coke and weed. Me, I'm just in here for weed. The other girl in my cell, she's in for coke. She's in serious shit, man.'

116

Hot Pants rolled her eyes and tutted. She glanced over her shoulder as if to coax me to go somewhere with her.

'What's her name?' I asked.

'Who?'

'The girl in your cell. I met a girl called Angel just, erm, a few nights ago and . . .'

'May be the same girl, but I don't know her name. She don't wanna speak to no one. Was she incredibly beautiful?' she asked, raising her eyebrows.

'Yeah! I mean, she was . . . pretty, like.'

'Not no more she ain't.'

'Eh?'

'Beg you a cigarette?' said Puppy.

'OK, little man,' said Big Bones. 'Wait there.' She skipped off down the corridor, singing, 'Like you have any choice.'

Hot Pants walked closer to the cell. 'So,' she said in a husky voice, 'you want tek I back to England with you, rude boy?' I'd love to have seen their faces in Searbank if I'd turned up with her. Mum would have had a panic attack.

Mum!

'Your Angel no look like no angel any more, yunno?'

'What happened?'

'Someone acid up her face,' chimed Hot Pants. 'And now she get arrest.'

Big Bones came back and passed Puppy a cigarette. He broke it into three pieces, got some brown paper from his bunk, and passed me and Breeze Block each a piece of cigarette and brown paper. They both made mini-rollies using the brown paper as Rizla. I copied them.

'You 'ave to lick it after every time you take a smoke,' said Hot Pants. She took the smoke from me and soaked along its edge

117

with her tongue, really slowly, then lit the rollie, took a drag, and licked again. 'See?' She handed it back through the bars. I tried it. It tasted like, well, it tasted like smoking a brown-paper bag, and it was, weirdly, quite comforting. I leaned against the gate and looked through the cold bars of the corridor as I toked and licked my sufferah cigarette.

From up there in the cell, I could see just beyond the end of the blue sea, its horizon a dark line that was just about to swallow the sun.

'Forget about her,' said Hot Pants.

'I wasn't thinking about her.'

'What you thinking about, then, rude bwoy?' she said, adjusting her wig.

'Nothing.' I wished I could think of funny, clever things to say, the way Increase did.

Increase!

I hadn't seen Increase since Monday afternoon. That was only one day ago. But it felt like another lifetime.

That night, I lay down on a concrete slab – the one on the right, the one on its own. The silver-grey smell of concrete and steel reminded me briefly of the smell of the little metal bits on the end of Mum's stilettos. That's one of my first memories: sneaking a taste of Mum's metal stiletto tip before someone caught me. The memory dulled as concrete dust coated the receptors in my nose.

Puppy gave me some old shirts and newspapers to pad out the slab. These must have been the establishment's idea of creature comforts. And they would have worked fine for an actual creature. As for a teenage boy from Searbank, they only made the experience even more uncomfortable; creased polyester under my back, plastic buttons indenting my face.

Just one more day, I thought as the sun died.

I've made something happen.

The moon took the sun's throne.

And I've had enough now.

The light of the moon made shadows of the bars across the cell, across me.

Just one more day.

A lone and beautiful voice drifted in from down the corridor, singing,

'Oh, the light

The light of life

Never shines light through my window

Only casts light on my shadow

Oh, the light

Oh, my light . . .'

Puppy made a bass sound with his voice and tapped a rhythm on the railings at the back of the cell with Breeze Block's weapon. Breeze Block knocked out a beat out on his Tupperware box and clicked his tongue.

The verse refrained, slightly changed, and with each line more voices joined in:

'Oh, the light

The light of life

Only hides under your bushel . . .'

And more voices joined in:

'. . . Only sheds light on my trouble.

And more.

'Oh, the light.

The light of life . . .'

Maybe the whole cellblock was singing now.

'You don't know me

Like you think you do . . .'

Apart from me, of course.

'. . . You don't know me

Like you think you do . . .'

I didn't know the song.

'. . . Don't know my light

Don't know my life

Like I know you . . .'

I was happy to just let the sounds move through me, shifting stuff inside me. I rested my tongue on the roof of my mouth, completing the circuit so the energy could tingle through me, the way Kissy had taught me.

Kissy!

My lips tingled like they wanted something, or like they were getting something. And for that short time, while everyone else sang, there was no better place to be than on that concrete slab with those shadows and stinking shirts, and those voices and sounds and the words:

'You don't know me

Like you think you do

You don't know me

Like you think you do

Don't know my life

Don't know my light

My light is you.'

They sang other songs too, including a few I was getting to know, and Puppy imitated the chants and wails of the lion-man.

Eventually, the voices fell silent. The sounds of traffic rumbled in from downtown Montego Bay. A horn blew in the near distance. Someone screamed in the streets below.

Then, finally, a voice sang slowly, softly, lonely:

'The weak don't follow the water . . .'

The voice sounded restricted, like the mouth wasn't opening fully. It sounded—

'The weak don't follow the water . . .'

—choked, and no one joined in.

'The weak don't follow the signs.'

A rock of guilt formed in my stomach as she sang.

I thought about Kissy again, or tried to.

I thought about Angel, or thought I should do.

Actually, I thought about Mum.

What would Mum say if she knew where I was?

All the times I'd been arrested in Searbank for nothing, and Mum had gone to the police station to complain. She'd made Dad write letters to the local police and even to the local MP, who wrote back to say that he took note of Dad's 'grave concerns', and fuck all changed. Now I was in the shit again.

But it's just a few spliffs. I haven't even done anything.

But I had.

I knew I had.

I'd made something happen.

I woke up stiff all over, stinking of sweat and concrete dust, and with the sight of Breeze Block crouched over the grey concrete toilet at the back of the cell.

I took off all my clothes and turned the shower on full blast. Full blast meant a dribble of cold water that meandered over my shoulder and didn't reach halfway down my back before drying up. I smeared water over the top layer of sweat under my armpits, then left the shower already dry and smelling worse than before I'd started.

Breakfast was the exact same mush we'd had for tea, in the same buckets.

Following morning mush, I did a hundred press ups and a hundred sit ups on my slab. I knew, now, that I could physically overpower Puppy and Breeze Block. And I knew that they knew it too. That felt good. I was king of the cell. I stood on my hands with my feet against the gate, grunting and sweating – 'Uh! Uh!' – as I did fifty upside-down shoulder presses – five sets of ten – just so they knew I could. No one was gonna be asking me to pull my pants down today.

Just one more day.

I was watching the subtle play of light on the dim grey ceiling when the cell door slid open like a sword through a scabbard. The lad's attempt at a cool stroll into the cell was thwarted by a hard push from a screw. Within seconds, the new lad's eyes had scanned the cell, registered me, and made contact with the other two lads.

The king was dead.

The lad was about my age, quite big, looked strong. He had half an ear missing – a fighting injury? Skinny legs though.

I could catch him with a kick to the leg, rush him, and throw him to the deck before the other two got me.

He was slightly better dressed than the other two; still had no shoes though.

The three of them chatted to each other in thick Jamaican patois so I couldn't understand what they were saying, but I got the gist. Puppy and Breeze Block were telling him I was strong. Half Ear was saying that between the three of them they could take me: take my yellow and green mesh top, take my Malcolm X T-shirt, take my pants, but his eyes kept drifting down towards my boots.

Three shoeless Jamaican boys versus me in my big red boots with the laces tucked in.

I walked towards the toilet as they chatted about how best to overpower me; side-eyeing me as they pattered, wondering what my next move would be.

'In Liverpool, la,' I said, putting on my strongest Scouse accent, leaving the words to linger as I pulled down my pants and squatted over the toilet, 'we don't watch each other while we're having a shit.'

Six eyes all flickered around the cell in embarrassment.

A small victory, but a victory all the same.

It wasn't the kind of thing I would've had the confidence to pull off in my old life. I was nervous, but I felt like I had a mushroom cloud hanging around me, protecting me. And besides, you can't just lie down and get kicked all your life. I'd tried that before and it had done me no good. But Joe Shirley was just a spoilt shit-bag from Searbank compared to these lads. These lads might kill me if I let them.

So I'd kill them if I had to.

I lay down on the solo slab.

They never tried anything.

Not straight away, anyway.

I nodded off on the slab and woke up to the three of them huddled around me. Half Ear was holding Breeze Block's weapon to my throat. 'Take off your shoes, pussyclaat,' he snarled. The sharp point followed my neck as I sat up. I took off my boots and handed them to Half Ear. The other two followed the boots with their eyes. Half Ear tried to conceal his joy and sustain his threatening face.

'Empty your pockets,' he said.

Putting my arms up to show no aggression, I gently moved the blade away from my neck. Half Ear tried to push back, but he was nowhere near strong enough. I pushed another few centimetres just to let him feel my strength. 'Hahaha,' he laughed as he stepped away. He put the boots on and snarled, 'Now, get your rass off my bed.'

And so that day went.

Just one more night.

No one sang.

I lay on the floor in the shadow of Puppy's slab.

Tomorrow was Thursday – family court. One more night before I was gonna be released to have a normal holiday: weed, reggae, girls, and 'Joe me sell the Bag Juice' on Walter Fletcher beach.

Flat on your back is the only way to lie on concrete that doesn't cause too much pain to your joints from the weight of your own body.

One more night.

I shoved a few old shirts under the back of my head and stared at the shadows of bars lingering on the ceiling, moving imperceptibly with the passage of the moon king.

A silent tear rolled down my temple.

I couldn't remember the last time I'd cried for my mum.

Just one more night.

So I thought.

Someone's mum made desperate noises on the other side of the wall: 'He only pickney, Lord.' – over – 'Have mercy.' – and over – 'He pickney, Lord.' – again.

It felt like I'd spent a whole day in that once-white room with no windows, listening to that sound seep through the wall.

I can't remember much else: blinking, listening, daydreaming about water. Sweat broke through the tacky layers of grime on my forehead as I leaned forward on my thighs. The big red boots looked up and winked at me.

When the guard had come to get me that morning – 'English man. Court.' – I was already awake. A galaxy of tiny insect bites had turned into red dots, like distant dying stars, as I'd scraped my fingernails up and down my arms.

I looked over from where I lay under Puppy's bunk. The big red boots were by Half Ear's bunk. He opened an eye and looked at me, expressionless. I stood up, took the boots, and walked out of the cell.

'Him a chile, Lord. He pickney.'

Someone eventually came to escort me to a room with a skinny fella sat behind a table. He was wearing a black pinstripe suit, a white shirt, and a black tie. He wiped the sweat from his forehead and put his hankie back in his inside pocket.

'Sit.' I sat down facing him. 'Name?' he said, patting his hair with both hands as if to make sure it was still there.

'Aeon McMenahem.'

He screwed up his nose – 'Ian McMenahem.' – and wrote it down.

'No, Aeon. Like EE-ON.'

He didn't change it.

'Age?'

'Sixteen.'

He had round little cheeks, a small pointy nose and chin, and wild eyes. He looked like a psychopathic budgerigar.

'And your legal guardian is whom?'

'Eh?'

'Legal guardian is whom?'

'You mean, like, my mum?'

'Yes, yes. Your mother is with you today?'

'Is she? No.'

His tiny eyes glared up at me from his budgie face, like he was really pissed off about having to talk to me. 'Your mother is where?' His nose and cheek bones were peppered with black heads.

'My mum? Er, at home, I think . . . I mean, she's in England, like.'

'England? So your legal guardian for the proceedings of this court hearing today will be whom?'

'I dunno, like.' I was getting confused. Maybe it was the heat, the dehydration, the screaming mother, or the way he spoke like he was Yoda. And what was going on with his hair? It looked like a shining freeze-frame of small swells on an oil-slicked sea.

'You have travelled to Jamaica alone?'

'No.'

'So. You are with whom?'

'Just my cousin, Increase.'

'IN-GREASE?' he shook his head. 'And his age is what?'

'Er, about twenty-four, I think.'

'And he is here?'

'Er, no, I don't know where he is. Maybe he's at the hotel. Peach's Paradise.'

'Peach's Paradise.'

He wrote that down while the mother wailed, 'Jesus, Lord.'

Increase was stood just inside the doorway of the courtroom with a couple of pigs. 'What the fuck is going on, Aeon?' He looked scared.

It was just like an English magistrates' court, apart from the fact it had the sound of a desperate Jamaican mum wailing through the walls: 'He pickney, Lord.' And the fact there was only one magistrate. And she looked like Grotbags from *Emu's All Live Pink Windmill* – but without the fun element. And she was Black. I'd definitely never seen a Black magistrate in St Helens Court.

Evil Budgie was sat behind a long desk facing Black Grotbags. I think there were two or three other people sat at intervals along the desk, and a few other people scattered about the rows of long benches facing the magistrate.

The pigs led me to the dock to the left of Grotbags. I sat down. She looked me up and down, then ordered me to stand up. 'And take off your hat while you are in front of my court, young man.'

The pigs giggled as I released my greasy wig. Grotbags snarled: 'You think it is amusing to see a young man reduced to such a degenerate and defiant state?' They looked down at their boots. She turned back to me. 'You people should wash your hair,' she sneered. 'So you think that you can come to this country and just break our laws, young man? Hm?'

I shrugged my shoulders. The skin around my eyes felt hot and dark.

'Pardon?'

'No,' I said to my feet.

'No, miss,' she snarled. 'You will look at me when I speak to you, and you will address me as Miss when you are in my court-room, do you understand?'

'Yeah.'

'Pardon!'

'Yes, miss.'

She looked down at Evil Budgie and grimaced, or it might have been a smile. 'Sir, have you made out a juvenile report on this delinquent?'

'Indeed I have, miss.'

'And may I now see that report?'

Evil Budgie grinned. 'Unfortunately,' he said, 'the delinquent is a minor. He is also an English boy with dual Jamaican heritage.'

What?

'I am required, therefore, to send my report, forthwith, to a court in England, whereupon it is to be verified, approved, and henceforth, returned back to this court where I shall, with due diligence, peruse, verify, and signaturise the aforementioned report, miss.'

What the proper fuck?

A gritty wave of sweat pushed its way through the pores on my forehead.

'And how long will it take for you to receive, review, and verify the report before my court can see it, sir?' You could almost see the dark energy moving between them.

'It is my estimation that such a process would be, making an allowance for the distance between Jamaica and England, completed by such a time as approximately the 26th day of the month directly subsequent to the present, miss.'

'The 26th of August, sir?'

The 26th of August?

'The 26th of August, miss.'

The 26th of August?

'And what is your suggestion for how to deal with the delinquent in the interim, sir?'

The 26th of August is over a month away.

'It is my suggestion that the guilty party be remanded, for the safety of himself and the law-abiding citizens of Jamaica, in a place of safety to be recommended by this court, until such a time as my report has been returned, verified, and signaturised, miss.'

My legs went weak.

'Thank you, sir.'

'And one more thing, miss. I have spoken to the cousin of the guilty party, who is eight years senior to the delinquent, and he has signed as legal guardian for the boy.'

'Good. Is that all, sir? In that case, I now order, by the powers invested in me, that the insubordinate youth be held at Copse, Place of Safety for Boys until further notice.' She got up and fucked off.

The two pigs grabbed my arms and walked me out of the courtroom. Increase's eyes were wide as they led me through the door, his mouth open, sweat running down his face. 'What the fuck is going on, Aeon?'

'I don't fucking know, la.'

Wherever this 'Cops' place is, at least it's not that last place I was in.

This place must be downtown as well.

Why are they turning here?

Why are they getting out of the car?

What the fuck are they doing?

'I thought I was going to the other place, "Cops". The Place of Safety.' One of the pigs leaned into the back of the car to grab my arm, but I pushed him away. 'Why the fuck am I here?' I wasn't having that pretend you can't hear me shit again. 'The judge said I was going to "Cops". The Place of Safety. I wanna go to "Cops".'

'Soon come,' snarled the pig.

The two pigs dragged me out the car and marched me back towards the concrete block.

My legs were shaking as I stepped into the cell. Puppy twisted a clump of hair. Half Ear picked at his nails. Breeze Block played with loose threads that dangled from the bottom of his jeans. It was like they'd never even seen me before. Had no interest whatsoever in an English lad with a huge pair of red Ellesse boots.

Maybe I slept under Puppy's slab that night.

Maybe a million insects made a meal of me.

Maybe I cried for my mum.

Miss Elwyn used to tell me that halfway through the story the hero has to die.

The road wound up into the hills.

Trees twisted out of grey rocks.

Stashed shacks peeped from behind gnarled bushes that held spiky fingers up to the sun.

To the left, a monumental valley expanded endlessly away in more shades of green than I knew existed.

A huge bird sat on a rock, its back – a long black and iridescent cloak – to the road. It turned its skinny sabre-nosed turkey face to the car, its round human-like eye taking me in, then turned away, spread its giant vulture wings, and pierced the valley with an angry, 'Caw'.

Only silence came from the front seats; silence and the odd grunt. The driver had the wide and stubbly neck of a wild boar. 'Oink,' he said to the other pig as the two of them wobbled along with the rolling, bumping, climbing of the road.

'Remember, though,' Miss Elwyn told me, 'that the hero always comes back from the dead.' She coughed into her hanky. 'That is the whole point of it all. The hero must always return.'

I fucking hoped so.

Puppy was on the left of me and Piggy on the right. Piggy had joined us just before we left Barnett Street that morning. He had the face of a miniature adult and the body of a famished imp. He was an eleven-year-old food thief. His ruined nose was the result of torture with a burning stick. It had happened at the place we were heading. That was why he'd run away. Apparently, if you run away and get caught, they send you to a place called the strong-room. Apparently, if you burn a boy's face with a smouldering stick so his nose ends up looking all Piggy, they send you to the strongroom.

People had mentioned this 'Cops' place. They said it was the best place to get sent. At 'Cops', you could walk around outside, play football, and sleep in a bed with a mattress and white sheets.

They said you could even buy weed and swim in a river at 'Cops'. At 'Cops', they said, they had real food.

But the strongroom? Why hadn't anyone mentioned the strongroom?

I know now that the place isn't that far from Montego Bay – only about twenty miles or so. I know that now, but my memory tells of an epic journey through the mountains. It could be that the pigs drove us around for a couple of hours to confuse us. Or it could be that time and memories are just that fickle; tricks the mind plays on us to create an illusion of control.

So this was the place.

The first thing I noticed was that the name wasn't Cops; the sign said COPSE. And someone had added a big yellow R between the O and the P. Then I noticed that the sign seemed to have rusted bullet holes in it. And someone had painted around the holes in yellow paint and written '9mm' with little arrows pointing to the holes. And underneath the word CORPSE the sign actually said PLACE OF SAFETY FOR BOYS (and Justice chuckles at the evil of her own irony).

We paused at the open gates as the driver pig uttered some oinks and grunts at two blokes who stood at the entrance holding long sticks.

Just like a movie set in some African outback, a group of shoe-less Black kids ran behind the car as we drove up the dirt track. One of them looked at me and screamed, 'Dem have a White man! Dem have a White man!'

The pigs led the three of us up to a big old wooden house, two-storeys and a wraparound veranda on the ground floor. It was like something from *The Waltons* – possibly even more sinister.

To my memory, the bulldog woman in the leopard-skin blouse was stood behind a serving hatch somewhere in the house when we were presented to her. She didn't even pretend to be arsed who we were. She summoned a guard and waved her finger over the three of us as she said, 'Tek them to the strongroom.'

They walked me along a gravel path that led us towards a large, one-storey concrete building with cracked plaster and flaking white paint.

A gaggle of kids crowded us shouting, 'White man. White man . . .' and other kids ran from the building. I wondered if the building was where they were taking us, but the Leopard-skin Bulldog had said, 'Tek them to the strongroom.' And something told me that the strongroom was another place.

We approached a little walled yard where the air condensed with the stench of sewage, sweat, and dark thoughts.

A towering, shiny figure with a long staff appeared, parting the crowd like a shepherd. 'Back, now. Move. Leave him, now. Leave him, now man.'

Behind him came a big lad with an ageless face.

The shiny stranger looked me in the eye. My heart thumped. The way he looked at me: without the wonder of the rowdy kids; without shock and amusement like the four other lads that followed behind him and the ageless one; without the hate of Black Grotbags and Evil Budgie and the pigs in Montego Bay, the pigs in Searbank; without the resentment of Increase and Joe Shirley; without the contempt of Mr Merryfield, head of history at Searbank High School. He just looked.

The vision left me as the two guards walked me into the yard. I say guards, but they were really just a couple of miserable old geezers in ripped jeans and Hawaii shirts, swinging sticks and spitting insults at little kids. One of them had two huge keys on a chain.

The place behind the gates came alive with the echoing sounds of shouting, scraping, and, finally, someone screaming, some-where under the ground.

One of the guards shouted through a slot in the steel door. I say shouted, but it was more like the dull echo of four hundred years of self-hate: 'Back to rass,' he droned. 'Get back, now. Move yuh bombo.'

He went on until all was silent but for the clanging of his key on the steel gate and the murmurs of, 'White man . . . strong-room . . .' from beyond the yard.

Behind the thick steel door, there was a gate of steel bars. The second key hung in it, clanged, and waited. They lined the three of us up with the entrance, me first, then Puppy, then Piggy. The key man swung the gate open, and the other fella shoved Piggy into Puppy, Puppy into me, and the three of us were rushed inside: 'Get in.' They locked the two gates behind us as we stum-bled down the steps.

The sound of keys clanging behind us echoed into the silence before us.

I used to go running at night along the brook in Searbank. I liked the way the thorns and twigs scraped my right side. I liked the way the wind and the street lights rippled along the brook to the left – as if a spirit ran alongside me. I liked the feeling of not knowing if someone was behind me, but I could never look back. It became a game: danger daring. If I could make it back home, beat my record time, and never once look back, that meant I could do anything.

It was a game, and that meant I could keep going now.

Filthy breeze blocks either side of us drew us down into the darkness.

This was the game.

Puppy's breath came fast and heavy behind me.

Down another step.

Come on, feet.

Down another step.

Keep walking, legs.

Down another step.

To the bottom.

The bathroom to the left was the source of the stench; like fermenting dragon shit.

Another few yards and we came to a breeze-block wall. We turned left then right then passed into the silence of the strongroom.

Seven rusty bunk beds stuck out along the left-hand wall, two lay along the right-hand wall. Red dust from the rusty bunk beds coated the sticky concrete floor.

At the far end of the room was another steel door. It had a big rectangular slot like a giant letterbox but higher up, and with no flap. Above the door was a badly painted picture of a gun and the words:

ROOM OF DEATH

Puppy was blubbing.

Piggy slid past the both of us, took a sheet from somewhere, and made a hammock under one of the bunks on the left; its base was too rusted to hold the weight of a person.

Puppy and I stood in the middle, waiting.

There were about nine lads to the left of us, all probably a couple of years older than me. Some leaned on the bunks, some sat or lay on bunks, and one was propped up on his elbows. They were all well dressed: shiny pants, fancy shirts, shiny shoes. In the far left-hand corner, three lads, all about my age, sat on the top bunk in jeans; no shoes, no shine, white vests. Three younger lads sat on top of the two long-ways bunks on the right; no shoes. One massive lad, built like a juggernaut, lay on a bunk underneath them, hands covering his face like he had faulty wiring; very old shoes.

No one was looking at me. It was like they couldn't register me yet.

The lads on the bunk in the left-hand corner got to work on Puppy. One of them, an ugly lanky bastard with stupidly broad shoulders, jumped down and pushed Puppy. 'Why you blubbing, pussyclaat? You want ya mama?' He slapped Puppy hard across the face so he stumbled back into me.

Puppy cried even louder, like the only hope he had was pity – I didn't fancy his chances.

'You want ya mama?' said Shoulders, turning to his mates and laughing. 'Poor likkle pussyclaat.'

'You want ya mama?' parroted the second lad.

The young kids on the right laughed along. The big lad underneath them held his face. Everyone else was dead still.

'Ya mama no here, pussyclaat,' said Shoulders. 'Nobody mama here. Because dis a special Hell. This here Gehenna, pussyclaat. A Hell design just for big man. And for pussyclaat likkle bwoys like you who waan be big man. You waan be a big man, no true, pussyclaat?'

Puppy sniffed with every sharp in-breath. He turned to me blinking, shaking his head.

The third lad was still sat in the shadows at the far corner of the top bunk. He stared at me hard. It was like he was the only one who really saw me. I was trying my best not to look directly at him.

'If you waan be big man like we, you mussa learn feh work

136

first,' snarled Shoulders. 'A no true?' he said, turning to the top bunk.

'Mussa learn feh work,' parroted the parroting lad.

'Come.' Shoulders dragged Puppy over to the bunk. 'Up, now, man. Up.' He climbed up with Puppy, handed him a once-white sheet, and ordered him to fan them. Shoulders laid back and put his hands behind his head, like a movie pharaoh being wafted by a slave.

Parrot did the same: 'Fan harder, pussyhole.'

The three young lads giggled.

Everyone else watched in silence.

The lad in the shadows was still staring at me. Then I sensed a change in his expression, and I couldn't help but look. 'What the fuck are you looking at?' he said as he leaned forward into the dim light. I could only see one eye. 'Get the fuck down,' he screamed at Puppy as he pushed him off the bunk. I flinched as Puppy bounced off the metal rim of the next bunk and landed in a crumpled heap on the rust-dust floor. He crawled past me and curled up in the corner of a lower bunk with no mattress and only half a rusted metal base.

Now everyone was staring at me.

One Eye had made me real.

'Where the fuck you from?' said One Eye, frowning.

'England, mate.'

'England, mate,' he said, copying the Scouse accent. 'You from Liverpool,' he said. Then, in the accent again: 'Fucking Scouser, mate. Fucking Mickey Mouser me, mate.' Then back to patois: 'Me nah your bomboclaat mate. And you no from Toxteth. You no fucking ghetto man. You a fucking pussyclaat.'

'Bomboclaat White man,' said Shoulders.

'White man,' parroted Parrot.

137

'White Man!' One Eye chuckled, like something had just occurred to him. 'Me used to live inna Manchester, you know?'

Manchester?

'Me know you fucking Mickey Mouse motherfuckers. Me used to fuck up Scouse pussyclaat for fun. Come the fuck here, you White Mickey Mouse bitch.'

Shoulders and Parrot sidled over as I climbed up onto the top bunk. 'You know why you see I man a sit here?' asked One Eye. He knelt at the end of the bunk and pointed at the wall: 'You see dat?' The wall had a row of five or six of them square ornamental bricks with four petals going from the centre to each corner. 'Look, Mickey Mouse.' I knelt next to him and looked. He was pointing into a dark room that could be seen through the square bricks. 'From here I can see the other side.' It was dead dark on the other side, but I could just about make out a table in the far corner of the room. 'Sometime when guard tek a break, dem come and sit in there and turn it on. You see? Television. This the only bed in Gehenna where man can watch television. And no one else in here see it unless me say so. That why you answer to me.'

'Right.' The thought – That's a stupid reason. – flashed across mind. I tried to disguise it by saying, 'Gotcha.'

Gotcha?

'Gotcha?' copied One Eye. 'Gotcha? You White piece of shit. Mek him work, den,' he snarled at Shoulders and Parrot.

Shoulders handed me the bed sheet saying, 'Keep us cool, now, bitch.' I took the sheet off him and half-heartedly wafted them.

'We have a White slave now,' said Shoulders.

'White slave bitch,' said Parrot.

A nervous little giggle burst out of me.

'What de pussyclaat him laugh at?' snarled Shoulders.

'I can't do that,' I said. I placed the sheet down on the bunk. 'I'm not wafting yous, la,' I said with another giggle.

'OK,' said One Eye. 'I know you fucking Mickey Mousers. You think you too tough to waft a Yard man?' He looked around the room to get them all on side. 'He think him too good to serve a Black man.'

'Fuck off, mate,' – I never meant that to come out – 'I mean—'

One Eye shouted, 'Get the fuck down.' He didn't try to push me though. I reckoned he really had been fighting with Scousers.

I climbed down and stood in between the bunks. He one-eyed me with a look of disgust: 'Tek off your boots.'

'No.' I swallowed.

His voice wobbled like he was gonna cry: 'Give me your fucking boots.'

'No.'

'Tek off your pant, empty your pocket, and tek off dem fucking boots, you Mickey Mouse White fucking pussyhole.'

'Listen,' I said, 'I've got nothing in my pockets, and I'm not gonna take my pants off. I've got two big stab wounds in my leg. I need to protect them.'

'Show us,' said a voice behind me. I pulled down my red jeans and showed them the wounds. I turned around to show everyone in the strongroom, and they all leaned in for a good look.

'Why you get stab up?' asked one of the young kids as I was fastening my pants, folding the waist over to keep them up.

'Someone wanted my gold chain,' I said. I took the half chain out of my pocket and showed it to the room.

'What happen to de man who stab you up?' asked another kid.

'I took the knife off him and stuck it in his face.'

The wound in my right palm opened up as I unfurled my fist, showing it around the room as proof. I could feel the respect in the room growing for me. For all they knew, stabbing faces might have been the reason I was in the strongroom.

One Eye gurned: 'OK, Mickey bitch. You think you so fucking rough you can prove it.'

Shoulders climbed down from the bunk and Parrot followed him.

The three young lads pushed at each other, all excited, fighting for some privileged position.

They've done this before – whatever this is.

There was a wire going to the one light bulb in the room, above the steel door. A break in the wire exposed the inner cords where it trailed past the young kids' bunks. One of the kids won the fight for the speck by the wire. He disconnected the wire and the bulb went out. Shoulders flew towards me with a punch. I lurched back, parried his fist away, and instinctively moved back in, but he was back to his position as the light flickered on.

So this is the game.

The light and dark game.

I gave up jogging after the fight with Joe Shirley, but I needed something.

Parrot was about to take his turn. He eyed me up while the light was still on, then, just as it went dark, he dived at me and swung a few wild punches. They all missed.

I'd been exercising five times a week since I was six years old. The doctor had said I had hyperkinesis, which was the medical term for bouncing off all four walls. The doctor had prescribed some drug to calm me down. Mum and Dad only gave it to me once, and I fell asleep with my face in my tea – which was a bummer because we were having ravioli that night. They didn't bother with it after that – the drug I mean, we definitely had ravioli again. Mum and Dad had to come up with some other way to use my energy up. By the time I was thirteen, running and swimming just weren't enough. They were boring and repetitive, and the clubs were full of swots and girls. Judo, Kung Fu, and Karate were all too fake – grabbing pyjamas, rabbit-punching, kicking in straight lines; bullshit. Kickboxing nailed it though.

Light off.

Shoulders lunged through the dark, his long arm shooting out in front of him like Dhalsim off *Street Fighter*. He caught me with a good one that split my bottom lip. I staggered back between the rows of rusty bunk beds.

Light on.

Light off.

Parrot jumped in and got one on the side of my head, but I caught him with a good stiff jab on the way out.

'Fuck him up,' the young kids were shouting. 'Fuck up de White man.'

Kickboxing worked. I was sure it was that training that had saved me from getting battered one time in the Ship alehouse in Searbank. A group of older fellas had kicked off on us for some vague reason. But they backed off when I kicked one of them in the ribs. There were too many of them for us to fight though. We bounced out of the Ship and pegged it down Turnpike Road.

We went back to my mum's house, gathered all the potential weapons we could find in the garage, and headed back to the Ship. I had visions of bouncing in there and shooting up the whole pub like the Kemp brothers in *The Krays* movie. Unfortunately, we didn't have a black van, or long black macs, or any guns. On the way back, the lads started to back out, one by one.

I wasn't about to go in there on my own.

A few weeks later, I bumped into some lads who were in the Ship that night. They told me that even over the other side of the pub there were people chanting as the fight started: 'Trigger, trigger, trigger. Shoot that nigger. Trigger, trigger, trigger. Shoot that nigger.'

If only I'd known.

There were people shouting at the other side of the big steel door now: 'Fuck up de White man.' Eyes popping up at the big letterbox slot: 'Fuck up de White man.'

Shoulders caught me again, this time in the eye.

'You may be a big man where you live,' shouted One Eye.

I used to imagine Joe Shirley's face on the punch bag, the spot pad, the air that my fists and feet jabbed at. I'd punch and kick till I had no physical energy left, then keep on going till I could feel the beastie just under the surface of my skin; till I could feel it nearly bursting out through the darkness around my eyes; till I could smell weed in my sweat; till I got that beautiful pain of extremes on my lungs – damage and repair, damage and repair . . .

'But in da strongroom,' One Eye continued, 'you just a White piece of shit.'

Parrot came at me for another go, and, rather than going back, I moved in and caught him on the bridge of the nose. He stumbled back holding his face: 'Bombo.'

'White Man tough,' shouted one of the kids.

I grabbed at the waist of my baggy red jeans to keep them up.

There was more bustling on the other side of the big steel door. A pair of eyes hovered motionless in the dark slot.

One Eye stood up on his bunk. They kept the light on. 'White Man,' he said, looking around the room. 'You know why we haffe punish you?'

'Yeah mon,' shouted a young kid.

'Me seh, you know why we haffe punish you, White Man?'

'Him know!' shouted another young kid.

'Because you,' One Eye continued. 'You owe your life to us.'

'Give it back,' shouted one of the kids.

'All your fancy shoe, your fancy clothes, your stupid spoilt child grin when you laugh at us,' he sneered. 'You laugh at us, pussyhole? Everything you have is owed to us. You know why, White Man? You know why? Because of this.' And he held his hands out in front of him with clenched fists, like he was wearing shackles.

Like I was the slave master.

He reached under his mattress and pulled out a big stick. 'You in Gehenna now, White Man.' He held up the stick like a ceremonial sword and passed it down to Shoulders, who passed it to Parrot. Parrot bounced from one foot to the other.

Heads bounced up and down behind the steel door, either side of the one still pair of eyes, watching me.

Parrot jerked like he was gonna go for me a couple of times. Then the light went out. He dived at me with the stick raised. Heads bobbed up and down at the door, and the still eyes floated forward from the darkness. My foot flew up in front of me, faster than thought, and hit Parrot in the chest. He flew backwards and skidded across the floor on his back. I kicked off the big red boots screaming, 'Aaaaaaaaggh,' so they flew across the room. I jumped over him and pounded my right fist into his face shouting, 'Yes!' Again, 'Yes! Yes!' And again, 'Aaaaaaaaaggh . . . ' – pounding him.

Out the corner of my eye, I spied Shoulders as he picked up the stick. I knew I had to move fast. The thought was there, but I needed just one more crack at Parrot's face. 'Yes!'

Now move.

I grabbed at the waist of my jeans and turned – too late.

A white light flashed inside my head. I stood up and staggered back a couple of steps, holding up my hands to deflect the next blow from the stick. It came. My legs gave way. I collapsed onto my arse as the stick knocked the big Rasta hat from my head.

Shoulders came for me again. My brain was saying move, but my body wouldn't play. He raised the stick over his head: 'Bomboclaat White Man.'

'That's enough.' One of the shiny shoe crew stepped in front of me. There was shuffling behind me as the whole crew sat up, stepped down from their bunks, shuffled forward.

'He's had enough,' said another one.

Shoulders backed up.

A couple of them helped me stand up, leaned me against a rusty bunk, and left me there, swaying.

One of the young kids jumped down from the bunk and stepped over Parrot, who was still peeling himself off the floor. The kid picked up the big red boots. He looked at me like he wanted to bring them over to me. He looked up at One Eye. One Eye glanced over him, fumbling about as if he was too busy putting the stick back in its stash to think about big red boots. The kid stood there, staring at the boots in his hand.

A new pair of eyes frowned through the slot, fingertips poking through to hold the head up. The voice was a rough and raspy growl. 'Give White Man him shoe, dem, pussycloth.' The kid with the boots wavered another few seconds, and then placed the boots on One Eye's bunk.

Voices were shouting on the other side of the big steel door:

'White Man fuck him up.'

'You see dat?'

'Me see dat, man.'

'White Man fast.'

'Him kick him like Van Damme, man.'

'Tuh rass!'

I was still light-headed, leaning on the bunk, looking at my black-socked feet in the red rust-dust.

Only when all the noise had died down and I felt like I could take my own weight again, did those other eyes reappear; the only ones high enough to watch me through the slot without effort. He said something to the lads on his side of the door. A few minutes later, they were shoving a sponge mattress through the oversized letterbox. The lads behind me pushed me forward to go pull at the mattress. It ripped halfway, but the other half came through, followed by an off-white sheet.

Then his eyes came to the slot again. I stepped forward and saw his face. The shepherd.

'Thanks,' I said.

'Pleasure,' said the shepherd.

He smiled.

And then he left me.

The one with the growling voice came to the slot and handed me a bud of weed and a piece of brown-paper bag. 'You earn it, English. Now see if you can get your shoe back from that one-eyed pussyhole.'

One Eye sucked his teeth.

The mattress and the sheet both stunk of piss, but they were a bed. The only bunk left that still had a base that wasn't too rusted to hold a mattress was the one next to where Piggy swung in his hammock; the one that Puppy was curled up on. The other lads told me to kick Puppy off the bed.

'He don't deserve no bed.'

'You fight for it.'

'Dat pussyhole no fight nobody.'

He'd been happy enough for me sleep on the floor in Barnett Street.

I nodded for him to move off the bunk.

He looked up at me with big Puppy eyes.

I pushed the smallest half of the mattress in his direction.

Puppy blubbed as he lay on the pissy half-mattress at the right side of my bunk.

Time passed . . .

. . . It could have been any time . . .

We didn't leave the strongroom in the morning.

As it turned out, we didn't leave the strongroom at all.

Day and night are blurred in the strongroom. Subtle changes in light.

Sounds.

Sleep.

Light.

Sounds.

At some time, on some day, there was a clanging on the gates and a shout of, 'Hinglish bwoi!' It must have been Monday.

At some point that day, I'd picked a piece of rusted bunk up off the floor to mark the days on the wall – something I'd seen in a movie. I tried to remember what day it was? We'd flown in from Manchester on Friday. That night I went to the Pier 1 with Sky, met Angel, got into a fight, went to the Cave, skinny dipped with Angel, got stabbed.

The taps didn't run in the strongroom.

On Saturday I got my stitches and left the hospital.

Piggy's bunk creaked to the left of me.

Then there was Sunday: trying to get a tan on the beach, buying a fat hat, a cane, and bag juice off an old bloke called Joe.

Sweat in my right palm stung the sliced nerve endings when I clenched my fist.

On Monday I got arrested.

The big red boots dangled from One Eye's bunk.

On Tuesday they'd taken me and Puppy to Barnett Street and banged us up with Breeze Block and the girls. Was it Angel?

Red rust-dust dissolved in the piss on the bottom of my socks.

Thursday was family court. Then back to Barnet Street; back to Puppy and Breeze Block and Half Ear.

On Friday they brought me here.

Now, I reckoned, it must've been Monday.

The air you breathe as your sleep in the strongroom tastes of stale piss and sponge.

A clanging on the gates.

A guard shouting.

I had wanted something to happen. The thought that I had somehow willed all of this was a strange comfort. And the only one.

The toilets don't flush in the strongroom. All three of them are piled high and overflowing with shit.

I don't think I'd ever gone so long without a decent wash.

Monday . . .

A key rattling on the bars: 'Hinglish bwoi! Come, now!'

Every day in the strongroom, the lads came up with an escape plot. The plot often involved the big lad on the bunk under the young kids: the juggernaut with the faulty wiring. He always had his hands over his face because they used to beat him till he screamed. Or maybe they used to beat him till he screamed because he always had his hands over his face. One day, I watched them bang his head against the rusted metal leg of his bunk to make it bleed. When the guards came, the lads rushed them. But the guards managed to get The Juggernaut out without coming to any harm themselves. The plot didn't work. I'm not convinced they wanted it to; escape plots were just something to do.

I sat on the pissy mattress.

I picked tiny shards of rusted metal out of my pissy, shitty black socks.

My whole body felt like it was coated in a layer of grime.

It could have been any day in the strongroom.

Piggy's bunk bed creaked as he swung in his hammock.

Same day?

Another day?

Days bleed into days.

Motivation comes and goes like days and nights, till the nights come longer, punctuated by sounds, subtle changes in dark and light.

They brought The Juggernaut back to the strongroom with a bandage around his head, that same day. No one tried to rush the guards and escape. It must've been night.

Puppy blubbed, curled up on half a pissy mattress.

On some day, I found half a Bible on the floor under my bunk.

Dad was a Seventh Day Adventist. We used to go to church every Saturday. That was the only place I used to see other Black people – mainly mean, curl-lipped old women who spoke in funny accents. And Mani, of course.

'Hinglish bwoi!'

Sleep.

Wake.

Sleep.

Wake.

Half sleep . . .

Monday.

A couple of times a day, the guards made everyone stand at the bottom of the stairs while they slid two buckets of ricey mush and two bottles of tepid water through the front gate. The same lad who'd stopped Shoulders from killing me with the stick gave me a plastic cup to scoop and eat the ricey mush with. His name was David P. Chadwick.

So it's now . . . Monday the 26th of July. I'm due back in court on the 26th of August. Thirty-one days to go. How long has it been, then?

I made a mark on the wall.

'What makes you think I was brought up in Moss Side?' said One Eye, one day. Good question. The same thing that made people think I was from Toxteth, I supposed; made random people at bus stops tell me about their cousins in Toxteth, ask me if I knew them. I never knew anyone in Toxteth apart from Mani and his family.

I looked at the big red boots that now dangled from the end of One Eye's bunk, and then looked back at him. 'I'm from fucking Wythenshawe,' he said, in a proper Manc accent.

Wythenshawe?

He'd been in the strongroom for three months. Three months without sunlight. Three months without decent food. Three months in that treacle-thick fermenting shit stench.

I'd picked the Bible up. I didn't know why. I'd stopped enjoying reading the Bible when I was eight. That was when I'd decided I didn't want to go to church anymore – after Mani stopped going. I hadn't seen Mani since that day we went back to his house, and Mani's dad caught us playing mummies and daddies in Mani's bedroom. But it took me till I was fifteen to find the courage to tell Dad I didn't want to go.

That was when Increase returned from London, grew the zig-zag out of his hair, and started going to church.

'For I was hungry and you gave me food,' I read, 'I was thirsty and you gave me drink, I was a stranger and you welcomed me, I was naked and you clothed me, I was sick and you visited me, I was—' I dropped the book on the rust-dust floor.

Piggy swung.

Puppy blubbed.

I made a mark on the wall.

One Eye said his dad was White. But One Eye wasn't light-skinned like me, he looked proper Black.

I couldn't believe it:

Where the fuck is Wythenshawe?

His dad had got depressed when he'd lost his job as a production-line manager in a factory, which I thought sounded like a shit job anyway. But his dad started drinking and ranting about foreigners taking White people's jobs. Then he started slapping his wife and son about. One Eye's mum had finally moved back to Jamaica. One Eye had two eyes then, when he became a ten-year-old lad from somewhere called Wythenshawe, living in Kingston.

One Eye had been in the strongroom for three months. Three months without running water. Three months without a loving touch. Three months in that leaden atmosphere.

But they had an escape plot. Every day they had a plot.

Monday the 26th of July.

Where's Increase? Have they even told him where I am? Has he told my mum what's happened?

Mum!

'Come! Hinglish!' Clang, clang, clang.

One day, one of the shiny shoe crew snatched my big Rasta hat while I dozed, and swapped it for some weed and some brown-paper bag for Rizla. 'Why you no wash your hair?' he asked as he shared the paper bag spliff with me.

Later that day, I took the black bandana from my back pocket and covered my hair with it.

The shiny shoes crew had all been sent to Copse together. They were from Kingston, on the other side of the island. They all looked about eighteen or nineteen. No one knew what they were in for, but everyone thought it must have been something serious.

David P. Chadwick was that kind of lad who didn't look hard or act hard. He looked like a nerd. But there was something about him that said you wouldn't wanna be on the wrong side of him when he flipped. He was wearing a pinstripe shirt, grey pants, and a blue tie – honestly, he wore that tie the whole time I was in the strongroom.

I flinched slightly as he popped into sight at my right side. He showed me a passport photograph. I nodded at it – I had no idea what I was supposed to say. He turned the picture over to show me what was written on the back of it in tiny, neat handwriting:

David Percy Chadwick

5/5/74

34 Westerly Road

Morant Bay

St Thomas

Jamaica

'I understand why it is so wrong what they try do to you. They don't understand,' he said, 'that we must stick together. We must not abandon one other. "For I was hungry and you gave me food, I was thirsty and you gave me drink, I was a stranger and you welcomed me, I was naked and you clothed me, I was sick and you visited me, I was . . ." '

What the fuck.

'When you get back to England, you will remember. We must stick together.'

He grabbed my right hand, unfurled the fingers of my clenched fist and placed the photograph in my palm. The corner of it poked into the slash wound. Then he lay back down on his bunk and stared into the thick atmosphere.

The plot, on one of those days, was to make a hole in the ceiling and climb through it. It took what felt like a whole day. And, obviously, failed.

Piggy swung.

Puppy blubbed.

Time passed.

We're supposed to fly home on the 9th of August. Mum will find out then – when I don't return – if she doesn't already know.

'Hinglish bwoi!' Clanging on the gates.

It's my birthday in four days.

'Hinglish bombo-blood and rass.'

That makes it Monday, then.

It was the first time since being in the strongroom that the guards had shouted me.

They made everyone stand behind the wall at the bottom of the stairs. My legs shook up a step, up another step, and up. When I got to the top of the stairs, the guards opened the gates: 'Out, Hinglish. Hout!'

I squinted at the ground as they dragged me into a hard wall of light. They led me back along the front of the main building, where a crowd of topless little kids gathered around us shouting, 'White Man out de strongroom. White Man out de strongroom.' More came running out of the dorm and across the grass, until we had a bustle around us shouting and laughing, 'White Man out de strongroom.' The guards whipped them off with their sticks, but they kept coming back, chanting at us. Their sounds softened as the guards walked me into the reception area of the big house, muffled behind the closed door and high walls: 'White Man out de strongroom. White Man out de strongroom.'

A flowery old couch with a torn-up plastic cover sat in front of the window. Increase looked up from the couch as I walked in. He touched his watch – the only thing he still had that had belonged to his dad.

In 1981 I was an energetic five-year-old with a loud laugh. I lived in a semi-detached house facing a big field in a leafy suburb. I had a Raleigh Grifter with no stabilisers and a Rupert the Bear that was so big I used to wear its yellow checked trousers. Insurrection wasn't the first thing on my mind when the Toxteth riots kicked off.

There's a photo taken in our front room: me and Dad with Increase and Uncle Saul. We're sat on the couch in front of a big box-shaped television. That's the only memory I have of Uncle Saul coming to stay, so I reckon it's that last time. That may even be the day the riots started?

Increase started talking about it more as he got older. He liked to quote the speech Margaret Thatcher made when she became prime minister, two years before the riots: 'Where there is discord may we bring harmony . . .' He used to contrast it with the discord expressed in 'Ghost Town' by The Specials. He liked to rant about the discord wrought throughout the country as poor people suffered from cuts to public services. He liked to talk about how when life gets hard people take it out on those closest to them because they can't reach the ones furthest away. So they blame their neighbours. Jamaican skinheads, Increase told me, blamed 'Pakis'. He told me that White lads took on the Jamaican skinhead style of music, clothing, and racism – and then blamed Jamaicans. White skinheads and the children of Jamaicans went to gigs to watch The Specials, and blamed each other. Increase liked to tell people how the '81 riots hadn't only been in a few 'Black' areas like people think: Brixton, Moss Side, and Toxteth. There were also riots in Cantril Farm, Dingle, and Birkenhead. And it wasn't just Scousers. Luton, Leicester, and Leeds kicked off. As did Southampton, Preston, and Wolverhampton. And, of course, Bristol, Sheffield, Nottingham and Newcastle. As well as Bradford, Blackburn, Maidstone and Stoke. And Chester, Shrewsbury, Edinburgh, Coventry, Knaresborough, Halifax, High Wycombe, Hackney, Hull . . . And then it got worse.

Increase liked to discuss how what his dad, Saul, did that week may have been the only honourable thing he ever did. Or not. Either way, it had got him killed.

Apparently, Saul had called me and Increase into our living room to watch the Toxteth riots unfold on the *News at Ten*. Saul never believed that those riots, or the ones in Brixton, were simply the reaction of Black youths rising up against racism and police harassment, poverty, and unemployment. Saul thought there was something else going on; something designed to split up working-class communities. Divide and conquer was apparently Saul's favourite saying. He took it from the British Empire. And he lived by it.

Saul was a gangster. Increase used to call him a one-man movement.

Throughout Increase's childhood, he watched as Saul's friends were killed off, imprisoned, or irreparably damaged due to that same lifestyle choice as Saul: to be one-man movements; one-Black-man movements. One of Saul's friends was shot in the leg, a strong young man one year, a weary paraplegic the next. Another of Saul's friends had his whole face reconstructed with metal plates following a beating with the leg of a metal chair from a 'friend' – lesser one-man movements.

They lived in a place called the Lozells Estate in Handsworth, Birmingham. Everyone there knew who Increase's dad was. People would stop Increase in the street just to tell him how much they respected his dad.

Saul gave money to local causes. He helped people who were having financial difficulties; people who nobody else was prepared to help. So everyone loved Saul. They had to, he owned them.

When Thatcher announced that the government was gonna allow people to buy their council houses dirt cheap, Saul saw a way of legitimising his money. He was gonna lend money to people so they could buy their houses. It's well worth the loan when you get to own a person's life thrown in with the interest.

Saul rushed off back to Birmingham, determined to prevent the riots from reaching Handsworth. According to Increase, Saul had played one album all the way up from Birmingham, *Handsworth Revolution* by Steel Pulse. But on the way back to Handsworth he played one song over and over again: 'King' by UB40.

Increase liked to explain to people in Searbank how people on the Lozells Estate always knew who had done what to whom, even when the police didn't. But when Saul McMenahem's body was found, no one knew who'd done that; not the police, not the community, not Increase.

Increase's mum got ill and Increase came to live with us. Until the day he joined the army.

'This is an absolute nightmare,' said Increase.

The plastic cover over the flowery couch squeaked as I shuffled away from Increase. He squeaked forward, put his elbows on his legs, and scoured his face with his hands.

'Do you have any idea how much hassle I've had finding this

place?' He had bags under his eyes. I hadn't seen him look so tired since he went AWOL from the army and came to our house on the run. 'And then I had to trust some nigger to drive me here. He's sat outside on his moped. It's that Penelope's cousin – you know that tart from the hotel?'

I know who Penelope is.

'I don't trust him. I don't trust her either. These niggers all want something from you.'

My mouth was too dry to suck the scab on my bottom lip. It stuck to the fur that coated my teeth.

'I saw that dungeon they've been keeping you in. I had to pay off the guards and some woman in a leopard-skin blouse so they don't put you back in there. What is that place?'

'The strongroom.'

Increase looked at my feet and his eyes changed.

He gave me that look, away from me. The look, away, that made my throat feel fat so I couldn't speak. So I couldn't tell him about the toilets that didn't flush, the ricey mush, the pissy mattress, the rust-dust floor, Piggy swinging, Puppy blubbing, One Eye and the light and dark game. But he was looking back down at my feet and he already knew. I had a story. And the last thing Increase wanted was for me to have a story.

He'll have to think of something fast.

'What did you do, Aeon?'

'What?'

'What did you do?'

His eyes were wet and his upper lip curled. He huffed a little bull breath and shook his head.

'What?'

He stood up and walked to the back of the couch so I couldn't see his thoughts.

'Some niggers came to the hotel. They said you had a fight with them in a nightclub.'

'I already told you—'

'They said you owe them money.'

What?

'They keep turning up and making me pay them.'

'But—'

'And every day they want more. They're bleeding me dry. Look at me, Aeon.' He walked back around to the front of the flowery couch so I could look at him. 'I'm scared to fucking eat in case I run out of money. I've asked the owner of the hotel, Mr Garter, if he can go into your envelope and release your money. But he's saying he needs your approval.' He scoured his face.

'I don't owe anyone any money. What are you—?'

'Anyway, never mind all of that. More important is how we get you out of here.' He curled the corners of his mouth upward.

He always does a sudden change of direction when he wants to confuse you.

'I've called your mum and dad.'

Mum!

Small rolls of dead skin and dirt gathered up in little black clumps as I rubbed my eyelids.

'I had no choice, Aeon.' He did that regretful smile. 'They're expecting us to arrive back in Manchester on the 9th of August. We can't just not turn up, can we?' he said all soft. 'And I can't go back either now because I've had to sign as your legal guardian, remember?' Hard again: 'Which means I'm stuck on this God-forsaken shithole as long as you are.'

'What did my,' I choked on the word, 'mum say?'

'Your mother? She was hysterical; she's a woman. And, obviously, she thinks it's all my fault. Lucky you've always got your daddy to pick up the pieces. Your dad's contacting the British Embassy, the Jamaican government, whatever contacts he's got here in Jamaica. Ha!' he said, pacing off down the room. 'You know, your mother asked me to find out the fax number for the court. I had to go back to that place to ask them for their fax number. They laughed at me. As if they'd have a fax machine; they haven't even got a phone. That probation officer was there – the one with the ridiculous hair – giving me down the banks. As if it was me who came to Jamaica acting like a don, fighting and carrying illegal drugs around, sleeping with a gangster's woman.'

'What do you—?'

'I brought you some provisions,' he said as he picked up a carrier bag from the floor: 'Soap . . . a toothbrush and toothpaste . . . a change of clothes.' He pulled out the sky-blue towelette Benetton T-shirt I'd only packed so Mum wouldn't get offended.

'Thanks,' I said, looking at my black socks.

The fumes from Penelope's cousin's moped were refreshment compared to what I'd got used to. I squinted into the sun as Increase left.

'White Man!'

I turned to face into the compound.

'White Man!'

Who the fuck is this?

His chiselled face was the type that would have been handsome, if it wasn't for the ugly spirit radiating through it. He was wearing shiny black pants, shiny black shoes, and a black shirt. His shiny black tie was knotted tight as if to stem the hatred from draining out of his shiny Black face. He coughed up some bile and spat on the floor at my feet.

His shouting had got the attention of the kids, and they rushed around me like rising waters:

'White Man.'

'Beg ya two dollar.'

'Beg ya two dollar, White Man . . .'

The Black man leaned in and down to get his face even closer to mine. His breath was the dark side of ginger. 'You come to me when I call you, White Man, is that understood?' He had a thin nose and thin lips; the kind of face that would look White, if it wasn't for the dark, almost actually black, skin.

'Take off your bandana.' He looked at my head and sneered. 'Why don't you go and wash your filthy hair? You people are disgusting.'

What people?

And with that, Black Man walked off to the big *Waltons* house.

'Beg ya two dollar, White Man . . .' murmured the swell of shirtless kids.

Six older lads, all topless and shoeless, walked over. The two tallest lads walked in front – the one with the staff first. He pointed the staff in front of him, parting the crowd like the Red Sea. 'Hello, friend,' he smiled.

The next lad, the one with the ageless face, stared at me.

The shepherd put his arm around my shoulder. I flinched. I don't think I'd been hugged like that by another male since Saul died and Increase moved in with us. That was when I stopped giving Dad a hug and kiss before bed.

'Let we go find you a respectable bed.'

The tide of excited kids rose and followed behind us. Sharp stones poked through my socks into the soles of my feet as we stepped onto the gravelly path, and some of the lads laughed as I winced and stepped back onto the grass.

As you get near the big one-storey building, you come to the courtyard in front of the strongroom. Fumes travel up from the strongroom and surround the area above it with a nauseating aura. I clenched my teeth and stepped back onto the gravelly path to avoid it. The shepherd touched my elbow as if to let me know he understood, and he was with me.

I wondered if I should wonder what he wanted from me.

We walked into the building. Inside was a large whitewashed dormitory full of wooden bunk beds with mattresses and white sheets. Shepherd led me past rows of wooden bunks to one in the far corner. 'This is my bed,' he said pointing to the top bunk. 'And this,' he pointed at the bed next to his, 'will be your bed.'

He climbed up to his bed.

'They all want something from you,' Increase had said.

But it isn't easy to mistrust someone who looks you in the eye like that, with eyes like his.

I climbed up to my new bunk and put the things Increase had brought for me – soap, toothbrush, sky-blue Benetton T-shirt – down on the mattress next to me.

'My name is Raphael,' said the shepherd, 'but, in here, people call me Shepherd. What's your name?'

'Aeon. But anything apart from White Man will do.'

'Ian it is,' he laughed, and some of the older lads laughed too. 'Nobody in here will call you White Man again,' he said, looking around. 'Apart from probably that fool in a black tie. I have no control over what that fool say or do. Who wear a black tie with a black shirt in this heat? Craziness!'

Kids ran off to shout the news to their friends: 'Shepherd say we nah feh call him White Man. Him name Ian.'

Shepherd turned to the other lads stood around the bunk: 'Straw Man, Trader. Fetch Ian up some bed sheet.'

Straw Man was the one who'd passed me the weed in the strongroom, the one with the angry voice. He had a wild picky afro, huge pectorals, and hardly a tooth in his head. The two of them walked straight over to a bunk that had another older lad lying on it. 'Darka, move,' said Straw Man.

'Nah, not I mon. Leave I,' cried Darka.

Straw Man slapped him across the head, then punched him until he squirmed on his bed, holding tight on to his white pillow and white sheets. Trader yanked the sheets from underneath Darka as Straw Man pounded him in every exposed body part.

'Nah mon, nah. Ow! Leave I, mon. Nah, nah.'

They ripped the sheets and pillow from him, marched back across the dorm, and put them on my bunk.

'Mek Ian bed up tidy,' said Shepherd to one of the younger kids. I stepped down from the bunk as the boy made my bed.

'Now,' said Shepherd. 'These boys don't have much. So if you want buy biscuits, sweets, maybe some bag juice, bun. These boys can go a shop and get you anything you like. And maybe you can share a little something. They help you, you help dem, y'understand?'

'Yeah.'

They all want something from you.

'But . . .'

Just do it, Aeon.

'Yeah, I've got, erm . . .' I reached into my left sock and took out the two hundred dollars that had been rolled up in there since I left Peach's Paradise on Monday night. Everyone's eyes widened, and some of the kids ran off to tell their friends: 'Dem never check White Man sock . . . White Man-Ian trick dem in de strongroom. Go tell, go tell.'

The sounds of the news spread around the dorm.

Shepherd leaned forward and looked me in the eyes. He had a way, a look, like he remembered something the rest of us didn't even know we'd forgotten. The only other person I knew who had that look, that way, was Kissy and it had the same effect. It made you feel safe to have them on your side.

The news of the money in my sock had now reached the basement from where muffled shouts rose up through the floor: 'White Man. Me kill you, you pussyclaat. Come here, White Man. Come down here, White Man.'

I clenched my teeth and held out the two hundred dollars for Shepherd to take.

'Give him twenty dollar,' he said nodding to a skinny kid. The kid's eyes lit up, and then he ran off, followed by three or four of his little mates. They were back about ten minutes later carrying buns, bag juices, and biscuits. The kid laid the mini-feast on my bed, reached into his pocket, pulled out some change and handed it to me.

'Maybe you give him two dollar for going to the shop,' Shepherd instructed me. So I did.

Shepherd stood up on his bunk and stepped over to sit with me on mine. He spread his hands over the feast, and I nodded that he should do whatever he wanted with it. He broke up the buns, opened the packets of biscuits and sweets, and handed them and the bag juice out equally between the excited little hands that gathered around the bunk. Each of the kids smiled and nodded their thanks, then ran off to share their catch with the smaller kids who, asleep or playing outside, had missed the whole thing.

The five older lads all sat on our two bunks as Shepherd handed them slightly larger portions. He smiled over at the little kids in the other half of the dormitory, and then turned to me.

'They won't ask you for much. They are used to having nothing. But is good to give a little something, y'understand?'

'Mm.' I wanted to say more but I was scared to talk. I thought I might cry.

There's a tree that stands alone in the field behind the dormitory. It looks like it's been there for hundreds of years; thick lumpy trunk and branches, dark green leaves. You can climb up the middle of the tree and appear in a hidden world above the leaves, where the branches curl and twist like they were designed to be sat in. A sitting tree.

As we all claimed a speck in the tree, Shepherd told me all their names: Trader (the clever one), Straw Man (the dangerous one), Saddle (the one with a funny shaped head), Ganja Baby (the little one), and Red Douglas (the strange and ageless shadow of Shepherd).

'Ganja?' said Ganja Baby looking at Shepherd with raised eyebrows.

Shepherd shrugged the question in my direction.

'Bears shit in woods?' I said.

'Bird shit?' said Ganja Baby frowning.

Forget it.

I held out my money, and Ganja Baby selected the right amount. He touched the top of my fist with his fist, then the bottom, and then the knuckles in the middle, and then nodded at me as if to say, *There's a piece of Jamaican culture for you.*

He dropped down from the tree, wandered off across the grass, down the path, past the big *Waltons* house, past a couple of guards, through the gates and out of Copse. He returned some time later and pulled himself up into the tree, a fat cob of weed sticking out from between two fingers like a cigar.

'Ganja,' he smiled.

'Ganja!' said the lads in chorus.

'Ganja,' Straw Man said again, rubbing his hands together.

Ganja Baby took a kingsize Rizla from his canvas bag, ground a fat bud into dust, sprinkled it generously into the Rizla, twisted it, licked it, lit up, inhaled, and – 'Ah!' – sighed.

He took three tokes, then passed the next go to me while he blew out the smoke. 'You 'ave weed like dis inna England?' he said.

'Not like this,' I said. I took a drag. 'Most of the weed in England is rocky.' They all stared at me, blank. 'Ya know, rocky-black, like?' Nothing. 'Ya know, like, er . . . a stick that you burn?'

Ganja Baby looked concerned for me. 'A rock and stick you burn?'

'And that's what they call weed?' said Trader. 'A stick?'

'We throw a bloodcloth stick for de birds, tuh rass!' said Straw Man, and they all laughed and sucked their teeth, slapped their thighs, and bumped fists with each other.

I took two more drags to make three, then passed the spliff to Trader.

'Well, you can get proper weed as well, like this stuff. But it costs a lot more money than it does here, so you only get a little bit at a time.'

'How much weed cost inna England?' said Ganja Baby.

'Well,' I took the stalk from Ganja Baby's lap and broke off a fat bud. 'This would cost about twenty pounds.'

'How much is twenty pound in Yard money?' said Ganja Baby.

'Well,' said Trader. He paused to take his third toke of the spliff, then passed it to Saddle. 'The English pound is currently worth forty-three Jamaican dollars,' he said. 'Therefore, twenty

English pounds is worth approximately . . . eight hundred and sixty dollar,' he said, nodding at me – as if I knew.

'Bloodcloth and rass!' said Straw Man. 'You pay dat?' He bumped a fist with Ganja Baby and slapped him on the back as they both laughed.

Trader had his chin in his hands, frowning in contemplation.

'Me met a man from England one time—' said Ganja Baby.

Then without even looking up, Trader said, 'Darka.' Ganja Baby rose like a hound to a whistle and launched a stone in the direction of the one they called Darka, who was about thirty yards away and approaching the tree.

Where did he get that stone from?

'Bombo. Nah mon,' shouted Darka covering his head and turning away. Another stone glanced his shoulder: 'Ah!'

Saddle had stones too and he launched one at Darka, which just skimmed Darka's afro. Then Straw Man launched one that bounced of Darka's arse as he turned away in defence.

'Ah, mon! Come on, gimme some o' da weed, mon,' shouted Darka limping towards the tree. He picked up the stone that had just hit him and launched it back, very nearly taking Saddle out of the tree.

'Send 'im bloodcloth Black rass away, now, mon,' said Straw Man taking the spliff from Saddle. Saddle flipped forward out of the tree, and Darka's next stone zipped past his head. Darka backed off to where the grass met the path and there were more stones to choose from. He scrambled for one, turned, and threw, just about keeping enough balance, fingertips scraping the rubble, grinning like he was starting to enjoy the battle.

Ganja Baby jumped down to back Saddle up. He pulled a selection of stones from his jeans pocket.

They've got stones in their pockets?

Between the two of them they saw off the one they called Darka.

Saddle rolled his shoulder, shrugging off the impact pain of a direct hit from Darka, as he repositioned himself in the tree and rummaged in his canvas bag for a Rizla.

'Dis man who live inna England,' Ganja Baby continued as he climbed back into the tree and took a bud of weed from his pocket for Saddle, 'him told me dat de English man like feh lick de woman punnani, dem, a no true?'

'Lick the . . . ?'

'De pum-pum, man. De pussy. De White, I mean de, erm, England man enjoy to eat a woman punnani, in between dem leg, no true?'

The lads reacted by making noises and cursing:

'Pssst, cho!'

'Blood and rass, no true!'

'Hahaha, no true, no true.'

Then they all went silent and looked at me, waiting for an answer.

'Do we like to lick a woman's pussy?' I said. It was like being asked if I liked to lick lollipops. 'Yeah!'

'No true.'

'Rhaatid!'

'No true, no true, haha.'

'Tuh rass!'

'You can't say dat,' said Ganja Baby laughing. 'You can't say dat because, inna Yard, man no want feh even share a smoke wid you if you lick a woman punnani.'

Shepherd shook his head.

'Well, I don't do it,' I said. 'I mean people do it. Like, I did it once, like, but I didn't, you know, I didn't . . .'

166

'Tuh rass!'

'Too dutty mon.'

'Dat a bloodcloth battyman business.'

'Dat no a battyman business, man.'

'Dat a rassclaat filthy business though.'

'Dat no battyman ting. Just a England man ting, no true, Ian?' said Ganja Baby.

Battyman? I'd heard that word. They said it in songs.

Shepherd shook his head again and said something quietly. It sounded like: 'A sickness, that.'

'You know what battyman is?' said Ganja Baby. 'You no know?'

'Him no rasscloth know what battyman is?' said Straw Man, and the others laughed.

All apart from Shepherd.

'Listen,' said Ganja Baby. I bought two batteries wid de money you gave I. Just to give us all a treat, you no mind?'

'Batteries? No, mate, that's fine.'

'Man have de bloodcloth battery, so where de stereo,' said Straw Man looking at Saddle. 'Where de blood-and-rasscloth music, man?'

Saddle reached into his canvas bag and pulled out a one-deck tape recorder. He put the batteries in and pressed play. A sparse rhythm came through, and a voice said, 'me love Black woman . . .' Saddle pressed rewind – wwrrrwwwrrrrwwwrrwwwrrrrrrrww DF Teck Tik DF – and the tape started from the beginning. It was the voice of the lion-man singing that song again:

'. . . lead . . . head . . . dead . . . battyman . . .'

A lone figure strolled up the path. It was another older lad, one I hadn't met yet. He wore a white caftan, white cotton pants, and Jesus sandals. He spied us lot in the tree as the song started on the tape. He picked something or other up off the floor, turned back down the path, and walked back to the dorm.

'De music of Jamdown is a very good way to learn we dialect,' said Ganja Baby.

Saddle and Ganja Baby were sat on my bunk the next day playing Saddle's tape to me. Saddle rewound the tape and played the song again. That music was unlike anything I'd ever heard in Searbank. I hated Searbank music. And I know it sounds strange, but the reason I hated Searbank music so much was because it reminded me of old Mrs Wilmington's jowls.

When we lived at the poor end of Searbank, before we moved to Searbank Stoops, we all used to play in Josh Harvey's garden. Harvey's mum and dad used to let us do anything, including jumping into the prized privets of old Mr and Mrs Wilmington next door. The Wilmingtons hated us doing it. But Harvey's parents seemed to enjoy winding them up so they actively encouraged it.

One day, as we played jump in the bushes, old Mrs Wilmington came hobbling into the garden, shouting. We were scared at first, but Harvey's mum egged us on so we felt like we could stand up to the 'old witch'. But when she came striding over to the hedge waving a hoe at us, everyone ran away. But I went in for one last jump, and I was still in the hedge when she got there. She grabbed hold of my hair and shouted over to her husband: 'I've got the piccaninny. Phone the police. I've got the little nigger.'

She had a hawk's grip, but I eventually pulled away, leaving a clump of hair behind in her talons. No police came. It was a minor incident, and the other kids involved have probably never thought about it since.

But it haunted me.

I must have only been about six at the time. I didn't even know what the word nigger meant. And I'd never heard anyone use the word 'piccaninny' before (and only a couple of times since). But those wobbly jowls stuck with me, the saggy eyelids, the hairy neck skin, and the sounds of those words – the way she said them.

When I got older, I started to see elements of that face in other White faces and particularly, for some unknown reason, in the faces of Paul McCartney, Bernard Sumner from New Order, and some fella that Dad used to listen to called Marty Robbins. And for that reason alone, I hated all their music. And for that reason, I hated all other music which, in my mind, was related to it: Talking Heads, Echo and the Bunnymen, Depeche Mode, and fuck Joy Division – the music of old Mrs Wilmington's jowls.

This stuff Saddle was playing though, it sounded the way I felt. It sounded like the roar of angry fire, the off-kilter crackle of dry wood flaming in the rain.

Saddle and Ganja Baby were teaching me the words of the song that Angel had danced me to in the Cave, the song that everyone apart from me had known. The song had a beautiful, hypnotic, and dangerous rhythm – and I was slowly starting to understand the meaning.

'Dem waan know, why de rude boy gone feh lead

We haffe buss up a battyman head

We haffe leave a battyman, dem, feh dead

Forfeit di law of the Almighty Dread . . .'

The lad in the white caftan walked into the dorm, saw us, picked up an invisible something from the floor, and walked out again.

'White Man!' Black Man's voice hit me like a slap across the back of the head. 'Here.'

Saddle and Ganja Baby chuckled as I slopped from the bunk and slumped off across the dorm toward the dulcet tones that summoned me.

'My name is Mr Garter,' said the visitor as he squeaked his skinny arse across the flowery couch. It was the yellow fella from Peach's Paradise Hotel. 'Sit down, Ian. We need to talk.'

The word 'Ian' was starting to wear me down.

'Your mother is very worried about you.'

The word 'mother' finished me off.

'You have got yourself into a very serious situation, Ian.'

I nodded at my black socks.

'This is not England. But you know that by now, don't you?'

Dirt and dust occupied the cracks and missing corners in the once-white linoleum floor tiles.

'This country does not have the same . . .' he thought for a second, 'restraint. Your mother is right to be concerned, Ian. This is a very dangerous place for a boy like you. Have you been mistreated or harmed in any way?'

I shrugged: 'No.'

He shrugged: 'Good. Now, do you know who I am?'

You just told me.

'I am a consul for the American government. Do you know what that means?'

I shook my head.

'It means, Ian, that I have a lot of power in this country. And I have decided to keep you safe. So, I am doing all that I can to get you out of here. I sincerely hope that soon you will be back at Peach's Paradise, and you shall be able to enjoy the rest of your holiday, whilst I keep you and your cousin away from the possibility of further danger.'

Mum.

'Did you hear me, Ian?'

'Eh? Yeah, thanks.'

'Is there anything else you would like to tell me?'

'My name's not Ian.'

He was already straightening up to leave. 'OK. Well, I have done all that I can do here. I will be staying in touch. You are in my care now, and I will make sure that nothing happens to you. Goodbye, Ian.'

He walked out to a big red American-looking car. The driver started the engine. I allowed myself to be engulfed by a cloud of red dust and fumes as they pulled away.

Mum.

'White Man!'

Jesus Christ.

Black Man leaned in behind me and spat at the back of my head: 'Dinner.'

Plates of food wobbled, span, and rattled when released from dinner ladies' hands. We ate in a long hall behind the big *Waltons* house. It was un-brushed and unlit, big brown stains on the walls.

Shepherd invited me to sit with him at the head of a long concoction of tables of various lengths, heights, and widths. The boys ranged from about eight years old at one end of the table to us lot at the other. The grey-green plastic chairs were all connected together by little loops on their sides. It felt like being back at junior school, but in an alternate reality where dinner ladies wear paisley bandanas and suck their teeth.

The food looked pretty much the same as what I'd eaten for every meal since being arrested. It was still ricey-mush with titchy bits of orange stuff, but now it had what seemed to be tiny bits of chicken as well.

Shepherd had a larger portion than everyone else, with bigger chunks of chicken and some tasty looking red sauce. He smiled at the dinner lady as she placed the plate down in front of him. 'Thank you, mummy,' he said. 'Ian, the English man, him need some a dis too, mummy. Thank you.' She patted him on the head and smiled, then launched the plate originally meant for me in the general direction of Straw Man. He frowned up at me as the plate wobbled in front of him. The dinner lady went back to the kitchen and returned with a special plate for me, all spicy red sauce and big chunks of chicken.

The food was better than any meal I'd eaten in the past week, though still less appetising than most meals I'd eaten in the sixteen years and eleven months before getting arrested in Jamaica. We even had dessert: a flavourless dry sponge that you needed water just to swallow, even though it had custard on it. Well, me and Shepherd had custard.

'No worry 'bout food for the others,' said Shepherd as I tried to not look at Straw Man and the others forcing down flavourless sponge with tepid water. 'Soon we mek sure dem all get something special, if you like. If you have a little money to help, we can mek something special happen. Then everyone feel OK.'

'Yeah man.'

'Irie man.'

'Irie, mate.'

'You need some more lesson in Jamaican dialect from Saddle and his tape,' said Shepherd. 'Saddle.'

'Yes man,' replied Saddle. 'Me see to dat straight after me finish dis dry-arse cake with water.'

Saddle and Ganja Baby took me to a patch of long grass behind the sitting tree. Saddle rewound the tape as I lit up a spliff. We went over the song a few times. I was starting to get a feel for the way they use the sounds, the words.

'We haffe bus up a battyman head

We haffe leave a battyman, dem, feh dead . . .'

'It's about shooting gay people?'

'Exactly!' laughed Saddle.

'Haha, him got it,' said Ganja Baby.

It seemed a bit harsh. But then I remembered the time in school when Joe Shirley said that some skinny camp lad from the year below us was gay. So I approached him and posed the question: 'Are you a fucking faggot?'

'Why, are you?' he said, and then slammed the fire exit door in my face. I ran round to the other entrance, but it was locked, so I kicked the door, shouting, 'You fucking queer cunt. I'll fucking kill ya, ya fucking faggot.'

We didn't really hate gay people though, did we? It wasn't serious, was it?

It was like in 'One Less Bitch' by N.W.A. when Dr. Dre rapped about pimping, gang-raping, and murdering women. He never really meant it, did he?

It's just a joke, isn't it?

But why did I think Dr. Dre was just joking, but the lion-man was serious? There was no way of knowing what the words in these songs really said about the way Jamaicans thought; or what N.W.A.'s raps really said about the way Black Americans thought;

or how much of what we said in Searbank High School reflected who we really were, and what we really felt.

'Because battyman deserve crucifixion,' said Saddle. 'Dat is de way we see tings in Jamaica.'

OK!

The sun was still low, just starting to reflect in the dew.

It had been days since I'd had a shit. Everyone else was still asleep as I penguin-walked from the dormitory, stomach churning and gurgling. I flinched every time my body weighed down on each foot and sharp stones poked through my socks. I stepped off the path and walked across the grass to the shed behind the strongroom.

There was a long bench across the back of the shed with a wide hole in the middle of it, and underneath the hole was a deep ditch full of shit. I crouched over the hole and a wave flowed out of me. My forehead broke out in a heavy sweat as my sphincter stung a memory of spicy red sauce that dripped, pipette-like, too long to keep holding my breath.

I tried to stay in the narrow corridor of non-fetid air between the shed stink and the dense stench of the strongroom. I pulled up my pants so they loosely covered my parts and hobbled off to look for wide leaves to wipe my arse with. The small and slightly dried out leaves I found would have to do.

Where are the showers?

Saddle carried a bar of soap and a towel in his canvas bag and, according to Ganja Baby, showered twice a day.

So they must have showers.

I John Wayne walked to the kitchens and helped myself to a glass of tepid water, then another, and a third.

It was so early that the sky was still layered in shades of orange and purple.

Something in my stomach churned again, but it wasn't my bowels.

What is it?

Kissy?

Increase?

Mum!

I wandered over to the sitting tree, sat beneath it, and rolled a fat little spliff to numb the guilt. And yeah, I knew the spliff would only make it worse.

Mum will probably be drinking too much.

I smoked it fast and rolled another spliff.

Mum won't be sleeping.

I lit up and toked hard.

She'll be getting her headaches.

And yeah, it did make it worse. So I took another toke.

The mauve morning turned yellow and blue.

I wondered what Dad had said to the British Embassy.

I wondered what the British Embassy was.

I closed my eyes for a second and wondered:

What if you could pull back time and space; tear it like a piece of paper with the story you're living written on it, chuck it away like it never happened?

There was a strange sound somewhere behind me, like a bird chirping and rasping at the same time. The sound ripped and warbled. Breaths of sound overlapped like waves and drew me into a scene.

Walking.

We were walking through the desert, me and Shepherd, holding hands, both of us carrying staffs. We lay down together on a patch of grass by a small oasis. I lay with my head in Shepherd's lap as he rummaged in my hair.

I opened my eyes. Sweat prickled my face. People were heading from the dorm over to the hall for breakfast. Shepherd turned out of the dorm and looked around until he clocked me under the tree. He lifted his head slightly in a question, and I looked down slightly in an answer. He turned and said something to Red Douglas, and then came over. 'You don't feel to eat?'

'Nah.'

'You feel to walk?'

I looked up. 'Yeah.'

We climbed over the fence behind the field and walked along a worn path. We walked for about half an hour, in silence, around a tended field with rows of crops in cracked earth, through a gap in a decaying fence.

The rain came.

It seemed to do it once a day, for just a few minutes; one hard rain. Shepherd ran to shelter under a tree – when it rains the Jamaicans run. I stood there in the warm rain, glad for the deviation from cumbersome sun.

'Get out the rain, you crazy English man,' laughed Shepherd.

I joined him under the tree. The dream came back to me: me and Shepherd in the desert, walking, finding shelter, and picking through each other's hair.

The downpour reigns short, and the heavy sheet of heat returns, once a day.

Two old men were sat on the veranda of an old wooden house. They eyed us suspiciously as we came to the place where the river runs. Shepherd sideways glanced me a hidden message. Shepherd never did say much, like he only talked when necessary.

'This place reminds me of another place, in another time,' he said looking down the river.

'Me too,' I said.

'Mm-hmm? Where it remind you of?'

'It's just a place near where I'm from.'

'In Liverpool?'

'Yeah, well, Searbank.'

'Oh.'

He sounded disappointed. I knew Searbank wasn't that interesting, but I don't think that was what he was getting at. I didn't know what he was getting at. It was gonna be another seven years before I'd even start to understand any of what was happening here.

'I used to go running there,' I said. 'Down by the river.'

'Was it as beautiful as this?'

'No. It was nice though.'

'Did you ever hear the river talk to you?'

Well I thought that was what he'd said. 'Eh?'

He smiled.

I guessed he must have only been about the same age as me, but he had the aura of an old man, I mean a wise one; his eyes, his posture, the way he smiled at me like I was a child, a child he loved. Maybe he made everyone feel like that?

'You hear that?'

It was the strange bird again, rasping and warbling.

'Yeah.'

'That call a doctor bird. A type of humming bird. It is a symbol of Jamaica. You have two dollar?'

I still had the bloodstained two-dollar note from the night I got stabbed. I took it from my back pocket and handed it to him.

'There it is,' he said.

And there it was on the two-dollar note; green body, red wings, purple head, and long tail curling underneath its hovering body.

'What colour would you say that bird is?' he said.

I looked up at him – a towering angel.

He turned the note over to show me the other side – a picture of smiling children of all shades – and he pointed the bottom right-hand corner, the phrase:

OUT OF MANY
ONE PEOPLE

I smiled in gratitude.

How do you get to be like Shepherd? Is it just luck or is there more going on? Shepherd was the top boy at Copse, and no one fucked with him. But he never hit anyone, or threatened anyone, or even threw stones at Darka. Not in the time I knew him for anyway – which felt like a lifetime. I wanted to cry. I wanted to hug him and say thank you. If I'd known how soon I was gonna lose Shepherd the urge would have been even stronger.

'What the matter?' he said.

'It's just my feet, my ankles,' I said, glad for the change of focus. 'They're really fucking itchy.'

The all-seeing eye was at full tilt. I was sat on a stone wall outside the dorm waiting for Shepherd to come back. I ditched my socks behind the wall and scraped at the red lumps on my ankles and the tops of my feet. Shepherd had insisted that I waited there while he fetched Saddle. Saddle was the only person there, as far as I knew, who had toiletries; he kept them in his canvas bag along with the rest of his belongings. And in there he, apparently, had something that would help with my itchy feet and swollen ankles: maroon leaf.

A load of lads were getting ready to start a game of footie on the field at the side of the big *Waltons* house.

'English wid us,' shouted Trader as he grabbed my hand and dragged me off the wall and over to the field.

'We want English. Dat no fair,' said a younger lad.

I didn't even wanna play. I was waiting for Saddle with his maroon leaf. I looked around for him as Trader dragged me in to the game.

Why did everyone want me on their side? If they thought I was gonna be good at footie because I was from Liverpool they were in for a disappointment.

Straw Man walked over and put his arm around me as he shouted, 'Me join de other team, and dem pussyholes can have English Ian, tuh rass!'

Our side still had a disproportionate number of older lads, but now the younger team had the mega-pecked, barely-toothed Straw Man who, as it turned out, was stronger, faster, and much more dangerous than anyone else on the field.

I glanced over to the wall to see if Shepherd had returned with Saddle and his maroon leaf. Footie was just about the last thing I wanted to get involved with.

If footie had just been like any other sport – tennis, rugby, badminton, or some shit – it wouldn't have annoyed me so much. But football isn't like other sports, is it? It's always there up in your face – footie. People didn't think it perfectly normal to start every conversation with a male they'd never met before by asking you what tennis player you support, what hockey team you like, or whether you're rooting for Duncan Goodhew or . . . whoever he used to swim against. So why did everyone wanna talk to you about fucking footie?

All the way through junior school it was there, making my mates not wanna play out until after *Match of the Day* on Saturday, or *Grandstand* on Sunday, or *Saint and Greavsie* whenever that shite was on. It was there in high school: catch-and-in at break time, heads and volleys at dinnertime, and after school they'd be playing one bounce behind the bus stop.

Even fully grown men would wander around Searbank wearing footie tops. They'd even wear the silky shorts when they played out the back of the Ship alehouse on a Sunday morning. Some of them even wore those stupid-arse long fucking socks, just to go to the shop.

And even when I just wanted go for a bevvy – not because I loved beer and pubs, but because there really was fuck-all else to do in Searbank – they'd have the shit pumping through huge red, green, and blue light bulbs onto a massive screen. Everyone in the alehouse would stare at the screen, hypnotised, half cut and shouting at a projected image like their lives depended on it:

'Who's the bastard in the black?'

'Penalty ref., come on.'

'Off side, ref.! Off side!'

'Move, Barnesy, you fat lazy nigger.'

That was why you'd always find me stashed in some corner rolling a spliff, or in the beer garden chatting to Jemma Simpson.

My feet were burning inside and out, and as red as the Ellesse boots. I leant down to scratch them, and to stop thinking about

Jemma Simpson: the first kiss at Searbank youth club disco, before I started seeing Kissy; the wank in the alley, when I'd only been seeing Kissy a few months; the next time I got off with Jemma Simpson, the time I really needed to stop thinking about.

The older lads were dishing out advice to the young 'uns, and Red Douglas was going through some kind of warm-up ritual.

My head was spinning with ankle itch, thoughts of Jemma Simpson, thoughts of Kissy.

I was trying to think of an excuse to not play when something happened that made me stay put. A load of kids gathered around Straw Man and started saying shit:

'Straw Man a beat him.'

What are they saying?

'Straw Man fuck him up.'

Are they saying fuck them up or fuck him up?

'Straw Man fuck up White Man.'

What?

The game started.

Team Straw Man's goalkeeper whacked the ball downfield and it soared in our direction. Everyone on their team sprinted after it, while everyone on our team backed up to meet it. The ball landed, without a single bounce, in the longish grass right in front of me. Even if I had possessed the skill to dribble a ball, it would have been impossible on this lumpy-arse ground, and with my increasingly lumpy-arse feet. So I did what I always did – I whacked the ball up field and legged after it.

My second step landed on something spiky, my fourth step on something even more aggressive, and then I stepped on something that – 'Fuckin' hell!' – absolutely knackered. I hopped around and swore a few more times. Being punched in the face, or stabbed in the leg, or hit across the back of the head with a big

stick are all unpleasant experiences. But the pain, and the antici-
pation of more pain, as you run barefoot over spiky-arse Jamaican
weeds – that's a unique evil.

Straw Man jumped up and down, probably on a whole clump
of sadistic weeds he wasn't even aware of, as he pointed at me,
laughing: 'Bombo. Hahaha. Tuh rass!'

I walked around for a bit as the game went on around me. I
had to practise acceptance of pain before I made any more moves.

Don't flinch.

Don't scratch.

Then the rock-hard ball came soaring in my direction again.
The whole of the other team sprinted towards me with a crazy-
eyed Straw Man at the helm. The ball landed. Straw Man tapped
it expertly past me and guided it down the bumpy field. It felt like
everyone in the game expected something from me. So I did the
only other thing I could do well on a footie pitch: I ran after Straw
Man, dead fast.

In school I always used to get picked for the team just before
Tommy Bog-Eye and Danny the Spaz. I, at least, had the skill of
scaring the shit out of the opponent by pegging it towards them
so fast they feared what might become of their shins. I always
went for the ball; it was just that I usually missed.

Straw Man's eyes widened. You could almost see a cloud of
adrenalin and pheromone vapour swirling around him. He frowned
and snorted like a bull. I went into pure monkey-man mode.

And I did aim for the ball, but, as was my speciality, I caught
Straw Man's shin. But Straw Man had tough shins, and he pushed
on towards our goal. I shot after him like he was the last 10A bus
from town, and I fell just short of a shoulder barge.

I reached out to hook his arm, but Straw Man deflected my
move with a back hand to the face. He was doing that fancy

footwork that they do when they wanna look good before scoring a goal. In my mind's eye, I saw Jay Reynolds, the best footballer in Searbank High School, doing one of his trademark sliding tackles. It was a manoeuvre I'd never successfully pulled off, but I was about to give it a go.

Straw Man hit the deck like I'd yanked out his soul.

'Bombo-fucking-White-rasscloth,' he shouted as he jumped up. He lunged for me, but I stepped back so he missed and stumbled, which made him even angrier. I had my fists clenched as I landed in stance, left foot forward. I sized him up, ready for him.

Straw Man was about to go for it, when he flinched like he'd seen a ghost walk up behind me.

I turned around.

Shepherd was stood there, unmoving.

'Fuckin' crazy English bomborass,' Straw Man half laughed, half sneered as he turned away and went back to the game.

Back in the dorm, Saddle sat down on my bunk and took a handful of dark reddish leaves from his canvas bag. He screwed up his face as he chewed them up. I screwed up my face as he spat them into his palm. He asked me to put my feet up on the bed, and then rubbed the mush into my ankles and the tops of my feet.

'It must be your foot too sensitive for de tiny beasties that live in Jamaican grass,' he chuckled. 'And de weeds also. And de stones.'

'Yeah, all right. Thanks, mate.'

'Thanks, mate,' he copied.

The itching started to wear off immediately.

'Why is it called maroon leaf?'

Saddle looked up at me, holding a thick and dark-reddish leaf, bracing himself to start chewing. 'Because of it colour,' he said. 'It kinda dark-reddish.'

'Mek him go chew de bomborass leaf himself, now, man,' said Straw Man striding into the dorm. No one else was in there apart from a few sleeping kids, so he must have left the footie match early.

'You know something,' said Saddle, 'you right, Straw Man. Why me chew a nasty red leaf, man?' He passed the bag to me. 'Enjoy, English,' he said as he slid off my bunk and sauntered out of the dorm. As I moved the leaf towards my mouth, I could already taste the bitterness in the air around it.

'You no chew, White Man?' Straw Man grinned. I looked him in the face, ready to pounce if he started again, but he smiled to show he was only joking. 'You no like it when dem call you White Man?' he said as he jumped up on his bunk.

'No.'

'Why it matter so much? Plenty people in de Yard would be happy to be called a White man.'

'What?'

'True. Too rasscloth true.'

'Why?'

'Why?' he laughed bitterly. 'Ptts, cho! You no know? De lighter a man skin, dem, de less curl up a man, dem, hair, the easier life is in de Yard. You no know dat? Cho! You no know much, Whitey, erm, Ian.'

'But I'm not White. Where I come from I'm seen as being Black.'

Straw Man nodded: 'Mm-hmm.'

'You know, so, I've always been, like, called nigger and things like that. I get stopped by the police and blamed for stuff.' Red Douglas walked in and sat on the bunk under Straw Man's. 'And

people like me can't get as good a jobs and stuff as White people.'
Red Douglas looked up at Straw Man with baffled eyebrows. 'You
know, I've had to live with being Black because I . . . I stand out,
you know what I mean?'

'I know what you mean,' said Straw Man. 'Because of your
clothes and de way you walk and ting, people tink you act Black.'

'No, because . . . because I am . . .' Red Douglas cocked his
head and stared at me. 'My dad's Black. My mum's White, but my
dad's from Jamaica. It's like Bob Marley.'

Straw Man scowled down at Red Douglas like I'd just farted.
'Because of your hair?' he said, looking back at me. 'You like Bob
Marley?'

'No, I mean, like, his dad was White.'

Wasn't he? I'm sure someone told me Bob Marley's dad was
White.

Straw Man looked like he was really offended. 'You no de same
as Bob Marley.'

'No, I mean, I'm . . . I know I'm not like Bob . . . they think
I'm—'

'A Rastaman?'

'No. I'm not a Rasta,' I sighed. 'It's like . . .' I carried on talking
to fill the embarrassing chasm created by the Bob Marley com-
parison. Red Douglas glared at me as I muttered more senseless
shit about how Black I was.

Straw Man's eyes eventually glazed over like his mind was
somewhere else, until he blurted out: 'It OK.' I stopped in mid-
flow. 'Me have a plan,' he said.

To make me Blacker?

'To get your shoe back.'

'My boots?'

'Me get back your shoe, dem, from de Strongroom. Protect your delicate English feet, dem. Cho!'

Red Douglas just stared at me like he was still confused.

'Protect you likkle White feet, dem,' said Straw Man. 'Hahaha, blood-and-rass.'

The three stitches in my left thigh were coming loose. The one stitch in the upper wound especially stuck out. The stiff plastic thread caught constantly on the weave of my baggy red jeans every time I took a step, every time I pulled on the waist to keep them from falling down, every time I shuffled where I sat.

Fuck!

I'd found a new place to sit. I needed a place. As an only child of parents busy climbing the public-sector ladder, I'd got used to having time to myself. After Increase had come to live with us, I had to find new places where I could be alone. And I found plenty in the caverns of my mind.

I held my hand upright as I sat down to stop the pulse of blood throbbing in the slash wound across my right palm.

Fuck!

The long grass behind the dorm was the only place at Copse where I could escape to the loneliness. It was the only place where there was no Black Man to bark orders at me, no Saddle and Scarecrow to ask me about England or tell me about Jamaica, no miserable guards swinging sticks at little kids as they, – 'Beg ya two dollar.'

But not today.

'What you doing back here?' snarled the guard.

I ignored him, shaking my head as I trudged off.

I found a small enclosure outside the kitchens at the back of the big *Waltons* house. I sat down on the concrete floor and leaned against the wall in between two stinking bins. Salty sweat stung the slash wound across my ribs.

Fuck, fuck, fuck. When the fuck is this gonna end?

As I rested my head on my knees, I noticed it was shaking side to side.

Why did I do this to myself?

Why had I taken the weight – like in the dream about the matchsticks? It had been an instinct. Something about daring to cross the threshold. Daring to leave the cave. I'd wanted to make something happen. And I had. It was happening. But I wasn't out of the cave. I was just in a new one.

I retreated further into the caverns.

At least no one would hassle me here.

'English Ian,' said Saddle, his face popping over the small wall behind me. 'Why you sittin' amongst de garbage, man?'

Fuuuck!

Saddle and Ganja Baby seemed happy with the progress I'd made. They both insisted that we carry on with my lessons, no matter how deliberately glum I looked.

Ganja Baby pulled a bud of weed out of his canvas bag. Saddle positioned his tape player in between two branches in the sitting tree and pressed play.

The music was so simple; just bass noises fading in and out, wood blocks and drum beats in scatty places, the odd sound from a keyboard in sudden interruption. No jangly guitar shit anywhere near it. And weirdly, the thing that made me want to move, to dance from the tiny muscles deep in the core of my body, was the silence in between the sounds. And then there was that voice, the voice of the lion-man.

'He loves his car and his bike and all his stuff?' I huffed.

'He love him "stuff", that's right,' smiled Saddle.

'But he loves his gun more?' I breathed.

'Ow. Nah man! A not him gun, dem,' said Ganja Baby blowing out a cloud of weed smoke.

'He said he loves his Browning?'

'That's what he said,' said Saddle.

'That's a type of gun?' I was sure Increase had told me that.

'True.' They looked at each other and nodded. 'True.'

'But a brownin,' said Saddle as he took the spliff from Ganja Baby, 'also means a light-skin girl. A brownin girl.'

My face was trying hard to hold my frown, to not show too much interest, to stay in my cave, but an incredulous smile caught me off guard and drew me out. 'Right. So he prefers girls with light skin?'

'Dat what him say.'

'But in that other song, he said he loves his woman because she's dead Black.'

'Exactly,' said Saddle. 'De brownin song caused so much controversy, he had to release a song for de dark-skin girl too.'

'People were that bothered?'

'Yeah man,' they said at the same time.

'You mussa understand,' said Saddle, 'is a big ting inna Jamaica. Some people want to look light skin so much that they buy special cream and soap to bleach dem skin.'

'Bleach?' I cried as Saddle passed me the spliff. 'Why would anyone do that?'

'Cho!' said Ganja baby. 'Why unu think man?'

I still didn't get it. To someone who'd wanted to be darker

most of his life, the thought of people whitening their skin was just insane.

'You see,' said Saddle, 'we are de product of a long history of people with light skin and straight hair always having all de power, all de money. Because dark-skin people were de slaves. And in de days of slavery, some master would have baby wid him slaves – light-skin master–slave babies. And sometime, they would be de master's favourite, would work in the house of de master as house nigger, you see?'

There was an N.W.A. song where they said something about 'house niggers'. And I'd always thought they meant people who liked house music.

'White Man!' came a yell from the big house.

I scraped my hands over my face: 'Ahh.'

Saddle and Ganja Baby laughed and touched fists as I dropped out of the sitting tree.

'White Man!'

'What?'

'Nurse,' said Black Man, pointing at the big house.

There was a young kid on the couch in the reception of the big *Waltons* house. He screamed in tears as an old nurse pushed on his stomach.

'It seems bad, nurse,' said the younger nurse.

'It is bad enough indeed,' said the old one. She looked at his little mate and said, 'Give him water. Go on now.'

The mate helped the sick kid to stand up. 'I want my mama,' said the sick kid turning back to the nurses.

'Your mama is not here,' said the older nurse before the young one could get any words out. 'Enough nonsense, now.' She shooed them from the room: 'Go on.'

The young nurse shook her head. Then she looked over at me and said, 'Oh my gosh, they have a White boy in here?'

'And what does your problem seem to be?' sighed the older one.

'I was sent here by that fella.' I nodded towards Black Man, somewhere outside.

'Do you have a specific medical issue?' she sighed, gesturing for me to sit down.

'Well . . . I got stabbed.'

The young one frowned and cocked her head all mumsy-like.

'Show me,' said the older one.

I pulled down my baggy red jeans.

The tension of the wounds pulling apart had made the stitches rip through the skin.

'Ooh,' said the young one pouting her lips, 'you get stab bad, White boy.'

The old one prodded around the edges of the wounds. The young nurse looked down at my curling toes. I was learning the many ways in which having no shoes and socks leaves you exposed.

'These stitches will have to come out immediately,' said the older nurse. 'Pass me the scissors.'

'Yes, nurse.' The young one rummaged in the bag and pulled out a pair of scissors. 'I can only find these ones, nurse, but they are a bit blunt.'

'They will do just fine.'

The scissors were curved at the end, for some reason. She poked the curved edge under the solo stitch so it poked into my flesh. She pumped her finger and thumb.

'I don't think they are sharp enough, nurse,' said the young one looking from my curling toes to the little bag.

'They will do perfectly fine,' said nurse as she hacked, sweat running down from under the wiry hair that stuck out from under her paper hat.

I looked through the window and gritted my teeth.

'Ooh, them stab you up bad, White boy.'

The stitch eventually gave way.

Miss Elwyn used to tell me the story of Chiron the centaur; half man, half horse. One day he wounded his thigh. The pain was unbearable. And no matter what he tried, nothing would heal it.

The old nurse began pumping on the other wound.

My next lesson came as I was sat on my bunk that evening. Saddle finished lathering himself in cream – as he did every morning and every evening – climbed up to my bunk with his canvas bag, and took out his tape recorder. He was happy with my progress, which called for my training to be elevated to the next level – which meant listening to a soundclash tape.

A couple of kids on the other side of the dorm got up from their bunks and did windy snake dances, firing finger guns at the gods – 'Bop, bop, bop.' – and Straw Man did a lying down in his bunk dance.

'You like dis?' said Saddle. He nodded as if to answer for me; as if nobody could ever possibly not enjoy listening to perfectly good songs being interrupted every twenty seconds; as if it was a genius idea to ruin good tunes with the blast of foghorns, gun-shots, and aggressive shouting; as if it was perfectly normal to restart, interrupt again, rewind, then replace the last tune with a completely different song before you even had a chance to hear the first one properly.

I nodded.

'One Love is de best soundclash inna Jamaica.'

'Is it, yeah?'

Some of the songs were versions of other songs, but changed so that they had the name One Love in them. I recognised one of them as one of the songs they sang that night in Barnett Street:

'Oh the light . . .'

But it had the name One Love added.

'The light of One Love

Surely murder any soundbwoy . . .'

And some stuff about a soundboy.

'Take the life of any soundbwoy . . .'

And killing him.

'You don't run tings

Like you think you do

You don't run tings

Like you think you do

Because my light

The light of my life

Is One Love sound.'

The bass kicked in: BOOM – ba-ba, ba-ba, ba,ba – BOOM, BOOM.

'Why you think dem say dat?' said Saddle. 'Talk about murder a soundbwoy and kill him system. Why you think dem do that?'

Because they're nuts?

I shrugged.

'It because dem sound system bigger and louder and play better tune than the next man sound system.'

'Right.'

'Dat why dem say it murder another system, and kill off a soundbwoy. You see?'

'Mm.'

'Dis no mean much to you? But it mean a lot to a Yardman trying to make a living, you see? No? Dat because you no know we history. You have to understand history, you see? If you no know wha'ppen behind your eye, how you ever goin see straight?'

I shrugged my shoulders.

'Sound systems became popular because of your World War II. You no know that?'

I shook my head.

'Because Jamaica lost so many of its young men to a fight started by crazy White men. So we lost a lot of our players of music, you know? And then, so many left to go tidy de mess and rebuild de mothercountry.'

'Africa?'

'Africa? Nah man. Britain. In de 1940s and 50s, Jamaica was still part of de British Empire. Jamaican people had been taught to see Britain as de mothercountry, and a land of opportunity. And back then, most Jamaican believe dis to be so. Dis was before we really knew our true place as Africans. Before de dreadman's teachings really reach mainstream people and teach dem we true history. De history of African kings and queens. De history of African slaves. Dat why people hate de dreadman so much, you see? Truth cut both way like a two-edged sword.

'One good thing to come out of dat war was all de new technology. Some of dat technology found it way to de Yard: phonograph, public address system, and so on. So now some Yardmans have access to equipment to record dem own music and press dem own record. And de man, dem, would press him own record and play dem out in de street or in de yard. And everyone could go a dance again. And so develop de popularity of dancehall. You see?'

I raised my eyebrows. 'Right.' I was fascinated. This was the kind of stuff I wanted, needed; and was embarrassed not to know.

'And man could make nuff dollar at dancehall. If people prefer him soundsystem and him record, dem go a dance and buy food and rum. So it became competitive, you know? Man wanted him sound to be bigger and better dan next man sound. So he say him system destroy, kill off, murder next man sound. Dat a why dem a say him sound-murder a soundbwoy. You see?'

Saddle stopped and ejected the tape.

'At first, most people record versions of American songs – soul and R'n'B – but with a Caribbean twist. As time went on, Yard people integrate dem own musical style on record more so. Rastafari have big influence on dat, also. But American influence always dere. Is a two-way ting, you see? Because dancehall culture travel to America and create rap, then rap return to Jamaica and influence dancehall. Rap not really new, you know? It go way back to African style of making rhythm wid your mouth over de drums. But now we mussa hardcore. Rap artists and dancehall deejays no live in no African utopia. Dat why man like Arkimedes Aslan talk about tings dat only ghetto people understand. You see? We mussa mek de music dat reflect our reality.'

I was coming to understand that this was the name of the lion-man in the songs: Arkimedes Aslan.

Saddle put the other tape in and pressed play. The bassline thrummed, and Arkimedes' voice growled.

'Tell me again what him say,' said Saddle.

'He's saying that he's gone to get some bullets to shoot a gay person.'

Saddle sang along: 'We haffe bus up a battyman head.' He

stopped singing when the lad in the white caftan walked into the dorm.

Straw Man shouted and fired invisible bullets from his fingers. 'Dere him go now. Bop, bop, bop. Bus up a battybwoy. Bop, bop, brrrrap.'

The lad in the white caftan picked up one of his invisible things off the floor, turned around, and walked out of the dorm.

'Bomboclaat, Poor Ting?' said Saddle.

'Is that his name?' I asked. 'Paul Ting?'

'No, not Paul Ting,' said Saddle. He leaned over towards Straw Man and bumped fists with him, laughing. 'He think him name Paul Ting.'

'Tuh rass, him a call him Paul Ting?' laughed Straw Man.

'Not Paul,' said Saddle. 'Poor Ting! Like you say "Aw, poor ting". You see?'

'Poor Ting,' I said. It was a perfect description. He was clearly the boy that people would say "Aw, poor thing" about. He was always alone. And he had that look in his eye; the look of one who sees a reality that no one else recognises.

Poor Ting.

'Me been down dere watching.' Straw Man accosted me as I equestrian-stepped over the hot shingle the next morning.

'Watching?' I said.

'Yeah mon. And me tink it time we a deal wid dat.'

'Deal with what?'

'You no want dem back?'

'Want what?'

'Your bomborass shoe, dem.'

'My boots?'

'Yes mon. Me can get your special boots back.'

'It's OK, mate, they're not special, really.'

I didn't wanna go anywhere near the strongroom.

'White man can't walk around here with no bloodcloth shoe.'

'I'm not . . . Honestly, I don't mind, mate,' I said, just as a sharp stone poked into the soft flesh on my left innersole. I tried to turn a wince into a grin. Straw Man flashed a sardonic tooth-deficient smile at me. 'English Ian. Is like me promise. Me look pon de strongroom. And you know what me see? Him no wear dem shoe.'

I really did not wanna hear anything about the stupid fucking huge red boots. And I didn't even wanna think about the strong-room. The very thought of it made me feel tight inside; every time I caught a whiff of the strongroom's thick stench; every time I woke up from dreams of Puppy blubbing and Piggy swinging; every time One Eye and his mates shouted insults well into the night:

'Why you out of Gehenna, White Man?'

'Somebody buy you out, pussyhole?'

'With money made from the blood of Black men, White Man?'

But Straw Man had his mind set. He said that One Eye had tied the laces together and hung the boots over the corner of his bunk. So we could sneak down there, get the stick Straw Man had in his hand through the wide slot in the big steel door, hook the boots by their laces, and: 'Hey presto as you White, I mean English, people say.'

I've never said that.

'So, you ready?'

No.

I didn't want them. I kept saying that I didn't want the fucking boots. It was better to endure the pain on my feet. There was something satisfying about the suffering. It felt like penance for something. Though I wasn't entirely sure what for. And Straw Man didn't seem to be in the mood for a deep-and-philosophical.

'Let's go, then.'

'Me?'

'Yes mon. You no want your bloodcloth shoe, dem?'

'No.'

'Well let's go, den.'

'Mate!'

We waded into the deep stench of the cellar.

I tried to control my breathing. I noticed I was sweating even more than before.

But why?

Because I was scared. You can't afford to focus on your feelings too much while these things are actually happening. But I can tell you I was absolutely shitting myself.

Because I was a scared little kid from a leafy village called Searbank. Because the snarling hard-bastard face that I'd practised in the mirror since I was fourteen was nothing like the real me. That was a face I'd fabricated as a veil for the fear: the fear of being unworthy, exposed, axed down. And because, to Straw Man, this shit was just life, but to me it was the darkest, scariest thing I'd ever experienced.

I told myself this whole thing was stupid; I really didn't want the boots. I think part of me actually believed what One Eye had said: that I owed them something. And some big daft boots and sore feet were the least I could offer.

Or maybe going along with Straw Man's plan was the least I could offer; who was I supposed to pay this debt to?

Straw Man edged along in sideways strides with his back to the wall. I followed, doing as he did. The bricks were lukewarm and tacky on the back of my towelette T-shirt.

I squinted in the dimness.

Is that a chair and a table in the corner? Is that the TV that One Eye watches, or is it a person sat in a chair?

Straw Man nodded his head and waved me towards the slot.

He wants me to look through?

'Come,' he whispered.

I allowed some external force to move my body. I leaned forward and peered in the direction of the slot.

'Look,' he whispered.

I could see the ceiling of the strongroom with its bent corrugated zinc where they'd tried to pull it down to escape.

'Closer,' he whispered.

I could hear Piggy swinging.

Why am I doing this?

'Closer, man.'

I thought I could even hear Puppy blubbing.

Straw Man placed his hand on my shoulder: 'Shh!' He pushed his stick through the slot and hooked the laces of the big red boots.

One Eye's head turned slowly. His gaze slipped passed the boots, the stick, Straw Man, through the slot and straight into my eyes. 'Fucking claat!' he shouted.

Straw Man slipped his hand through the slot and grabbed the boots off the end of the stick. But One Eye grabbed them as well, and the two of them pulled against each other's strength.

'Get de boots,' Straw Man shouted.

One Eye screamed, 'White bastard. You owe me.'

'Grab dem, White Man.'

Time must have slowed down because it felt like I was stood there for ages, watching them pull at the soles and toes, red leather and laces of them big fucking boots.

'Grab dem,' Straw Man shouted again. I reached through the slot to grab the boots, but I found myself holding a hand instead. I pulled the hand and it came through the slot. Straw Man wrenched the boots from the grip as I tugged once more. One Eye's arm bent the wrong way with a sickening crack.

One Eye made a horrible high-pitched noise: 'Wiiaaahhh,' then cried, 'Fucking White bastard.'

One Eye screamed more than ever that night: some abuse, some threats – but mostly pleas for help.

The next day was Friday the 30th of July; the day before my seventeenth birthday.

The big red boots caught the corner of my eye from where they now hung on the corner of my bunk.

One Eye screamed. I breathed out a sigh but my gritted teeth netted the guilt and back-drafted it to my heart.

'White Man!' shouted Black Man. I screwed up my face with hate – always a welcome relief from gut-curdling guilt.

My first visitor of three that day was stood by the window in the grimy, grey reception area of the big *Waltons* house. His huge lips parted to reveal huge white teeth as he smiled, his huge round cheeks moving further up his face, his huge round nose crinkling, and his huge white afro wobbling as his huge round belly heaved with a: 'Hohoho.'

He was like a big Black Santa.

I was Searbank's first Black Santa. In fourth year at Searbank Primary School, we had this American fella called Mr Hanratty over on a teaching exchange in Miss Elwyn's class. He used to teach us about how America didn't even exist until some fella called Columbus tripped over it, or something. Then he'd go to the next class, and Miss Elwyn would unteach us everything he'd said.

He did a boss play with us, though: *Father Time*. We read through the script to see which children would play which parts. I knew which role I wanted straight away. It was only a walk-on role, but, as far as I was concerned, it was the most important role in the whole play. My legs shook with excitement as I waited for my turn. And when it came, I stood up for added impact and blasted my line off all four walls – 'Ho, ho, ho.' – looking around the room, gathering my audience in – 'Merry Christmas, everybody.' It was so loud and so full of energy, it was so good the whole class stood up and started clapping and cheering.

'Well,' said Miss Elwyn, 'I think we've found our Father Christmas. Well done, Aeon. OK, sit down now, children.'

Mr Hanratty looked puzzled. 'I think we should probably let some other children give Santa Claus a go; for obvious reasons, don't you think so, Mrs—'

'Right, that is it,' said Miss Elwyn, 'I've had enough. Would you please step out of my classroom, Mr Ratty.'

'Hanra—'

'Now! Thank you.'

We couldn't make out the words they were saying outside the classroom, but we caught the sound of Miss Elwyn's angry voice cutting through the wall like a razor saw; Mr Hanratty's low buffalo growl creeping under the door. Then we thought we heard a word, just one word, but it was a special word because Miss Elwyn had told us that no one was allowed to say that word to me ever again. Everyone turned and looked at me as if they felt sorry for me. I didn't even know what the word meant.

It was the same word that Debbie Blaine's dad, the school care-taker, had used the day he stormed into our classroom and ordered Miss Elwyn to stop making his daughter sing songs about 'them—' And Miss Elwyn ordered us lot to sing 'Pick a Bail O' Cotton' even louder as she marched Mr Blaine out of the room.

We never saw Mr Blaine at the school again.

Now I feared we might lose Mr Hanratty as well. And all because of a word that had something to do with me. But we didn't lose him. And by the time Mr Hanratty walked back into the classroom, all wide smile and audible breath, I had the part.

'Hohoho. Hello, Aeon. I'm Teddy,' said the visitor. 'Like a bear.' His big smile dominated the reception area. 'I'm your daddy's cousin,' he said, putting his arm around my shoulder.

He was Black, man. Blacker than Black Man. Blacker than Darka. Blacker than anyone at Copse.

'Me and your daddy grew up together in Scott's Hall, in the parish of St Mary.'

He was the Blackest person I'd ever seen.

'We were all raised by our nanna. Eleven of us in one bed; can you imagine that? And your father was the eldest of us all.'

He was so Black. I wanted to walk around Copse with him at my side, like: *Who's a White man now? Look at him. Look at him! That's my dad's cousin. My . . .*

'What does that make you to me, if you're my dad's cousin?'

'That makes me your cousin, Aeon. This is Jamaica. Everybody is everybody cousin in Jamaica, man, hohoho.'

My cousin.

'Your daddy is seriously concerned,' said Teddy. 'So it has been requested that I attend this fine establishment of incarceration and rehabilitation, this wonderful "Place of Safety", our island's pride and joy, and employ the wonders of my knowledge, rhetoric, charm, and persuasion to get you out of this God-forsaken hell hole.'

'What are you gonna do?'

'I can't do anything. De law is de law. I spoke to Mr, erm, the man in charge here; dark, dark Black man?'

Not as Black as you.

'Him say we have to wait see if the man who own your hotel, Mr Corset,' said Teddy.

'Mr Garter?'

'Yes him. We have to wait to see if Mr Corset can get you a court date. I can't get you out of here. But your parents say dat . . .' He glanced around the room to make sure we were alone, then whispered, 'They say dat you must get out of the country and back to England by any means.' He looked down at me with raised eyebrows. 'Do you understand?'

He sat upright and slapped his thigh to break the mood. 'So, hahaha, hoho. What you do to get yourself in a place like this, my likkle rudy?'

'I got caught with some weed.'

'Hohoho, haha. You get caught?'

It's not funny is it?

'I think they just wanted to get me. I don't know. I got stabbed a couple of nights before I got arrested and—'

'Me hear dat. Hoho, haha. You get stab. Oooh, me laaaaugh.'

Who laughs when they hear about someone getting stabbed?

'I've still got the wounds in my leg.'

'Hohoho.'

'And my hand.'

'Hehehe, haha.'

'And my side.'

'Oh, oh no stop it, you killing me, likkle rudy. Hohoho. Ooh, me laugh.'

I noticed.

He wiped a tear from his round cheekbone. 'And how are they treating you in here, likkle rudy?'

'It's OK now. It was bad at first.'

'Oh yes. Dem beat you up?'

'Well, I got in a fight and I got hit over the head with a big stick and—'

'Bombo. Dem beat you good with a stick, tuh rass, haha.' He jumped out of his seat and slapped his thighs in amusement. Then he went all serious again. 'You know these boys may be dangerous? You don't know why they may be in here. You must be careful.'

I'll remember that.

It was hard to believe that Teddy Bear was related to Dad. Dad was tall and slim and handsome, kinda noble-looking. This fella looked like he was from another planet.

'Your daddy was the oldest of all of us cousins,' he said. 'And the smartest. He was a lay preacher, you know? From time he was only fourteen, him preach at the church in town, in front of White folk and everything. That is why the preacher get him a place at the school. Your daddy was the first person from our humble village to attend a proper high school. The first ever! Him never tell you any of this?'

'No.'

'Ptts, it no surprise me. Him probably too hoity-toity to talk about him simple life in a Jamaican backwater. We didn't know much about the outside world back then. It was a quiet life, you know? Inward and backward. But to us, to all of us, Britain was the mothercountry. Cho! We never knew that Britain was more like a wicked stepmother who hated her charge. And we, the naive stepchild, still loved our abusive protectress, you know?

'And your daddy, well, due to him education, he could recite poem and excerpt from all sort of fancy book and play and ting from Britain. He would come home from school and teach us tings: William Shakespeare, Percy Shelley, Maynard Mandeville. I only knew these names because your daddy taught them to me. And he made me remember them, because I was the second eldest, the next in line. Your daddy used to make me recite de poem, dem:

"What could be free when lawless beasts obeyed . . ."

His voice boomed.

"And even the elements a tyrant swayed?

In vain kind seasons swell'd the teaming grain,

Soft showers distill'd and suns grew warm in vain:

The swain with tears his frustrate labour yields,

And famished dies amidst his ripen'd fields,

What wonder then, a beast or subject slain

Were equal crimes in a despotic reign?"

'Oh, de sounds, de beautiful, beautiful sounds of those words. Your daddy liked to read H. G. Wells, Charlotte Brontë, Oscar Wilde, the Bulldog Drummond stories. And that's all well and good; but he never really understood what he was reading. What does it mean to know the words and inspirations of the real children of the wicked stepmother, when you no know the meaning? We didn't even know they were talking about us. About us in relation them. But they knew it. And we did not.

'But, you know, everyone looked up to your daddy. Everyone expect him to do something special. And he did.

'But Britain, psst, cho, such a wicked stepmother. What is it to love she who will never love you? To aspire to emulate those legitimate children of hers; they who will never believe that you can reach their lofty standards, for you are already handicapped by birthright? No matter what you achieve, they will always be waiting for the primitive beast in you to rear up and smite or deflower some innocent White maiden. Or else they will pity you for being the result of their ancestors' subjugation of your ancestor. And dat wicked stepmother, she instigate her impingements, which come with tutting tongue, knowing nod, wagging finger, shaking head, and steel chains to keep you restrained for the rest of your time. Chains on your mind.

'Remember what Maynard Mandeville say:

"The humbled races of the white man's design,

Must follow with our waters, follow our signs." '

He bounced out of reception with a 'hehehe' and a 'hahaha'. I followed.

'You come and stay with me in Kingston,' he said as we left the big house. 'Me give the address to your cousin already. Come stay. We go a Scott's Hall, and me show you what real Jamaican culture look like. In Maroon land.' Then, turning back one last time before he got into his car, he shouted, 'If you get out of here alive that is. Hohoho.'

What the fuck just happened?

At some point that morning, they took One Eye from the strongroom. He screamed in pain as they cuffed his hands behind his back and piled him into the back of a police car.

If you travelled the world on a mission to find the polar opposite of Teddy Bear, you could do no better than to return with the yellow skin and porcelain frame of my second visitor that day.

'Your mother is very worried, young man,' said Mr Garter.

I didn't know what to make of Mr Garter. He painted himself as my saviour, but I wasn't so sure. I didn't trust his weird face. I couldn't put my finger on what he was. He looked like Ben Kingsley in *Gandhi*, but even more racially ambiguous. And that voice. It was a bit Jamaican and a bit American, but there was something else, a sort of racist Australiany/South Africany thing going on. And his voice went up and down, like . . . I couldn't quite put my finger on it, but it reminded me of something, someone off the telly.

'How could you put your mother through such anguish?' said Garter. 'She has done her best to raise you well.'

And I didn't like the way he spoke down to me. Yeah, I did feel guilty about Mum. But what the fuck did this fella know about my mum? What the fuck did he know about being me? About being brought up in Searbank, where the only other Black people were my dad, who'd spent a lifetime perfecting the art of acting White, and Increase, who hated me for being less Black than him and hated all other Black people for being . . . Black.

'I am going to get you out of here for your mother's sake.'

Now? I can't go now.

Of course, part of me wanted to go now. Obviously, part of me wanted to get as far away from this shithole as possible, as soon as possible. But, another part of me was clinging on to Copse, clinging on to this horrible situation – clinging to Shepherd. If I left now, I would never see Shepherd again. But fuck this situation.

How do you hold two conflicting cravings in your mind at one time?

I rubbed my eyes.

'And I have promised your mother that I will keep a close watch over you until such a time as you appear in court.'

Which is when?

I heard myself breathe in.

'I have spoken to the magistrate . . .'

I blinked hard.

'. . . and made an arrangement.' Garter wiped his sweaty palms on the lap of his inflexible beige pants.

'You will be granted bail when you appear in court next Thursday.'

Next Thursday.

I heard myself breathe out.

'I will sign for your bail, and you will live under my aegis for the remainder of your time on this island. Do you understand?'

I couldn't even be arsed trying to guess what an 'eejis' was.

'Yeah, mate, er, Mr Garter, nice one.'

'A boy in the care of an older benefactor would call that man sir at all times where I come from.'

And where's that, then?

'Do you understand me, Ian?'

'Yeah.'

In the time I'd been at Copse, I'd never seen any one of the others, Shepherd, Straw Man, Trader, Red Douglas, Ganja Baby, Saddle, Darka, or, indeed, Poor Ting get called for a visit. And now, Black Man comes goose-stepping from the main house, shouting, 'White Man,' for the third time that day.

I didn't know whether I believed Increase's story: that he was being harassed by gangsters. True, it did seem out of character that he would be so worried about something that was happening to me – he looked like he'd aged about ten years. But the thing about Increase was, he actually lived his lies; he played them out in his head so much they became his reality.

Increase squeaked forward on the flowery couch. He supported his head in his hands like it was made of rock. 'Your mum and dad are really scared, Aeon. They think you might get killed in this place. They don't want us to stay in Jamaica a day longer than we're supposed to. Do you understand what that means?'

'Mm.' I nodded at my bare feet.

'Aeon?'

Bare feet on once-white linoleum tiles all ripped at the corners, showing floorboards underneath.

'Aeon?'

I squeezed my right fist tight so that the sweat from my fingertips seeped into the sliced flesh of my palm, because if it hurts it must be doing some good.

'Has that big daft cousin been? Teddy?'

'Yeah.'

'He came to the hotel too. He said we can stay with him in Kingston. But I don't think I wanna get involved with his useless fat Black head. I don't trust him.' Increase's eyes searched around his skull for a few seconds. 'I don't trust any of them, Aeon.' He clenched his jaw and looked at me as if to say: *Do you understand that I'm not just saying this for effect; I really do hate these people.* 'Aeon, you can't trust anyone in a Godless pit like this island. Do you know anything about the hate and cruelty that created these people?' He stopped and breathed deep to gather himself.

'That fat bastard tried to lecture me about Saul, you know?' He snorted a joyless chuckle.

'Your dad?' I said.

'The Black bastard who sired me, you mean? Yeah, him.' Increase sniffed. 'Fuck him anyway. The main thing is we've gotta get you out of here.' He nodded in the direction of the door to indicate Penelope's cousin, who was once again waiting outside on his moped. 'He reckons he can help. But I wouldn't trust that nigger as far as I could kick him, either. They could all be all in on it together: him, her, Garter, your fucking gangster mates. But what choice have we got?'

'Mr Garter said I'm getting out on Thursday.'

'He turns up at the hotel every morning,' said Increase still glowering at the door that led to Penelope's cousin. 'I'm sure he wants something. He probably expects me to pay him money. Not that I've got any.' His breathing was heavy again. 'Especially now those gangster friends of yours are turning up at the hotel every day.'

'What gangsters? I don't—'

'And yesterday, I saw the main one leaving Garter's office – the one that looks like some sort of primitive subspecies. So that proves that Garter's in on it. That's why they keep coming back. Don't trust him, Aeon. They're all corrupt, every one of them, even the White ones.' He wiped his hands down his face and scratched down and up the stubble under his chin. 'Has he been here?'

'Garter? Yeah, he was here before. He said he's gonna get me out on bail next Thursday.'

'Thursday? Ha! If he really wanted to help you he'd have done it immediately. He wants to let you stew in here till your gangster friends have taken us for everything we've got. They're getting your money too now.'

I looked up.

'Bothered now, aren't you? I've run out, Aeon. They've taken everything I've got. Then they came and told me to get money out of your envelope in Garter's safe. And when I went for it, Garter watched me the whole time. But he never mentioned needing your permission, this time. You see, I observe, Aeon. I know he's in on it. And he's watching them envelopes too; to make sure we don't get to our passports and flight tickets. He wants to keep us in this shithole country.'

He nodded at his own thoughts.

'Well, if you're out next Thursday that will give us three days before our flight's due. You know that being released on bail means you can't leave the country, don't you?'

Does it?

'And your mum and dad want us to get on that flight whatever it takes.'

How?

'You know what that means, don't you?'

No.

Before he left he gave me a carrier bag with some biscuits, boxer shorts, socks, and my white Reebok Classics with little Union Jacks on their sides.

I walked into the dorm with the Reebok Classics on. A gaggle of young kids ran up to me begging to try my shoes on. I sat up on my bunk where the big red boots dangled.

Straw Man walked in and did a double take from trainers to the boots, boots to the trainers.

That night, they brought One Eye back with his arm in plaster. And they rushed him straight into the strongroom.

One Eye shouted through the night. But it sounded different, or maybe I was hearing him differently. Because I didn't only hear hate and violence, I heard sadness and desperation.

Shepherd looked over at me from his bunk. I wondered how it would be to be here now without Shepherd.

It was just after breakfast and Saddle and Shepherd were sat on the wall in front of the dorm. As I walked over to join them Straw Man appeared behind me. He looked down at my feet; all clad in white Reebok Classics with little Union Jacks. He sat down next to Shepherd.

I sat down next to Saddle. 'What day is it today?'

'Today it Saturday,' said Saddle.

'Saturday? It's my birthday today,' I said, expecting at least some pleasure from saying it out loud.

'Today is Shepherd birthday too,' said Saddle.

I leaned around Straw Man and Saddle to Shepherd. 'Is it your birthday today?'

'Yeah man.'

'It's mine too. How old are you?'

'Seventeen today.'

'Me too.'

'Really?'

'You mussa twin souls,' snarled Straw Man.

I took out what was left of the two hundred dollars. 'We should have a party, then,' I said.

'Indeed,' said Shepherd.

Straw Man's glare burnt into the top of my white Reebok Classics.

'What you think, Straw Man?' said Saddle. 'We goin throw a party for Ian and Shepherd birthday.' Straw Man shrugged his shoulders. 'Ian say we can use him money feh buy cake and biscuit,' said Saddle. Straw Man looked glum. 'Chicken and dumpling,' said Saddle. Straw Man looked up and wobbled his head about all nonchalant. 'Beer and weed,' said Saddle. Straw Man almost smiled.

Saddle went to the shop to buy flour, chicken breasts, and Red Stripe beer. Ganja Baby headed up to the farm on the hill to buy weed. Straw Man and Red Douglas climbed over the fence at the side of the compound and waded through brambles as high as themselves, risking the chop of a machete and further legal proceedings if they were caught stealing plantain. Three of the kids ran off, whooping and laughing, to buy biscuits and cakes, sweets and bag juice. Even Trader and Darka were in on it, sneaking into the kitchen to steal knives and pans.

'Come,' said Shepherd.

I followed him, as the others prepared the party, through the secret exit in the bushes beyond the sitting tree. We walked the same old route.

'So when you a leave us?' said Shepherd.

'I'm going to court next Thursday.'

'The White man help you?'

'Yeah. He's a—'

'Shh,' said Shepherd, his finger to his lips. He pointed. It was the long-tailed multicoloured bird again; wings shimmering, beak in the head of some purple flower. It fluttered off and sat on a branch, looking around us. Then it made that sound, the one I'd heard before falling asleep under the sitting tree: a round warbling, jaggedy ripping and rippling.

'Syzygy,' whispered Shepherd.

Eh?

We reached the ridge of the hill and passed the wooden house. The two old blokes eyed us, leaned into each other to say things, shook their heads and sipped Red Stripe, eyes always on us.

We sat by the river.

'When are you out?' I asked.

'Soon come, me think. I don't know why, something just tell me so.'

Even the sun that soaked into my light-blue Maccano T-shirt wasn't hot enough to account for the intense heat pumping up from my chest, bellowing up to make my face even hotter.

We sat down next to each other in silence.

We heard the magic bird singing for us again, making a bubble of harmony and a crackle that pierced it. We lay down next to each other and watched the little fluffy clouds move and morph. I drifted off.

When I opened my eyes, Shepherd was sat upright, leaning on his staff, staring at the river. I forgot what I'd dreamt immediately. Maybe on purpose. Maybe it was something like what I'd dreamt under the sitting tree: Shepherd and me. How good it would be to be those people now; to lie down together, to hold hands, to look through each other's hair. But that type of shit was for another life.

The sky sunk from unnameable purples to deep blue dusk.

It was still warm as we crawled through the bushes and back into the field behind the sitting tree. Everyone else was already there, preparing the feast. Straw Man lit a fire as Trader coated the chicken legs in jerk paste and skewered breasts on whittled sticks. Saddle shaped up dumplings. After some arguing over fire space,

Darka lit his own fire to boil yams and breadfruit, leaving Saddle to fry his dumplings. Trader then used Darka's fire to fry the plantain. Ganja Baby saw that the guards were plied with enough beer and weed to keep them at bay.

The deep sweet smell of frying yellow fruit reminded me of Dad's kitchen, which reminded me of Dad's smell.

Everyone who tasted Dad's food loved Dad's food. But the appreciation of Dad's food was often accompanied with the phrase: 'I don't normally eat foreign muck.'

And our next-door neighbour had once suggested that foreign food smells 'weird'. And that, suggested this neighbour, was why foreign people smelt 'weird'. It was around this time that I started to take more interest in my Dad's smell.

I never mentioned it to anyone. Dad's smell became a guilty secret. Because that smell was the one thing about my dad that, to my mind, set him apart from my friends' dads. Not his hair or his skin or his crisp expensive suits – but his smell. I never did work out if it was different or if my mind had made it different: maybe less greasy than my friends' dads; maybe a bit tangier? But the link was made: the link to 'weird', the link to 'foreign', the link to 'muck'; all of which meant different, which meant shameful.

But now, that food and that smell were the most concrete connection between the me who worried over human odours in Searbank and the me who sat to eat, unwashed, by a fire in Jamaica.

The jerk chicken and dumplings were nowhere near as good as Dad's, but it was still the best meal I'd ever had; eating, drinking, smoking, chatting, and laughing around that fire.

When we'd finished eating, Straw Man sent three kids to share out the leftover chicken and biscuits, sweets and bag juices with their friends. 'Dem like kings among de pickney tonight,' he said as they ran off.

As we passed spliffs around the fire, Saddle joked about Straw Man and me nearly fighting on the football pitch. Straw Man and Ganja Baby reminisced about my arrival at Copse. Comments were made about how obvious it was from the time I arrived that Shepherd and I had a special connection. That even as I was marched to the strongroom, the spark was felt by everyone there, and it had fizzed through Copse, Place of Safety for Boys, ever since.

Someone started up a song and we all joined in:

'The weak don't follow the water . . .'

I took the black bandana off my head and handed it to Shepherd. 'Happy birthday.'

He tied the black bandana around his head and said, 'And me have something me can give to you.'

'No.'

'Please.'

'Are you sure?'

Shepherd had been carrying that staff since I arrived, and I didn't know for how long before. I was scared to take it.

'I don't need it any more, brother.'

I took the staff in both hands like a ceremonial sword. It had an intense, high-pitched energy that made my hands tingle like empty pins and needles.

'Thank you.'

'So sometink go on last night, then, boys?' said Leopardskin Bulldog. I'd hardly experienced anything of her murky presence since the day I arrived at Copse, when she'd ordered three frightened boys to be sent to the strongroom. Now she stood at the head of the breakfast table, eyeing us all. Why hadn't we even considered putting back the pans we'd taken from the kitchen, covering the fire pit, or hiding the chicken bones, beer bottles, and spliff ends?

'No point trying to hide it all now,' whispered Ganja Baby.

'What was that, boy? Do you have sometink to say?' she snarled.

Ganja Baby shook his head and stood up. The rest of us left the dining room behind Ganja Baby as Leopardskin Bulldog spat insults at us.

'Yo,' said Red Douglas, 'maybe we should give them some space to clear up the mess.'

'And go a swim?' said Saddle.

'Too bomborasscloth true,' laughed Straw Man.

We left the compound through the hidden exit behind the sitting tree. We followed the narrow paths to where the red dust became solid clay. Green leaves flowed over onto barefoot-worn paths. The undergrowth aliens creaked and cackled and cautioned.

Dragonflies veered past my head like they couldn't see me. A spider swung down from an invisible perch and walked along my arm like I was just another plant.

Shepherd took control of my new staff – his large hand wrapped around mine – and flicked a thin snake from the path. 'One good reason to carry a staff,' he smiled.

The two old men on the wooden veranda watched us over their Red Stripes and cigarettes. One nodded to where Shepherd's hand touched mine. The other shook his head.

We turned and manoeuvred our way down the embankment to the slow-flowing blue-green river.

Halfway down the embankment, I sat on a fallen tree trunk as the lads carried on to the water.

'You no swim?' said Shepherd.

'Nah.' I looked at my leg. I didn't want to risk the wounds getting infected.

'Of course, man. Dem wound serious?'

'They are since that nurse had a go at them.'

'Ha,' he nodded. 'OK.'

Trader and Darka took off their jeans and walked into the river in shorts. Saddle was already in the river, lathering up a bar of soap. Ganja Baby sat on the end of the jetty and sprinkled some weed into a Rizla. He turned away to protect his spliff as Straw Man jumped in from the end of the jetty, still in his jeans.

'Your hand start to heal yet?' asked Shepherd.

I opened my right hand cautiously and showed him the slice that ran diagonally across my palm. It was finally starting to knit together.

Red Douglas stood at the edge of the river and stared up the hill at us. He spooked me out the way he did that look. It was like he was seeing something different to everyone else, something in me.

'And your feet, dem any stronger yet?' smiled Shepherd.

'Nah,' I laughed.

'You need to strong up dem feet for your journey, Ian.'

'Journey?'

Red Douglas shouted up at us: 'Yo, English Ian. Me challenge you to a race.'

'Him no swim due to him leg,' shouted Shepherd.

Red Douglas muttered something that sounded like an insult as he turned and walked toward the jetty.

Shepherd turned back to me: 'Me know about your name, yunno?'

'My name?'

'Yeah man. McMenahem.'

'Oh, that name. I thought you meant, you know, my real name.'

'Your real name?'

'Aeon. My real name's Aeon. Like EE-ON. Not Ian.'

'Hahaha. Me thought that name, Ian, no right for you. But is your surname me a talk 'bout. Me used to visit St James as a yute, just close to where your name come from. You ever meet anyone in England called McMenahem who not your relative.'

'No.'

'You ever wonder why?'

'No. What does it mean?'

'You no know? For real?'

'No, what is it?'

'Soon come.'

Red Douglas shouted up at Shepherd again: 'Yo!'

'Right now, me go win this race on your behalf,' said Shepherd. 'So now me know your real name, you haffe call me by my true name. You remember it?'

I did remember. 'Raphael,' I said. A ripple from the sound moved through me.

An almost invisible smile.

Raphael ran down the hill, right to the end of the jetty, and pushed Red Douglas into the river. He jumped in, securing the black bandana on his head as he resurfaced.

Straw Man took the soap from Saddle.

Ganja Baby lit the spliff.

Trader splashed Darka who shouted, 'Nah mon.'

Raphael and Red Douglas started their race. Their front crawl was sloppy, and I knew I could've beaten both of them easily, even with my breaststroke. Part of me wanted to run down there and jump in. The part that wanted to carry the Universe's weight in matchsticks; the part that wanted to slowly lean forward and drop from the top of the multi-storey car park at the Tontine Market in St Helens; the part that wanted to go to Jamaica and make something happen. The part of me that had to be resisted.

Chiron, Miss Elwyn used to tell me, was a centaur: half man, half horse. He was the oldest and wisest of all the centaurs; an original Titan and, therefore, immortal. But his immortality became a curse when he was wounded in the thigh, because the longer he lived with the wound, the worse grew the pain. Eventually, he found a solution. Prometheus had been chained to a rock where every day a vulture flew down and ate his liver, which grew back overnight ready for the same punishment the next day. This was Prometheus' penance for stealing fire from the gods to give to humans. The only way the cycle could be broken was if someone else took Prometheus' place. And if that place was taken by an immortal, their immortality would be cancelled out and they would die. A deal that suited the needs of both Prometheus and Chiron.

I can't say which one went first – Red Douglas then Raphael or Raphael then Red Douglas – but one after the other they both slid smoothly through the silver-blue surface of the river, and never came back.

The ripples from their raggedy hands and feet subsided almost instantly, and the river rippled slowly like a melting mirror.

Like nothing ever happened.

I stared at that one spot until my brain caught up with my eyes.

I scanned other parts of the river where the reflections of the overhanging trees shimmered with almost as little movement as their other selves.

They're trying to trick us, I tried to trick myself.

I imagined them popping up somewhere under the trees, giggling. But that was not gonna happen. Raphael and Red Douglas were not the giggling types.

My eyes darted about where the sky bounced its blue illusion back up to itself from the cool, uncaring surface of the river.

How much water, how much time passed before me as I stared?

The black bandana bobbed up at the nearside bank.

Trader shouted up at me, 'Where dem go?'

My stomach was tight.

Ganja Baby pivoted around on the jetty, shouting up at me, his voice going up in pitch every time he shouted, 'Where Shepherd and Douglas go? Where Shepherd and Douglas go? Where Shepherd and Douglas go?'

My eyes were hot.

The other lads joined in, shouting at me like I was supposed to know something, like I was supposed to do something.

I couldn't move.

Trader screamed up at me, 'Where the fuck dem go, White Man?' as if I'd done something to them. He turned away from me – I was too pathetic – and shouted at Saddle: 'Where dem go?'

Saddle looked up at me with desperate eyes and said, 'Shepherd?'

Saddle and Ganja Baby paced up and down the riverbank, shouting.

Trader and Straw Man turned in the water, bobbing round and round.

Raphael's staff tingled in my hands.

'Before the hero can return,' Miss Elwyn used to tell me, 'he must seize the magic sword, the holy chalice, the enchanted staff.'

But Raphael was gone.

And this wasn't my staff.

Darka was still on the jetty. He raised his hands to the sky and shouted, 'Dem dead, mon.' He sounded excited. 'Dem bomboclaat dead.'

The two old fellas were still sat on the veranda of the old wooden house drinking Red Stripe as we walked back up the embankment. 'You lose your friends?' one of them said.

'Yes mon,' said Straw Man. 'You see dem?'

'Dem dead, mon.' He smacked his lips together with exaggerated indifference.

'Yeah mon,' the second old fella piped up, puffing on his ciggy. 'Nuff people drown in dat river, mon, ptts, cho!' His words lingered like he was deliberately drawing them out. 'It have a spinning undercurrent. You no see it from de surface, eh-eh. Ptts, but dangerous,' he said, looking directly at me. 'Very dangerous to swim in.' He took a sip of his Red Stripe and sighed, 'Eeeeeh.'

Saddle sped up to a jog as we reached the gates of Copse.

Straw Man and Ganja Baby fell in behind.

Trader sped up to a fast walk.

Darka strolled in behind them.

I was the last to walk through the doors of the big house and see Black Man absorb the news, his gaze fixed solid on a point just over our heads. He turned to Leopardskin Bulldog. She screwed up her nose like she was sniffing a corpse. 'Well now,' she said, 'you see what happen when you break de rules?'

I've tried to remember what happened at Copse in the three days after. I've tried, for the sake of the story. But it's all just a jumble of stuff. Stuff and noises. Noises and Aeon sat under a tree, withering in the sun like strange fruit.

Withering and listening to evil little sounds about the bodies of Raphael and Douglas being found downstream, bloated and blue.

I know some new arrivals came at some point, a new gang. I can't remember what any of them looked like, but I remember the sounds of new people. New people to tell me to empty my pockets, to give them my pants, to give them my T-shirt, the white Reebok Classics I wore on my feet, the red Ellesse boots I wore around my neck.

But it was all just noise.

Empty noise.

Because Thursday had gone. It must have gone because Saddle came, looking all concerned, saying they should have been there hours ago to take me and some others to court.

Straw Man came as well. He said something about the big red boots. But whatever he said, it was all just noise.

Because Raphael was gone.

And now even Thursday was gone; Saddle had said so.

Saddle came again and shoed some kids away from me; told them to stop with their noise:

'Shepherd duppy gon get you.'

'Shepherd duppy come for you.'

Saddle tried to convince me to throw away the staff. 'Just leave it 'pon de ground and get some rest, Ian.' He said it was freaking people out, making them think I was possessed by the ghost of Raphael.

But it was all just noise.

Like Garter's promise of court on Thursday.

What was Thursday? Noise.

One Eye and his mates in the strongroom shouted shit through the night, and all through the next three days and nights: 'Bring the White motherfucking bastard to me.'

No one tried. Who was gonna fuck with a mad White man who wears shoes around his neck, who doesn't flinch when you slap him across the head, who carries a dead man's staff and stares at you, as you spit in his face?

'White Man.'

Noise.

'Shepherd duppy gon get you.'

Empty noise.

'Dat de mad White man.'

'Gimme your shoes, bumberclaat.'

The noise became a second skin, one you wear outside and in. Even in the silence it kept whispering.

'He's confused about his sexuality.'

'. . . read the books . . .'

'Get in the car.'

'Wog head.'

'You have no gifts.'

'Tick-tick.'

'. . . let some other children give Santa Claus a go . . .'

'Get up and fight, you Black bastard.'

'Trigger, trigger, trigger . . .'

'Except for all the niggers . . .'

'Tock-tock.'

Then came a sound roaring like a forest fire . . . no, a rumbling like a river . . .

'English. Ian. Come, English. English.' Saddle leaned over me, touched my arm, and smiled, gently.

'Look. It come, Ian.'

I looked up. A truck.

Somehow, the dead Thursday was still alive. And I was leaving, big red boots dangling around my neck; wound throbbing in my right hand where it clutched at Raphael's staff.

Chiron was the wounded healer. 'Chiron,' Miss Elwyn used to tell me, 'is the one who gives to others as a means of release from his own pain.' But I hadn't given anything.

Me and some other lads were loaded onto the back of a white truck.

We rumbled off, back down that same dirt track that had taken me into Copse fourteen days earlier.

The pitiless sun was everywhere, reflecting everything, bouncing off the foreheads of Saddle, Ganja Baby, Darka, Trader, Poor Ting, and a sea of kids and newcomers as they watched us leave.

If I had decided to swim, to race, to take that risk, I would have won. And Red Douglas and Raphael would have still been alive.

But I hadn't given myself.

And all the other things I hadn't done.

Like how I hadn't told him I fucking hated him.

Like how I hadn't told her I loved her.

Like how I hadn't told him I loved him.

After the death of Raphael, I hadn't given anything to anyone at Copse.

Straw Man stepped from the crowd and stared at the big red boots that dangled around my neck – as heavy as a ship.

224

BLACK GROTBAGS, THE EVIL magistrate, had acted like she'd never even seen me before – like it wasn't her who'd recently sent me to a place where I could have got murdered over a pair of fucking boots. She granted me bail.

I used Raphael's staff for support as I lugged my Reebok Classics over the tiny dried-up rivers of blood in between the stones underneath the eaves before reception at Peach's Paradise. The big red boots dangled around my neck, weighing me down.

Evil Budgie, the evil probation guy, had reminded us that Increase had signed as my legal guardian, so if we tried to skip bail we'd both be banged up for at least six months each. And at seventeen, I might not be so 'lucky' as to be sent to a place as 'safe' as Copse.

Increase had looked down and scowled at his slip-on brogues the whole time, occasionally touching his watch.

Now he was scowling out from the balcony, scowling over at the poolside bar from where music floated up and through the patio doors. The sound of bass, skank, and melody reverberated like three voices hitting me in the head, the heart, and a third place – 'I've Got You Under My Skin'.

Mr Garter had been at the court as well. He would now be responsible for keeping me 'out of trouble'. And if I didn't show up in court on the 26th of August, he would be responsible for my two-thousand-dollar bail.

Creatures cackled in the bushes as I walked along the outdoor corridor to the room.

I opened the door. It felt like I was trespassing in a place that didn't want me. The room was dense with the dark energy of a man who hated me. The room smelt like Increase sleeping and breathing out evil dreams about me.

I showered in silence.

Back then, I could go for days or even weeks without washing and still only smell like I'd been swimming in a sea of Lynx Musk. But now, no amount of soap and water could get rid of the reek of sweat, concrete dust, bunk rust, piss, shit, soil, and blood.

As I'd once heard someone say that it helps your dreadlocks matt together if you don't wash your hair, shampoo hadn't been anywhere near my head for three months before going to Jamaica. Now, a sachet from the tray of miniature freebies disappeared into my greasy, matted wig leaving not even a suggestion of suds. I emptied five more sachets onto my head, rubbed and scratched at my scalp. The slash in my right palm stung and tingled. I pulled my fingers through the coarse entangled clumps, tore it out in dead-skin peppered chunks.

Seven sachets of conditioner later, the hair started to separate in my fingers, knots unravelling into strands.

Suds ran down my leg, made their way around the raised wounds, where the skin had been as torn by the stitches as by the stab wounds.

The chemical smell of laboratory flowers puffed up in the steam around me.

I unblocked the plug hole, threw clump after clump of dead hair into the wicker bin.

The mirror in the bathroom almost laughed out loud at me. My hair stood up in a shaggy clump on my double crown like an ethnic Mr Majeika; it straggled down in wavy threads on the right like the latest version of Michael Jackson; it spiralled out on the left like *Guinness Book of Records* fingernails.

Whenever Mum dyed her hair she used to wrap a towel around her head from the back, twist it into a tail at the front, and flip that back over her head. One of the reasons I'd always wanted long hair was to give me a valid reason to wear a towel the way Mum did; and also so I could swing my hair around like Jon Bon Jovi in the video to 'Living on a Prayer' (I didn't hate all White music).

Increase stared at me as I walked out of the bathroom in a towel turban and towel skirt.

I searched through my Head bag: clean boxer shorts, white socks, white vest, blue jeans, woolly black hat.

'Garter wants to see us in his office,' said Increase. 'Whenever you're ready.'

Garter's office was a windowless little dungeon underneath the reception area: no light, no air. A white bulb screamed down on my woolly black hat from the low ceiling. Increase was in the chair next to me, bolt upright; long plaid socks perfectly parallel to long khaki shorts. He checked his watch.

'Are you with us, young man?' said Garter from the other side of the desk. 'Well? Are you listening to me?'

'Yeah.'

'Well, I suggest you pay good attention.'

'Mm.'

'It is, unfortunately, incumbent upon me to act as your patron and protector for the remainder of your time in this country. Do you understand what that means?'

I can guess.

'I am in charge. And it is imperative that you behave yourself. I'm sure you have learned a valuable lesson from all of the trouble you have caused everyone.'

'I certainly hope so,' said Increase flashing me a look.

'That goes for you also, young man,' said Garter turning to Increase. 'You must also pay penance for your responsibility in this matter.'

'Pay penance? You mean pay dollars? Is that why you're helping those gangster rude boys to extort us?'

'I have no idea to what you are referring, young man.'

'Ha! See,' said Increase. 'He's lying. I told you he would. I told you, he's in on it.'

'All that I know, young man,' said Garter in his uppy-downy voice, 'is that the responsibility the court has invested in me means that my good reputation is at stake. And I shall not be expecting any more trouble to be brought to this establishment.'

Who does his voice remind me of?

'Now, you are to return to court in three weeks' time.'

It's the way his voice goes up and down.

'This means that you have plenty time to enjoy the rest of your stay in Jamaica.'

A memory of 1980-something slid past my mind just long enough to see the bamboo couch in Mum and Dad's old living room. And me, kicking away the wicker with my swinging heels, transfixed by a bulbous TV screen.

'However,' said Garter. 'I will expect the two of you to report to Elias, my security guard, by 10 pm every night.'

The person on the TV was the person with Garter's voice.

'Do you understand that? Well?'

Trying to sound commanding.

'You will stay out no later than 10 pm, and that way we may keep you from causing any more trouble. You English boys think that you can go anywhere in the world and act like you own the place.'

It was a woman.

'But in a place like Jamaica, jumped-up ragamuffins like you two do not last a second. Is that understood?'

Increase stared up at Garter like he was ready to hit him: 'Is that a threat?'

Garter leaned forward on his desk, ignoring Increase, and looked at me. 'How are you going to sort your life out? Hm? Do you intend to go to college? Get an education?'

'Educate derives, etymologically, from the Latin words educare and educere,' – this was Increase answering, obviously – 'which denotes that education should, in part at least, mean to draw out.' He made a claw to demonstrate the action of drawing something out of my head.

I inched away from Increase's claw hand.

'Whereas, indoctrinate means to force in the doctrine extolled by the ostensible educator,' said Increase pushing his claw at me as if to shove something into my head.

I hated the way he always used me as an example, thought it was OK to push himself at me like that.

'We don't adhere to state-sponsored mind-control programmes, do we, Aeon?'

And the way he'd try to make out that I agreed with him when I didn't even know what the fuck he was on about.

'I prefer to read books,' he said, 'to make up my own mind. I've also been busy serving in the world's pre-eminent armed forces.'

His voice broke for a split second. He'd barely said a word about the nearly three years he spent in the army since he went AWOL.

'The same armed forces that needed America to save them from the European forces encroaching upon their "green and pleasant land" not so long ago?' said Garter.

'America is Europe encroaching on someone's "green and pleasant land",' said Increase.

And, yeah, Increase was an annoying bastard. But I definitely preferred this old Nation-of-Islam-style Increase to the pious Christian Increase he'd recently invented.

Increase had stayed in touch with Graham X, even though Graham had been angry about Increase joining the army. I remember mum being furious that Increase had gone AWOL, and 'brought the law to *our* house', so that he could go looking for 'some religious zealot with a made-up name. Christ!'

In later years, Increase told me that it was only a year before he went AWOL that Graham had been corrupted. And Increase had seen it happen.

Graham X was the first person in Toxteth to set up a vigilante squad to tackle the crack issue. Most people didn't even know what crack cocaine was in 1989, but to anyone who had family or friends who were addicted to it, crack was the devil's work. As was the case with Graham X and his addicted stepsister.

Lost Found Muslim Lesson 1; Number 2: 'Savage means a person who has lost the knowledge of himself and who is a living a beast life.'

Graham decided to find out who was selling the crack and shut them down. By that time, Graham had a small following including some pretty hard lads from the area. And it just so happened to be while Increase was on leave from the army that Graham led his squad on their first raid.

And Increase joined them.

They watched the dealer's house until they were sure he was alone. Then they bounced over the road and kicked his door in.

'It was like stepping into another world for them,' Increase had told me. 'I mean, I'd seen the spoils of criminality when Saul was alive; I'd been in houses dripping with status symbols while living with you lot in Searbank.

'But Graham was raised in an insalubrious slum. The authorities had so much contempt for the people of L8 that many of the shops destroyed in the '81 riots were still charred shells in 1989. Picture it: this was a three-bedroom Victorian terrace with no front yard on one of the roughest streets in Toxteth. But when that door flew open and the squad saw what was inside . . . Hew!' Increase exhaled. 'It was like they'd flung open the gates of heaven. The man had a white deep-pile carpet that looked like you wanted to sleep on it. He had the biggest television set even I'd ever seen. He had a Betamax and a set of mahogany shelves full of videos. The man had a chandelier hanging from the ceiling in his tiny front room. A chandelier in Toxteth!

'I saw the squad's reaction, and I knew that there was only one way this was going.'

Lost Found Muslim Lesson 2; Number 11: Question: 'Will you sit at home and wait for that mystery God to bring you food?'

'Answer: Emphatically No!'

'They all just stood there staring into the house,' Increase said. 'I think they were more shocked than the man whose front door had just been kicked in. They wandered around his house with their jaws on the floor. Oh, and listen to this, they even took their shoes off before going in,' Increase laughed. 'One of the lads shouted from upstairs – and he sounded like was actually going to cry – "He's got a bed made of fucking water, kidda." ' Increase laughed louder.

'I was the only one who stayed in the front room to keep an eye on the dealer, make sure he didn't run off. And he just sat there grinning at me as if he knew exactly what was happening. Yeah, he was about to take a beating from men in socks. Yeah, he was about to have his money and drugs confiscated by religious zealots. But this was to be the first and last time Graham's squad tried to shut him down. Graham's squad had been to the mountaintop and seen the other side. And he knew exactly what they were thinking: "Where can we get hold of some of these drugs to sell?" '

But Graham X didn't watch gangster movies. Graham X didn't listen to 'gangsta' rap. So Graham had never heard lesson number two: the one that advises against getting high on your own supply.

'That's why, when I went AWOL and found out he'd gone missing, I had to find him. I was the only one who could have warned him,' said Increase. 'I should have warned him. Graham had no one he could really trust. And he'd made me give him my word that I wouldn't let him wander too far from the path.'

Lost Found Muslim Lesson 1; Number 11: 'My word is Bond and Bond is life, and I will give my life before my word shall fail.'

Garter took a measured breath and turned back to me.

'Your cousin has already decided to waste his life as a preacher of antiquated and dogmatic liberalism. I hope that you will be more sensible and major at one of your fine English universities.'

'Dogmatic.' That's it. The dog woman! His voice sounds like

the woman who did the discipline with the dogs on the telly. What's her name?

'We will continue to keep your passports and flight tickets in the signed and sealed envelopes in our safe, where they are secure,' said Garter.

He manoeuvred around his desk and led us up the steps, out of his office, through reception, and out to Elias, the security guard in his green plastic chair.

'Elias will be keeping an eye out to ensure that you two boys return to your room no later than 10 pm each night.'

Elias raised an eyebrow like it was news to him.

'And,' Garter went on, 'he will be reporting back to me immediately if you boys so much as step beyond this car park after 10 pm.'

Elias picked up his *Jamaican Gleaner*.

'Here at Peach's Paradise I keep a good house and—'

Woodhouse! That's it. Barbara Woodhouse – 'Walkies'. My stomach juddered out a giggle that burst up and through my nose before I could stop it.

'And if . . . Are you OK?' said Garter.'

I hid my face in my hands.

'If you need to access the envelopes to withdraw money, you will only be permitted to do so in my presence."

Stop it. Stop thinking about 'Walkies'. But the laugh burst through my hands.

'What in the name . . . ? Is he crying? I should think so. A small show of humility goes a long way. I am here between the hours of 10 am and 2 pm every day. Is that all clear and understood?'

My face gave way to an involuntary guffaw.

'Good heavens, are you . . . Is he laughing at me?'

Stop it, stop it. You're making it worse.

'Get back to your room. I have never been so insulted in all my life.'

It made no sense that it could still be Thursday. I'd sat at the sitting tree for a whole day. Even Saddle had said that Thursday had gone. Then there was the bumpy journey back down from the hills and into Montego Bay – a short journey, maybe; maybe a long one like on the way to Copse? There was the court appearance. The walk back from court. The shower. The lecture in Garter's office.

After that I'd phoned Mum and Dad, who'd still insisted that I get out of Jamaica as soon as possible. 'Do you understand what we mean by that, Aeon?' Mum had said. 'As soon as you can, son. By any means, OK? Do you hear me?'

Mum and Dad spoke in code. I wondered why Mum didn't just say what she was thinking. Like when I'd told her I was going to Jamaica with Increase. She didn't like it. But she didn't say anything. I suppose people of that generation just got used to saying nothing; being seen and not heard, speaking only when spoken to.

Mum's dad was a butler, an organist at the local church in Dunfermline, and a cross-dressing bisexual. He was found with his head in their gas oven when my mum was eight years old. And from that day on he was never mentioned again by an adult family member. So, of course, Mum said nothing.

When Dad was nine years old a strange woman shouted at him for climbing on a big rock. The woman ordered him to come down. She then beat him across the head for doing something so 'dangerous'. He had no idea who the woman was. Turns out it was his mother.

Dad said nothing.

When my mum was doing her nursing training in Hull, there was a male charge nurse who used to regularly make inappropriate comments to female trainees, and once he even put his hand up my mum's dress. But, in those days, if you complained you would be summoned to the charge nurse's office and told that you simply were not suited to the nursing profession.

Mum said nothing.

Dad's dyslexia was so severe that he found it very difficult to read books. But back in the 1950s and 60s, if he'd admitted that he struggled to read in school he would have been hit with a whip with the end soaked in water, he would have never become a lay preacher at fourteen, and he would never have been accepted on the Nursing Lecturer MA. So, Dad memorised Keats and Coleridge word-for-word, he gave faithful renditions of Ecclesiastes and Apostles from memory, he made sure he knew his Anatomy and Neurology off by heart.

And Dad said nothing.

People of Mum and Dad's generation grew up believing that finding purpose in life meant dedicating yourself to some bloke who may have said some stuff two thousand years ago; that belonging meant accepting that you belong to some bloke – who may be the same bloke who said the stuff, maybe his dad, or maybe he was his own dad – who invented the world six thousand years ago; and that the meaning of life was to work till you drop, avoid most fun stuff, and wait for the reward you may finally receive when you're dead – if you're dead lucky.

Mum was brought up in the Mormon church. Following my dad's first visit to that church, in 1967, the congregation agreed that my dad should never be allowed to attend again. Purpose. The pastor at my dad's Adventist church said that to marry my mum to my dad would be like marrying a donkey to a horse. Belonging.

Mum and Dad said nothing.

It should have been night-time. But time moves differently in the heat of the forge. And as I crossed the roundabout, totally ignored by Randy and his girls, the sun was still there somewhere, hidden from sight but still filling the sky. People were still skulking around. Cars were still beeping. Reggae music was still blaring from shops where people still talked without buying shit. A mad man in a towel was still drawing something in the dust on a dirty shop window with a red, white, and blue pole, still not spinning.

Maybe one barber was busy on the one customer's cropped afro, and maybe the second barber was busy leaning on the back of an empty chair, chatting to the two fellas sat at the back of the shop like they didn't even need a haircut. Whatever was happening, everything went silent when I walked in.

They all looked at each other with raised eyebrows; mouths open, and heads shaking as I sat in the second barber's chair. I pulled off the woolly black hat. My hair sprang out and sat there like the nest of a mad bird. The barber stumbled back a couple of paces and raised his hands in shock.

'Bumberclaat!' shouted one of the men sat at the back of the shop. He laughed hard, sprung up from the chair, and slapped his thighs as the second man jumped up, slapped him on the back, and shouted at the barber: 'What the bloodclaat you going do with dat?'

The barber eyed me from behind, an artist taking in a tricky subject. 'What you waan me do with it?' he said.

'Take it all off please.'

'All off? You really want me take it all off? OK,' he nodded. 'It probably for the best.'

The shop was quiet the whole time the barber snipped, no talking but for the odd murmur from one non-customer to the other as the barber shaved. Hair rolled over my shoulders and fell to the ground in big, dandruff-dappled clumps as he shaped and stood back to consider.

The other barber squinted appraisingly. His customer stayed in the first chair, even after his haircut was done, hand on his chin, watching. Two new customers came in, got hushed, and sat down to observe a master at work. He snipped and shaved the back and sides one way and another, then another, in every direction until they tapered seamlessly up to small block, like a mini high-top with an angle sloping down from left to right.

He massaged some orange liquid into my hair that smelt manly and healthy and hairy like, well, like barber shops. He dusted the back of my neck with talc and brushed it off. And when he shook out the towel, there were no annoying bits of stubbly hair down the back of my vest, not a single one.

Everyone in the shop nodded in appreciation. Then the barber himself nodded and looked around the shop with his hands out in front of him as if to say, *You see how me deal with that!?*

He showed me the back of my head with a small mirror, moved around to the side, then turned the mirror towards the window as some lads bounced past. I caught the markings of the mad towel-man's finger: a spiral obscuring the reflection of my face in the window, and all this reflected in the mirror.

The bell rang as the door opened and the lads walked in. 'Him pretty,' said the leader. He wasn't pretty. 'Little light-skin Liverpool yute,' he said. 'You see me?'

The mood in the shop twisted, and the barber looked at me like I'd tricked him.

The Leader and his three mates eyed me through the big mirror. I didn't recognise any of the mates, but his evil kipper was coming back to me; even though I had only seen it once before, and only for a few seconds, before I'd smashed a rum glass into the side of his head in the Pier 1. But no, I'd seen his face before the Pier 1. I'd seen him on our first day in Jamaica, when we'd got lost downtown. He had watched us from in front of one of those tiny houses with bars on the windows. I'd tried to ignore the desolate glare that told me that he knew that no one should have to live there; and that he knew that I never had.

'You see me now?' he nodded.

He kept his eyes on mine through the mirror as he stepped up to the chair. I thought about standing up, but the chair was still pumped up high and this didn't seem like a great time for an awkward stumble down.

'You remember dat pretty, pretty gal you meet at Pier 1?' His eyes showed no feeling. 'She no so pretty any more. And maybe me no look so pretty to you, you see me, English?'

The scar from the rum glass was a jagged line across his left temple.

'You know what this?' he said, dangling a little bottle with liquid inside. 'Bumberclaat, him no know,' he said, looking around the room. His boys laughed. He leaned over me and dangled the warm bottle at the side of my face. 'Liverpool think him a rude boy, and dun even know what acid look like. You ever see woman walk around Jamaica wid face all melt up like old candle? Dat due to dis, you see me? Is a weapon we use 'pon a woman,

238

dem. Dat why we get some acid for you. Because you English pussyclaat vain like a woman, no true?'

He was right; if being vain means you don't want someone to melt your face off with acid – too fucking right.

'So me tell you what me a go do. You give me three hundred dollar, and me let you keep your pretty red face one more day, seein?'

'I haven't got it on me, I'll have to—'

'No mind dat. We meet you later,' he said.

He leaned forward and picked up a pair of scissors from the shelf in front of us.

'Oh,' he said, pressing the end of the scissors into the soft skin at the top of my right ear, 'me owe you dis.' He zipped the scissors across my temple so they sliced the skin. 'Near an eye for near an eye,' said The Leader. And his mates all laughed.

I watched them through the window as they bounced off, back into the depths of downtown.

The mad man in the towel came to the window again. 'Bumberclaat! Move,' shouted the barber. The mad man moved on, but not before he'd crossed out the spiral pattern with an ominous X.

It was 1990.

Dad was watching *Never the Twain* when the doorbell chimed 'Rule, Britannia'.

'Increase,' said Dad, trying to restrain the pleasure in his voice; he looked around to see if Mum had heard. 'Come in, come in, son. Why do you always use that damn bell?' he said, putting his arms around Increase. 'I've told you, son, this is your home.'

I started as the handle of the dining-room door crashed into the plaster on the hallway wall. Milk sloshed up the sides of my bowl of Kellogg's Multi-Grain Start.

Increase grinned over my dad's back and looked blankly into my eyes.

It had been over a year since Increase had gone AWOL and the police had come to our house looking for him. He'd served his time in Colchester Military Prison and been dishonourably discharged. That much I understood. Why he went AWOL, he wouldn't tell any of us.

That night, I heard Mum and Dad arguing. Mum was saying that maybe it wasn't his fault, that maybe Increase wasn't born a bad person, that maybe it was just the inevitability of being brought up by someone as damaged as Saul. 'But there's something else,' she said. 'I can't put my finger on it, but there's something manipulative about him.'

'Do you smoke?' said Increase as he sat down on my double bed the next day.

I wasn't sure if it would impress him or annoy him, so I said, 'I've been trying to give up,' as I pulled a packet of Regal Kingsize out of the inside pocket of my school blazer.

'No, I mean do you SMOKE?' He grinned, laying a bag of weed out on my bed.

I didn't know whether to expect disdain or respect, so I just said, 'I have wanted to try it.'

Increase would hang around for a couple of weeks, then he'd be off again for a few months. He said he was doing business down in London.

'I'm not sure what kind of business he's in,' Dad had said, 'but he seems to be doing well.'

He did that! Every time he came back he seemed to have more money and nicer clothes.

Then one time, he came and sat on my bed in a pair of bright yellow dungarees, a yellow and black leather hat, and a pair of velvety Travel Fox boots.

'Do you smoke?' he said, grinning.

'I am tryna give up.' I smiled as I pulled my skinning-up tray from under my bed, littered with ripped-up Rizla packets, loose tobacco, and a skinny stick of rocky.

'No,' he said. 'Do you SMOKE?' And he dropped a little white stone onto the tray.

Supreme Mathematics; Number 8: 'To build is to elevate the mentality of self, and others around self . . . To Destroy is to ruin by allowing negativity to outweigh the positive.'

'What kind of business do you *think* he's in?' Mum had spat.

It's people like these that give Black lads a bad reputation. People used to say that a lot back then. It had always confused me that: how can one person, or even a gang of people, give a whole race a bad reputation? I'd seen loads of White dickheads, plenty of them in gangs. But I'd never heard anyone say that they gave all White lads a bad reputation.

My heart thumped hard as they banged twice on the door of our room at Peach's Paradise, then let themselves in.

I glanced over their faces and found myself agreeing: it was people like these who gave Black lads a bad reputation. I'd been going to the First Avenue bar in Old Swan since I was fourteen. From there we'd go on to one of the nightclubs in Liverpool: The State, the 051, the Hard Dock. These were mass gatherings where people took ecstasy, danced to piano house, rave, or hardcore, and muttered the ceremonial words: 'What 'ave you had?' Other rituals included rubbing sweaty faces together while talking in too familiar embraces and, of course, bottling each other at the end of the night. I'd bought weed in the Eagle and Child in Page Moss, and once I even drank a whole pint in the Quiet Man alehouse in Huyton – a quick one, obviously. Point is, I'd seen absolutely loads of White dickheads. But none of them were anywhere near as intimidating as this lot.

Was it something to do with them?

Or was it me?

I gave The Leader his three hundred dollars.

'What about unu bredrin?' he said.

'What do you mean?' I asked.

Increase stood up on the balcony and glared at me through the patio doors with that *I hate niggers* look. And I got it now. Because I hated them too.

Increase stepped through the patio doors to say something. But one of The Leader's 'bredrins' – a bloke with a head the size of my body – lurched over to him, pulled a knife out, and held it to Increase's throat: 'We no need no clever talk from you, clever nigger.'

'You know, we can gut you like herring now and nobody do a ting about it,' said The Leader. 'Nobody ever tell you, man can kill any nigger in Jamdown and get away scot-free? As long as you leave di scene of di crime, and no stand around wait for police with blood drip from your hand.' The three bredrins laughed.

I gave them all the money I had in the room.

They were gonna come back tomorrow and take more.

And they'd keep coming back every day until we had nothing left.

Then what?

They left laughing, slapping each other's backs, touching fists.

My legs were still shaking as I sat on the bed, not looking at Increase.

'You didn't believe me, did you?'

I could hear my own breath.

'This is all your fault, Aeon.'

I could hear Increase's breath.

'It wasn't me who came to a third world country and started trying to act like some sort of rude boy, was it? But it's obviously me who's left to think of a way to undo this disaster you've created.'

'We should go to Kingston,' I said. I wanted to say other things too.

'You never have any ideas, do you? It's always up to me, isn't it?'

'Dad's cousin . . .' I tried to clear my throat of the unsaid stuff bubbling up in it, 'that Teddy fella. He said he gave you his address.'

'I've had enough to deal with in my life without being put under even more pressure just because you're an entitled fucking shit-bag.'

'There's a shop near the roundabout where you can hire motorbikes.' My throat creaked under the pressure.

'No one in this world – no one – has ever been there for me. But God protects useless bastards like you, doesn't He?'

'Fuck off,' I whispered.

And you're the fucking hero of the fucking world, aren't you? Increase the Invincible. Who the fuck do you think you are? You think that you're better than me because you're from a shit area and your dad was a cunt? Bullshit, mate. You're just a fucking knob-head like everyone else. That's what I'd like to have said. But all I could muster was that quiet: 'Fuck off.'

We had three more days – Friday, Saturday, and Sunday – to work out how to get our passports and flight tickets from Garter's safe and get on that flight back to Manchester without being noticed. If we tried and failed we'd both be arrested and sent to prison. The only other choice was to be taken for every dollar we had until we couldn't even eat, then get stabbed up by a primitive nutter and his horrible mates.

'There's a place down by the roundabout where they hire motorbikes,' I said.

'You said. So we go to Kingston and stay with that big daft cousin for a couple of days. Then what, Aeon? Then what? It's a shitty plan.'

Obviously it was a shitty plan. It was barely worthy of being called a plan. And I tried as best I could to think about it logically, weigh up the pros and cons. But the weighing-up part of my brain wasn't playing. A silent voice told me we were going to Kingston. Kissy would have said it was the Universe guiding me. But Kissy said all kinds of weird shit.

I wondered if those Rastas were still in the room downstairs.

I could do with a spliff.

Even in the beige hotel room light of the next morning, with Increase still listing flaws in the non-plan as I pulled on my white Fruit of the Loom T-shirt, black Adidas shell suit bottoms, and white Reebok Classics with the little Union Jacks, I knew I was going to Kingston.

Josh Harvey – the lad whose mum used to let us jump in old Mrs Wilmington's privets – was allowed to do all sorts of stuff. When we were about ten, his dad bought him a moped. We used to take it out on the field facing our house. But Harvey being

Harvey, he eventually rode it into the Del – a wide ditch full of horse shit. And when we got it out, it was never the same again. I hadn't ridden a motorbike of any kind since. But I could still remember the thing you do with your foot: up for first gear, down for second, down again for third – something like that.

Bogey had sold me a massive bag of weed for forty dollars. It was well more than I'd wanted to buy. But how could I refuse what looked like about a quarter ounce of fine weed for the equivalent of an English pound?

I sat on the balcony and rolled a spliff.

I was going to Kingston even if I had to go on my own.

Just like how I should've done this whole thing on my own.

Well now I could.

Then I lit the spliff. I sucked and inhaled – doubt wafted in; exhaled – guts gone. I inhaled every single thing that could possibly go wrong, exhaled every bit of will I had left.

And then I knew that riding a motorbike to Kingston was gonna get me killed.

And I knew I had to go.

All the way down the hill, I thought about how I was gonna blag the fella in the shop that I was twenty-five years old when he saw the age on Increase's driving licence.

'Me know a lot of tourist, dem, go to Kingston for Sunsplash festival,' said the fella.

He hadn't even looked at the licence, and he already had the key in his hand ready to give me the bike.

'The what?' I said.

'Dis bike no mek it there and back, yunno? It too far.'

'I'm not going there, mate.'

'The boss no want him bike push too hard. And it too dangerous to ride a small bike all the way from here to Kingston. Some
of these road is treacherous.'

'I'm not going to Kingston.'

'You no go a Sunsplash?'

'I don't even know what a Sunsplash is, mate.'

'Now me know you tell a lie because everyone know what
Sunsplash is. You go a Kingston?'

'No, mate.'

'You go a Sunsplash?'

'I don't . . . No, mate. I'm not . . . I've gotta—'

'Well, me hope you tell the truth. Two day you want it for?'

'Please, yeah. I'll return it on Sunday night.'

'Sunday night? That three day including today.'

'Yeah, OK, three days. How much is that?'

'How much you want pay?'

'Well how much is it?'

'How much money you have?'

Fucking hell, I hate Jamaica!

I could feel the fella in the shop watching me from the front
window of the reception area. I tried to look casual while hoping
I remembered how to get the thing started. Surprisingly, I got it
going and into first gear. I looked behind me. The fella in the shop
was nowhere to be seen.

A car screeched on the outside of me as the blue Honda 50
wobbled onto the roundabout. I kicked the pedal up and down
trying to find second gear. The driver held down the horn for an
extended beeeep and cut me up to go left. A fresh tsunami of
sweat suddenly breached the pores on my forehead.

I wasn't new to driving on the roads. About three months earlier, I'd bought a brown Austin Maestro for forty-five quid from Sophie Titwank. Its suspension squeaked and the exhaust backfired. The stereo was just a plastic cover. It came off in my hand the first time I tried to turn a knob. It must've been the brownest car in the whole world.

A minibus revved its engine threateningly as I veered a sharp left. I twisted the throttle so I was going twenty-five miles an hour as I hit the hill. The speed dropped to twenty, fifteen, about ten miles an hour by the time I was halfway up. By the time I got to the hotel, the bike was going so slow I thought it might topple over.

How am I gonna ride this thing all the way to Kingston?

I got off and pushed it the last few yards into the car park.

Elias, the security guard, grinned at me from his green plastic chair.

I didn't even know where Kingston was. From what the fella in the shop said, it was pretty far.

But, first problems first, now I had to deal with Increase. And here he came, closely followed by The Leader, who was followed by the guy with the massive head and a couple of other types who go around giving Black lads a bad name.

'Speak of di devil,' said The Leader.

Increase looked at the bike, then back to me again with his mouth open.

'Mek we go talk some business,' said The Leader.

Elias got up, shrugged his shoulders, and wandered off.

'So. Unu have we money?' said The Leader.

'Yeah,' I said, taking twelve hundred dollars out of my pocket.

'Good,' he said, taking the cash. 'Now we go get di rest.'

I looked at Increase. He had an envelope in his hand.

'You see, we pickney mother, she sick and she need money feh help with di pickney, dem,' said The Leader. 'And you see we bredrin here. Dem have pickney with sick mother too.'

'Too sick,' chuckled one as he flicked a ciggy end at my feet.

They all laughed.

'So,' The Leader went on, 'we need some extra cash, you see me? For we pickney, dem. You no care about a Black man pickney, pretty boy?'

They definitely weren't the first of my concerns.

'But is a lucky ting, you know? Your smart-mouth cousin get some travellers' cheque. And me know a man who get you a better rate of exchange than di bank give for your travellers' cheque. So you fetch your travellers' cheque too, and is a win-win situation, you see me?'

'Follow we,' said The Leader.

He straddled a big red Suzuki motorbike, and one of his mates got on behind him.

Increase nudged past me to ride the Honda 50. He nodded for me to get on the back. The other two followers jumped on a rusty white scrambler.

We followed them down the hill, onto Randy's roundabout, and left, downtown.

Right turn.

Broken concrete.

Left turn.

Distorted basslines.

Right turn.

Deep downtown.

I thought back to my first day in Montego Bay, the first time we went downtown. I remembered the weight of the sun on that first day. It was no lighter now. I thought about the recurring dream that I'd remembered as we walked downtown that first day. In the dream, I'd be carrying an infinite bundle of matchsticks. And the fear of the weight didn't come from the fear of being crushed. I feared what might happen if I was mad enough to not fear carrying the weight of the Universe.

That day, as we walked downtown, I'd accepted the challenge. I'd agreed to take the weight. And look where it had got me: stabbed, mugged, imprisoned, knocked out, bereaved, slashed, and now this.

We followed The Leader.

Shops crumbled to dust.

Left turn.

Women wore melting faces.

Right turn.

Men wore defences like coffins.

Straight on.

Dogs died in the street.

New caves form in my mind: Fear of doing; fear of not doing. Fear of living; fear of not living. Fear of leading; fear of following.

We followed.

Rusty gates hung from a crumbling once-white wall. And there we stopped.

Increase passed his travellers' cheques behind him without turning to look at me. I took the envelope, got off the bike, and followed The Leader through the gates.

There were people milling around, crowds squeezing in and out of the market. A woman carrying two brown-paper bags barged into me, sucked her teeth, and muttered some insult as she passed.

The smell of traffic on the street faded, and the volume came up on the smell of fish stalls where men and women shouted their prices. We passed stalls with pots and pans, baskets piled high, dangling rolls of coloured cloth at all angles overhead.

We arrived at the smell of fake leather going soft in the heat. The stall looked like it was made of jeans, T-shirts, and belts. They were all Armani, Moschino, Marco Polo, and Hugo Boss; they must have been because they had those words written all over them in massive letters.

'Yes?' asked the man at the stall, his belly hanging over the belt of his pants. None of his clothes had massive words on them.

'Irie, uncle,' said The Leader.

'Who dis?' said the uncle, eyeing me slowly.

'Man from Liverpool, England. Him need exchange travellers' cheque. You can do dat?'

'You know me can do dat,' said the uncle. Then, under his breath: 'And me know what you can do, too.'

'Haha,' said The Leader. 'None o' dat, man. Man is a bredrin from Liverpool.' He put his arm around my shoulder. 'A no true?'

I smiled and nodded.

The uncle paused while he eyed the nodding tourist and the smiling Leader. Finally, he shook his head and said, 'Come, man. Come, cho!'

I manoeuvred my way around a mountain of jeans to the back of the stall.

'How much you ave?'

'Er.'

Turns out we had sixty quid in travellers' cheques.

The uncle raised his eyebrows and checked The Leader's face for a reaction. 'OK,' he said, looking at me to see if I was sure.

I nodded.

The uncle narrowed his eyes. His second chin wobbled as he rubbed the bone one.

'At de bank, now, dem give an exchange rate of forty-two dollar to de pound,' he said. 'I can give you forty-seven dollar to each pound so dat is, erm . . . you want to change the lot? Uh-huh. That is . . . two thousand eight hundred and twenty dollar,' he said, already thumbing through a pile of notes retrieved from somewhere behind a leaning tower of T-shirts.

He counted the money for what felt like ages. I started to feel wobbly and slightly sick from the smell of melting belts. I tried to make a bit of conversation to make the interaction less uncomfortable: 'Busy day?'

'Hush, man,' he said, handing me a huge wad of Jamaican notes. 'Hold dis.'

The uncle shouted over to the man at the stall facing his: 'Watch dem as they leave.'

'Nah man,' protested The Leader. 'Nobody haffe watch I. Man is I bredrin.'

'Watch dem,' the uncle insisted. 'Me watch your stall.'

The second stall holder followed us all the way out of the market, with The Leader making exaggerated conversation with me, and turning around to suck his teeth at the man following us.

Increase was edgy, still sat on the Honda 50, flanked by the followers. He stared at his tassel brogued foot where it rested on the broken kerb.

The second stall holder was stood at the entrance to the market, still watching us, expressionless. The Leader turned back as he bestrode the red Suzuki and sucked his teeth at him one final time. 'Get back to your own business, man.'

He looked over his minions and grinned, then turned to me as I got on the back of the Honda.

'Now we go somewhere where you can pay your debt to we pickney,' he said. 'Follow we.'

We followed lefts and rights.

We followed past ramshackle shops.

We followed to the place with tiny houses with bars on the windows.

We kept following.

I held on tight to the leather strap across the seat and kept my back straight, careful not to touch Increase. There was a tense stiffness in the calm way he turned the corners, slowly following. The travellers' cheque envelope bulged in my pocket, now swollen with Jamaican notes.

I wanted to shout in Increase's ear: *Fuck this, let's just leave them. Let's just turn the wrong way and fuck off, all the way to Kingston.*

We followed to the place where people stood outside shelters made of corrugated zinc backed against a long wall. I recognised the place. This was what I'd come to Jamaica for. It was to see places like this that I'd left Searbank. But I'd seen it now, and I didn't need to see it again.

The thing I had to make happen had happened.

But it was still happening.

And I didn't know how to make it stop.

We approached a crossroads. The two bikes we were following shot straight across without even checking if anything was coming. Increase decreased speed slowly till we stopped. He looked both ways.

The lad on the back of the second bike turned around, then leaned into the driver, who shouted and waved to The Leader on the bike in front. They both pulled over in front of some shops that looked like they were held together by the brightly painted words on the old planks that hung from them.

All four lads were looking at us now.

Waiting.

And we were looking at them.

Not at each other.

But we both knew.

We'd stopped following.

'Come, man,' one of the lads waved at us. The Leader started to turn his bike around. A car behind us beep-beep-beeped, and someone shouted, 'Move, man. Move it.'

The Leader kicked his red Suzuki into gear, wobbled, and skidded up speed towards us. Increase leaned to the right, kicked the bike into first gear, and skidded off in front of a car – beeeeep – 'Bomboclaat.'

I put my arms around Increase's waist and leaned forward as if to add to the speed. We turned left, mounted the kerb, and knocked over a wooden box that some blokes were using to play dominoes. They jumped up, and one of them lunged at us and managed to push my back as we passed. He fell but jumped back up to chase after us as the bike wobbled back onto the road. Another bloke threw something at us as the bike gathered speed.

Another crossroads.

An old man on a wooden cart swept into sight, zooming through the busy traffic. The cart looked like one of those things they used to ride along train tracks in silent movies. It's not a sight an English brain can quickly register. 'Move! Move!' he shouted. He leaned into his wheel and just missed us.

A once-black car swerved in from the right of us, horn blaring.

Neither of us looked back as we turned and turned, going nowhere as fast as the little Honda 50 was willing.

We came to an old theatre. It was the same place we'd passed on that first day. Where the Rasta had appeared in the niche and said, 'Go straight, then right.'

We went straight, then right.

We chugged up the hill that led to Peach's Paradise. A red lorry came storming up behind us so close it ran us off the road. The bike toppled on its side, and we toppled off onto the sandy-grassy verge, the drag of air trying to pull us under the lorry's wheels.

We looked down towards the roundabout.

They weren't there.

Increase sighed long and deep, and then looked at me with black eyes, tense jaw, gritted teeth.

We both knew that Kingston wasn't just a shit idea, it was a dangerous idea.

Neither of us spoke as we stood the bike up and got back on. Increase started the engine.

He pulled up at Peach's Paradise and ran off to the room to get the note that uncle Teddy had given him.

I went back too, tied my black Adidas shell suit top around my waist, and – 'I'm just gonna get my, erm . . .' muttered some shit as I grabbed the bag of weed from the bedside cabinet. I did wish there wasn't so much of it. But I had it now. And I didn't wanna leave it in the room. And besides, I didn't have time to take a bit out and wrap it up without Increase seeing.

We got back on the road.

The A1.

Eastward.

To Kingston.

A SUN-SPLASH SOUNDS LIKE the thing that was happening to us now as we chugged across the top of the island. It's subtle. A wind-slap sweeps in from the sea to the left and chills you just enough to disguise the fact that your skin's getting frazzled by the sun-splash.

A red, yellow, and green hand-painted sign on an old fence plank sat propped against the sign for the A1. One arrow pointed to Cockpit Country, the other to Kingston.

The sea was so candyfloss blue it looked like it'd be sweet to taste.

A shoeless dreadlocked boy wandering along the road stopped to frown at the whining moped as we passed.

The odd tumbledown hut made of abandoned planks and rust-dusted sheets of corrugated zinc must have served as home for the odd lonely man, fisherman, Rasta man.

At one point, there was a row of little shops. They were made in the same way as the lonely shacks and seemed to be selling cigarettes, drinks, and touristy trinkets, but Increase didn't stop.

On the right it was just bush and hills and the odd road sign pointing to Historic Falmouth, Trelawny Rio Bueno, Runaway Bay, but Increase didn't stop.

A sun-splash sounds like the thing that happened to Jonah when

God made a worm kill his tree. That story used to freak me out when I was a kid. I mean, what kind of spooky fucker watches you everywhere you go? Forces you to do stuff you can't be arsed with?

It was because of that God fella that the climax of every wank was followed by guilt. It was because of God that I could never sing 'I Know Him So Well' by Elaine Page and Barbara Dickson out loud. Never. Not once. Not even when I was on my own because He was watching. God, the all-loving father of everything. He who created flowers and birds, songs and mountains, rivers and sunsets, colours, cold morning wind, pleasant summer sun, ripe fruits, tall trees, greenwood, meadows, eyes to see and lips to tell and all that. Didn't like any gay shit, though, did He?

This is the same fella who had Jonah thrown off a ship and swallowed by a whale.

The moped sputtered on.

Further in, the sea dropped from soft and sweet blue to a hard, bitter, and interminable darkness. Something in me wanted to sink into it and disappear; let the waters take me, the same way they'd taken Raphael and Douglas.

Then the fear kicked in.

The fear of no fear.

I told Kissy about the dream once – the one where I'd be carrying the weight of the Universe in an enormous bundle of matchsticks. I'd fallen asleep on her bed and the dream had come to me. I shook myself awake – the way I always did when it happened – and forced my eyes to open. Kissy was lying next to me.

Look at the blue sea, I thought as the moped rattled on. Forget about Kissy. Kissy's gone.

But every thought ran like the curved line of the horizon back to Kissy, back to the dream, back to the weight.

I threw my head back and sighed into the wind-slap. A

tropical-sized bug zoomed down my throat. I coughed the creature up and spat it sideways so that it disappeared behind me. But even that didn't clear the memory of Kissy lying next to me, my gold rope chain hanging from her neck, Dad's serpent key dangling at the end.

We passed a sign for Plantation Village.

But Increase didn't stop.

I told Kissy about the fear.

'Are there any other feelings?' she asked.

I nodded.

'Can you describe the feeling?'

I didn't have a good word for it:

Knowing . . . becoming . . .

'Is it possible that you're scared of accepting your destiny?' she offered.

'What does that even mean?' I asked.

'I don't know,' said Kissy. 'It's your destiny.'

'I don't know either.'

'Well maybe you should just allow the Universe to show you the signs.'

The serpent key swayed with her words.

We passed a sign for Discovery Bay.

Increase didn't stop.

Increase only stopped when we had to, because we now had no idea where we were. The town was called Ocho Rios. I'd never heard of it, but Increase seemed to know that we shouldn't have been there.

It was busier than Montego Bay, bigger streets, brighter shops, more stalls, and more tourists milling around. We stopped outside a cavernous cream-coloured shop with tourists pouring in and out. It had large Arabic-style windows displaying gold jewellery. A young lad sat outside, scraggy stumps where his feet should have been dangling over the kerb. He was holding a sign that said:

PLEAS GIV JENERUSLY

Increase unfolded Teddy's note and pointed at the bit that said:

If you get to Ocho Rios you have gone too far.

Too keen to traverse the line of latitude eastward.

Hahaha.

Get back on the A1.

Increase shook his head like it wasn't welcome on his neck any more. He didn't say anything, or even look at me. But I could feel the resentment pouring out of him – like all this shit was, somehow, my fault.

He was right, of course.

I had made it happen.

Increase turned the Honda 50 out of the town and headed around a left bend to where the buildings stopped. We crossed a stone bridge shaded by huge green leaves, a river running underneath.

Increase was still shaking his head as we turned a left bend and climbed a hill.

The Honda 50 made a whining sound. A haze of stinking smoke wafted up from underneath the seat. I thought Increase was gonna shake his head right off. He yanked the bike over to the side of the road so that it swung towards the bushes like a bladdered old geezer lunging at a bus stop for an angry piss.

We got off the bike, and Increase lifted the seat. The smoke was coming from somewhere around the battery. Increase twisted a plastic knob. It came off in his hand. He looked at me.

What?

A couple of local lads came running over as if to help us.

'No,' said Increase. 'Come on, let's go before they start harassing us.'

We got back on the bike. Increase kicked it into first gear and pushed us off with his foot. The two lads shouted and sped up after us. About forty seconds into the chase, it became clear to us all that a smoky old Honda could go up hill in first gear just faintly faster than the running speed of your average Jamaican lad.

'Fuck you, man,' the lads shouted after us.

The bike whined on.

We got back on the A1.

We trundled along till we came to a dusty, busy, stifling place called Spanish Town. The bike was struggling, still smoking, but it kept going.

Cars, motorbikes, and trucks beeped at each other on an expanse of gritty road that seemed to be a gap where a roundabout should have been.

Two pigs in an old motor stopped next to us at some traffic lights.

I could feel the bulge of weed in my pocket.

Shit.

The pig in the passenger seat was staring at me. I didn't look at him, but I could feel his eyes on me.

Shit.

I thought about putting my hand over my pocket to hide the bulge, but that would have looked too obvious. I thought about just taking the weed out and tipping it on the road, but that would have been stupid.

Shit.

The lights changed, and the police car rattled off over the crossing.

Increase turned around as he pulled off; he must've wondered why I was shuffling around so much. I got the weed out of my pocket and squeezed it between my hand and the leather strap on the seat.

We followed the signs to Kingston. The buildings got bigger, and the colours got brighter; then, just as quickly, the colours deteriorated into dirty grey walls masking whatever commerce had once gone on behind them.

We passed another police car. They were pulling over and saying something to some local lads.

I pressed the bag into my palm and compressed the weed as much as I could.

We passed a third police car – I couldn't take it any more.

Why did I bring this fucking weed?

I pretended to cough and slid the bag of weed into my mouth. I pushed it over to my right cheek with my tongue, but it made my face bulge like a hamster's stash.

I tried to say my own name to test if it was possible to speak with so much weed in your mouth.

'What?' shouted Increase.

'Nompum.'

It wasn't.

The roads got busier, the air got dustier, and the buildings got brighter again as we eventually found ourselves back at the same non-roundabout as before. Increase raised his right hand to the sky, then hit himself on the head three times – 'No, no, no.' – not, I don't think, to stop the shaking his head had been doing on and off since Ocho Rios.

260

We were following the signs again.

It's hard to breathe on the back of a bike when your mouth's stuffed with weed.

I'm gonna have to do something.

I half swallowed the bag, just to test if it would go down my throat in an emergency situation. My gag reflex kicked in to push the obstruction out of my throat. Only it pushed it the wrong way, and the bag of weed slid straight into my stomach.

Shit!

The signs took us back to the non-roundabout again – twice. 'You bastards,' screamed Increase as he drove straight over it.

He stopped the bike at the side of the road and slumped over the handlebars. We'd been travelling for hours, splashed by the sun and slapped by the wind, with no food and no drink.

Increase attacked his pocket and yanked out Teddy's instructions. We read:

Reach Spanish Town.

Follow the signs. Get terribly lost.

End up back at the first sign.

Take out Teddy's instructions.

Remember what he told you:

Never follow road signs in Jamaica.

Hohoho.

From then on, we followed Teddy's instructions to a tee, and, six hours after leaving Montego Bay, we came to a dual carriageway that took us to the city of Kingston.

I thought about the weed in my stomach. I'd never eaten weed, but I'd heard about people doing it. And it did, apparently, get you very stoned.

The bike sputtered to a stop right outside a row of small houses with bars over their windows.

Increase turned to me and snarled, 'Well that was fun.'

Teddy's living room smelt like Dad's kitchen, just slightly darker.
Teddy's wife, Millicent, sat the two of us down. The dining-room
table was a solid dark wood covered by a sheet so thick it had
bounce, a plastic sheet over that, and a tablecloth with embroi-
dered pink and yellow flowers over that. The matching silver salt
and pepper cellars in the centre of the table were polished up too
shiny for use.

Tripe though? I was sure that that was what she'd said.

Teddy was late home from work 'every day', according to Millicent, and would 'soon come'. 'You may eat in his absence,' she
told us. 'I'm so sorry he is not here to greet you. And I feel so rude.
But if you boys will please excuse me, I really must get ready for
work.' She went upstairs and left us at the table with the tripe.

Tripe though?

I didn't understand why anyone would name their food after
something that means utter shit? I was about to find out.

It smelled nice. It looked nice: yellow rice, red, yellow, and
green salad, and something that looked a bit like the gorgeous
curried goat Dad used to make and tell people it was lamb
because: 'English people don't want to know they're eating a goat.'

Tastes good: spicy, herby, chewy. Very chewy. Jesus – super-
chewy. Un-fucking-chewable. What is this tripe?

Increase spat a piece of tripe back onto his plate. It sat there
undefeated like it hadn't had teeth anywhere near it. I was about
to do the same when Millicent came back into the room in a blue
nurse's uniform. 'How is your food, boys?'

'Mm,' said Increase scooping up a forkful of rice. 'Uncle Teddy is a lucky man to be married to a culinary genius. Just how do you manage to make a sheep's gut so appetising?'

Sheep's gut? I nearly retched on the rubbery morsel in my mouth.

Increase grinned across the table at me.

'Oh, you know,' said Millicent. 'One must do whatever one can when one's family come to stay.' She stood there looking at me, waiting for my comment. I had to just swallow the lump whole.

'Mm,' I said. 'Thanks.'

'Well, there is plenty more in the pot if you want second helpings.'

'Oh, not for me,' said Increase. 'But it's Aeon's favourite, isn't it, Aeon?' Increase winked at me. 'He was too shy to ask.'

'Oh you mustn't be,' she said. 'Let me get you some more.'

No!

Increase peered around into the kitchen from where we could hear Millicent doing stuff with a pan, a ladle, and some tripe. He took Teddy's directions from his pocket, forked his tripe onto it, folded it up, and placed it on his lap. He mixed the sauce in with the rice just as Millicent came back through with a steaming pan of tripe.

'How much you want?' she said as she spooned a huge dollop onto my plate.

'Oh, no, that's enough, thanks.'

'It's OK, Aeon, don't be shy. He's so shy.' Increase bared his teeth at me.

Increase patted his stomach and licked his lips as Millicent stood there watching me push the stuff around my plate.

'This is simply delicious,' said Increase eventually. He stood up and gave Millicent a hug like he'd known her all his life. She hugged him back, tilting her head like she'd never been so flattered to be touched. He smiled over her shoulder at me. 'Eat up, Aeon,' he grinned. 'He's always been such a slow eater. Slow at everything really.'

My jaw tensed either side of the rubbery chunk of sheep's gut on my tongue.

'Such a lovely boy,' said Millicent as she rubbed Increase's tight curls. Her bingo wing wobbled, and there was already a sweat patch developing on the armpit of her uniform. I clenched my left fist under the table and swallowed down another piece of tripe. My tear ducts reacted angrily, and I had to blink the water away.

'Hohoho,' came a voice from the front door. 'Hello, little long-lost ones from the wicked stepmotherland.'

Teddy prowled over to where I was sat, placed a hand on my shoulder, and sniffed at my plate: 'What she feed you? Tripe? Ptts, cho! Woman always buy this nasty, waste of time, chew your face off nonsense.' He took my plate into the kitchen and scooped the remains of the meal into the bin. 'We get some jerk chicken on the way.'

Millicent rolled her eyes and shook her head. 'Me go a work,' she sighed.

She smiled at Increase as she left, ignoring me as if I'd deliberately made Teddy bin the tripe.

'Well,' said Teddy as he walked in from the kitchen with three glasses filled with ice. 'You two ready to go a Sunsplash?'

'Sunsplash?' said Increase. 'Wasn't that started to celebrate Jamaica's independence from the British Empire?'

'That is right,' said Teddy. He took a bottle of rum from a dark wooden drinks cabinet underneath shelves that housed a complete collection of the *Encyclopaedia Britannica* even older than Dad's collection. He poured three glasses.

'I don't drink, thanks,' said Increase.

Teddy poured the rejected rum into his glass and passed the other one to me.

'A proud day for Jamaica,' said Increase.

'Indeed,' said Teddy.

'Seems ironic though, doesn't it?'

'What does?' said Teddy.

'I mean, it's ironic,' Increase explained, 'that Jamaica celebrates independence. Considering it's got exponentially poorer and more violent ever since it left the British Empire. In fact, there's your answer,' said Increase as if he hadn't said this same shit a million times before. 'You need to ask Britain to take you back on as a colony.' Increase grinned and chuckled his way through each sentence like it was all just a joke.

'Mm-hmm.' Teddy raised an eyebrow.

'Though it is highly improbable that they'd want you back, isn't it?'

'Indeed. Why would they take responsibility for the child they stole, beat, raped, and then left out for the John Crow to eat? Why would anybody do that?' Teddy sipped at his rum.

Increase was enjoying himself. 'Do you have a bathroom?' he said.

'Do we have a bathroom?'

'I was wondering, with this being a third world country . . .' smiled Increase.

'Oh, I see,' smiled Teddy, just as broadly, 'you need to make sure your bowels already empty before you venture into the heart of darkness?'

'Well, can you blame me?'

'True that. Let me show you where this bathroom we are so lucky to possess is.' He grimaced. 'We even have a spare bed for you two to sleep in,' he said as they left the room. 'A real bed, just like they have in England: pure, clean, untainted white sheets and all.'

When Teddy walked back into the room, he sat in a throne by the bookshelf. His face morphed into the most serious expression I'd seen him pull off so far.

'So he is the clever one?' I sank deeper into my chair. 'But, remember, this is your story.'

I really could not be arsed with any more cryptic shit from Teddy. I didn't wanna talk to anyone, least of all this big daft relative. Why would I have any interest in the opinions of the man who thought it was funny that I'd been sent to Copse, that I'd been stabbed and battered? If I told him about Raphael drowning he'd probably piss himself laughing.

'You don't understand our ways. Why we think the way we do. Because your experience of life is so far removed from ours. And you probably hate us for it?'

He wasn't wrong.

Teddy sighed: 'Never mind. It is a special gift, you know?'

What?

'He is the clever one,' he said, nodding to where Increase had sat. 'But you write the story, and that is a real special gift.'

I didn't like the way he was whispering at me like I was part of some plot.

'Me think that why Negus want to see you,' said Teddy.

Who?

'He sent me a message. He say him go show you the road back.'

The what?

Teddy winked.

I wondered if the weed in my intestines was getting into my bloodstream, making me paranoid.

I didn't feel stoned.

'Soon come. Now it time for Sunsplash.'

Teddy waved his ticket in the direction of a couple of massive blokes at the gate. We did the same with the tickets Teddy had just bought us from some kid in the car park, and walked through onto the huge field.

I still didn't feel stoned. I actually felt quite energised – eyes clear, mind sharp. I thought that maybe the weed had stayed in the bag and the whole lot would come out the other end the next morning.

Beyond the gate was a funnel of humans either aggressively trying to sell stuff or just hanging around trying to guess the origins of anyone not Jamaican:

'Canada?'

'Bag juice,' shouted one fella. He grabbed a kid by the T-shirt and pulled him closer to us. The kid nearly dropped the box he was carrying, heavy, I supposed, with bags of sugary warm juice.

'Japan?'

A few of the traders held up cardboard boxes, torn at the corners to make them flat, and shouted, 'Reggae-bed, reggae-bed.'

'USA?'

A small Rasta swung his body around from the centre and snaked his arms around the dance like a Kung Fu imp. One fat dreadlock sprouted up from his head, branched off, and waved above him like a palm tree. He stepped into the funnel to perform his trick. A small crowd gathered around him. He held out one closed fist and stirred the other hand around over the top of it. The fist, finally, exploded into five fingers to reveal the mysterious contents conjured up in the palm – a deal of weed wrapped in clingfilm.

The small crowd laughed.

Increase shook his head.

'UK?'

A gang of local lads barged through the crowd, bobbing their heads from side to side, sucking their teeth, saying 'Cho', killing the atmosphere. The walls of the funnel re-formed somewhere else as a Japanese guy bought the weed from the imp.

The enormous field was closed in by a circular fence with stalls all the way round.

The huge crowd cheered as three young women stood to the right of the dimly lit stage and started up an angelic high-pitched harmony:

'You don't know One Love

Like you think you do . . .'

The crowd cheered, and some fired finger pistols at the night sky.

'You don't know One Love

Like you think you do . . .'

The ground rumbled, and the grass quivered as the bassline kicked in.

'Don't know my light . . .'

The music was haunting and humble at the bottom end, violent and vain at the top end.

I didn't know much about music. I knew what I liked: 2Pac, Rebel MC, 'Devotion' by Nomad Featuring MC Mikee Freedom. I knew what I didn't like: Michael Bolton, M People, 'Hold On' by Wilson Phillips (who bought that?). And I knew what I wasn't allowed to like: 'Time After Time' by Cyndi Lauper, 'Total Eclipse of the Heart' by Bonnie Tyler, 'Show me Heaven' by Maria McKee.

But I didn't understand how music had such a strong pull on my feelings. Music somehow connected me to parts of myself that were usually unseen, unheard, even unfelt. And this, this Sunsplash music, hit somewhere even deeper than 'You're the Best' by Joe Esposito in the fight scene from *The Karate Kid*. It made feelings bubble up from somewhere so distant I couldn't even find a memory to connect them to. The matchsticks dream was the closest thing I knew: the heavy, heavy weight; the lightness of the weight; the unknown source of the weight; and the light.

'The light of my life . . .'

Sang the women on the stage:

'Is One Love sound.'

The singing women were followed by some Rasta band. 'Hohoho,' shouted Teddy as he danced off into the crowd, 'here come Mystic Revealers.'

Increase did his best to appear bored and unimpressed by the amazing spectacle. Even when some fella called Shinehead wowed the crowd with his big smile and even bigger sunglasses, and got kids to join him on stage as he sang about being a 'Jamaican in New York'.

The compere came on to introduce an act. His introduction was so short it seemed a bit disrespectful. The noisy reception that each act had received so far was uncomfortably contrasted by the relative silence that now sat over the crowd. I craned my neck for a better look as the act walked on stage.

'It is such an honour to perform here in Jamaica,' said one of the two lads. They didn't look like the other acts. They were wearing long shorts, baggy T-shirts, and baseball caps. They looked like a couple of Canadian college boys, and the lad doing the talking was White. 'I am the first White act ever to perform at the Sunsplash, and we really do appreciate the kind offer. My name is Snow,' he said, then looked at his mate, a skinny Black guy. 'And this is MC Shan.'

They performed some song called 'Runway', which Snow reckoned was a global hit. The crowd pretty much ignored him. MC Shan was starting to look a bit embarrassed. But Snow sounded unapologetic as he said, 'OK, OK, but I know you all know this next tune.' I knew this next tune: 'Informer'. It was one of those songs that everyone liked; even people in Searbank liked it.

This version, this night, though, had a deeper, subbier, dirtier bass than the version I'd heard on *The Chart Show*. Snow blasted into his chorus, his voice fuller, growlier, more aggressive. All at once, the crowd jumped up into the air and blasted booms at the stage, brrrraps and booyackas at the sky.

BOOM, BOOM.

Snow smashed it.

The music at Sunsplash didn't stop.

The bands performed twenty-four hours a day, all seven days of the Sunsplash.

Basslines drive on like desert-tired camels. Guitars jab like aggressive shards of sand on desert winds, while melancholy riffs endlessly return like the sunrise. Horns blow with keys and carry harmonies of war zones. Singers celebrate the sounds of love, death, and homelessness. Harmonies wail on behind in desperate defiance.

The ground quivers. The air vibrates with the frequencies of love and hate colliding, resting in each other's arms, becoming one.

This is what I came to Jamaica for – this resentment, this rage, this resolve. This is the stuff that blokes in rap songs were on about. This is the stuff that London Blacks who talked about Stephen Lawrence on the *News at Ten* possessed as a birthright.

And Increase.

And Malcolm X.

And lads on Granby Street.

And now it was mine too.

Something had to happen.

And it had.

I'd made something happen.

How many lads from Toxteth could say that they'd been stabbed in Jamaica? How many London Blacks could say that they'd been to prison in Jamaica? How many could say that they'd had sex with a *Playboy* model in Jamaica?

Funny how your mind changes the story innit?

My mind had been somewhere else as the compere had introduced the act.

Imagine one woman on a dark stage, an ecstatic crowd at her feet. The light stretches the shadow of her long body and carves the sharp angles of her regal, feline face. And as soon as she starts up the singing, you recognise the song:

'The weak don't follow the water . . .'

The crowd sing along.

'The weak don't follow the water

The weak don't follow the water

The weak don't follow the signs.'

Miss Elwyn used to tell me: 'The hero will seize a mighty sword, Aeon, an ancient stone, a contended crown. It will seem to be the glory one had sought all along. And the danger is, you see, that it may consume our hero entirely. So one must overcome the temptation to stay in the land one has fought so hard for so long to reach. However, Aeon. Aeon, look at me, not out of the window. Aeon, look at me. Good boy,' she caught my eyes, smiled, and spoke really slowly. 'The hero, in order to be a true hero, must relinquish the spoils of the exploit. And the hero must always return.'

The singer orders her band to: 'Hol' up, hol' up, hol' up.' The band rolls the beat and bass down a short, steep hill to a stop.

'The hero must take the road back home,' Miss Elwyn used to tell me.

'You know,' says the singer, looking around to address the band as well as the audience, 'I wish me likkle bredrin Arkimedes was here right now.' The crowd cheers in agreement. Then louder: 'Me say, me wish me likkle bredrin Ark-I-Media . . .' She brings the band back in with a drop of her hand. A stocky young man bounces on stage flanked by tall beautiful women in long colourful skirts and bikini tops. He's wearing a kaftan and a turban. He has dangly things that look like the fancy curtain ties from Mum's front room hanging around his neck. His stout rock of a body sways from side to side as he waves his arm over his head like a rebel flag.

There he is – the lion-man.

'De weak don't follow de water or de signs

Johnny never know what him got, until it dies

Johnny didn't do it love, but for de lies

De weak don't follow de water or de signs . . .'

I leave Increase and wade in deeper.

Flag hands wave all over the rebel field.

Feet rise and fall all as one.

The crowd roars along with the lion-man.

A wave of electricity tingles up from the grass to the base of my spine, up my back, over the top of my head, down the front of my body, and back to the soles of my feet.

'The sword may not feel like a sword at all,' Miss Elwyn used to tell me.

Arkimedes' lion voice pounds out the words:

'Some learn de hard way

Some like de dark days

Some learn de ha-ard waaaaaay . . .'

'But fires cleanse as purely as water,' she told me.

'Some learn de hard way

Some like de war stay

Some learn de ha-ard waaaaaay . . .'

'Hell is as homely as Heaven to a hero,' she told me.

'Some learn de hard way

Some like dem heart flay

Some learn de ha-ard waaaaaay . . .'

'You may want to stay there,' Miss Elwyn told me time and time again. 'But the hero must always take the road back home.'

Why was it always me she had these 'little chats' with?

'Some learn de hard way

Some like de dark days

Some learn de ha-ard waaaaaay.'

I paid the taxi driver as Increase stomped off to let us in using the key Teddy had given us.

All the way back he'd moaned about how he'd spent hours looking for me at the Sunsplash. He'd finally found me as the sun rose on the Splash. I was lying on my back on a torn-up cardboard box. Reggae beds are as unlike real beds as they sound, but there, that night, it was a reassuring discomfort. I was smoking a spliff some Japanese lad had passed me and watching a guy called Mad Cobra sing 'Flex, Time to Have Sex'.

And I still didn't feel in the least bit stoned.

It must have been about five in the morning when Increase opened Teddy's door just wide enough to slide through, and we both spider-stepped into the living room. The kitchen door swung open; we both sprang upright.

'Hello,' said Millicent, all cheery. 'You boys want breakfast?'

'Er, no thanks,' said Increase. 'We should probably get some sleep first.'

Millicent showed us to the spare bedroom and laughed hard when Increase asked if there was a duvet. 'Duvet? Duvet? Ha. This is the tropics, you know? "Duvet?" Cho!'

Increase moaned that he was never gonna get any sleep on a rock-hard mattress with no duvet, especially now, in broad daylight. He sighed long and heavy as he slipped off his slip-ons. And the next thing I heard from him was snoring.

The music of the Sunsplash vibrated in me still. But now came something else. That heaviness; like the heavy matchsticks from my dream – too light to share, too heavy to bear.

Increase breathed out dreams.

I pulled the black Adidas shell suit top around my shoulders.

I wanted to be back at the Sunsplash. I could have lived in that field, with that music. It gave substance to the weight; and weight is easier to handle when you can name it. But lying in a bed, next to Increase's dreams, with a long-haired White bloke named for Jesus looking down at me from the opposite wall – heart on fire – it was just nameless, petrifying weight.

The weight sat up and looked around for something to blame. Maybe I felt bad about what Increase had said: that he'd spent all night looking for me; that he'd thought I'd got myself into more trouble; that Teddy was an old man and it was disrespectful to stay out all night while we were guests at his house.

'Hohoho, haha. Me just return from Sunsplash,' said Teddy as he strode into the bedroom. Increase sat bolt upright and took a loud and hypervigilant breath; the way he regularly did since the time he went AWOL.

Time must have passed. What was bright but mellow sunlight was now a slap to the eyeballs that my whole face tried to fight against.

'Me thought you boys would still be there,' chuckled Teddy. 'Come, let us drink some real coffee, Blue Mountain style.'

Increase took a long breath and followed Teddy downstairs.

I rolled onto my side and sat up. I blinked at the floating motes of dust as they lit up in the hard lines of sunlight streaming through thin nets. My eyes felt huge, like their blood vessels were about to burst and my eyelids had swollen to protect them. I could move OK, if slowly. The bag of weed had, evidently, not stayed closed in my stomach. My head didn't hurt though. I actually felt quite good, in a strange out of focus kind of way.

I glided down the stairs in slow 'Mr Soft' steps.

The sun flooded through the windows, sinking the kitchen.

I stared into the blurred reality as Teddy hohohoed around the place, making three coffees.

'Your motorbike will be fix by tomorrow morning,' said Teddy. 'I've had a friend of mine come over and pick it up. The man is a mechanical genius. Whatever wrong wid your bike, he will have it right. But now, the day is pushing on. And we have a journey ahead of us.'

'Where are we going?' said Increase squinting in the harsh light.

'Where do you think?' said Teddy. 'You boys don't want to leave Jamaica without seeing the birthplace of your fathers, do you? The womb that produced generations of your people. The village of Scott's Hall. The Parish of St Mary. We are going into the Blue Mountains. The birthplace of the McMenahem Maroons.'

WE WERE SAT AT the back of the top deck of the number 50 bus along Turnpike Road as I stuck three Rizlas together. I wasn't even making a serious point at the time, I was just saying it because Kissy was pissed off with her mum about something, and it's just one of those things you say: 'You can't choose your family, can ya?'

'I did,' she said. 'Choice is all we have got. I chose to be Kissy, and you chose to be Aeon. You chose to be born to your particular parents and raised in this particular backwards little commuter village. And you chose to do that at this particular time, so that the Universe could experience just the particular aspect of consciousness that only you being Aeon from Searbank, right now, can provide.'

'Do you really believe that?' I said, rolling the tobacco of a Silk Cut around in the Rizla. Kissy was always saying this kinda stuff.

'Of course I do.'

Kissy didn't have normal beliefs.

'It's weird though, innit?' I said. 'I mean, why would anyone choose to be from Searbank?'

'Maybe because you knew that I was coming here.' Kissy smiled as she pulled up her tweedy ankle-length skirt and put her feet up on the seat. 'But obviously, you don't remember me, either.'

The bus went round the huge roundabout at Searbank Stoops. It turned left at the farm with the sign where someone had sprayed the word FUCKIN in between PICK YOUR OWN and STRAWBERRIES.

'But nobody sees it like that apart from you,' I said. I burnt some rocky and sprinkled it on top of the tobacco.

'People around here don't. That's why places like Searbank are full of victims. Like Angela. You remember how scared Angela was that day on the field, when the Kentons took her nan's necklace.'

'Mm.' I rolled the tobacco and weed around into a pencil shape.

'That's because she's a victim. Because she believes that stuff just happens to her randomly, out of her control.'

'Well it does, doesn't it?' I said, licking the skins to seal them.

'If that's what you believe, then you've already given your power away to others, and to random chance. But if you completely believe that everything that happens to you is created by you, then no one, no-thing, has any power over you. It's all your creation. That means that you can do anything.'

'Is that why you stayed there that day?'

'You mean the day I saved your skin?' she smiled. 'The day you first bothered to look at me? The day you realised that you loved me? That day?'

'Yeah, that one.' I slid a roach into the end of the spliff.

The bus went past the sandstone Freemasonic nursing home.

'Is that why you never got off when them sixth-form shit-bag mates of yours left yous on your own?'

'They're not shit-bags, Aeon. They're my friends. They were just scared. And they never left me. I stayed.'

I wasn't convinced: 'Mm.'

'So why did you and your little scally mates stay, then? You were scared.'

I frowned: 'Not that scared.'

'You mean not as scared as you were of being called shit-bags?'

I winced. 'But you're a bird. And your mate was shittin' herself. So, you put yourself and Angela in danger, and got her nan's necklace nicked by the Kentons, just to prove that you're in control?'

'No, Aeon. It was your mates who had something to prove. That's why they stayed. That's how they made themselves into victims. They didn't even know they had a choice. They gave up control to the Kentons, and random chance, and other people's opinions. I believed that the situation, at least my situation, was exactly what I'd conjured up. What the Universe had conjured up through me, as me. And if I am the Universe, then what's the difference?'

'I was there for my own reasons,' she went on. 'And I think it worked out quite well.' She slipped one of her knitted shoes off with the opposite foot – Kissy didn't wear normal shoes.

'So just believing that you've got all the power, gives you the power. Is that honestly what you're saying?' I lit the spliff.

'Yes,' said Kissy.

'Because . . .' I thought I might've understood what she was getting at, 'then you can accept everything that happens.'

'Exactly. Even if we think of the situation as something conjured up by the Universe, or nature, or God, that still means me, you, us. Because we are the Universe, nature, God. So what is the difference?'

'So now you're saying that you're God?'

'Only to the same extent that I'm not God. That I'm just a passing thought before a dream in an endless mind.'

'You're a trippy bird, you, you know?'

She ignored me, too deep in thought and flow. 'What I'm saying is that both are true. And the way you perceive a situation at any moment is your choice.'

'It's still only a belief, though, isn't it? Doesn't mean that it's true.'

She raised her naked foot, with no nail varnish, and stroked the tips of her toes gently over my cock, making it go hard in my pants. 'Define truth,' she said. I couldn't define fuck all with weed in my lungs and a raging hard-on.

'So why were you there, then, you nutter? If you created all that; why? Why choose that madness?'

She took the spliff from my fingers and gave me one of her looks. 'I didn't create anyone else's reality, Aeon,' she said. 'Just mine.' She removed her foot from my lap and hid it away under her tweedy skirt: 'And if you haven't worked out why I chose to be there yet . . .'

If I'd known then that that would be the last time she would ever talk to me like that, the last time she would ever look at me like that, the last time she ever would touch me like that I might have made different choices.

The shopping mall.

The bus stop.

The concrete walls and tough little trees that popped up from bone-dry, concrete-dusted earth. They floated by the window of Teddy's car through the film over my swollen eyeballs.

'What do you boys know about the Maroons?' asked Teddy.

'They were traitors,' said Increase from the front seat.

The weight around me was a spongy blanket.

'They were heroes,' said Teddy. 'From the time Spanish pirates first stole Akan people from the African Gold Coast, and exported them as slaves here in Jamaica, those Africans fought for their freedom.'

'Maybe some did,' Increase sneered. 'But they were mostly just slaves, weren't they?'

The back of Teddy's car was an airless vacuum.

Teddy went on: 'And they fought alongside others oppressed by the imperialists, like the Taino Indians – the original inhabitants of Jamaica – and indentured Spanish labourers.'

'Because they had no choice,' said Increase.

The heat from the back seat was a soft electrical tingle.

Teddy popped in a TDK tape and pressed rewind as if to prove he wasn't taking the debate too seriously. He turned to the back seat like it was me he was having a conversation with – not much chance of that.

'When the English invaded, a hundred and sixty years after the arrival of the Spanish, the African slaves saw an opportunity to escape and join those already living in the mountainous interior of the island,' said Teddy.

'And immediately started helping the British in their imperial mission,' said Increase.

'Indeed, some did. And due to his quick-wittedness, Juan Lubolo and his followers were granted freedom nearly two hundred years before the abolition of slavery.'

'And ten years later, he was dead.'

The tape clicked at the beginning, then started its forward journey of turns and returns. An organ wobbled about like a gospel song, and then a country and western style guitar kicked in – as if this journey wasn't already trippy enough.

'I think that if Juan Lubolo was alive today, he would be

someone very similar to you,' Teddy said to Increase, 'intelligent, singular, recalcitrant.'

The bloke on the tape started singing, 'I Walk Alone'. He didn't sound very Black.

The road was narrower now, two lanes each way. A large and brightly painted villa here, a small wooden shack there, palm trees and scrub in between – all floating past on a wavy sea of sun haze. The Blue Mountains throbbed in the distance; so far off they were actually blue.

Teddy half turned to me in the back again. I tried to smile to show him I was there with them, but my face wasn't playing.

'From the time the British took over this island in 1655,' said Teddy returning to his lecture, 'they suffered seventy-six years of violent slave uprisings and raids by Maroon groups. The Maroons would raid their plantations and free other slaves to boost their numbers. They became an unstoppable force.'

'But most of the Blacks remained as slaves,' said Increase turning to me.

I blinked in response.

'The Maroons,' said Teddy, 'took over two parts of the island: one in the western, Leeward mountains and one in the eastern, Windward mountains we are heading into now. These places were very difficult for the British troops to enter.'

'And perfect for some uncivilised Africans to live in,' said Increase.

'What, you think people no know about this thing we call civilisation before any European name it so? You no know that Africans founded civilisations hundreds, even thousands of years before Columbus set sail? You never hear about the ancient city of Timbuktu? You never read anything about Benin, Great Zimbabwe, Kilwa? You no know nuttin' about Kush, Wagadou,

Aksum? How about Meroe? How about ancient Egypt, the ancient Land of Punt from where Egyptian culture descended? You no know Blacks were building pyramids when England was a mud pit? Cho! You English boys only read a racist, white-washed version of history. A nonsense, man.'

The roads were tiny now, and we had to slow down every time a car came in the other direction. Teddy blew the horn before we went round each bend.

'Under the leadership of Granny Nanny, in this district,' said Teddy, 'and Cudjoe, in the western mountains, the Maroons fought a war against the British that lasted from 1731 to 1739. An eight-year war against the most efficient fighting force in Europe, that ended with the Maroons undefeated.'

'It ended,' Increase raised his voice as the engine whined up a hill, 'with the Maroons signing treaties and agreeing to capture other runaway slaves for the British.'

The weird country and western music was still playing. It sounded like something Dad used to listen to. I never understood why Dad listened to that racist music. Or, as it goes, why Increase – the Nation of Islam version – used to insist the music was racist. It also sounded like the music from *The Dukes of Hazzard*, which, apparently, was also racist. Why would anyone call *The Dukes of Hazzard* racist?

'The Maroons were the first peoples to officially break the yoke of European colonialism and gain autonomy,' said Teddy.

'Wasn't it a Maroon called Lieutenant Davy who killed Tacky, the great leader of an African, Fante tribe?' said Increase. 'And didn't that put an end to Tacky's uprising, to the great pleasure of the British imperialists? And wasn't the famous Davy from your village,' he went on, 'Scott's Hall?'

'Hmm,' Teddy grunted as he slowed down.

A goat crossed the road and trotted over the edge of an unknown drop.

'They're Hanging Me Tonight,' sang the bloke on the tape.

My mouth was dry. I leaned my head against the window and felt the bumps and vibrations of the motor, the road, and the weird music in every cell.

'The Maroons helped quash numerous uprisings once they were protected by treaties, didn't they?' said Increase. 'I sometimes wonder if those treaties helped to prolong slavery in Jamaica.'

'I wonder if . . . No. I know that the rebellion of the Maroons, and others like them, is why slavery was abolished at the time it was.'

We passed houses that had been half built and left with metal poles sticking up where walls should have been.

We passed abandoned buildings with dirt creeping up from the floor to darken the unpainted grey concrete.

'And what about the second Maroon War, Uncle Teddy?' said Increase. 'How did that end? I forget now.'

'You don't like to hear anything positive about your own people, do you, Increase?'

'Wasn't it with the Maroons surrendering to the British?'

'The British fought dirty,' said Teddy. 'Brought in bloodhounds from Cuba to hunt them down. How could they—'

'And weren't some of them deported?'

'They were tricked,' said Teddy.

The song playing now was all dramatic. It was interesting, the way he sang it.

'Too gullible, then?' said Increase.

The song seemed to be telling a story. It was a pretty good tune, to be honest.

'Or too trusting,' said Teddy. 'Maybe not as akin with dishonesty as the enemy.'

But if *The Dukes of Hazzard* was racist, this stuff was off the scale:

Did he just say 'yipee yi ya'? What could sound more racist than that?

'Ghost Riders in the Sky'.

Is this it?

Teddy looked up as he slowed to a stop on the bumpy road outside an abandoned house. It was a big old thing, in a street of big old detached things. The whitewash on the walls around the garden flaked. A snake careened away underneath a rusted gate.

Increase grunted as he lifted his head – he must've nodded off.

'Nearly all of the teachers in your daddy's school were White men,' said Teddy, still looking up at the old house. 'All except for Mr Stuart.'

Increase turned and widened his puffy eyes, like: What's this all about, now?

'Jamaica was an excellent way for the rich and privileged families of empire to rid themselves of reprobates,' said Teddy. He turned his gaze from the house and looked at me. 'People think that we can excuse the behaviour of the imperialists and slavers because people were somehow less conscious of their actions in those "olden days",' he scowled. 'But people were then as people are now, pttss, cho! So just imagine if it was now.' He looked at Increase. 'Just imagine that some arrogant, pumped-up nation with an overfunded military had recently invaded some small island and slaughtered most of the inhabitants, or infected them with some new virus. Then they start shipping people from a

warzone, which they funded and encouraged, in another contin-
ent to this new outpost of their empire. Dem plan is to force those
poor victims of war to produce unnecessary goods to sell back to
the privileged classes in the homeland. Oh, and torture, rape, and
murder will all be legal and actively encouraged. Simply because
the profits are huge.'

Increase turned and glanced at me again, like: I still haven't got
a clue why we've stopped here.

'Now, ask yourself,' said Teddy. 'What kind of person is going
to actually go to such a place to buy some of these abused and
divested human beings? Hm? Of course, only the lowest of the
low, the most deranged and sadistic psychopathic reptiles in de
whole of high society. And if you belonged to those wealthy
classes in the eighteenth century, and if you had such a maniacal
crazy-man in your family, Jamaica was the place to send him.

'Well,' Teddy said to me as Increase slid down slightly in his
seat and folded his arms. 'Remember me tell you, your daddy was
the first person from Scott's Hall ever to attend the high school?
Well, by that time the rape and ownership thing were not so com-
patible with contemporaneous sensibilities, hmm. But outposts
of empire, like Jamaica, were still used as a dumping ground for
Britain's freaks and outcasts.

'And here is the point,' said Teddy. Increase took a loud, deep
breath as if to say: Not before time.

'Nearly all of the teachers in Aeon's father's school were White.
They were all White and British: highly educated, highly respected,
and very strange. All apart from Mr Stuart. Who lived here.' He
pointed at the house. 'Mr Stuart was a local man. A Black Jamaican
man. And he was the smartest of all dem teachers. And,' Teddy
chuckled, 'well considered to be the sanest. He was tall and handsome and well versed in the history of the British Empire.

'And here is the point.' Increase sat upright as Teddy pointed at him. 'It was Mr Stuart who taught Aeon's father that African history started when the Europeans arrived. He taught his pupils that no Black African had ever seen a written word, built a stone building, or worn a decent item of clothing before the Whites turned up.' Teddy turned to me. His voice was booming now and almost cracking with emotion. 'It was Mr Stuart who taught your father that Africans lived in trees.' He looked at Increase as he repeated, 'Lived in trees! It was Mr Stuart who used to make his pupils sing "Rule, Britannia" and "God Save the Queen" before class. And if the pupils got the words wrong, it was Mr Stuart who would crack dem with the whip. And we all respected Mr Stuart more than any other Black man in this whole area. Because Mr Stuart only knew what he was taught. And we only knew what we was taught.'

Teddy let out a long sigh. 'One morning,' he said, in a quieter and lower tone, 'as your father walked to school, a haunted wail and an unsettling chant polluted the morning air, overpowering the eight o'clock crow of the village cockerel. Your father told me how he followed that sound and arrived outside this here house. Mr Stuart's house. A crowd had gathered around the sound of the wails, which came from Mr Stuart's wife; a beautiful "mulatta", as we used to say back then. And she was being supported by her friend Irene, another beautiful "mulatta". The chanting? That came from right there,' Teddy pointed to the second floor of the house, 'Mr Stuart's bedroom windowsill. And there your father observed the most respected Black man in the whole area stood stark naked, rocking back and forth and bouncing and chanting strange, strange sounds. Something that sounded like "Grassanami bunka ooh ah. Grassanami bunka ooh uh. Grassanami bunka ooh ah. Grassanami bunka ooh uh. Grassanami bunka ooh uh . . ."'

The strange chant gave me a shiver over my whole body.

'It took three hours for a truck to arrive from the asylum in Kingston,' said Teddy. 'They carried Mr Stuart to the truck by his arms and legs and threw him in the back like a lump of rotten meat.

'Mama, our grandmother, saw Mr Stuart in Kingston about three years later. He was wearing raggedy trousers, no top, and no shoes. His eyes were blank and his body was scarred all over from the beatings. Beatings was the technique the asylum's used to use to chase the devil out of a person.'

Teddy shook his head as he put the car into first gear and pulled away. 'Chase out the devil,' he sighed.

We turned onto a red-dust road. A few kids ran up to the car shouting, 'Teddy, Teddy,' as Teddy slowed down to a near stop and handed out coins taken from underneath the tape player.

'Who de White man, Uncle Teddy?' said one of the kids.

Increase chuckled.

'This is your cousin,' said Teddy. 'This is Aeon McMenahem.'

She pressed up against the car window to get a better look at me. I looked her in the eyes. But still, she didn't see me.

The houses looked just like Teddy's but smaller; one-storey, detached concrete blocks painted cream and red and blue, bars over the windows and doors.

We pulled up and walked through the village. Teddy waved at people, then turned to me and Increase saying, 'That is your cousin Christine, she is a Byfield,' and 'That was your cousin Nial, he is a Hibbert,' and 'There is your cousin Grenville, he is a Lattibeuadiere,' and 'This is your cousin Shirley, she is a Nugent.'

Increase was the only cousin I'd ever known, and now I suddenly had a whole village full of cousins.

'Everybody is everybody cousin in Jamaica,' said Teddy. 'Hohoho.'

OK, a whole island full of cousins. And I didn't know any of them.

People invited us into their homes for ackee, yam, plantain, mannish water. But Teddy kept saying, 'Maybe later. We go see Negus.'

'Oh!' they'd say. 'Negus,' and they'd frown or raise their eyebrows and nod. 'Negus.'

Before Increase moved in, I used to regularly hassle Dad to tell me stories about growing up in Jamaica. It was always the same stories. I loved the one about his first pair of shoes, how they were made from an old car tyre, and how he lost them accidentally-on-purpose in a river. And the one about how they used to get excited when the butcher gave them a bull's penis, and they'd make soup from it, and they called the soup 'mannish water' because the Maroons believed that the bull's penis had the powers to make you more 'mannish'. I thought that was the funniest thing in the whole world.

But this one time, just one time, he told me the about the big parties they had in St Mary and all over the island in 1962, when Jamaica gained independence from the British Empire. And one time, just this once, he told me about the posters on the walls in his school advertising employment opportunities in Britain. All you needed to do, they said, was be willing to work or study in Britain and they'd give you a British passport. And the posters requesting the much-needed labour of Caribbean citizens of the British Empire all had a big picture of the warm and welcoming face of the minister of health, Enoch Powell.

Then he told me about how he'd left Jamaica in 1963, alone. Dad had fully believed that he was part of something bigger than him, bigger than Jamaica, bigger than anything the world had ever seen – the biggest empire in the world ever, Britain, the mothercountry. Dad had sailed for three and a half weeks from sunny Kingston with hundreds of other Jamaicans and arrived in grey Southampton, alone.

The customs man spat on Dad's shiny winklepickers.

Dad never told me that story again.

We walked out of the village up a tiny footpath, through some bush, and along a small road that overlooked a huge green valley.

The valley reminded me of the drawings I used to do as a kid. I'd fill a side of A4 paper with arched lines for rolling hills. Then I'd use a different shade of green for each hill. The pictures were inspired by the patchwork fields I'd seen from the back of Dad's car as we drove through North Wales on our way to the annual Adventist Church Family Camp. The difference here was that every shade of green you could imagine was caught in every tiny space. There wouldn't have been enough greens in all the felt tips in all of Toy & Hobby to recreate one inch of the place.

I had seen these vast Jamaican greens on the way to Copse. The difference, I suppose, was that then I hadn't recently digested a quarter ounce of marijuana in my sleep.

We came to a small wooden house where chickens wandered around the front yard.

'This is the home that my grandfather, both of your daddies' grandfather, built with his own two hands,' said Teddy proudly. 'The home we all grew up in. Now it is where Negus live.

Everyone else live in modern concrete homes now, but Negus like it here. He like the seclusion.

'Be warned. Negus is obeah. Him have strange ways. But he knows the history of our people better than anyone else in the village.'

Teddy had explained that an obeah man is like a witch doctor. So I was expecting Baron Samedi from *Live and Let Die*. Instead we were introduced to this little old fella in a pair of baggy jeans, tatty Nike T-shirt, and a velvety Kangol top hat. He was a bit of a disappointment to be honest.

'May we come in?' asked Teddy.

'Yes, Teddy, come, come. And bring those two English boys with you,' said Negus.

The house was just one room with a dirt floor. There was a bed, a rocking chair, and a bedside cabinet with a small pile of ancient books. And that was all there was.

'Can I get you something?' asked Negus.

It didn't look like there was anything to get.

'Just a drink please, cousin,' said Teddy.

Negus walked around the bed and, when he opened the bedside cabinet, it seemed that a dim light shone from inside it. He pulled out a jug of red juice and a glass. 'Sorrel and maroon root,' said Negus as he poured Teddy a drink. It looked homemade and gorgeous and, somehow, cold. My mouth was so dry.

He offered us to take a seat on the bed while he slid into the rocking chair.

'So you are Increase McMenahem?' said Negus. 'And you must be Aeon?'

I wondered how he knew our names. I'd never heard of him till Teddy mentioned him the day before.

'I am William Plantagenet Nimrod Darius Earl of de Baron

Sandwich Dante Nebuchadnezzar Mandingo Confucius Chandragupta Balaclava McMenahem. But everyone know me as Negus.

'My mother was de sister of both of your great-grandmothers. Her great-great-great-grandfather, him name Virgil, was born in de bush that is now my back garden. It is he who gave you your name – McMenahem. You know why unu name McMenahem?' he said.

I looked at Increase, but here was something even he didn't know.

Teddy finished his drink and gave the glass to Negus. Negus went round to the bedside cabinet, pulled out a clean glass, and poured a drink of the red stuff for Increase.

'Hmm,' sighed Increase as he sipped the juice. It looked delicious.

'Me no know what your fathers have taught you, if anything?' said Negus. 'Me can understand why your pappy would not know these things,' he said, looking at Increase. 'Saul was taken from Jamaica when he was just a yute of seven. And his father marry a White woman, out there inna England, who hated Saul. She used to beat him and call him name, you know? Racist name. She made him leave their home to fend for himself when he was just thirteen. That why Saul became so tough. Your father never tell you all that?' said Negus, as if it wasn't a question.

Increase shook his head, rubbed his wrist, and looked at the floor.

Negus looked at me. 'And your father,' he said, 'he was always ashamed of where he had come from. He was the first person from this village to go to a proper school, in de town. This was because him very smart, intelligent. He was tall and handsome, a good runner, a good cricketer, everybody loved him. But at de big school he mixed with boys who were rich, mostly White boys. It was tough enough to try to fit in with those boys. De last thing him want do was admit he was from a Maroon town. Even his best friend did not know he was from Scott's Hall.' Negus chuckled. 'Can you believe that?

'And what about becoming a successful "professional" inna England? You think that wasn't tough enough without people knowing that you was born and raised in some countrified backwater? Cho!

'They both had their own reason, true, true. But me tink is a good ting you two come to see me. You both look like you need some lesson.'

He straightened his back in his rocking chair and rested his hands over his knees.

'My great-great-great-great-grandmother was a wise woman, a healer, and she was born a slave. She was de mother of de man born over here so, in what is now my back garden.' He pointed at the back wall. 'Virgil, as I mentioned, was de first McMenahem – let me explain. You know a who Menahem?'

'Menahem is the son of Samson,' said Increase.

'Exactly, he does know sometink. And who was Samson?' he said looking at me.

'Samson, that's, er, the strong fella, from the Bible,' I chipped in.

'Exactly, Samson was a strong "fella". Now, de first thing you mussa overstand is that de story you read in de Bible is all version of old, old story. Dem been told, retold, and remoulded, mainly by word of mouth, over thousands of years before de old goatherds of Canaan wrote them on their parchment so.'

Increase sat up straight and frowned.

'Now, of course, de stories change to fit de experience, environment and understanding of those who are telling de story. But all over de world is same, same story. And you know why? Because every person, and every group of peoples, go on de same journey throughout their existence. We all born of a woman. As children we all know that de one being who can bring life and death at will is de mother, de woman, de goddess: Isis, Gaia, Mother Mary. And we all know that de one person who can take de great mother away from us, and therefore serve as de greatest danger to our peace and wellbeing in de bosom of de mother, is de father, de masculine aggressor: Set, Uranus, Yahweh.

'And, likewise, we all experience de extremes of night and day. De night is cold and dark and dangerous – evil; de day is warm and light and comforting – good. You overstand? We all see that everything lives and dies and is reborn again. Every day de sun dies and is reborn, and every year she dies for three days and is reborn; you may call it winter Solstice or Christmas. And de moon, him die every day, and go through him slow death and rebirth every month. De plants and animals we kill to eat, de next day there is always more, gods willing. And we live and die too. And children just appear in de belly of a woman. Like magic, we are constantly reborn. All life is immortal.

'And every peoples have their enemy. De people from over de sea or over de hill, who they fear attack from; or who they are told to fear by dem leaders – because fear is a great way to keep a community working together. Me simplify, but is basically de way it work. Some people say all story are different. But I suppose it just depend on perspective – some are always seeking difference, some are always seeking de unity in all tings.

'So, in this same-same story, we create a hero of ourselves and an antagonist of de other – Israelites and Philistines, Blacks and Whites, cowboys and Indians – child's play, you overstand?

'Now, Virgil's mother came from a family line that had always secretly kept some semblance of story from Africa alive, even when dem slaves and dem African story not allowed. And she taught de stories to Virgil. She also took a great interest in de Bible stories taught by de slave masters, and she see a similarity. So she teach him to overstand de power of a story. And de power of a name.

'Now you must know, of course, that she was a Maroon. That is why we are Maroons. And so are you. We have been Maroons ever since de day she run away from de plantation to fight in de second Maroon War.

'She would have had surname of her former master: possibly Hibbert, James, Byfield, or something like that. Virgil, her son, did not accept that as him name. So he make up him own name. And him consider Menahem because him de son of a strong man – de strong man being Africa. But Virgil not only a son of Africa, because when his mother freed herself, she was pregnant with him. Pregnant by her master. Virgil was light-skinned too. Like you,' he said looking at me. 'Many of de Maroons were light-skinned in those days because rape was so prevalent on de plantation. Now, although Virgil would never know or respect him father, he accept him birthright as him fate. That is why he settled for McMenahem; because Mc mean son of. So he is de son of de son of a strong man. Twice removed from Africa. You overstand?

'And that is why you must respect your name: Aeon McMenahem, Increase McMenahem. Because a name hold power: de power to understand your destiny, and to manipulate the fickleness of the three Fates.'

It was weird, the way Negus spoke. It tapped into something deep inside me, something that came from the same place as the matchstick dream, the Sunsplash music. It was heavy. But I felt that I was starting to understand something about the weight.

Then again, maybe I was just wrecked and it was all nonsense. How much weight could I give to the word of a man in a velvety Kangol top hat who only owned three pieces of furniture? Then again, one of them did seem to be a magic cupboard.

He took Increase's empty glass and put it in the magic cupboard. My sandpaper throat rubbed up on itself as I gulped. Negus took out a clean glass and poured the gorgeous looking red juice. He smiled at me and sipped it, delicately.

For fuck's sake.

The hard Jamaican rain that fell for a few minutes once every day now battered down on the zinc roof like ten thousand angry drummers.

Negus turned towards something in the corner of the room.

A dog?

Where did that come from?

He tilted his head at the dog like a blind man listening for movement. 'Time feh go?' he said to the dog. 'It say it time we go,' he said to me.

I looked at Increase and Teddy. Increase frowned. Teddy shrugged as if it wasn't even his idea in the first place that we came to this madman's house.

'Not dem two. Just you,' said Negus, looking at me. 'It only want you.'

I looked up at the thundering ceiling. 'Don't worry,' said Negus, 'It say de rain stop now.' But it was still hammering down – until the moment we stepped out the door.

I followed Negus into his 'back garden'; a vast valley where the sun was already lifting the mist.

The sun wasn't heavy here, like it was in Montego Bay – like a ship. It was heavy like an ocean – overwhelming everything. I felt like I might collapse from dehydration or heatstroke or tiredness, or just being so ridiculously stoned.

I followed him through thick foliage, long grass, overhanging trees. Negus pulled back a branch to walk through, then let it go so a handful of wet leaves slapped me in the face. He turned back to me, grinning.

'It say you look like someone.'

'Mm?' I said wiping my face.

'What's that,' he said to the dog. 'Oh, it say de man name Gary . . . what's that? Gary Will Not?'

I stopped. And I knew then that there was definitely something weird going on. How could Negus have known about my phobia of all things relating to Gary Wilmot?

He had his back to me now, but I could feel his grin seeping through the back of his head.

He took me to a circle of trees with a patch of grass in the middle.

'Pick one,' he said.

'A tree?'

'Pick one!'

I pointed at a tree.

'Good choice. Sit down.'

'Next to the tree?'

'If you like.'

I sat down and leaned my back against my chosen tree.

Negus nodded at the dog: 'Mm-Hmm,' he said, and then turned back to me. 'It say you still no see because you still no open your eye, dem. It say you mussa start close your eye five hundred year ago. And unu still fear feh open dem. It a say it work so hard to help you keep them open, but now you no even see him.

Because you see so much that you nah waan feh believe can be true, and now your eye just nah waan feh open. That why, even after all that happen on dis trip, you still no see how oppressed become oppressor, how solid become fluid, how in darkness one must look to light – you still no see me?'

'Erm?'

The dog was sat in front of me. It was the weirdest looking dog I'd ever seen. It reminded me of a goat. Its coat was black, but kind of iridescent like a pigeon's neck. And its eyes looked human – dark purple with yellow circles around the pupils. The only other eyes I'd seen like those were Raphael's and Kissy's. It tilted its head like it was checking me out.

'It say it want me tell you it name.'

'Oh . . . right.'

He nodded at the dog: 'Mm-hmm. OK, me tell him.' He looked at me and said, 'It call Pistle.'

Pistol?

I nodded my head and smiled like – *That's nice.*

'It wonder if you know what it short for?'

I shrugged my shoulders.

'It short for epistle. You know what that mean?'

I shook my head.

'It say you should read the books in the study.'

Fuck off! Is he quoting Dad now?

'Now,' he said. 'You have any gifts?'

What!

'Gifts,' he said. 'For your family.'

What the fuck?

Now he was quoting the customs guy from the day we arrived in Jamaica.

My heart fluttered.

'Pistle,' he said, 'want give you a gift. But it insist on a fair exchange.'

Sweat ran into my eyes. I was so tired I could hardly even move my mouth to talk, and I was still exactly as stoned as the moment I woke up that morning.

In my right pocket I had whatever money was left after paying for petrol, Sunsplash tickets, and food and drinks at the Sunsplash. I knew I had to keep something to pay for the repair of the Honda 50. I rummaged in my left pocket and pulled out its only contents: half a gold rope chain and a bloodstained two-dollar note. I placed them on the floor in front of me, moving like I was on a bouncy castle. Pistle sniffed them briefly, then lapped the gold chain up into its mouth, swallowed it whole, then bared its teeth at me in what looked like a human smile.

A rock dropped into my stomach.

'Pistle say dat was exactly what it want. And you can keep de change.'

I put the two-dollar note back in my left pocket.

'Now. Look at it,' said Negus.

'Look at it?'

'Look at it.'

'The dog?'

'Just look at it till it done.'

'How will I know . . . ?'

'Ptts, cho, you know nuttin. Hush, now man, and look at de bloodclaat dog.'

So I sat there and looked at the dog-thing.

After a while my back started to hurt, but I felt like I shouldn't move. I looked over at Negus. His eyes appeared to be closed in the shadow of the rim of his velvety Kangol hat. Maybe he'd fallen asleep.

I felt embarrassed.

Ages must have passed.

I stared at the dog.

I felt like laughing.

I wondered if it was all a joke, me being the punchline.

I stared at the dog.

More ages went by.

I got worried about leaving Increase and Teddy for so long.

I considered getting up and walking away, but I wasn't sure where I was.

I felt angry for some reason, like I wanted to scream.

I stared at the dog.

Water glazed my vision and the dog's face went into soft focus.

Then the dog's face changed.

I see the face of a Black man with wide cheek bones, as if it's superimposed on the dog's face. His jaw is clenched, his nostrils are flared. He is trapped. Behind bars. Behind him there's a dark cave with no visible end.

The face changes to the face of another Black man, eyes far apart and wide with horror. He is crouched in a white cave. It has jagged rocks dripping from the ceiling like icicles.

Now comes another face. A Black man in a kitchen. There is movement and voices all around him. But he is suddenly unaware of his surroundings. He looks at me like he has just noticed me. Like he has just noticed where we are. In the caverns.

We are all in there together, me and all the other men. And it is like I can feel all their feelings at once: the drop of the stomach when the rollercoaster dips, the rush up the spine when you come during a perfect blowjob, an anger and hatred too powerful to compare to anything Aeon has felt before; more than a death wish, an entitlement, and a fear of weight, or a fear of lack of fear, or a fear of fear itself.

'Now you feel it,' said a voice next to me.

I realised I wasn't in the cave any more. I was sat on a beach looking out at the sea.

'The others don't feel it yet, because they refuse to accept that the end of our people has come,' said the old man sat next to me. He was speaking another language, but I understood what he said. 'Only you and I feel it. It is easier for you, because I have taught you. And because you are not so attached, because you are not fully one of us.'

I looked down, surprised to see I had a small pair of naked breasts.

Another scene came, further on in time. The old man stood up, supported by a walking stick. He walked out into the ocean leaving me, the young girl, to sit watching, desperate and confused. The old man kept walking until the ocean had swallowed his legs, and then his torso, and then his head.

And he never came back.

Eventually, people came up behind me asking me where the old man was, as if I'd done something to him. Some of them started walking up and down the shoreline shouting his name. I tried to remember the sound of the name but the sounds left me, the vision left me.

I was aware of the feeling of my own face. It felt like I had a wild grimace or maybe a stupefied smile or an animal's growl. Water dripped off my chin.

Salt water?

The ocean?

Sweat?

Tears. Tears gushing down my cheeks.

Negus opened his eyes and looked up slowly. 'You see it?'

Pistle smiled at me.

'You see it!'

'What was it?'

'It was you, Aeon McMenahem.'

I closed my eyes and tried to shut out the weird feeling, but when I closed them the image was there. But now I was above the scene looking down at the girl as the sea covered the head of the old man. They looked like Native Americans.

I opened my eyes and tried to keep them open. I was scared to blink. It felt like I could just drift off to this place where I was someone else, and Aeon could be lost for ever.

'Me?' I said.

'Yes,' said Negus. 'That was you, de way you once were. What else did you see?'

'An old man.'

'Good. Did he say anything?'

I couldn't take any of it in, it was just too weird.

'Yeah . . . something about the end of our people. What did he mean?'

Negus cocked his head at the dog, then looked back at me. 'You have a lot to learn. That was five hundred years ago.' He thought a moment, like he was considering how much to tell me. 'You have a lot to do. But you have to work it out for yourself. Or not at all.' He shrugged. 'You coming to de end of a long journey, Aeon. We all are.' Negus stood up. 'And you know what happen at de end of a long journey, don't you?'

'What?'

'Soon come,' said Negus. 'Soon come.'

'Time for some proper music,' said Teddy changing tapes as we got back into the car. The bloke on this tape did sound Black, proper Black, and poor, and happy. I wasn't sure exactly what the song meant, but it sounded like he was singing 'Pressure Drop' directly to me.

My thirst had been quenched as Increase and Teddy had headed back to the car. Back at Negus' house, he had finally given me a drink from the magic cupboard.

'How does it do that?' I'd asked.

'Do what?' said Negus.

'The cupboard. How does it make the juice cold?'

The bloke on the tape sang to me all the way back to Teddy's House: 'In The Dark', '54 46, That's My Number', 'Daddy's Home'.

Miss Elwyn used to tell that Moses, Noah, and Jonah were of the water and Shadrach, Meshach, and Abednego were of the fire. 'But you,' she said. 'You, Aeon, are of both.'

A thick line of white clouds dissolved in the searing sun over the roof of the Blue Mountains.

'But why me?' I asked.

What made me so special?

'Because you, Aeon, you are a person. The others are just stories.'

'What, this?' Negus had said as he'd opened the magic cupboard to show me inside. 'You mean my refrigerator?'

And as we got back on the dual carriageway towards Teddy's house, I got it. And I cried again, silently, as the Black bloke on the tape used his rich voice to send me back in time: 'Take Me Home, Country Roads'. And I smiled.

Teddy's friend came the next morning. He had fixed the bike, but lost the key in the process and had to hot-wire it. It worked though – just about. The Honda 50 coughed and spluttered, like a veiny-faced old smoker running for the last bus, as it juddered out of Kingston, through Spanish Town, up to the A1, and westward.

At the hill that rolls down to Randy's roundabout in Montego Bay, the engine cut out and refused to turn over another rev. We freewheeled down the hill, pushed the bike up onto the kerb, and rolled it into the hire shop.

The fella in the shop turned to the clock. It said 4:59 and 30-odd seconds. We were early. He gave his teeth a little suck. He looked us up and down one at a time, stopped at my windswept, wind-tanned face and said, 'You enjoy Sunsplash?' He frowned. 'In Kingston? Come out!' he shouted, pointing at the door as if come meant for us to go. 'Come out!'

The black and red Head bag was still at the end of the bed where I'd left it, but it was on its side. Shepherd's staff lay on the bed. The drawers were all open, uneven.

I unzipped the Head bag. It was empty. All gone. N.W.A. T-shirt, baggy red jeans, all of it, Malcolm X T-shirt, hooded mesh top, bandanas, denim shirt, Nike stuff, Le Coq Sportif stuff – all gone. They'd even taken my socks and boxer shorts from the zip pocket on the end of the bag. And even my JD Sports shoulder bag was gone. I looked under the bed: the big red boots were gone.

Increase checked the bedside drawer where he kept his dad's watch. His posture and breathing changed enough for me to know there was something wrong.

He picked up his bag and put it on the bed. He opened it, looked inside, grabbed it, turned, and flung it behind him:

'Bastards!' The bag crashed into the vanity table smashing the mirror. 'Fucking Bla . . . fucking bastards.' He rushed over and grabbed at a drawer, yanked it out, and hit the vanity table with it – 'Ah fuck–fucking cunts.' – repeatedly.

I didn't know where to turn my face, but I couldn't just walk out of the room. So I had to be there with his pain. I had to accept that whatever I did, whatever mad shit I made happen to make myself worthy of even being in this story, my pain would never be any match for his. My dad had never shot anyone, or sold drugs, or been to prison, or brought skanky women back to our house, or been found dead in a park with both of his wrists slashed.

I closed my eyes for a couple of seconds. But every time I did that she was there – the girl on the beach – inside my head. It was gonna be a while before I'd even start to understand who she was. But what I felt was this: she lived in me, she lived in Teddy and Millicent, One Eye and Raphael, Piggy and Puppy, Leopardskin and Black Man, Sky and the nurses and the maid, Bogey and Randy, Big Bones and Hot Pants, The Leader and his followers, the singer and the lion-man, the singing Rasta, the Rasta at the theatre, the Rasta with the cane, Bull Cosby and the customs man, Big Pig and Rab C. and Rab 2, Joe who sold the bag juice and Peach who owned the Paradise, Increase and Saul and Negus and Dad . . . she lived in all of us. And I knew that I was her, now, in Peach's Paradise, feeling her as she felt us from that beach into the future; our anger, our longing, our loss of knowing her.

She sits there listening to the old man who tells her that the water brings death for all of their people. He tells her that she must choose: to die with them or to live and become us. She sees us now, and she doesn't want to be us. And she knows that she will choose to be us.

My right temple tingled where The Leader had sliced me.

And I knew then what I hated about The Leader and his mates. It was the same thing that Increase hated about Black people in general. They were me. They were him. But now I knew that I'd chosen to be them, us, our past, and this present.

Someone tapped three times on the door.

It was weird, but I felt that I could see them all more clearly than before. I saw them in me. And, yeah, maybe they didn't see me in them, or maybe they chose to ignore the me in them, or maybe the me in them was too painful for them to look at.

But I saw them.

Increase looked at me like he'd just noticed I was there. He stopped and scraped his fingernails over his head.

I opened the door and Penelope slipped in. She didn't know where to look: at Increase, at the shards of smashed mirror and splinters of drawer on the floor. She looked at me. She still had her Timotei girl hair, her big eyes, her long fingers. But she wasn't a fantasy any more. She was just a person. She wasn't a fantasy and I wasn't gonna rescue her, or anyone else, from anything.

She walked over to the vanity table and placed down two big brown envelopes, a roll of white tape, and a black biro. 'I will return shortly,' she said as she left.

We opened the envelopes, retrieved our passports and flight tickets, and padded the envelopes with some flyers for local attractions, some Peach's Paradise menus, a red airline sock. We resealed and re-signed.

Increase sat on the balcony and stared out at the swimming pool.

I spied a note on the floor amongst the shards and splinters. I picked it up and read:

Thanks for the gifts niggaz

Penelope returned. 'Mr Garter would like to speak to you both immediately.' She opened a *Jamaican Gleaner* newspaper and folded the envelopes in its pages.

'OK,' I smiled.

But we had no intention of speaking to Garter. Not then. Not ever again.

It felt like dawn when I woke up, fully dressed. Increase was already on the patio, staring out at the pool.

It was Monday the 9th of August. The day to return to Searbank. Or the day to go back to prison. I checked the time on my flight pass: 15:18.

Peach came knocking herself. 'Mr Garter insists that you two boys show your faces at his office immediately. Is that understood?' She wobbled her orange face slightly. 'I said do you understand?'

Looking at each other, it was obvious we couldn't disguise what was happening under the surface for long.

It was now 10 am; five hours before the flight to Manchester. We just had to avoid Garter for a few hours. And then hope the plan worked.

We rolled up a couple of towels and headed out, like it was just another day and we were simply taking a stroll to the beach in the same wrinkled and reeking clothes we'd been wearing for the past four days now.

Elias nodded at us from his green plastic chair.

We walked down the hill, past the spot where the blood of two boys had now been washed away in the daily rains.

We walked as aware as our senses allowed with heads down,

as if looking down would prevent The Leader and his mates from noticing us.

We walked past Randy's roundabout in silence, ignored. We turned right and passed the bike-hire shop, soft-footed. We walked past Cornwall beach with no tourists and no shark nets, past the burned down bar, past Doctors Cave beach where tourists and locals mingled, past Walter Fletcher beach where the only Jamaicans were bar staff and Joe who sold the bag juice. We walked all the way to the posh restaurant with the yellow, black, and green flag to where the road tailed off towards the police station. We turned and walked back in silence.

I stopped at the market stall where I'd once seen a man carving a sculpture from a log with a piece of broken glass. The carving was still there – a beautiful dreadlocked woman smoking a pipe. I had to take something home for Mum. Increase glared at me as I counted through the last of my money and gave most of it to the man in exchange for the carving.

'Mr Garter really wants to see you boys,' warned Elias as we returned with perfectly folded towels.

'Thank you,' I said as we walked on, past reception.

'Rude boys,' chuckled Elias.

It was nearly midday. I checked the time on my flight pass. Still 15:18.

Increase went and had a drink down at the poolside bar, like it was any other day.

The wait was getting too hard to handle. I sat on the end of the bed and played all kinds of scenarios through my mind. None of them were promising.

My stomach felt tight and empty. I didn't know what was worse, the weight of the matchsticks or the emptiness I felt now.

'Sky insists that I come back up here,' said Increase as he walked back into the room.

'Sky? Why?'

'He wants to speak to us about something.'

There was a light knock on the door. Increase opened the door and Sky slipped in. He wasted no time. 'So what is your plan?'

'What do you mean?' said Increase.

'Please McMenahems,' said Sky. He glanced at the door. 'We don't have much time; I can't leave the bar for long. You are flying home today, yes?' I looked at Increase. Increase looked at me. 'McMenahems, please trust me, we don't have time to waste.' He moved to the middle of the room, glancing at the door again. 'Mr Garter wants you to stay. To go back to court, yes?' he half whispered. 'Now, I am sorry to rush you, but what is your plan? Penelope tell me you already have your passports and flight tickets, yes?'

'Yes,' said Increase.

'So how do you intend to leave without being seen?'

'We intend to go over that fence behind the bar, into the hotel next door,' said Increase. 'Then we'll have to get to the road and get a taxi to the airport.'

'No, that's no good,' said Sky shaking his head. 'Someone will see you. And if, by chance, no one see you on this side, they will see you on the other side. They have too many security guards over there, and some of them are dangerous. Everyone here knows what goin' on. No one have no secret in Jamaica. You need a better plan.'

'We don't know what to do,' I said. There was no point trying to hide the fear, it was dripping off me.

308

'I have a plan,' said Sky. He reached in his jeans pocket, pulled something out, and handed it to me. It was Dad's serpent key. 'If you trust me?'

'I trusted you,' said Kissy.

I felt like all the air, the blood, everything carrying energy through my body had suddenly drained through my feet, through the floorboards of Kissy's bedroom, slopped down over her parents' record player, and drowned out 'Aquarius' by the cast of some play.

Of all the things that lads in Searbank could say about Jemma Simpson, not one could say that they'd had sex with her. So when she offered herself to me around the back of the Bodega off licence, it seemed rude to refuse.

I could only manage half a hard on, and she was so dry it cut the end of my dick. I was gonna have to wait till that healed before I did anything with Kissy. But how could I do that? Me and Kissy did something nearly every day.

Maybe I should just tell Kissy, I thought.

Kissy liked saying things the way they were. And she knew I got off with other girls. How would a bit of rubbish sex be any different? But I couldn't talk honestly the way Kissy did. I just didn't have her ways.

Kissy put her arms around me as I stepped into her bedroom, like she was hugging me. But then she stepped back and pulled an invisible something from the space behind my back. She looked at the space in her hand. 'What's this?' she said.

'What's what?'

She wiped her hands clean of it, clean of me, clean of a future that once was. She unclasped the gold rope chain with Dad's serpent key dangling from it and handed it to me.

'I trusted you,' said Kissy. 'But you have to go now.'

She's still there, every time I close my eyes, the girl on the beach.

She sits outside the cave and her song susurrates within the walls of every chamber.

She sings her story.

Her ancient voice bounces off the sandstone walls and limestone stalactites; rock interwoven with twisted steel and iron, the remains of ancient statues, copper wires, and twisted VHS tape. She sings of how sorry she is to have created us. Her sonorous sounds echo with the screams and howls of 45s with cat o' nines, blast and bang, slash and crack; cries and wails of failed revolutions bounce around uneven walls papered with *Encyclopaedia Britannicas*, Page Threes, and Milky Bar Kid wrappers pasted with spit and spunk, Carlsberg Special Brew and the volcanic insides of Maccy D's Apple Pies.

She sings to let us know that it is never too late; that there is always a way out. If only we would listen. Listen to her. Because she is us. And even though we have forgotten her, and even though she forgot herself, we can still leave these wretched chambers. Together.

'Remember, there always is a way,' she sings, 'Remember; follow the water,' she sings. 'Remember. Follow the signs.'

I put my hand over my pocket and press it against the serpent key.

Waiting was the worst bit.

The black and red Head bag sat there on the floor like a beached whale with an empty belly.

Increase rubbed his wrist.

Raphael's staff lay on the bed.

'And what are you gonna do with that?' asked Increase.

'What do you mean?'

'That stick.'

I shrugged my shoulders.

'You can't take it with you, you know?'

Can't I?

'They won't let you on an aeroplane with a piece of tree.'

Won't they?

'It could carry foreign parasites into Britain.'

I hadn't thought of that.

I searched around inside myself to see how I felt about the fact I was gonna leave Raphael's staff on that bed. There was no feeling. Raphael wasn't in the staff. Raphael was in me. In the chambers of my heart.

We waited.

The room was ready to let us go. That room did not give a fuck about me. I'd only stayed there Friday, Saturday, and Sunday; by Monday I was locked up. Then I was there Thursday night and Sunday night.

And now it was time to go.

Increase came out of the bathroom and grinned at me: 'You ready, nigger?'

'Are you ready, Chalky?'

Increase stared at me with no expression for a second before his jaw quivered. I shook my head as my stomach shook out a little laugh. He moved towards me. I didn't even flinch as he rested his shaky hands on my shoulders. We leaned into each other, foreheads touching.

Increase stood up straight. He looked around the room. 'At least we haven't got any luggage to carry.'

'Just this,' I said picking up the Rasta head. 'For my mum.'

Dad turned his Ford Granada into our double drive. We were returning from what was to be the last time I'd ever go to Church Teen Camp. Something was wrong. When we first moved to Searbank Stoops, there were only eight houses in our street, a large area of overgrown grass on the other side of the road. The builder had promised to sell the rest of the land for further development, but he was holding out for the best price. That was gonna take a while yet. But there was something wrong: a rectangular patch of scorched earth in the grass facing our house.

That wasn't there when we left.

There was something about Mum's closed-mouth smile as Dad and I walked through the front door – 'And how was Church Camp, dear?' – something was wrong. 'I've made some changes, dear,' Mum called after me as I headed up the stairs. I ran to my room.

No!

My red, grey, black, and white IKEA rug was gone.

'It will be easier to keep clean now,' said Mum.

No!

My black IKEA shelves had been replaced by the old oak shelves from the conservatory.

'You've got more space in there now,' said Mum.

No!

And my bed. My amazing double bed with the wooden legs.

'Where the fu—. Where's my bed, Mum?'

Mum glanced through my window to the patch of burnt ground facing the house.

What!

I turned back to where my double bed should have been as Mum left my room.

My jaw dropped. Everything that had been underneath my double bed was now laid on top of the crappy Formica single bed she'd replaced it with. Everything: *Men Only* magazines with pages stuck together, rounders bat with SHS (for Searbank High School) written on the handle, butterfly knife with blade blackened by lighter fire and rocky-weed, my skinning-up tray with ripped-up Rizla packets, loose tobacco, and a tiny bumnut of rocky.

The crack! Where's the fucking rock?

It had been nearly a year since Increase had left the rock on my tray. I'd picked it up and smelt it, I'd licked it, I'd even burnt it and inhaled the fumes, but I hadn't smoked it. Sometimes I used to just look at it and wonder. He'd given it to me like it was as normal as giving someone a ciggy. But it had felt wrong for some reason. I couldn't get my head round it. So I hadn't smoked it. And now:

Where's the fucking crack?

I got on my hands and knees and searched the grey carpet, but there was no way Mum would have missed a single millimetre when she got into one of her cleaning frenzies.

She must've vacuumed it up or something.

There was no way she would've known that it was drugs anyway.

I wouldn't say that I calmed down, but I did stop panicking about the crack.

Increase came to visit more often. Every couple of months we'd see him. And every time he seemed to have more money in his pocket.

The hinged numbers on the bedside clock flipped and flopped. 13:32. Increase put his passport and flight ticket in his pocket.

Penelope came to the room one last time. 'Good luck,' she said with her head down.

'I'm, erm . . .' muttered Increase.

She looked up at him.

'I'm a . . . a fool.'

'The vexation of a fool is known at once,' she said.

'But the prudent ignores an insult,' he said.

I thought about something Teddy had said just before he waved us off from Kingston: 'If the fool would persist in his folly he would become wise.' I thought that maybe I was starting to understand what they were all talking about – but I'd have to find out what folly meant.

The clock flip-flopped: 13:52. I checked the time on my flight ticket. It still said 15:18.

We waited.

We were both stood in the middle of the room staring at the door when it knock-knocked.

'You ready?' said Sky. He looked around him, down the hall. 'Let's go. No wait.' He pushed us back into the room and came in with us. He held up his hand to make sure we stayed silent. I stopped breathing.

The door tap-tapped.

'Quickly!' said Sky. He opened the door and the three us rushed out. It was Eunice, the maid. Her mild eyes now looked sharp, her face battle-ready. She turned to us and whispered, 'Good luck,' then turned her mild eyes back on, turned, and walked down the corridor folding a towel.

A door opened and someone stepped out, just too late for us to turn back. It was Bull Cosby, the mammoth American, the guy who had tried to lecture us at the poolside after I got mugged, the guy who Increase had told to 'shut the fuck up'.

Fuck.

Bull Cosby looked us up and down, at the Rasta head, at the filthy Fruit of the Loom T-shirt, at Sky.

We stared at him as the unmistakable clop-clop of Peach's stilettos turned out of reception and in our direction. I swear I saw her orange arm swing around the corner. Bull Cosby turned and bounced in her direction, his voice booming, 'Mrs Peach, honey. There is something I must bring to your attention. Your ice bucket does not work. The ice has all melted again and . . .'

'Now, now,' whispered Sky.

We followed him down the corridor. Bull Cosby had one arm around Peach's shoulder as he led her back towards reception. Behind her back, Bull gave us the OK symbol.

'This way,' said Sky.

He opened a gate into a staff only area and guided us through. He led us down some steps and through a small maze of washing machines and clothes stands.

'Move. Quick, quick.'

We rushed through another metal gate and down a thin alley that stopped at a fenced-off embankment of trees and bushes.

'Over the fence and straight ahead. Go! Now!'

We both turned to thank him. I wanted to give him something, but I didn't have anything to give. Apart from the Rasta head, all I had left was the filthy clothes on my back – black Adidas shell suit, white Fruit of the Loom T-shirt, Reebok Classic trainers with little Union Jacks.

'Go, now.'

Seven dollars.

I had five Jamaican dollars in my right pocket and, in my left, a bloodstained two-dollar note. I took the pathetic offering from my pockets and held it towards Sky.

'You need that for the taxi. Just go. Please.'

'Let's go,' said Increase turning to run. He looked back at Sky and nodded.

'And Aeon,' said Sky.

I turned back.

'I see you. Remember that I do see you, Aeon McMenahem.'

We climbed over the fence and fought our way through spiky weeds, angry little bushes, sharp rocks. We came to a fence that led onto the road and climbed over.

On the other side of the fence, a Hillman Hunter was parked up waiting. The back door was open and the driver stood by. 'In,' he breathed.

The driver shut the door behind us and told us to lower our heads out of sight. He stepped into the car looking all around him, then pulled away at casual speed. He adjusted his rear-view mirror to get a good look at us.

'You remember me?' he said.

The radio in the car was on quietly, but I could just make out the outro of the song:

'Some learn de hard way

Some like de dark days . . .'

316

'You know you owe me five dollar, rude bwoy?' said the driver. 'Some learn de hahard way . . .'

It's not cool, a broken heart.

It's not like Slash stood outside a little white church, legs akimbo, hair flowing over his guitar – 'November Rain'. It's not like Michael Jackson wiping away tears live on stage – 'She's Out of My Life'. It's not like Skin'ead O'Connor crying into a camera lens for five minutes – 'Nothing Compares 2 U'.

It's more like a sickness that creeps up on you at random intervals, so some cheesy storyline about Scott and Charlene in *Neighbours* makes you feel like you've been punched in the heart.

So you wake up screaming from dreams of Kissy locking herself in a room with your dad and refusing to let you in, although you're on the floor outside the room screaming and crying, begging, but she just doesn't fucking care any more.

It can hit you any time of day, this disease; every time you remember that no one will ever love a skinny little freckle-faced nobody like you the way Kissy did; every time you rewind your VHS of songs from *The Chart Show* and replay 'Show Me Heaven' by Maria McKee.

Fuck you, Maria McKee.

It turns you into an obsessive nutter that calls Kissy's mum's number every day and slams down the phone as soon as it rings.

It makes you walk all the way to Kissy's street every day, as if you're on your way somewhere else, just in case you bump into her, because you haven't even got the guts to just knock on the door and beg her to forgive you.

Because who could take that again? Being blocked at her front door. Seeing that floppy-haired, sixth-form pussy stood behind her as if to protect her. From me? Seeing how she felt sorry for me when I blubbed through that pathetic sentence: 'You're so beautiful.' Hearing her say, 'Don't do anything stupid, Aeon,' while 'Boys Don't Cry' by The Cure plays upstairs (you bastards). And it's clear that what she really means is: *I've grown out of you, Aeon. I deserve better than you, Aeon. This sixth-form pussy is a better person than you, Aeon.*

And knowing she's right.

And knowing that, in truth, you don't even want her back.

You want this pain.

Because the pain is part of the story.

This is what you've made happen.

And it ain't fucking cool.

Just necessary.

The large clock in the terminal silently shifted its hand. It was 6:52 pm.

It had been hard enough just getting into the terminal. Who knew that there was a five-dollar charge just to get into the terminal? If I'd known that I wouldn't have given the taxi driver my last five dollars. And Increase had used his last five to pay for the ride. If I'd known, I wouldn't have bought the Rasta head that Increase now glared at as the realisation dawned on us – we were fucked.

I recognised some of the tourists from the flight into Jamaica. Most had already gone through to the terminal so I had to act fast. I approached a middle-aged couple from Manchester, but their faces turned stony with fear as the manic Scouser jabbered at them. The young Black couple next to them got up and trotted off with their heads down before I could even ask.

I ran over to the double doors to see who I could catch coming through. And there they were, tipping a tall Mike Tyson in a frayed old waistcoat for carrying their bags. 'Thank you, Jeremy,' said one of the big Black girls. 'Yes, thank you,' said the other, before both sets of eyes settled on me.

One of them suggested they should maybe give me the five dollars, but really didn't see why they should help my 'repugnant and racist friend'.

Increase looked scared.

The girls took pity on us.

So, we'd passed through to the terminal.

Then the tannoy had announced a delay to the Manchester flight. A delay that kept us guessing – for four hours.

The terminal was vast, but my tiny world had been closing in on me moment by moment – no tick by no tock.

A hot, dark mist hung over my face. I leaned forward and put my head in my hands.

From one chamber to another. I hunched over like I could actually feel the eerie cold of limestone stalactites on my back.

I didn't even have it in me to keep looking around the place in fear of being spotted and arrested.

My mind played through the scenario at Peach's Paradise when Garter finds the room abandoned. His grimace as he opens the envelopes in his safe to find that we've left him some menus, flyers, and a red airline sock.

And what would happen to Penelope? To Sky? To Eunice? People had risked their jobs for us.

And for that we deserved to be caught.

They might send me back to the strongroom.

And what about the lads I'd left behind. Was One Eye still in there nursing a broken arm, cursing a spoilt 'White' boy? Was

Puppy still down in that dungeon, frightened and isolated, crying for consideration? And what about Scarecrow, was he still at Copse dreaming of the big red boots I hadn't known how to give to him?

They couldn't just run away like I was doing.

I savoured the pain as I clenched the fist of my right hand, salty sweat seeping into the slash wound.

A person could easily get killed in a place like that – especially a person like me. And even if we did make it home alive, Increase was never gonna forgive me.

The slice on my right temple tingled.

And what about Raphael?

'Aeon, come,' said Increase as he jumped out of his seat.

The two of us snaked from our seats and weaved through tourists and trolleys into a duty-free wine shop.

'It's Garter,' breathed Increase as we ducked behind a shelf. 'He's here. With the police.'

A hard pulse fluttered in the top of my left breast.

'I don't know how they didn't see us.'

Maybe they weren't there?

We crouched down and peered through the gaps in the duty free shelves.

Could I trust anything Increase said?

'They were right in front of us.'

I suppose I'll never know.

'Look,' I said. 'People are going up the stairs. They must be getting on a flight. We can try and get on.'

Increase looked around. 'We've got no choice. You go first. Just look straight ahead and run. This is it now. Go!'

One after the other we sprinted across the terminal, up the

wrong side of the stairs, and followed the flow of bodies lined up along the right side of the corridor. We jogged straight up to the stewardesses behind the desk and handed over our flight passes. One of them eyed the passes and, amazingly, sent us off down the flight corridor to the plane.

The stewardess at the end of the flight corridor looked over the passes and directed us to our seats.

Graham X was dead. It was 1992. I only knew how bad it was because it was mentioned in Mum's *Daily Mail*. For some reason, the *Mail* had decided to run a story that wasn't a story at all, just a litany of horrific crimes committed by Black men against other Black Men. Graham X's rape and mutilation was top of the list.

'Cursed be Canaan,' said Increase looking at the open page of Mum's *Mail* where it sat on the kitchen counter. Dad stopped at the kitchen door and looked pleased that Increase was quoting the Bible. 'The lowest of slaves shall he be to his brothers,' said Increase, grinning back at Dad. 'Blessed by the Lord my God be Shem,' said Dad.

Mum clunked a plastic funnel into the top of her new coffee percolator.

'And let Canaan be his slave,' said Increase.

Dad slipped into his double-breasted pinstripe-suit jacket and straightened his tie pin as he said, 'May God make space for Japheth, and let him live in the tents of Shem.'

To my memory, it was this very week that Increase ditched his dungarees and Travel Fox and started wearing tweed jackets and corduroy pants.

I could hear the Kirby vacuum being pushed up and down my grey bedroom carpet by the cleaner.

'Indeed,' said Increase, 'and let Canaan be his slave.'

Somehow, everyone apart from us had heard the announcement to board the Manchester flight.

But we were on the plane – a good thing.

A bad thing – 'Woeful greetings from the cockpit,' said the pilot. 'It is incumbent upon me to apologise for the delay to this flight. A bag has been stowed on the plane which, apparently, seems to have no owner,' he explained. 'As soon as security have woken up and done something about it, we will get this bird in the air and spirit you all back to sunny Manchester.' He sighed: 'Don't hold your breath.'

I'd spent the past hour sat bolt upright, eyes bulging out of my head like Pob. A trickle of sweat dripped from my chin as I grabbed the seat in front of me and looked around it again, expecting to see Garter and a policeman walk onto the plane.

'Listen,' said Increase, 'I'm scared too.' He rubbed his wrist, unconsciously. 'I've never been more scared in my life. But, please, try not to look so obviously paranoid.'

I nodded. I got what he was saying. I did get it. But I had to have another peek.

'Look, Aeon. I don't know how Garter got into the terminal, but even the police can't just walk onto a plane. Really.'

'Mm.' I had another look.

'Update,' said the pilot. 'Apparently there was no extra bag. Genius, eh! So, flight 1063 to Manchester will now resume. I am advised to exclaim my gratitude to all passengers for the patience you had no option but to exercise.'

The girl's voice vibrates inside the distance fractures of my mind – 'Follow the water . . .' she sings – 'Follow the signs . . .' And I still don't know exactly what she means. But I do know one thing: I have to interpret the song she sings my way.

The hard pulse in the top of my left breast fluttered another time.

'They can't touch us once we're on British soil, Aeon. Honestly, I know that for a fact. OK?'

The plane taxied onto the runway.

'OK?'

Revved.

'OK.'

Gathered speed.

'I'm OK, la.'

And took off.

In 1986, when I was nine and a half, the NASA space shuttle *Challenger* exploded in the sky seventy-three seconds into its ascent and killed all seven of its crew members. One of those crew members was Christa McAuliffe. The image of the rocket exploding has stayed with me ever since. And the thing that disturbed me most was the thought of a normal person, a woman, a teacher dying in such a way. I didn't understand why God would allow such a thing to happen.

Dad was impressed by the speech given by President Reagan. Reagan compared the crew's death to the death of Sir Francis Drake on that same day three hundred and ninety years earlier.

'Who's Sir Francis Drake?' I asked Dad.

'Shh,' said Dad leaning towards the telly. Dad almost swooned as he sighed, 'Oh, beautiful,' then sank back in his armchair as Reagan finished by quoting some poem.

'Francis Drake was a pirate, a slave-trader, and an heroic explorer,' Miss Elwyn told us the next day. 'And if any of you heard the president's speech you may have noticed that he said something very beautiful at the end – words that were not his own.' She then read us the poem 'High Flight' by John Gillespie Magee Jr.

Later that day, Miss Elwyn told me that all heroes seek immortality. 'Francis Drake, Queen Elizabeth, William Shakespeare.

'Achilles chose immortality over life. Psyche found immortality through love.

'A few will dare to burn at the stake, to swallow whole the ocean, to traverse the underworld. Fewer will return, remember, and dare to share their experience. They are the ones who bring back the stories.'

Miss Elwyn coughed into her white hanky and then slipped it back under the sleeve of her cardigan. She probably thought I hadn't noticed the blood.

At Manchester Airport, customs stopped and searched the bags of every single young Black man coming off that flight – every single one. And every single White person, old person, and woman walked through without receiving so much as a second look.

The customs guys asked us why we had no luggage, just a wooden Rasta head. We didn't feel like sharing the story with them.

'Well, I think we'll just take a closer look at this carving, OK, lads?' one of them said all friendly as if he was doing it because he liked us.

They were gone for ages. We watched as the customs

inspectors made their only arrest from that flight: a short-legged, quick-eyed brown guy dressed like he was from Cuba in a brown suit and a cheap trilby – the world's most blatant drug-smuggler. His suitcase was full to the brim with blocks of weed wrapped in cellophane – he hadn't even bunged a towel over them.

Everyone else who'd been searched had gone through to Arrivals ages ago.

The customs guys came back. They'd drilled a hole through the top of the Rasta head to search inside it for drugs. They hadn't found any. So then they'd drilled a bigger hole in between her eyes.

'At least you've got something for your mum,' grinned Increase.

The customs guys looked gutted that they hadn't found any drugs. So they kept us there for further questioning.

'Bet you're glad to be back on English soil?' said Increase as customs finally released us. 'At least now you know you're a nigger again.'

He said it loud so the two skinny White guards could definitely hear.

I turned away from him.

I turned away from them.

I left the Rasta head where it sat on the search desk and walked through the passage into Arrivals, Terminal 2, Manchester Airport.

Something had to happen.

EPILOGUE

And so, I made something happen.

Aeon is partly based on me. And, yes, I did spend my seventeenth birthday in a Jamaican detention centre. Even while I was in there I knew that, as long as I survived, the experience would form the basis of my first book. What I did not know is that it would take thirty years to get from that prison cell in Jamaica to being published by Picador.

Aeon is – I was – a self-fulfilling prophecy. I was taught by my history teachers that people who look like me and my father have achieved nothing worth mentioning in the whole history of civilization. I was taught by the police that I was born to be a criminal. I was taught by wider society that I deserve to be ridiculed daily due to the amount of melanin in my skin. And indeed, I – and Aeon – did become exactly what was prophesied: underachiever, criminal, 'nigger'.

It is beyond the scope of this little epilogue to prove just how incorrect the assumptions above were. For now, let's just bear in mind the words of Teddy: 'Blacks were building pyramids when England was a mud pit?'

If you would like to know more, get a book on it.

Nowadays, I work in prisons with my organisation, RiseUp. We teach people how to create and fulfil their own prophecies, how to see their past challenges as the origin myth of their own inner protagonists, how to become the heroes of their own journey.

And we, indeed, are coming to the end of one such journey. Slavery and serfdom, colonialism, and the ideology of inexorable growth have had their day. As all dogs do.

The people of Jamaica have been on a journey as torturous and arduous as that of any peoples in the history of civilization. And yet, they have produced some of the most vibrant minds, the most electrifying cultural output, and one of the most influential ideologies of our times.

For many, the world over, these times seem as treacherous as ever. But we must remember that heroes turn challenging tides into opportunities. Heroes turn base metal into gold – and it is always hot in the forge. Heroes combine the fires of the forge with the cooling force of the waters and return home with ever-more steadfast swords.

And behind the force of these forges, waters, and swords stand our ancestors. They were always with us. And they are here now, smiling upon us as we start to wake up and acknowledge them.

Now is the time to RiseUp.

We can only do this together.

Thank you for joining me as we start this long journey.

Something has to happen.

ACKNOWLEDGEMENTS

Thank you to my wonderful wife and best friend, Poppy, for putting up with my obsessive ranting and striving for so many years. Thank you to my son, Gabriel, for understanding. Thank you to my daughter, Fionnula, for loving. Thank you to my mum and dad for love and life; to my sister for being my other mum and my inspiration; and to my brother for teaching me.

Thank you to my agent, Clare Coombes at Liverpool Literary Agency, for believing in LOCKS and making this happen.

Thank you to Ravi Mirchandani, Salma Begum, Andrea Henry, Hope Ndaba and everyone else at Picador who has supported this project and made my dream come true.

Thank you to my first band, The Shakti: Mak, Phil, Sharlene, and Dean. Without you guys I may well have never dared to enter and remain in the arts world (and where would I be now?).

Thank you to Stuart Coady and everyone at RiseUp for your ongoing support and encouragement.

Thank you to Commonword, Writing on the Wall, Live Theatre, Newcastle, Blackfest, Liverpool, the Everyman Theatre and all of the arts and cultural organisations who supported LOCKS from the start.

And to the people of Liverpool: I could not have made it this far without your support.

Thank you to Ross Dawson and Bella Adams, my lecturers at Liverpool John Moores University: you don't know how much your belief in me helped me to start and complete this project.

Thank you to Sue Gerrard for guiding my writing, and to Sherry Hughes for helping me name this book.

Huge thanks to everyone who has encouraged me and shown interest and enthusiasm over the years I have been talking about and working on this project.

And thank you to you for reading this book. Without you I would still be talking to myself.

GLOSSARY
Speaking Jamaican Patois and Liverpool Scouse
By a Non-Jamaican Plazzy Scouser

I suppose I should start by defining the three terms used in the title: Scouse, patois, and plazzy. The word Scouse derives from 'lobscouse', a dish made from leftovers. As David Simpson explains in his book *All About Scouse*, the dish 'was probably introduced to Liverpool and north Wales via Scandinavian, German, and Baltic sailors'.*

It seems that everywhere you go in the world they have something like lobscouse; a way the poor have found of turning leftovers into something delicious.

Patois is the language of the poor, the Jamaican poor. The word derives from the French *patois* meaning colloquial dialect. In *Understanding Jamaican Patois*, L. Emilie Adams explains that Jamaican creole would be an appropriate term for the dialect in question. However, Adams goes on:

> Technically the term "Creole" refers to mixed African/European language. But because the term was used to refer to "Europeans born in the West Indies" it seems rather inappropriate as the name for the language of the Africans in Jamaica. The French term "patois", though widely used in Jamaica today, is not a proper name of this language either. It is a common noun which can refer to any

---

* Simpson, David, *All About Scouse* (Tyne and Wear: My World, 2013), p. 2.

language in the world which is considered a "broken" or "degraded" version of a "proper" language.*

So, a people who were once enslaved ('broken' and 'degraded'), barred from communicating in their original African languages, and also barred from reading and writing in European languages, once again managed to take the leftovers and make something delicious of them.

And plazzy is Scouse for plastic, meaning fake. So, a plazzy (plastic) Scouser is someone who was brought up on the outskirts of Liverpool but still has a Scouse accent. Someone like Aeon. Someone like me.

The following glossary probably doesn't feature every confusing or colloquial term used in *Locks*, but what is here is in alphabetical order rather than order of usage.

1. Babylon

And so, having just discussed the food and language of the oppressed, we serendipitously get to start by discussing the oppressor: Babylon. To quote Leonard E. Barrett, Sr in *The Rastafarians*: 'As a group the Rastafarians see Jamaica as a land of oppression – Babylon.'†

I would go further to say that the Rastas see the whole of Western capitalist civilization as Babylon.

The term is used by Rastas as a reference to the biblical story of Babylon. To quote the apocalyptic vision of the apostle John in the final book of Bible, the *Book of Revelation* (18:1–3):

And after these things I saw another angel come down from heaven, having great power; and the earth was lightened with his glory. And he cried mightily with a strong voice, saying, Babylon the great is fallen, is fallen, and is become the habitation of devils, and the hold of every foul spirit, and a cage of every unclean and hateful bird. For all nations have drunk of the wine of the wrath

---

* Adams, L. Emilie, *Understanding Jamaican Patois* (Kingston: LMH Publishing, 1994), p. 5.
† Barrett, Leonard E., *The Rastafarians* (Boston: Beacon Press books, 1997), p. 3.

of her fornication, and the kings of the earth are waxed rich through the abundance of her delicacies.*

And as I write this, in October 2022, I cannot help but think that the Rastas might be on to something there.

2. Barm

And so to return to the food of the poor, I can't believe I have to explain what the word barm means. But, so I am told by my editor, southerners have no idea what a barm is. And, according to Microsoft Word and its squiggly red lines, barm isn't even a real word. Well, as Microsoft Word and all you southerners will have noticed, *Locks* is jam-packed with words that are not 'real' words. But what makes a word real? The dictionary? Microsoft? Southerners? Or simply the fact that people make that sound to describe a thing? I'm going to go with the latter. And a barm is a bap, a bread roll, otherwise known as school dinner in the 1990s.

What? What do you mean you don't have dinner in school? I'll come back to that under the letter D. Bloody southerners . . .

3. Battyman

And so, from some innocuous Scouse to some incredibly offensive patois. Battyman is a derogatory Jamaican term for a gay man. It was important for me to use the term as it was such a prolific term in Jamaican music during the time that *Locks* is set. Stuart Borthwick, in his brilliant book *Positive Vibrations: Politics, Politricks and the Story of Reggae*, supplies a list of homophobic Jamaican dancehall songs.[†] The list covers a fifteen-year period, and it is six pages long.

Laws against sodomy were introduced to Jamaica by the British

---

* Holy Bible, King James Version (London: Eyre and Spottiswoode, 1976), p. 1819.
[†] Borthwick, Stuart, *Positive Vibrations: Politics, Politricks and the Story of Reggae* (London: Reaktion Books, 2022), pp. 246–51.

Empire. Apparently, sixty-seven countries still have anti-sodomy laws,* many of which inherited those laws from the British.†

I was recently at a Tudor display in Liverpool's World Museum (it was, incidentally, a display celebrating John Blanke, Henry VIII's Black trumpeter) when I saw a sign that read:

> The Buggery Act was introduced in 1533. It outlawed the "detestable and abominable vice of buggery". While there were very few formal charges under the Act during Henry's reign, it became an important tool in his attack on the monasteries.

Fascinating, eh! Tools invented by the powers that be in order to dominate each other, eventually become tools to dominate us, and we then use those tools against each other.

Homophobia was also rife during my upbringing in northern England in the 1980s and 90s. I have chosen to make a point of this in *Locks* for a couple of reasons. One being that sexuality is one of the many ways in which this society has simplified and polarized identity. Overcoming dualistic thinking and moving toward fluidity and unity are key themes throughout *Locks*. But I also wanted to highlight how the fear of being, or even seeming to be, gay has held men of my age back by diminishing our ability to be comfortably intimate with one another. As is the case with Aeon regarding Shepherd.

4. Bevvy
British slang; an abbreviation of 'beverage', used to define the alcoholic kind.

5. Bladdered
This is what happens to you when you drink too many bevvies. You get bladdered, meaning highly intoxicated.

---

* https://en.wikipedia.org/wiki/Sodomy_law.
† https://www.buzzfeednews.com/article/miriamberger/british-colonial-era-anti-sodomy-laws-still-reign-around-the.

6. Bloodclaat

This is a derogatory patois term. It derives from the term 'blood cloth', as in a woman's sanitary towel (sorry, I am simply reporting the facts). Throughout *Locks* the terms 'bloodcloth', 'bumberclaat', 'bomboclaat', 'bombo', 'rassclaat', and 'pussyclaat' all have the same meaning and derivation. As do the compound words 'bomborass', 'bomborasscloth' and the highly verbose adaptation, 'Bombo-fucking-White-rasscloth'. And, just in case you are wondering, I was personally anointed with all of the above terms during my real-life Jamaican journey back in 1993.

7. Boxies

Short for boxer shorts.

8. Bredrin

A Jamaican term of endearment meaning friend. It derives from the term 'brethren' meaning brother or, in Christian terms, a member of the flock or congregation.

9. Bumnut

I am so sorry. Why do I do this? Well, I've finished the book now, and I agreed to writing this glossary and the upshot is embarrassing myself by admitting just how many offensive terms are secreted within the pages of this dangerous and salacious rag. A 'bumnut' is a little piece of faeces that's stuck to your bum hairs. It is used in *Locks* as a term for a tiny piece of marijuana resin, which looks very much like . . . well, you get the picture. Deary me! What would Mary Whitehouse say? I am ashamed of myself. And yet, as I write, I cannot dispense of this massive grin. There's something wrong with you, Ash.

10. Bunged

Threw.

11. Cardy

Short for cardigan. I use 'cardy' in *Locks* when describing a police officer because something about the sound of the abbreviation – 'cardy' – just seems more dismissive.

12. Chippy

Short for chip shop (the place where the poor pay for something utterly delicious made of spuds).

13. Cho!

A Jamaican exclamation. It's used to accentuate the speaker's annoyance, loss of patience or sardonic humour. It is used, in *Locks*, mainly by older characters. Its first use in *Locks* is when the customs inspector is annoyed that Aeon doesn't understand his hints for a tip: 'The inspector sucked his teeth an extra-long, loud time: "Pttttssss, cho! You have no gifts."'

14. Copped-off

To have kissed someone passionately. See also 'Got off' and 'Necked'.

15. Dead

In Scouse, 'dead' is used to mean really / very. Critiquing Christianity, the narrator of *Locks* says: '. . . and that the meaning of life was to work till you drop, avoid most fun stuff, and wait for the reward you may finally receive when you're dead – if you're dead lucky.' I simply could not resist playing with the Scouse slang and double meaning. It's my book and I'll play my way, OK?

16. Defo

Scouse abbreviation of 'definitely'.

17. Dickie Lewis's

Of all the references in *Locks*, this is the one that is there purely for the pleasure of my Scouse readers. Because who else would have a clue what and where Dickie Lewis's is. Lewis's is a department store that first opened in the mid-nineteenth century in Liverpool, and maintained Liverpool as its flagship store. The store was bombed during the Blitz and rebuilt in the 1950s. The new building featured a statue of a naked man to symbolise Liverpool's resurgence after the war. The statue was, apparently, titled *Liverpool Resurgent*.* But, true to the Scouse way of doing things, because the statue's dick is exposed, we know him as Dickie Lewis.

18. Dinner
Again, just for the southerners, dinner is an afternoon meal. Dinnertime at school is at midday when you go the shop, and eat your cheese barm – which is a bread roll, remember.

'So,' I hear you ask, 'why do you call the thing you keep your cheese barm in a lunch box?'

And with the characteristic Scouse humour that also carries the threat of imminent violence, I answer, 'Because you're a smart arse. Now go fuck off, your tea's ready.'

19. Down the banks
I did not know this was just a Scouse thing, but it had my editor baffled. To give someone 'down the banks' means to severely criticise them. It is apparently an Irish and Scouse thing. Lots of Liverpool dialect comes from Ireland due to the high number of Irish that moved to Liverpool in the nineteenth century to escape poverty and famine.[†] We have just made another link between poverty, food, and language, haven't we?

20. Duppy
A Caribbean term for a ghost or spirit, particularly a malevolent one. Some online sources suggest that it has West African roots, though the evidence is hazy. During Bogey's rant it represents the negative energy of brainwashing colonial education. Later on, the children at Copse say

---

* https://en.wikipedia.org/wiki/Lewis%27s.
[†] Simpson, David, *All About Scouse* (Tyne and Wear: My World, 2013), p. 10.

to Aeon that, 'Shepherd duppy gon get you.' This means that they think Shepherd's ghost is with Aeon. And, to them, that is not a good thing.

21. Dutty
Patois for dirty.

22. Ee-ar
Scouse for hey you.

23. Footie
Short for football.

And, just so you know, I am not a red or a blue. Just leave it!

24. Got off
As it is used in *Locks*, 'got off' means two different things in Scouseland:

One, to leave a place: 'Is that why you never got off when them sixth-form shit-bag mates of yours left yous on your own?' (See below for a definition of shit bag.)

And, two, to kiss someone passionately: 'It was about a week or so after the first time I got off with Kissy.'

25. Haffe
Sometimes written 'ha fe', is patois for have to.

26. Head-the-ball
A stupid or crazy person.

27. Irie
The quintessential Jamaican word, 'Irie' adorns touristy trinkets and T-shirts galore. It means good, pleasing, excellent. Dis *Locks* glossary is Irie, man.

28. Jamdown
And Jamdown is the place where they say 'Irie'. Jamdown is one of the colloquial names for Jamaica. These also include Jamdung and Jamrock.

29. Kipper

I have struggled to find back up for the Scouse definition of either this or the following Scouse term in any literature. But 'kipper' and 'kite' both mean 'face'.

30. Kite

It means face. C'mon, Scousers, back me up here.

31. La

This is a term of endearment placed at the end of a phrase, similar to mate. It is said to be short for lad. However, most of the meaning is derived from the tone in which a word is spoken. So 'la' emphasizes endearment, for example, when Aeon is talking to Sky, but it emphasizes enmity when he says it in the cell in Barnett Street:

> 'In Liverpool, la,' I said, putting on my strongest Scouse accent, leaving the words to linger as I pulled down my pants and squatted over the toilet, 'we don't watch each other while we're having a shit.'

32. Legged it

Scouse for ran away.

33. Like

In *All About Scouse* David Simpson describes 'like' as 'a kind on verbal full stop, Like.'[*] That's a good enough explanation for me, like.

34. Ma

Scouse for mother.

35. Macca

An abbreviation for any surname that starts with Mc or Mac. Everyone in Liverpool knows someone called Macca.

---

[*] Simpson, David, *All About Scouse* (Tyne and Wear: My World, 2013), p. 35.

36. Made up
Scouse for pleased.

37. Necked
The Scouse term 'necked', as it is used in *Locks*, means to drink something quickly. In Liverpool it can also mean to 'get off' with (passionately kiss) someone.

38. Offy
Also spelled offie, a Scouse abbreviation of off-licence: a shop selling alcohol to be consumed off the premises.

39. Overstand
A fascinating word. It is one of those magical ways in which the Jamaican Rastafari have morphed the English language into something uniquely representative of their life experience and world view. To understand is to know what something means or does, or how something works. To overstand is to have deeper insight into the context, derivation, and meaning of a thing or event. To quote from an excellent definition on urbandictionary.com, posted by evilelove on 11 Dec 2006:

> Understanding can drive the car, maybe fix it, maybe even design or improve it within its basic structure. Overstanding realizes that the design is imperfect in the way it is for reasons beyond simple engineering. For example, overstanding knows that we could have cars that use less or no gasoline but that we won't because it is not in the interest of those who control the making of cars to make them last longer, be more efficient, less expensive etc. They make their money when you buy, fuel and fix the car, so why would they help you take their money away? Never mind pollution or helping poor folks out.*

---

* https://www.urbandictionary.com/define.php?term=overstand

If you understand *Locks* you will know that it is a story about a naive boy searching for identity and getting in trouble. If you overstand *Locks* you will know that Aeon's journey, his experiences, the songs and sounds he hears, the people he meets, and even his name are all pointers to deeper layers of meaning.

Overstand?

40. Pegged it and Pegging it
Scouse for ran fast and running fast.

41. Piccaninny and Pickney
Both terms are used in *Locks*. And, as they are connected, I shall cover them together. Pickney is patois for 'child'. L. Emilie Adams suggests that it is an abbreviation of pickaninny.* Pickaninny comes from the Portuguese *pequenino*, meaning 'very small'. The term was originally applied to Caribbean people and their babies. The term 'piccaninny' came to be used as a racial slur.

It is interesting that Jamaican people still use the term 'pickney' to describe their children, when it has derived from a term that became derogatory. Is there something of the self-fulfilling prophecy of colonialism happening here? Just a thought.

42. Pusssyclaat
Please see 'bomboclaat' above.

43. Rassclaat
Rass is patois for 'backside' and claat means 'cloth'. So a rassclaat would be an arse cloth, but it refers, in literal terms, to a sanitary towel (again, please see 'bomboclaat' above).

---

* Adams, L. Emilie, *Understanding Jamaican Patois* (Kingston: LMH Publishing, 1994), p. 59.

44. Rhaatid

Also spelt raatid, rhaatid is an exclamation like 'woh!' or 'gosh!'. Adams says: 'Although popular etymology often derives this word from the Biblical "wrath", pronounced raat, it is more likely a polite permutation of ras, à la "gosh" or "heck".'*

45. Rocky

A Scouse term for marijuana resin.

46. Rudy, rude boy, and rude bwoy

Jamaican patois for a lawless young man.

47. Scally

A Scouse term for a lawless young man, short for scallywag. Scallywag is thought to have Scots-Gaelic origins.†

48. Scouser

See the start of this glossary.

49. Selecta or 'selectaaaaa!', as it is shouted by the deejay at the soundclash in *Locks*.

The selecta is the DJ or the person who selects and/or passes the records to the DJ in the dance hall or at the 'soundclash'.

As an interesting aside, in Jamaica, the word deejay means the toaster, the person who speaks in rhythm over the record.

50. Shit-bag

In Scouse terminology, a shit-bag is a coward. To someone in Aeon's scally (see above) mindset, an unwillingness to place oneself in unnecessary danger is enough to have them deemed a shit-bag. And, as this is

---

* Adams, L. Emilie, *Understanding Jamaican Patois* (Kingston: LMH Publishing, 1994), p. 60.
† Simpson, David, *All About Scouse* (Tyne and Wear: My World, 2013), p. 47.

the only point of contention Aeon can find with the sixth-former lad that is hanging around his girlfriend, Kissy, he uses it repeatedly.

51. Slowy
A slow dance you have with an amorous interest at the end of the disco.

52. Smack heads
Derogatory Scouse term for heroin addicts.

53. Sufferah
Patois for 'sufferer': literally, one who has suffered, as in those poor and oppressed in dis here Babylon.

54. Teef
A patois way of saying 'thief'.

55. Tosser
Literally one who masturbates, used all over the UK as a term of abuse.

56. Yard/Yardman
Yard means 'home' and, particularly, the homes of the poor, such as those sang about by Bob Marley in 'No Woman No Cry'. In Britain we use the term tenement yard to describe the cramped and under-resourced conurbations that were built by our ostensible leaders and representatives to keep the poor huddled together in oppression and ill health.

The word 'yard' also came to mean Jamaica in general, and a 'Yardman' is a man from Jamaica.

57. Yo
I am going to end this glossary with a word that is neither Scouse nor patois. And I would imagine that most of you believe this word needs no explanation. This word, however, deserves to be better understood. Moreover, it perfectly sums up the purpose of *Locks* and the message that it and the stories that shall follow it are really pointing to.

Nowadays, it is thought of as a greeting predominantly used by Black Americans. But check this out. I recently read, in the excellent book *The Hero with an African Face* by Clyde W. Ford, that the sound 'Yo' was used by the Bambara people of the region of Africa, now known as Mali, to define the sound of the vibration from which the whole universe emanates. Ford explains:

Astrophysics continues:

Then from a single point came a big bang, an explosion of immense proportions. Only faint glimmers of that explosion remain, detectable as a consistent level of background noise in the universe.

Bambara sacred wisdom answers:

The entire universe began from a single point of sound, the root sound of creation, Yo. Yo is the first sound, but it is also the silence at the core of creation.*

So, Yo is the Bambara's version of the Om from the text and prayers of the Hindu and Tibetan Buddhist faiths. Yo is the Bambara version of the 'Word' that is referenced in John 1:1 of the King James Bible: 'In the beginning was the Word, and the Word was with God, and the Word was God.'†

The purpose of this glossary is that you may understand some of the colloquial terms used throughout *Locks*. The purpose of including the word Yo is that you may start to overstand the true purpose of my debut novel.

Do you understand?

Do you overstand?

---

* Ford Clyde W., *The hero with an African Face* (New York: Bantam Books, 2000), pp. 170–72.

† Holy Bible, King James Version (London: Eyre and Spottiswoode, 1976) p. 1546.